THE ONE DAY OF THE WEEK

THE ONE DAY OF THE WEEK

RAFAEL SANCHEZ FERLOSIO

translated from the Spanish by J. M. Cohen

Abelard-Schuman *london new york toronto*

First published in Spain under the title of *El Jarama* by Ediciones
Destino S.L.

© This translation Abelard-Schuman Limited 1962

First published 1962

Library of Congress Catalogue Card Number 62:11782

london: Abelard-Schuman Limited 8 King Street WC2
new york: Abelard-Schuman Limited 6 West 57 Street New York 19
toronto: Abelard-Schuman Canada Limited 81 John Street 2B

In rivers, the water that you touch is the last
of what has passed and the first of that which comes:
so with time present.   LEONARDO DA VINCI

Two distinct groups – nine young people
and some older men and women – visit a
crowded resort area outside Madrid on a
Sunday in late summer.

"*I will give a brief description of these rivers, taking them in their order and beginning with the Jarama. Rising in the gneiss on the southern slopes of the Somosierra, between the peaks of La Cebollera and La Excomunión, it flows through the province of Madrid, passing La Hiruela and the mills at Montejo de la Sierra and Prádena del Rincón. It then enters the province of Guadalajara, crossing the Silurian slatebeds as far as the former convent of Bonaval. Then, flowing through deep gorges in a bed of calcareous limestone which extends from Pontón de la Oliva, it takes its course past Tamajón to Congostrina in the direction of Sigüenza. A little below Pontón de Oliva it is joined by the Lozoya. It then makes an oblique turn towards the south to form the plain of Torrelaguna, eight hundred metres downstream form Uceda, where there is a wooden bridge. From its junction with the Lozoya it serves as a boundary between the two provinces. A few kilometres above El Espartel, however, it flows into the province of Madrid, entering a bed of quaternary diluvial sands, and following a shifting channel which renders the area useless for agriculture. Only at Talamanca has it been possible to deflect its waters into a short mill-stream which drives a mill with two wheels. At Talamanca also there is a bridge which now serves no purpose since the river shifted its course many years ago to make itself a new channel. Between Talamanca and Paracuellos it is crossed by several ferries, and lower down by the Viveros bridge, which carries the main road to Aragon and Catalonia at a point exactly sixteen kilometres from Madrid . . .*"

* * *

"Do you mind if I pull back the curtain?"

He always sat in the same position, with his back to the dark inside wall, and his face to the door and the light. On his left was the bar-counter, parallel to the direction of his gaze; and he placed his chair at an angle, so that his right arm rested on its back while his left lay along the counter. Thus he was enclosed in a sort of niche with his body protected on three sides. On the fourth side he wanted light. He wanted a clear passage in front of him for the light to reach his face; it annoyed him that the curtain should prevent his seeing outside the door.

"Do you mind if I pull back the curtain?"

The boss nodded assent. It was a heavy piece of sacking. They had soon discovered his mania. One morning, just after he had taken his usual seat in the corner, the boss had pulled the curtain back himself without waiting to be asked. He did it ceremoniously with a studied gesture, and the man took offence.

"If you don't like my pulling back the curtain you could have said so, and I'd have gone somewhere else for my drink. But clowning won't get you anywhere with me."

"But, Lucio, can't you take a little bit of a joke? Of course I don't mind, man. We always put it up in the summer, to keep out the flies. If you like it pulled back it doesn't matter to me. Only it makes me laugh, this craze of yours for looking outside. Aren't you sick of what you see there? Always the same tree and the bend in the road and the wall."

"It isn't a question of what you can or you can't see. I don't even notice if I see anything at all. But whether it's a craze or not, I like to have it open. It's stifling otherwise, and you don't know where to look. There's nothing to fix your eyes on. Besides, I like to see what goes by."

"What doesn't go by, you mean."

The conversation ceased. The boss propped his hairy arms on the counter, and leant the full weight of his body on them. A streak of sunlight fell on the cement floor. When the whistle of a train struck his ears, the boss spoke: "Quarter to nine." The two men imperceptibly changed their postures. A woman's voice called from the passage: "Perhaps you'll tell that man when he turns up to stay here for the evening and serve in the garden. Because Justina can't. Her young man's coming to fetch her at four."

"Couldn't the fellow choose a weekday to take her out? He knows very well I need her here on Sundays."

The woman came in with her head on one side, struggling to get her comb through a knot in her greying hair. "There's no reason," she said, "why the girl should stay here like a martyr every Sunday. She's got as much right to go to the movies as anybody else."

"Nobody's stopping her going to the movies. I'm only saying that they might pick another day."

"And how do you expect him to have the time on another day, on a working day, to take her to Madrid and bring her back, when he doesn't stop work till half past seven or after?"

"All right. I didn't mean any harm. Let them do as they like. All right."

The woman had untangled her hair and could now address her husband with undivided mind. She went on therefore in a different tone: "And what's more, the real reason why he takes the child out on Sundays is because he doesn't like to have her serving in the garden, with all the customers eyeing her and making dirty remarks. And there, let me tell you, I'm entirely on his side."

"Oh, he doesn't like it, eh? Who is he to tell me what my daughter ought and ought not to be doing? I call that a bit much. Wants to teach me how to bring up my own child, does he?"

"You need someone to teach you, and that's a fact. You don't know much about girls, or you wouldn't keep her going from table to table like a café waiter. It's time you learnt once and for all that girls should be handled with care."

She was arguing with her husband across the counter, shaking her big black comb in his face. "No one would believe that you treat your daughter like this, Mauricio. And I'm glad he's taking her out. It shows his good breeding, and I'm all for it, see!"

"So now he's turned up he's going to give us all class."

Lucio looked at them each in turn.

"Class? Bah! The child's going out today and that's that."

[8]

She retired to finish her combing. Mauricio glanced at Lucio and shrugged his shoulders. Then they both looked towards the door.

"There's a new damned fool idea in this house every day," he said with a sigh. Both were silent. The square of sunlight had grown a little bigger; it was reflected on the ceiling. Flies were buzzing in a whirl of dust and light. Lucio changed his position.

"There'll be people coming to the river today."

"Yes, more than last Sunday, if that's possible. Seeing how hot it's been this week . . ."

"I bet there'll be a lot of people today."

"Yes, it's too hot to do anything, even here in the country. So what must it be like in the town?"

"The river will be swarming with people."

"It must have been ninety or ninety-five in the shade there yesterday and the day before."

"Yes, they'll come today. Crowds of them'll come today to swim in the river."

The calendars showed off their vivid colours. The reflection from the patch of sunlight spread among the shadows making everything shine with the usual brightness of a bar. The white bottles of *cazalla** and *anís* shone proudly on the shelves, displaying like precious stones all their facets and their transparent dimpled shapes. Mauricio was pulling out the yellow thread of a duster which had caught on one of the nails. The cracks between the boards were caked with soap and dirt. On Mauricio's arms was a wavy imprint from the part of the grain least worn away with use. He inspected the pattern with amusement, and voluptuously scratched his reddened skin. Lucio was picking his nose. Framed in the doorway he saw burnt earth and olive trees, and the houses of the village less than a mile away, overshadowed by the ruins of an ancient factory. Beyond this were fields undulating as far as the horizon, which was veiled by a thin dirty streak. This might have been mist or dust or the chaff from threshing. Above stretched a smooth, relentless sky like armoured steel, without a single wisp of cloud.

A burly man blocked the whole door with his shoulders. He had

* A type of *anís*, at its best approximating to an aniseed-flavoured *schnapps*.

looked right and left as he came in. The place was darkened as he crossed the threshold.

"Morning! Where do I leave this?"

He carried a block of ice wrapped in sacking on one shoulder, pressed against his neck.

"Morning, Demetrio! Leave it here for a minute till I can break it up. And bring in the rest before the sun gets at it."

Mauricio helped him to take off the sacking, and the man went out. Mauricio searched in every drawer for his hammer. Demetrio re-entered with another block.

"We didn't hear your truck. Where have you left it?"

"In the shade. Where else d'you expect?"

"Of course, of course. But you gave me a start. Have you brought the crates as well?"

"Yes, two crates, one beer and one lemonade. That's right, isn't it?"

"Yes, quite right. Now go and get the other block or it'll melt. Where the hell's the hammer? Faustina! Everybody here takes things from where they belong, and no one bothers to put them back. Faustina!"

He lifted his head and saw her in front of him.

"Here I am. What's the matter? You don't have to call me more than once. I'm not deaf."

"Where did you put that hammer, I should like to know?"

"Look!" she said, pointing to the shelves. "Staring you in the face."

"That's a strange place to choose for it. What are the drawers for?"

"Anything else?"

"No-o!"

As she went out Faustina touched Lucio on the shoulder, and with a backward jerk of her thumb towards her husband, murmured: "Just like him!" Lucio gave a wink and shrugged his shoulders. The truck driver put down the last block of ice beside the other two.

"Don't bring the crates in yet. Help me to break up the ice, if you would."

Demetrio grasped the block, and Mauricio broke it up with his hammer. A chip of ice fell on Lucio's coat sleeve, and he watched it rapidly melt away to a small drop.

"You don't get the good out of them when they're whole. The cold is distributed better this way. Now you can bring me the crates."

Demetrio went out again. Lucio pointed to the door and said: "He's a good lad."

"A good lad but a bit thick. Good though, through and through."

"Not much like his father. That old man . . ."

"Lucky that old man died when his son was young."

"Very lucky."

"Broad shoulders and troubles to match."

"But he wouldn't harm a fly. He's a real good lad, he is."

"And he doesn't make difficulties. If you ask him to do something, he does it straightaway. Couldn't do it quicker if it was for himself. Other lads at his age strut around, and think you're trying to boss them . . ."

A new darkness announced Demetrio's return.

"D'you mind lending me a hand, Señor Mauricio?"

"Bring them in."

The boss came from behind the counter and helped him put down the crates. There was a sound like the cackling of geese, as one by one the bottles were slowly transferred from the crates to the ice-box. When he had stowed the last away Mauricio poured out a glass of *cazalla* for Demetrio.

"Would you be able to spare some time this evening to lend me a hand?"

"I was meaning to go dancing this evening, Señor Mauricio. I'd rather you found somebody else."

"Chasing a girl, I suppose, seeing you'd rather go dancing than earn a bit of money. But never mind, that's not my business. My daughter's going to the movies, and I don't know who else to ask."

"Why can't Señor Lucio help you? He never does anything."

"I did enough, I can tell you, when I was your age."

"What did you do? Tell me."

"Lots of things. More than you've ever done."

"Tell me one of them then . . ."

"More things than you."

"I don't believe it."

"Listen, boy, you don't know anything so far. You've got a great deal to learn."

"That's enough now. Take what I owe you, and stop quarrelling with Señor Lucio."

He put three five-peseta notes down on the counter. He had taken them from the drawer with his wet hand. He dried his hands on a cloth, and Demetrio picked up the money.

"Well, you can help me another day. Enjoy yourself at the dance. I'll manage as best I can on my own."

"I must go and put the truck away now. It's getting late. See you tomorrow."

"So long."

"You can't force the boy. He does more than he needs to for other people already. She always thinks that you can make use of anybody you like at any time. If the girl takes it into her head to go to the cinema, he has just as much right to do as he fancies. Sunday's a holiday for everybody. You can't impose on people. He may come here for the tips, but he's still doing me a favour if he spends the whole blessed Sunday serving food and drink."

"You're quite right. Women treat everything as if it were their own property, people included."

"Yes, but take her own daughter. No one must even look at her. You heard what she said just now, didn't you?"

"Yes, that's women all over, and you won't change them."

"And I shall bust myself this evening trying to serve the whole lot."

"You certainly will. And there'll be a crowd today, I promise you. It's not ten o'clock, and you can feel the heat already."

"What a summer! It's more than anyone can take."

"Still it suits you all right. The hotter it is the fuller your place gets."

"Yes, of course. If it wasn't for days like this, you might say, it wouldn't be worth my while hanging about behind a bar. It really wouldn't. What's more, things aren't what they used to be or anything like. There are too many *merenderos** along the river and the main road. Once upon a time mine was almost the only one.

* A *merendero* supplies drink to customers who bring their own food.

[12]

You never knew this place in its better days."

"Yours has one advantage though. It's out of the way."

"That's no advantage. I really believe the crowd prefer the others even with the din all round because they're near the river or the main road. Especially people who've got cars, since they don't have to come up this stretch of bad track."

"When will they pave it, eh?"

"Never."

On the stubble the dust from the threshing whirled round, whipped up by a little faint breeze which had been skimming the ground between the wall and the road. The eddy whirled for a moment like a giant funnel in the doorway, and then died, leaving a spiral trace in the dust.

"There's a bit of a breeze," said Lucio.

Justina came in from the passage.

"Good morning, Señor Lucio. You here already?"

"Here comes the sun," he answered as he looked at her. "Morning, beautiful!"

"You've got to give me thirty pesetas, Father."

Mauricio eyed her for a moment, opened the drawer, and took out the money. Holding it in his hand, he eyed her again and began: "Now look, dear, just you tell her from me ..."

She ran off, leaving her father with the words on his lips and the money in his hand, but returned almost at once.

"She says you must give me fifty, not thirty."

Mauricio opened the drawer again, and added four five-peseta notes to the six in his hand.

"Thank you, Father. What was it you were saying to me just now?"

"Nothing."

Justina looked at the two of them, tilted her chin, opened her eyes wide to express surprise, and departed again.

Suddenly an engine rumbled. It revved two or three times, and the noise stopped in front of the door. Voices sounded from the sunshine.

"Wait, let me help you."

"No, no, Sebas, I can manage on my own."

Mauricio went out to look. A girl in trousers was getting out of the sidecar of a motor-bike. He recognized the young man's face. They both came towards him.

"Well, young fellow, so you're back again?"

"There you are, Paulina. He still remembers us. How are you?"

"Of course I remember you. I'm very well. And you?"

"As you can see. We've come for the day."

The girl wore a pair of man's trousers much too large for her, which she had rolled up her legs. On her head she had a blue and red hand-kerchief, tied in a band round her temples. The ends fell to one side.

"Come for a breath of the country, eh?"

"Yes, and to have a bit of a swim."

"Nobody can stay in Madrid on a day like this. What'll you have?"

"I don't know. What will you have, Pauli?"

"I had breakfast before I came out. I don't want anything at all."

"Never mind about that. I had breakfast too." He turned to Mauricio; "Have you got some coffee?"

"I think there's some made in the kitchen. I'll go and see." He went into the passage. The girl brushed her companion's shirt.

"You have got yourself in a state!"

"It's a real joy, girl, riding a motor-bike! You don't notice the heat. But once you stop, then you begin to bake. The others won't be here for quite a time."

"They ought to have left earlier."

Mauricio came in with the coffee-pot.

"There *is* coffee. I'll give you some now. Have you two come on your own?"

He put out a glass.

"No, there's a whole crowd of us. But the others are on bikes."

"Oh! Take as much sugar as you want. You didn't come on that motor-bike last summer. Have you just bought it?"

"No, it's not mine. What do you think I am? It belongs to the garage where I work. The boss lets us take it out sometimes on Sundays."

"So all it costs you is the petrol?"

"That's right."

"Well, and I was just saying we hadn't seen last year's crowd here this summer. All the old faces again, eh?"

"Some of them, yes, and some that you won't know. There'll be eleven of us, won't there Pauli?"

"Eleven altogether," answered the girl. "There should have been twelve really. But at the last moment one of the fellows' girl friend dropped out. Her mother wouldn't let her come."

"And that tall fellow who was such a fine singer, is he coming?"

"Oh, Miguel!" said Sebas. "Yes, he's coming. What a memory you have!"

"What a good singer that boy was!"

"He still is. We passed them a long way back on the Barajas motor way. They won't be here for a good half-hour, I shouldn't think. It's ten miles to the bridge, isn't it?"

"Yes, it's still ten," Mauricio agreed. "Quite easy on a motor-bike. It must be a nice ride."

"Yes, it's a fine run on the bike. But the moment you stop the heat gets up and hits you. Still, so long as you're moving there's a cool wind on your face all the time. But tell me, I was going to ask you—You don't mind, do you, if we leave our bikes here like we did last year?"

"No, of course not. Do just what you please."

"Thank you very much. And do you still have the same wine?"

"No, it's not the same. It's better if anything. But it's very much the same type."

"Good. Perhaps you'd fill us . . . four bottles, I should think, for the morning."

"Yes, just as many as you like."

"But four bottles, Sebas? You must be mad. What do we want with all that quantity? You always have such big ideas."

"Don't be so silly. Four bottles go down without your noticing it."

"All right. But I know you. You take care you don't get drunk. See? Because when you do you always get quarrelsome and spoil the party.

"Don't work yourself into a state, miss," interrupted Lucio.

"Leave him alone and let him enjoy his wine. Whatever he drinks now he'll have drunk before you get married, and that'll leave quite a drop less for him to drink afterwards. Isn't that right?"

"Today's one day, and the day we get married's another."

"Don't you listen to him," said Mauricio. "He's a dangerous customer, and I know him. Never go to him for advice."

"They know you too well here," said Lucio with a laugh, "that's the trouble. They just see right through you."

"Well, just go somewhere else then, and see if you get a warmer welcome."

Lucio took the girl on one side, and said to her quietly, muffling his voice with the back of his hand: "He says that because he gives me credit. That's why, you see."

Paulina smiled.

"What is it you're whispering to the young lady? Can't you see her fiancé doesn't like it?"

Sebastián smiled also.

"That's right," he said. "I am a rather jealous type . . . so take care."

"Oh dear, he's jealous, is he, and he doesn't like it! I only wish that were true."

Sebastián gave Paulina a look and pulled her to him by the shoulders.

"Come here! Come here, silly! Now supposing we go out and see if the others are coming!"

"Just as you like. What's the time?"

"Twenty-five to ten. They can't be long now. See you later."

"So long."

They went out, and walked towards the level-crossing.

"What a funny old man!" said Paulina. "Did you notice the odd sort of grimaces he was making?"

"What did he say to you?"

"Nothing. Something about the other man giving him credit. But what a heat, Sebas, what a heat!"

"Yes, I wish the others would hurry up. I want to get in the water as soon as I can . . ."

"You wouldn't be so silly as to go in before eleven, would you? It might stop your digestion."

"What care you do take of me, Pauli! Will you be just as careful of me when we're married?"

"And what effect does it have, eh? You don't pay the least attention to what I say. I can't see that it does any good."

"What you say always does me good, love. I'm always pleased that you've said it."

"Now come, what's the use of being pleased if you don't put what I say into practice?"

"But it makes me love you even more. That's the good thing. Now isn't that something?"

"Oh my goodness, what an idiot you are, Sebas! What a silly thing to say!"

"I love you. You're the sun in my sky."

"We've got one sun already, and that's enough, love. We don't need any more today, really we don't. Look, here comes the train!"

"Shall we count the wagons?"

"What a silly idea! Why?"

"Oh, just for fun."

★   ★   ★

"That's a nice couple if ever I saw one," said Lucio.

Mauricio was busy rinsing the bottles.

"They used to come last year," he said. "But they weren't engaged then as far as I remember. They must have fixed it up since."

"Only one thing against them. The awful trousers she was wearing. They are ugly! Why do girls wear such things?"

"For the motor-bike, of course. It's more comfortable to ride in trousers, and more decent."

"Yes. But I don't like to see girls dressed like that. Looks like a soldier."

"They are a bit big for her, I admit. She must have borrowed them from her brother."

"Give me a modern girl in a pretty skirt! Anything else spoils the figure."

"They're losing their taste up in Madrid. They don't know how to dress any more."

"Don't they now? In Madrid, let me tell you, you'll see women dressed with more taste than you've ever seen in your life in the country. Cloth, cut, everything, just right!"

"You see plenty of sights like this girl too. After all, Madrid's the centre. It's the capital of Spain, and everything finds its way to the Capital. You'll see the best there and the worst, you're bound to."

"But there are more good things than bad in Madrid."

"As we see it, perhaps, when we come up from the country. But go and ask the Madrid people themselves. However, you've got the proof before your eyes. They come out here to spend their Sundays, don't they? And why? Because they've had more than enough of the Capital. If they were happy there, they wouldn't come away. And it's not just one or two. Thousands of them come out every Sunday to escape the heat. So you can't say definitely what's good and what's bad. People get sick of everything, even of capital cities, in the end."

Mauricio had finished filling the bottles and was wiping them with a cloth. There was a silence. Lucio stared at the square of country framed in the empty doorway.

"What a soil!" he exclaimed.

"Why do you say that?"

"Say what?"

"What you said just now."

"What a soil, you mean? Probably because I was looking at the fields."

"You don't say!"

"No, don't laugh. What are you laughing at?"

"I was laughing at you. You're a bit dull this morning."

"Does that amuse you?"

"No end."

"Very pleased to hear it."

The whole countryside had taken on the harsh colour of the stubble. A repulsive, shadowless ochre, lying in a troubled impalpable lethargy under its cloak of threshing-dust. The hills lay one above another, billowing into the distance, like a succession of animals' backs, each resting wearily on the one beneath it. Hidden among this herd, the Jarama flowed its secret course. And on the further bank too uncultivated fields repeated the colour of the stubble, as if the corrosive summer sun had reduced all variations of the earth's colour to a single dirty ochre.

"Like a smoke?" asked Lucio.

"Not yet, thank you. A little later."

"Well, I won't roll my first then until you start too. The later you begin the better for the cough. Tell me, will Faustina or your daughter be going to San Fernando?"

"In a little while I expect. Why . . .?"

"Do you mind if I ask them to bring me a packet of tobacco?"

"That's up to them. Ask them yourself when they go. But won't you be going too at dinnertime?"

"I don't think so. My brother and his wife are spending the day in Madrid with her family. They must be in the train by now."

"So you're not expecting a meal?"

"Yes, my meal's down there. If they could fetch that for me too as they go by . . . My sister-in-law'll have put it out ready on the kitchen table. If they'd do that then I shouldn't have to go."

"And what else, your lordship? Don't you think they'll have enough to carry without having to bring you your dinner from home?

"Oh, all right then! Forget it. If I feel like it I'll go myself. If not, I'll eat it tonight. It's all the same to me."

* * *

The freight train went by, and the whole group of cyclists appeared on the other side of the level-crossing. When she saw them Paulina began to shout and wave her arm.

"Miguel! Alicia! Here we are!"

"Hello, boys and girls," someone shouted from the other side.

"Been waiting for us long?"

The poles of the level-crossing were slowly lifted. The cyclists crossed on to the railway track, steering their bikes by the handlebars.

"Stuck-up aren't we with our motor-bike!" said Miguel as he approached Sebas and his fiancée.

They were all sweating. The girls wore coloured handkerchiefs like

Paulina's with their ends dangling. Almost all the men were in white shirts. One had a blue and white vest with horizontal stripes like a sailor's. He had covered his head with a pocket handkerchief knotted at the corners. His trousers were tucked into his socks. But the others had cycle clips. A tall girl who came last was making faces because of the jolting as they crossed the rails. She was cursing her cycle.

"Oh lord, this is an old wreck!"

She was wearing some peculiar blue glasses that ended in raised points at either side. They prolonged her eyebrows, and made her look like someone out of a Japanese fairy-tale. She also wore trousers, and when she met Paulina she said: "You see I've kept my promise."

Paulina looked at the trousers.

"They do fit you beautifully! And they suit you perfectly. Mine look awful beside them. Who did you get them from?"

"My brother Luis."

"They look good on you. Turn round and let's see."

The girl swung her hips with a studied movement and without letting go of her bicycle.

"You'd do for a model," said the lad in the sailor's vest with a laugh. "Some curves!"

"Compliments later, or we shall get run down by a train," answered the girl as she left the track.

"Did you have any punctures?" asked Sebas.

"No, no! It's Mely's fault. She would stop every twenty yards to say that she was no good for this sort of trip, and we mustn't tire her out."

"And what sort of trips is Mely good for?"

"As for that . . ."

"But anyway, nobody forced you to wait for me. I could have got here just as well on my own."

"You wouldn't have got very far on your own in those trousers, I promise you."

"Wouldn't I? And why not?"

"Because there'd have been at least a couple of men wanting to keep you company."

"All right. I shouldn't have minded, so long as they weren't like you."

"Good. But what are we doing here in the sun? On we go!"

"Doing? Clearing up Mely's future."

"Well, you can leave that till afterwards, when we've got a little shade."

Several of the cyclists were now back on the road.

"Tell me, did you pick the very worst machine in the place?"

"I took the first one they offered me, chum. Perhaps you'd rather have walked here on your flat feet."

"Come on, we can ride now. There's no reason for walking."

"It's the worst bone-shaker I've ridden in my life. It's as bad as one of those brown ones they give you in the army. And that's saying something."

"How's the food looking?"

"We don't know," answered Sebastián. "It's still on the bike. But we shall see if there've been any casualties. I don't think there have."

Pushing their bikes, Miguel and another of the girls walked beside the friends who had come down to meet them. The rest had all mounted now, and were riding ahead.

"Things did get a bit of a jolting," said Paulina. "The food tins were clanking about like the devil!"

"So long as none of them came open . . ."

"Do you know, the boss remembered us. He recognized me as soon as he saw me."

"Did he now?"

"He remembers you too. He asked after you, didn't he Pauli? The fellow who sang, he said."

The others had reached the bar. The lad in the striped vest was leading, and took the road to the right. A girl went past it.

"This way, Luci!" he called. "Follow me. This way, see! Here we are."

The girl turned her bike and took the same road as the others.

"Where's the garden?"

"Behind this wall. Don't you see the trees peeping over the top?"

The whole group had arrived and stopped before the door.

"Oh, it's nice here."

"Mely always comes last, you'll notice."

One of them looked at the front and read: "Customers may bring their own food."

"I could swallow a glass of water this very minute, a glass the size of a cathedral."

"Make it wine for me."

"At this time in the morning. No, it's too early."

They went in.

"Mind honey, there's a step."

"So there is. Thank you."

"Where do we leave the bikes?"

"Outside for the moment. They'll tell us where later."

"I've never been to this place before."

"Oh I have, quite often."

"Morning!"

"Good morning to you."

"Fernando, please give me a hand. I've got my skirt caught up."

"It's a bit fresher here already."

"Yes, at least you can breathe."

"I do remember his face."

"Well, well, how are you?"

"Expecting you, as you can see. I was quite surprised not to have had a sight of you yet this summer."

"Please could I have a glass of water."

"With pleasure. Now where's the tall fellow who used to sing? Didn't you say he was with you too?"

"Yes, he is. He's coming along behind with his fiancée and the pair with the motor-bike. They don't mind the sun, you see."

"Difficult for anyone to like it on a day like this. Now this is your wine in these bottles."

They stood in a glistening line along the counter, four litre-bottles of red wine, all alike.

"The others ordered them as soon as they arrived."

"Well, we'll start on them now. Who wants a drink, boys?"

"Now just a minute, idiot!"

"What for?"

"Keep these bottles for the river. If we want wine now let's have it by the glass."

"All right. Just as you like. Do you want wine, Santos?"

"If it's allowed . . ."

"I'm drinking water!"

"Don't drink too much, you're sweating."

"Those fools haven't got the food out yet. I don't know what they've been doing all this time."

"Tito, do you want a glass?"

"I prefer water for the moment. We'll talk about wine later on."

"And you girls? Water, wine, lemonade, orangeade, coke, pine-apple juice?"

"Anyone'd think you were doing the selling. You make a first-class barman, chum!"

"If these young ladies don't want wine, the only thing I've got for them is lemonade."

"What I'm going to do, boys, is sit down. I'm not going to drink anything till I've cooled off."

"That's sensible. Do you want lemonade, Lucita?"

"Yes, lemonade."

"It's much better than the water, of course, because I keep it cool," said Mauricio, leaning over the ice-box, "while the water is at room temperature."

"It must be boiling then."

"This is good," said Tito. "It quenches your thirst."

"When you're still hot," resumed Mely, lying back in her chair, "you shouldn't take things that are too cold."

Her body was long, and her hips were broad, and her flesh revealed its firmness through the cloth of her trousers. She laid her two bare arms on the cold marble of the table. Santos addressed the boss.

"Would you mind us putting our bikes in the garden same as we did last year?"

"No, of course not. Whenever you like."

"Come on then, let's do it now, and each take our own."

[23]

"You know where the garden is. Here at the end of this passage."

"Yes, thank you very much, I remember."

As they went out to fetch their bicycles the other four came into the bar.

"You might get the stuff out of the sidecar, Sebas," said Santos, "while we shove the bikes in the garden."

Miguel came in and went up to the boss with a smile.

"Well, how are you? I hear you've been asking after me . . ."

"Very well, thank you, and I'm glad to see you. I was only saying to your friend just now how surprised I was not to have had a visit from you people this year."

"But now here we are!"

The others lifted their bikes past the counter and into the passage leading to the garden. It had three old brick walls, and on the fourth side was the back wall of the house. Parts of the garden were shaded by honeysuckle and American vines that climbed along horizontal wires. And there were three little trees, acacias.

"What a quaint little place it is," exclaimed Mely.

The tables were placed along the walls in the shade. Some discoloured trestle tables, and two larger tables of pine-wood. Around them were folding chairs, and rustic benches made of half a trunk, secured to the earth close to the wall. Through an open window at the back of the house the wife could be seen in the kitchen, and through another corresponding window on the other side of the garden door shone a chromium bed and a yellow bedspread.

"Prop them up here."

They left their bicycles leaning against the frame of a game of Frog. Santos put his fingers into the creature's bronze mouth.

"Look out, it bites."

"Shall we have a game now?"

"This afternoon. We'll get a good one this afternoon."

"All right, now you've found it, I suppose you'll make a thorough nuisance of yourself with it, won't you!"

"You're right. Once they start playing Frog, then we've had it!"

They went along the passage, the one in the striped vest remaining behind.

[24]

"Look a minute, I say just a minute."

Santos glanced back, and looked at him from the dark passage through the frame of the door. He was clasping the slender trunk of one of the trees in the sunlit garden, and his feet stuck out at right angles.

"Come on Daniel. Stop messing around. I know you're a great athlete."

"You couldn't do that," said Daniel as he came in. He followed the others into the bar. The food tins had been brought in, and Mauricio piled them on a corner of the counter.

"We might go down slowly now," said Miguel. "What's the time?"

"It's just ten," answered Santos. "I'm ready when you are."

He finished his glass of wine.

"Come on then. Let's go. Somebody take the bottles."

"We'll come back for the stuff at midday. I don't know whether we should eat by the river or whether it wouldn't be better here. We'll see."

"You can please yourselves. Anyhow you know the stuff's safe here."

"See you later then."

"Yes. Make the most of your time and enjoy yourselves."

"Yes, thank you. We will. Goodbye."

Lucio watched the outline of each one against the light, as they went through the door and turned left along the road. The frame of the door was empty again, a blinding yellow square. The voices grew distant.

"Youth was made for pleasure!" said Lucio. "They're at the right age. What a beauty that other girl in trousers was. She's got the looks and the style to carry them off." He sketched an outline of her figure in the air with both hands, in the direction of the sunlit door.

"You see, then. You see it's all a matter of who wears them. Now give me that cigarette."

Lucio searched painfully through all his pockets for his tobacco-pouch and cigarette papers, hunching his shoulders to reach into some remote corner from which he finally fetched them up. Mauricio lifted them from the counter, saying as he rolled his cigarette: "You mustn't smoke too early. The longer you hold out the better for your health."

"And what is the time, in point of fact?"

"That's an odd question, coming from you. How can the time matter to you? How can it ever have mattered to you what the time was?"

Lucio twisted one side of his face into a grimace.

"So it surprises you all that, does it? Well, I'll tell you, it's because I'm getting old."

"You're not old. The trouble with you is that you don't stir a muscle all day long. You're sluggish from never getting any exercise, that's what you are . . ."

"Exercise? Don't need any. I've taken enough."

"When?"

"What do you mean by when? Before . . ."

"Before what?"

"Before all the trouble. And inside. Don't you suppose we had to take exercise? People imagine that in there all you have to do is to sit and wait for them to bring you your meals."

Mauricio watched him closely, letting him go on talking, and waiting for what would come next: "D'you think we didn't sweat in there? Why in prison you never stop work except at night. It's worse than outside. And you don't get paid for it either." He raised his eyes from his cigarette to Mauricio's face. "Well, what are you staring at?"

Mauricio returned to finish his job of wiping the counter.

"Oh, nothing, I . . ." He retreated to the middle of the counter. "I'm just going to fill a couple of bottles. We shall have customers in a minute. Justina! Justina!"

A voice sounded from within: "Coming, Father!" She appeared in the doorway.

"Tell me. What did you want?"

"Your mother. Because if you're going to San Fernando, it's getting a bit late, and I need those things for midday. And look, Señor Lucio wants you to do an errand for him. Tell her what it is."

"Nothing, dear, nothing . . . Only if it wouldn't be too much trouble, you might drop into the *Exprés* and get me a packet of tobacco. The green."

"Of course I will."

"Wait, I'll give you the money."

"When I come back. There's no hurry," said the girl, and disappeared into the passage.

Lucio turned round and called to her again: "And a packet of cigarette papers, Bambú . . ."

"But didn't you want them to bring back your dinner as well?"

"Oh, be quiet! It doesn't matter. Don't mention it to her. Just don't mention it."

* * *

They walked fast, impatient for a sight of the river. They crossed the road and took a path on the opposite side . . .

"Is it far?" asked Mely.

"By those trees. Do you see?"

Some tree-tops appeared straight ahead. There was obviously a steep drop down to the trees and the river bed.

"Is it big?"

"You'll see."

They did not see anything till they got to the bottom of the slope, when it suddenly appeared. There hardly seemed to be a river. The red colour of the soil stretched from bank to bank, unbroken by the current; it was as if the same earth were flowing liquid in the river.

"What a funny river!" said Mely. "And is that a river too?"

"It must be all stirred up," observed Luci.

They had stopped on the edge of the embankment, ten to fifteen yards above the river, and were looking down.

"Well, that is a swindle, isn't it? No river or anything. I *am* disappointed."

"What did you expect? The Amazon?"

"You girls can never have seen the Jarama before," said Daniel.

"The Jarama is always like this. It's always this colour."

"I don't like it a bit. It looks dirty to me."

"That isn't dirt, my girl. It's the clay it brings down.

"It looks dirty but it isn't. You'll find it's very good water."

"Oh, but I wouldn't think of drinking it. I wouldn't dream of it."

"Not good to drink, Mely," said Daniel laughing, "good to swim in."

Tito pointed to the left, upstream. "Look. That's where the train goes over."

There was a brick bridge of six great arches, and in the distance the Viveros bridge, with the houses along the main road beside it. The wood at the bottom of the hill covered a long spindle-shaped island, which divided the river into two unequal branches. The nearer, which was narrower and constricted by the embankment, had dried up in the summer heat and no longer flowed. Consequently the island was joined to the bank on this side, and could be reached for almost the whole of its length merely by crossing a little bed of red and sticky mud. Only towards the right did it still contain a little water: a backwater which separated the end of the island from the bank, leaving it as a pointed peninsula. Facing the tip of this peninsula, where the backwater joined the main stream, the water spread in a wide calm pool bounded by the concrete dam, built for a grain mill or irrigation works. To get down to the trees the path became a little irregular stairway cut into the side of the hill.

"Let's hurry now. The sun's scorching."

The steps were flattened, almost worn away. A great laugh rose from below when one of the girls slipped on the mud, sat down in the two grooves made by her heels, and showed her legs. She took it badly at first, surprised at her fall, but when she heard the others laugh she lifted her head and laughed too.

"What a clumsy idiot I am! What an idiot!" she said, still on the ground. Santos took her hands and tried to pull her up. But she was laughing too much to get on her feet.

"What an idiot I am!" she repeated happily.

"Have you hurt yourself?"

"No, no! It's all soft."

"What a view you gave us, Carmela," said Mely. "We could see everything up to your vaccination mark."

"So what? Nothing very dreadful in that, if you didn't see any farther."

"It kept us all waiting anyway."

"Come on, girl. Get yourself up."

"Gently, gently, please," and she began to laugh again.

"You can rinse your skirt in the river when we swim," advised Alicia. "It'll dry in no time."

"Remember the time Fernando fell head over heels, the day we went to Navacerrada? That was another – what do you call it – historic occasion."

"Remember? Of course I do. We take it in turns, you might say."

"And I remember it too, let me tell you, especially the cuts I got from those damned stones."

"You didn't like it at all when we laughed at you."

"Did you expect me to find it funny?"

"Why is it that everyone laughs when somebody falls down? You've only got to come a cropper and all the others split their sides."

"It's because people falling down remind us of the clowns in the circus," said Mely.

There were already several groups under the trees, sitting close together in the shade on newspapers and outspread rugs. There was hardly any turf, only bare, dusty soil. All that persisted was an occasional tuft of twisted grass smothered in dust. On the dust lay wine-jars, water melons and leather bags. A dog was trying to get its teeth into a ball. Boys ran barefoot in the sun between two improvised goals. The tree-trunks were thick with carved letters, the oldest of which had already healed over, becoming an integral part of the tree itself. They were beginning to look like natural marks. They were being absorbed into plant life. The water flowed, a reddish orange, plaiting and unplaiting the skeins of its current – the long muscles of the river. On the edge were reeds, clumps of vertical stems that stuck out of the water, and caught the floating weed, which lay in dark patches. Banks of clay stuck up in places above the water-level, like oblong red paunches in the sunlight.

"That's where we sat last year, between those four trees."

"There isn't much grass and that's a fact."

"The cattle eat it."

"Or it gets trodden down."

Here they spread Santos' beach-robe between two trees, and Mely sat on it at once, waiting for nobody.

"You're like a cat, Mely," somebody said. "You always choose the best seat just like a cat."

"The rest of us girls can go to hell for all you care. Leave us a bit of room please."

"All right, dear. I'll get up if you insist. There you are." She sprang to her feet and walked away.

"No need to get huffy now. Come and sit down again, just where you were, and don't be a nuisance."

She took no notice and went into the trees.

"Did you see that? I wonder what they said to her to make her so cross."

Daniel had gone off and was inspecting the bark of a tree. Mely went over to him.

"What are you looking for?"

He raised his head in surprise.

"Eh? Nothing."

Amelia smiled.

"Don't get sore, boy. Mayn't I see?"

"Go away and mind your own business."

He put his back against the tree to cover it.

"Oh you *are* hateful!" laughed Mely. "So it's a secret? I'll find out though, don't you worry."

"Don't be mean."

Mely searched among the initials on either side of Daniel.

"What do you bet I find it?"

"Don't poke your nose into what doesn't concern you."

"How bad-tempered you all are today! You're all horrid."

Thoroughly annoyed, she made a half-circle and rejoined the others.

Streaks and patches of sunlight broke up the shade. Carmen had spread herself on Santos' beach-robe, and was gazing into the tree-tops. Mely's head had appeared above her, against the dark leaves.

"Lie down, Mely. There's room for two. It's marvellously comfortable."

Amelia looked at her but did not answer. She then surveyed the bank, the clump of trees and the groups of people.

"Where can the others be?"

"What others?"

"Zacarías and his gang.'

"Oh them! I don't know. Are you sure they're coming?"

"Of course they are. By train. They arranged that last night with Fernando. Didn't they, Fernando?"

"Yes, they promised they would. They promised to meet us up at the *merendero* and join up with us for the evening."

Mely continued to gaze.

"I can't see a sign of them anywhere."

"They said they were going to some place they knew first," said Tito scratching the dust. "But we can get on quite well without them."

Amelia turned brusquely towards him and gave up looking. She lay down beside Carmen on Santos' beach-robe.

"It isn't comfortable, even in the shade," she said.

"I think we'll swim soon."

"It's still too early."

Santos was watching a furious game of football played in a clearing among the trees by a group of kids in bathing trunks. The ball was bright red. "Get it, get it, boy!" muttered Santos. As they ran they kicked the dust up into the sunlight. Almost the whole group was now on the ground, either full-length or propped on their elbows, and facing the river. Only Fernando was still standing beside Tito, who was drawing round his sandal with a bit of stick, outlining it in the dust.

"Do you want to know what I think?" He surveyed the whole group.

"I think you're a ghastly sight, the whole lot of you. A real dopy mob!"

He scratched the back of his neck, threw out his chest and stretched.

"Well, you might at least leave me somewhere to lie. Then we could be one big happy family."

He circled round the others looking for a place.

"You're worse than a greyhound with all that twisting and turning before you can lie down. Can't you go away somewhere?"

"Here, we'll find you a corner here if you're so choosy. But do stop wandering round and making us all sea-sick."

"Free of charge too, seeing that it's for you."

They made a space for him on the beach-robe beside their legs.

"Thank you, Mely darling. I knew I could count on you."

He sat down. An old photographer strolled through the trees, dragging a cardboard horse. He wore a yellow canvas jacket over his sports shirt, and carried his camera on his shoulder, holding it by the tripod.

"Pity we didn't bring a camera."

"Yes, it is a pity. My brother has a box that he brought back from Morocco."

"It might have occurred to you to ask him for it."

"Yes, it might."

"I didn't remember. He took a couple of rolls with great keenness in the first ten days he was home, and then he put it away in a drawer and forgot all about it."

"Talking about that . . ."

"Those boys who develop it on the spot, it's chucking your money away. They make you look awful."

"Yes, they're hopeless. But it's nice to have a few photos to remind you of times like this, when you're out for the day. You enjoy looking through them afterwards. There's old so-and-so with his usual dopy face . . . It gives you a good laugh . . ."

"Yes, it does. We've never had a photo that included the whole gang, Samuel, Zacarías, and the lot," said Fernando.

"How do they come in? They're not part of our gang?"

"Maybe you don't reckon they are, but I do. I've known Samuel since we were kids."

The photographer did not speak. He just stopped in front of each group with a questioning glance, and pointed with his thumb at the camera on his shoulder. Sometimes, if they seemed to hesitate and didn't say no to him immediately, he would add with a shake of the head: "In a jiffy," as if everyone understood him perfectly. Then he would depart with his horse, shrugging his shoulders and taking another suck at the pipe which hung from his teeth. The smoke from his pipe spread in all directions, like the fumes from an old engine.

"I think we can have a swim now," said Sebastián.

"Hang on a bit. Don't be impatient. Wouldn't you rather have a drink first?"

"Yes, you're right. I would. Pass me the bottle."

"Where's Dani gone off to?"

"I bet none of us remembered to bring a glass?"

"I've got a plastic one," said Alicia. "It's my medicine-glass, you see. But I left it up top with the food."

"We don't need a glass. There's a straw in one of the corks. Don't you see?"

"There's Dani. Look at him."

He was wandering among the trees and groups of people. Now he had stopped to watch the game of football.

"Daniel! Dani!" called Sebastián.

Daniel turned round and lifted his chin interrogatively.

"Now you'll see how fast he comes ... Here, Daniel!" He waved the bottle in Daniel's direction. "Come over here, and take a drop of refreshment."

Daniel hesitated but finally made his way back to the group.

"See, he's coming all right," laughed Sebastián. "It never fails. You've only got to show that fellow a bottle and he follows you like a lamb."

Daniel said nothing when he came, but passing to the back of the group took a place on the edge beside Miguel.

"What were you wandering about for all on your own?"

"Nothing. Just having a forage."

"Inspecting the girls, eh? Here, have a drink."

"Poor fellow, coming out without one ..."

"Don't need one." He lifted his elbow and took a swig. After a deep gulp he drew breath, and wiped his chin with his hand.

"You've almost finished the bottle. Hand over. What's it like?"

"Warm."

"Well I wouldn't know what to think. If it had been cold ..."

"Look here, why can't we put the other bottles in the water to cool?"

"That's an idea. We will."

"Now Santos, old lad, you're the nearest, and you're not doing anything at the moment. Let's see you get moving."

"Now, chuck it! Chuck it! I don't give a damn if it is warm. It tastes just as good."

"Afraid I gave you a shock. Do you find moving such hard work?"

"Yes, it's very hard work. You've no idea."

"That man was born tired."

"No, boy. I wasn't born tired. I got tired afterwards. All the week I get tired, always shifting around."

"Well, do you suppose the rest of us spend the week sitting on our backsides and staring at our navels?"

"I don't know. Anyhow, I've come for a rest. There's only one Sunday in this week and a man has to make good use of it. Someone else can go. Pass me the feeding-bottle."

"All right, chum, all right. I'll go myself," said Sebas.

He got up and carried the other bottles to the river.

"Aren't you girls going to have a drink?"

"You might have asked us at the beginning."

"Sorry, honey."

"Not at all, sir. Where wine's concerned the men come first, and the women have the dregs. Everybody knows that."

"Just our bad manners again."

The heat became more oppressive. Carmen lifted her arms, and clasped her fingers together. Santos looked towards the river, and blinked his eyes at the sun. "Now's the time for a swim," he said. "I'm going to get my clothes off anyway."

"He's right. What are we all dressed up for? Even if it's too early to go in, we'd be certainly cooler in our trunks."

Mely got up, stretched and looked all round. "Still no sign of Samuel and his gang," she said.

"You seem to want them very much!"

"With all that crowd by the river, it wouldn't be very easy to pick them out."

"Better if he'd only taken two bottles. This one's at its last gasp, as they say."

"How it does go! Gives you quite a surprise."

"It's because there are so many of us."

Mely lay down again and Sebastián returned.

"What's the matter. Have you finished the bottle?"

"I have."

"Happen to have a packet of Bisontes, Mely?"

"Yes, over there in my bag. Pass it here."

"Good," said Fernando, "Mely will now give us an American-type cigarette."

"Sorry, boy, but they're for us girls. You guys are just as happy with your black tobacco."

"Where do we undress?" asked Santos, getting up.

"There, behind the bushes. I'll come with you."

"Well, darlings, may I have my beach-robe, please?"

"Not on your life! We're not stirring. We're too comfortable. Besides, you don't really need it."

"We've all got dreadful lazybonitis this morning."

"Witty, aren't you?"

"Come on, Alberto, let's go."

Santos and Tito went off to the bushes at the bottom of the slope.

"What's the matter with Daniel?" asked Santos.

"Oh, I don't know. What do you think?"

"Haven't you noticed how moody he is? He isn't saying a word."

"That's his nature. You know how he is. One moment he'll be making more row than anybody else, and the next he goes dead on you."

"Well, he's certainly done it with a vengeance today."

"Leave him alone, and he'll cheer up."

A mother and daughter were busy peeling potatoes. The girl, who was about fifteen, was in a swimsuit. She had thin legs covered with a golden down. There were some peelings and a bottle of oil beside them, also a pink towel and an aluminium soap-box. Somebody in the river was shouting and waving his arm, with his body half-submerged in the orange water. "Mother, mother, look at me!" the voice rang very clear. "I can see you, darling. Be careful . . ." The bodies were almost the colour of the water.

"In these bushes," said Tito.

There were a couple of brambles with a great deal of dust on their rough, dark leaves. Near by were the remains of another bush that had been on fire. The stumps of its branches, almost completely carbonized, formed a black patch. Tito looked at the frail body, as Santos took off his shirt.

"You are white."

"Of course I am. You chaps go to the baths. But I've never got the time. This'll be the first swim I've had this summer."

"But I haven't swum more than two or three times myself. The fact is I start off with a good colour. You'll go red like a lobster you see."

"Yes, that's why I wanted my beach-robe. I can't stand too much sun the first time."

Alberto clasped his shoulders. He looked all round him.

"I don't think the girls will want to undress here. You can be seen from everywhere."

"They've probably got their bathing things on under their dresses. They've only to dodge behind a tree, and that's that."

"They must like being hot then. Mely's a bit upstage this morning, isn't she?"

"Why do you say that?"

"I don't know. She's done nothing but ask about Zacarías and his lot all the morning. Didn't you notice?"

"Well, what about it?"

"I dunno, chum. It's as much as to say that she didn't want to come. But she could have gone with the other gang, couldn't she?"

Santos shrugged his shoulders. "That's up to her," he said. "And I can't say I'd miss her."

*　*　*

Coming from Coslada, the most direct way was to follow the railway track as far as the level-crossing. Usually he didn't bother about his shoes. When they were new, he'd looked after them, and now that they had just been cleaned, he took a little care of them again on account of the sharp stones on the track. Sometimes when no one was looking he walked along one of the rails, trying to keep his balance. The level-crossing keeper's daughter had a red dress, and she shooed away the hens that had started walking over the linen stretched on the ground. The vine leaves above the door were smoky from the trains. The girl saw him coming and stopped to look at him. She did not laugh at seeing him balanced on a rail, but called out immediately: "There's a train coming."

The man in white shoes turned round sharply. She was pulling his leg. And the girl ran into the house, like a kitten bolting for home. At the level-crossing the man left the track and turned to the right. Here too he was careful where he stepped, for fear that the dust of the road might dirty the white of his uppers.

"Morning."

"Good morning."

He saw Justina and her mother coming out with the baskets. The girl looked him up and down and moved off, covering her head with a coloured handkerchief to protect herself from the sun.

"Anything fresh."

"Nothing, as you can see . . ."

"Shall I pour you a glass?"

"Yes."

He looked outside. He saw the two women on the road. He placed his fingertips on the counter. When the glass struck the wood, he turned towards Mauricio: "Did Julio come last night?"

"Which Julio?"

"The foreman."

"No, the foreman didn't come. The other one did."

"Will he come tonight?"

"The foreman? I suppose so."

White Shoes put his lips to the wine, and looked once more towards the door.

"Not half hot."

"Yes, middling hot, you might say. It seems to wait for Sundays to be particularly stifling."

"Yes, its no respecter of the Sabbath," said Lucio. "The river will be a sight today. It'll be swarming with people."

"I expect so," said the man and turned to Mauricio. "Are you sure he's coming?"

"Pretty sure, as I told you. Today being a holiday, it's almost a certainty."

He looked at White Shoes and went over to the sink. The man said no more. All three seemed to be waiting for something.

"You know, some of us have behaved like fools all our lives," said the man in white shoes after a short time. "Give me another glass, Mauricio, if you please."

Mauricio took the bottle and examined it closely. Then he remarked, in considered tones: "I suppose you know what you're talking about."

"You wonder why I said that? I have every reason to. Why did I come to Coslada? Why the hell did I ever come?" He resumed his silence.

"Only you can say."

"All I can say is that I ought to have stayed in my own country. I should have been better off. But you always find everything out too late."

Lucio and Mauricio looked at him, and Mauricio tried once more: "Have you had such bad luck then? What has happened to you exactly, if you don't mind my asking?"

The man lifted his face from the glass, and peered at Mauricio most judiciously from underneath his brows. He sighed: "It's nonsense. But that sort of thing in a village can be very awkward. I'm a fool to pay attention to it, all the same."

He swallowed his saliva. There was a pause. He looked out at the fields and went on: "It's all politics. Petty politics, of course. Barn-door politics. But politics all the same, one man wanting one thing, another wanting another. There's a lot of talk in a barber's shop, more than there should be. If you don't stop them they say this, that and the other, and if you do stop them they walk out. But if you don't stop them you're involved. They only seem to come for one reason, just to spill all their nastiest thoughts, all the poison in their

[38]

systems, everything that so far they have been keeping to themselves. You've only to lather and shave them – that's enough – and you find yourself involved. You're absolutely caught."

He gesticulated as he talked, and kept glancing uncomfortably at the door. His words came in fits and starts. "Well, this morning Abelardo came to see me. You know him?"

The others nodded.

"What he came to say was that three or four of them were talking about boycotting me, and seeing that I lose my customers. According to them the air at my place has had a bad effect on a lot of people in the village." He paused and looked at them without drawing breath. "You can see what it means to my business," he went on, "if the air at my house is bad for people . . . Even this seat could understand that. But what do they expect me to do? Lift my customers out of the chair and throw them into the street with their mugs half lathered, or what? Am I supposed to stuff a towel into their mouths?"

"There's nothing to beat the gossip in a barber's shop," said Lucio. "It's the kind that does the most harm."

He might have been talking of a small animal, a flea or a louse.

Mauricio returned to the point: "But what was the trouble this time?"

"That fellow Julio . . . It's all nothing. Guillermo Sánchez rents a shop from him, and doesn't want to get out. So Julio goes around spreading rumours to make him look ridiculous. He tries to discredit him everywhere. Well, Julio was opening his great mouth the other day when I was shaving him – it was last Friday – and abusing Guillermo. He didn't notice the man in the chair behind him who is hand and glove with Guillermo, so it seems. And this man of course goes straight off to tell his pal the story. So you can imagine . . ."

* * *

Daniel lifted the bottle, and fell back still drinking. Finally he choked and sat up, breathless with coughing.

"Serves you right," said Alicia. "You shouldn't have been in so much of a hurry."

[39]

Miguel slapped him on the back.

"All right, Miguel, don't bother. It's all over. Went down the wrong way."

"You are silly to be drinking wine so early," said Paulina. "If you'd waited till we have our food, you'd still have had plenty. You fellows don't seem able to get along without it."

Daniel turned to face her.

"You can talk to Sebastián like that if you like, but don't use it on me."

"I only said it for your good, and so that you don't spoil the fun. But don't worry, lad, I won't say another word to you. Do whatever you like."

"What she said wasn't so awful," protested Sebastián, "that you've got to answer the girl like that."

"I don't spoil anyone's fun, Sebastián. If I felt like spoiling the fun I'd go off on my own, see? But what about her? She pours cold water on everything."

"Don't get so worked up, Daniel," interrupted Miguel with a laugh. "If there's any cold water going, we might pour it into the wine."

Everyone burst out laughing.

"Yes, we might. It wouldn't be a bad idea."

"He speaks like a book. You're in great form today, Miguel."

"He can always find an answer. He's a wit!"

"The others are coming back now. I want to go and swim." They came out through the trees, undressed.

"Wait a bit and let them try it first. The longer we wait the warmer the water will be."

"No, no! Let's go in all together. It's no fun if we don't."

"Of course we must all go in together," said Sebastián. "It's far more fun."

"Are you ready?" Miguel asked the others as they arrived.

"Yes, but wait a minute. If we're going in somebody must stay here and look after the stuff. We can't just leave it."

"We'll all take it in turns. Then there'll be no problem."

"You needn't bother," said Daniel. "I'll stay behind. I don't feel like bathing yet."

"Right. Now let's go and get changed. Come on, Sebastián."

Fernando, Sebas and Miguel went off. The heat grew even more stifling, and they had to keep on choosing a new place because the sun struck through the foliage, and the shade was alway shifting.

"Where does this river go?" asked somebody. "Do any of you know where it goes?"

"Into the sea, like any other river," answered Santos.

"Funny! We could have guessed that. I mean what places does it pass?"

"I know the Henares goes into it just past San Fernando, and I know that it goes into the Tagus, but nowhere near here. Near Aranjuez or Illescas I think."

"But tell me, is this the river that goes through Torrelaguna?"

"I don't know. I think it must be. I know it rises in the Sierra."

On the other side there were no trees. From the coolness of the shade they saw a few bushes on the bank itself, and the blinding plain beyond like a hare's skin losing its fur in the sun. The water only flowed through the central arches of the bridge. It had left the first two piers on the farther side completely dry. The shade of the arches sheltered other groups of people who had camped on the sand with the bridge towering above them.

"There were plenty of corpses in this river, they say, during the war."

"Yes, chum. The heaviest fighting was farther up, at Paracuellos del Jarama. But the front ran all along the river as far as Titulcia."

"Titulcia?"

"Never heard of it? One of my uncles – my mother's brother – was killed there in the offensive, at Titulcia itself. That's how I know it. We were having supper when the news came. I shall never forget it."

"To think that this was the front," said Mely, "and that all those men were killed!"

"Yes, and here we are bathing quite peacefully."

"As if nothing had ever happened. And perhaps just where you put your foot, there was a corpse once."

"That's enough," interrupted Lucita. "What's the point of bringing all this up now?"

The three others came back and Miguel asked: "What are you talking about?"

"Nothing. Lucita doesn't like stories about corpses."

"About what corpses?"

"Those that were killed in the war. I was telling them that quite a lot were killed here, an uncle of mine among others."

"Yes, that's true. But tell me now, what's the time?"

"Five to twelve."

"Well, what about it? Supposing you girls were to think about getting undressed? And you, Daniel, have you made up your mind? Are you going to stay here and look after the things?"

Daniel turned round: "Eh? Yes, I will. I'll stay for the moment. I'll have a swim later on."

Sebastián had begun to leap about and do acrobatics. He rested the palms of his hands on the ground and tried to turn a cartwheel, with his feet in the air. He gave a Tarzan grunt.

"What's the fool playing at?" asked Carmen.

"Nothing. He think's he's a wild Indian."

"He's got a screw loose."

He had turned his cartwheel, and leapt down to the water. He tried it with his foot and returned delighted.

"Oh boy! The water!"

"Well, what's it like?"

"Marvellous. Phenomenal."

"Is it warm?"

"No, not warm. Betwixt and between. It's ideal. What on earth is the matter with you girls – not having your swimsuits on yet? Come on! I'll give you just five minutes and not a second longer."

The girls began to move. They got up lazily. Sebas ran off again and got embroiled with a dog. He had stumbled over the creature and it was barking all round him. Sebastián withdrew his legs as if afraid that the dog was going to take a bite at his naked flesh. The others mocked him from where they stood, and Fernando called out: "Good dog, bite him!" A fat gentleman with a Buddha-like belly and a deep, hairy navel ran up to Sebastián, covering his back with a coloured towel as he left the shade.

"Oro! Come here, Oro," he called to the dog. "Heel! Oro, good dog! Don't be afraid of him. He won't hurt you. He's never bitten anyone. Oro! What did I say? Quiet, Oro, quiet!..." He flourished the lead over his dog but did not hit him, and the animal finally obeyed. The man smiled at Sebastián and returned to his party.

"I wish he'd bitten you, really I do. I should have been quite delighted."

"And why, darling?"

"That would have taught you not to behave like a fool."

"But I wasn't annoying anybody, darling. Besides, it was the dog that started it."

"You were annoying me. I don't like it when you make everybody stare at you."

"Don't be so silly! Go off with the others and get yourself undressed. Be quick about it too, and then perhaps we can have our swim."

Sebas sat down again, panting, and his fiancée went off after the others. Miguel folded his trousers carefully and arranged his things at the foot of a tree.

"Here, Daniel! My things are all together. See?"

Daniel turned round reluctantly.

"Right."

Santos and Tito were now pretending to box among the trees. Miguel looked at the scattered group, and at the others' jumbled clothes and shoes.

"Look, Sebas, what about putting your things here, next to mine?" He pointed to the place beside the tree.

"What's the point?"

"Do as you like. They'd be better there ... At least I think so."

"Don't worry. I don't feel like getting up at the moment."

Miguel gave a gesture of resignation and continued to look at the things scattered on the ground. He hesitated. Then suddenly, without a word, he began to collect the piles of their clothing, and carry them to the tree. He arranged them garment by garment till each pile was like his own.

"Isn't it better like this?"

Sebastián turned round absent-mindedly.

"Eh? Oh yes, much better like that." His voice changed: "Tell me, is Santos a good swimmer?"

He waved his hand towards the trees, where Santos stood with Fernando and Tito. While he was boxing he had almost tumbled over a family's picnic. "What next!" grumbled the wife. "There goes my wine-jar."

"How brown you are! What have you done to get so brown?"

Two of the girls were holding up Santos' beach-robe as a curtain while the others undressed behind it.

"No, I'm not really brown. I've hardly been in the sun."

"Oh well, you must tan quickly. But I don't get brown till summer's almost over."

The girls holding the beach-robe looked at each others' bodies and the swimsuits which appeared behind it, as their garments fell one by one.

"Now that's really nice. Tell, where did you buy it?"

"At Sepu. How much do you think I paid?"

"Don't know. Two hundred?"

"Less than that. A hundred and sixty-five."

"That's cheap. It almost looks like wool. Now you hold it up for me. I shall feel quite shy. I'm so very white."

Mely and Paulina had already come out in their swimsuits and were inspecting one another.

"Hurry up, girls."

They wanted to go over to the men all together. Luci had a black woollen costume. The other two, who were browner, had printed cotton ones, elasticated and puckered all over. Mely's was green. They did not know what to do next, and kept looking at one another in doubt while they gathered up their clothes. As they looked, each compared herself with the others. They laughed excitedly and kept pulling their swimsuits straight.

"Wait for us girls. Don't go till we come."

Now they had dissolved into giggles. Alicia and Mely were whispering to one another, and the rest wanted to know what was amusing them. Then Carmen and Luci tried to hide behind the others. But

[44]

Alicia noticed it, moved aside and, catching Luci by the wrist, pushed her forward. Luci took fright and hid behind a tree.

"Don't be so silly. Come here!"

"What's the matter with Lucita?" asked Fernando.

"She's shy because she's so white."

"How ridiculous!"

But now she felt even shyer at having to appear alone for everybody to look at. She was all laughter and blushes, and only her head peeped from behind the poplar.

"You go on, all of you. I'll follow behind."

Suddenly Tito cried out: "After her, everybody!"

Fernando, Santos and Sebas rushed shouting after Tito towards the tree where Luci was. She ran a little way in the direction of the water, but the four men quickly caught her, tipped her over and picked her up by the arms and legs. Then they carried her down to the river shouting and struggling, while Miguel and the rest of the girls watched them from the shade of the trees.

"Let me go! Let me go!" shouted Luci. "Don't duck me. No! No! Help!" No one could tell whether she was laughing or crying. All that they did was to wet her a little and put her down on the bank.

"How rough you are. You nearly sprained my wrist!"

Tito moved back towards her. "My poor darling!" he said jokingly. "Show me now and I'll make it better. Don't you want me to make it better?"

She drew back sharply. "Let me alone. It's all your fault. You're a lot of savages you are."

Tito did an imitation of Lucita's girlish tones: "They're a lot of brutes, aren't they darling? Shall I smack them? Yes, I'll smack them. Take that and that, you nasty men!"

He burst out laughing.

"Can't you stop making fun of me?"

"All right, Luci, my beautiful. We'll be serious now. Don't get upset. May we beg your pardon . . . ? Everybody's to beg Lucita's pardon! On your knees!"

"We're with you."

All four knelt down, still laughing, in front of Luci, and she tried to get away. But they followed her, still on their knees, with their hands clasped in a mocking pretence of sorrow. She looked all round at the people to see if they were watching.

"You do look a lot of fools!" She gave an uneasy smile. "Do stop making exhibitions of yourselves."

She dipped one foot in the river and sent a splash in their direction. "Mind, I'm going to splash you . . .!"

They jumped to their feet with a shout and ran away, Miguel and the rest of the girls had now come up.

"Keep that sort of game to yourselves," said Mely. "Lucita's easy to tease. Only hooligans like you would do it."

Sebastián gave a shout as he rushed down to the water: "Last one in! You know . . .!"

They all ducked: Miguel, Tito, Alicia, Fernando, Paulina and Sebastián. Only Mely and Lucita remained on the bank, watching the confusion of bodies, cries and foam.

"I don't like the feel of all this mud on my feet," said Mely. "I keep being afraid there may be some little animal hiding in it."

* * *

The smoke drifted across the encampments. It dispersed among the tree-tops with a smell of cooking and burnt brushwood. In the middle of the next party, a *paella* was bubbling vigorously, and the woman in black was avoiding the smoke and flames that surged up in her face. Daniel saw her working hard, and throwing back her hair which got singed at the ends. Each time she bent down to plunge her spoon in the thickly bubbling stew, she showed her breasts, very white beneath her stove-black dress.

The little girl in the sky-blue swimsuit came up dripping and threw her thin arms, glistening with water, round her mother's neck. She kissed her scorched cheek. "Oh, don't do that, darling. You're making me all wet!"

The girl's naked legs leapt round the fire. She picked up the dog's lead and ran off towards the river. Her mother followed her with her eyes in and out of the trees, until the little thin body turned golden in the sunlight.

Down there, in the scorching light that burnt the eyes, there was a multitude of heads and chests in the reddish water, and the flash of limbs threshing the current. All along the river there was a chaotic swarm of bodies, and from everywhere came strident cries, interspersed with more distant echoes of shouts metallically magnified from under the arches of the bridge. A colourless sun, very high in the sky, shone at the zenith like a little trembling mirror. But down below, the light was red, thick and blurred. It crushed the earth like a giant's foot, pressing all shapes and outlines to the ground. Daniel had thrown himself on his stomach and was hiding his face. Suddenly an unfamiliar clanging, an unexpected and deafening din, came to his ears. Torpid though he was, he sprang quickly to his feet, and in the blinding light saw everyone along the river waving their arms. They were waving to the train, which rumbled noisily over the bridge, above everybody's head, with a long double reverberation, with an interminable weary rattle that drowned every cry. It passed, leaving behind unheard greetings and arms waving at the transitory, unknown figures in its hundred carriage windows. The bridge seemed still to tremble after the last coach, as if shivering with fever. A bewildered silence was filled afresh by the same shouts as before. Daniel saw a woman on the bank, with her skirts tucked half-way up her thighs, soaping a naked child. The broad plume of smoke which the train had left along the river slowly dispersed.

* * *

Two men came in, one in the uniform of the *alguacil*, the municipal constable, and the other a tough customer in a shirt stained with sweat under the arms. He slapped White Shoes on the shoulder.

"What's the trouble now, barber? Which of your teeth's aching today?"

"My wisdom tooth," he answered with a forced smile, casting a side glance at the boss. "We were talking about life."

"Ah, that's interesting. It's always an interesting subject. But Mauricio knows more about it than we do. That's why he gets tougher every day. Doesn't he now?"

"Tougher? Tougher about what?"

"Tougher with the cash, and well you know it."

"I'll be blowed. But talking of toughness . . . What will you have?"

"Carnation brand." He turned to the constable. "And you?"

"Carnations are over. I'd rather have wine."

He had a stupid voice; and his last word sounded like a noise, a sound produced by a thing not a person. Silence fell. Mauricio's hands stopped in mid-air, as if he had forgotten what he was doing. They were conscious of the roof above their heads; they seemed to hear the tiles up there cracking in the sun. The whole landscape had flattened itself like the side of a newly baked loaf against the rectangle of the door. No voices came from the river, nor from the level-crossing, nor from Coslada and San Fernando. The bottles glistened on the shelves. At such moments someone always asks: "What's the time?"

"I killed a goat this morning."

"Twelve o'clock exactly."

"I'm telling you in case you want a haunch. I could send you one down."

"This morning? But it's not a slaughtering day."

"It damaged itself last night. They sent a message to ask if I wanted it, and I took it. I couldn't leave the beast in pain until tomorrow. Well, are you interested?"

"Not a bit. I couldn't sell it. The people who come here bring their own food. If they ask for anything except drink, it's for tinned stuff and olives. There's very seldom any call for cooked dishes. If there was you know very well I'd buy my meat from you."

"Yes, of course I do. But this is very good meat, a two-year-old goat with plenty of flesh on it. Only last night the animal was left tied up in the yard. It seems to have got entangled in the rope and broken its leg."

"Whose goat was it?"

"It belonged to Luis at the inn. He's got six more, but he can never manage them. He hasn't an idea how to look after animals."

"Yes, we all know that. Is there anything he does know about? The man has one craze after another, and he loves complicating things . . . If I buy this today I can sell it again tomorrow. He wants to make his money overnight, and that's where he comes unstuck. It's not the right way. If you want things to pay you a profit, you must keep them quietly and look after them. It's no good being impatient or greedy. Possessions are no good on their own. You've also got to know how to make use of them."

The constable nodded agreement, pointing to Mauricio as living evidence of this fact: "No, they're no good on their own," he said in confirmation. "You've also got to-o-o . . ." He made a grandiose gesture with his hand. Mauricio turned towards him.

"Just listen to him. What can you know about it? Have you ever had any possessions at any time in your life . . . ?"

Lucio tilted his head in order to see something outside between the heads of the other two. He pointed to the square of the door and said: "Look, they have their meat too, although it's Sunday."

They all looked. Not far away, above the yellow hills, vultures were wheeling in the sky. They were describing a spiral cone, whose inverted head pointed to a fixed spot on the ground.

"He does choose some odd things to show you," said Mauricio. "I don't care even to look at them. The mere thought of them makes me throw up."

"They're disgusting creatures."

"Everyone lives on what he can," said Lucio. "They may feel just the same disgust at what we eat. It's all a matter of habit. We're taught that certain things are bad. So we dislike them, and they disgust us. But we might just as well have been taught something quite different."

Mauricio got impatient: "Oh, for God's sake drop the subject. We've had enough of this sickening nonsense. It makes me feel ill."

The butcher gave a loud laugh, and White Shoes continued to gaze reflectively through the door.

Lucio persisted: "After all, there isn't such a difference. We eat the stuff two days earlier and they eat it two days later."

The butcher laughed again.

"Look here, if you don't shut up . . . " threatened Mauricio.

"We're all flesh, aren't we? Or are you made of something different. Let him answer that one. Aren't I right? Well, perhaps you'd better tell him then. You're a butcher, so you'll know better than anybody."

They laughed. The constable broke into the conversation nervously, with shining eyes: "They ate a cat last winter, here at this very table."

He pointed with his finger. He was agitated by what he said.

"Here . . . !"

Mauricio looked him in the face.

"What do you mean? What are you driving at? This is a story you've invented."

"Here!" repeated the other. "You thought it was a hare. But it was a cat and I know it."

White Shoes looked back into the room and said without a laugh: "If all the cats and dogs that we ate in the war were let loose in this room . . . They tasted better to me in those days than beef does today. But if they were put in front of me now I'm sure I should be sick."

"You see, Mauricio?" said Lucio. "That confirms what I say. It's all a matter of habit. You get used to anything quite quickly when you have to."

White Shoes was watching the vultures again. They wheeled down from the clear sky, and plunged into that low layer of dusty air towards something on the ground, as if at the bottom of an enormous pot.

"You heard what the barber said?" persisted Lucio. "Pour us a glass, do. You needn't be afraid there'll be a big crowd today. With that face of yours you'll frighten them off."

"Will you have one too?"

White Shoes turned round.

"I beg your pardon . . . Yes, thank you. I will."

And he looked away again.

"I'll have another *cazalla*," said the butcher.

Mauricio filled the glasses, and the constable took a gulp, his eyes fixed on the girls on the coloured calendars. Mauricio turned and followed the line of his gaze.

"Well, do you like them?" he asked.

"Yes," answered the constable. "I like them. Yes."

He grew nervous as he spoke, as if suffering from a spasm. There was a smile in his little eyes.

"Well, if you like their pictures so much, old man, you'd like them better in the flesh."

"Him?" exclaimed the butcher. "He's the type that prefers pictures. Yes, sir! That's true, isn't it? Pictures can't do any harm."

"He's quite right," said Lucio. "With pictures there are no complications."

The butt of their remarks looked at them without knowing what to say.

"Sometime or other he must have burnt his fingers, I suppose," persisted the butcher maliciously.

"What, me?"

He emptied his glass, assumed an enigmatic smile and straightened his cap, to imply that they were wrong. Mauricio and the butcher laughed at him, as if he were a child. The man in white shoes once more removed his gaze from the vultures, and took another sip from his glass.

"They really might bury those carcases."

"And who do you think would go in this weather, and dig holes under the burning sun, with the earth as hard as it is? Whose job do you think it ought to be to bury a useless carcase? It's hard enough work looking after them when they're alive without having to worry about them when they're dead."

"It should be a matter of hygiene if nothing else."

"Hygiene? There's no such thing in the fields. Hygiene's all right in a barber's shop. But in the fields those birds out there are carrying out the only hygiene possible."

"A fine sort of hygiene!"

"So what? You'll find the whole place completely clean tomorrow. You may call them disgusting creatures, but vultures do no harm. On the contrary, they perform a service. If it wasn't for them we should have carrion lying about for a month."

White Shoes expressed his doubt by a grimace, but said nothing, and turned his gaze once more towards the door. The constable nodded agreement, and pointed an approving finger at the butcher.

★ · ★ · ★

Mely swam awkwardly, splashing all the time. She had put a plastic cap over her hair. While they were still on the bank Luci had said: "How well that cap suits you! Where did you say you bought it?"

"My brother brought it back for me from Morocco."

"It's very nice. It must be American!"

"I think it is . . ."

Then the two of them had gone in gradually, laughing as the water rose to their legs, to their thighs, and to their waists. They stopped and looked at one another. They laughed even louder, each egging the other on, as if they were being tickled. They splashed and clutched one another, shouting as they did so, till both were wet all over and panting with laughter. Now they joined the others at a spot where the water rose just above their waists. Only Alicia and Miguel, who were the best swimmers, had swum downstream towards the dam, where the water was deeper.

The people talked and shouted at one another in the crowded river as if the swelling babble of voices were not a thing of their own making, but the living roar of the river itself, against which they had to shout even louder in order to make themselves heard.

Luci was with Santos, Carmen and Paulina. The four of them had linked arms and were jumping up and down in unison, ducking their heads and then leaping up in the foam. Mely had gone some way off, and was trying, on her own, to improve her swimming. Tito and Fernando were laughing at her efforts.

"She fancies herself as Esther Williams," mocked Tito. "Probably thinks that's who she is."

"Idiot!"

Tito went over to her, grasped her by one ankle and began to pull her along. He laughed.

"Leave me alone, you pig, leave me alone!" cried Mely, waving her arms to keep her head above water.

Fernando came up behind and jumped on Tito's back, ducking

him completely. Mely, released, watched Fernando's up-and-down struggle, and guessed at Tito's efforts underwater.

"That's right. Hold him down, the silly fool!"

Fernando was suddenly tossed in the air, and Tito's head appeared in the foam.

"I'm glad he did that. You thoroughly deserved it!" said Mely, as the gasping Tito recovered his breath.

He swung round quickly.

"Fernando, Fernando, he's coming after you . . ."

They clung to one another in a violent and excited battle. Their two bodies turned over and over in a whirlpool of muffled splashing. Their slippery limbs, their taut muscles and heads, appeared and disappeared as they struggled for breath. Finally Mely was alarmed by the sight of Fernando's anguished face as it emerged for a moment from the tossing water only to sink again.

"Santos!" she cried. "Sebastián! Quick, quick, or they'll drown each other."

The others rushed up, and the struggle immediately ceased. Tito and Fernando looked at one another, exhausted, panting, coughing and speechless. They rubbed their necks and chests with their hands.

"That wasn't funny," said Santos to them both. "It was too much of a good thing!"

Fernando looked at him out of the corner of his eye and, still speechless, pointed a finger at Tito.

"One of them might quite easily have got drowned," observed Paulina. "Don't you know that's dangerous in the water?"

"They started on me," said Mely, "but they got the worst of it."

Fernando was finally able to speak: "He always goes too far. He never knows when it's more than a joke."

"You began it. Did you expect me not to do anything?"

"I only held you under for a minute. You're always playing these tricks in the water. Why did you have to try them on Mely?"

"You're not going on quarrelling about it now, are you?" interrupted Santos.

"He's just a savage," protested Fernando. "He hasn't got the sense of a louse. Wasn't it him that started attacking me in the river?

It could have been very nasty for both of us. You can't get apart you know, because you're struggling so hard to get your head above water and breathe. The damned fool!"

"Look, Fernando, let's drop the subject if you don't mind," said Tito. "Will you shut up?"

"No, I won't. I won't shut up."

He went up to Tito and flourished his arms in his face.

"Fernando's quite right," said Mely.

Sebas edged himself between them.

"Now come," he said. "It's all over. Forget it and stop quarrelling."

Tito glanced bitterly at Mely.

"All right," said Fernando. "But don't speak to me again today."

"Don't you worry, I won't speak to you for a month," said Tito.

He looked sad as he turned half round and made for the bank, helping himself through the water with his hands.

"Just like him!" said Fernando to the others.

Paulina watched Tito's departure and said in pained tones: "What a silly business! I don't know why you've all got to quarrel this morning. Everybody was so happy. It was just stupid, that's all."

"That applies to him, not me."

"Quite right," said Mely. "It was that fool Tito who . . ."

"Well, don't you make trouble either," interrupted Santos. "You always like setting people against one another. It gives you pleasure."

"I don't set people against one another, I tell you. Tito started mucking about, and I won't have him pawing me, understand that!"

"All right, all right," Santos cut in. "But don't shout at me. It's not my business. It's between you and him."

"Exactly!"

She went off with Fernando.

"That girl gets sillier every day," said Santos to Carmen. "She thinks she's the world's wonder."

"I've always told you so. This isn't the first time. She imagines all the men are running after her. She wants them to too, and she tries to make them."

"She's got no decency and she's as conceited as they make 'em."

"I can't stand her, really I can't."

"Nor can I!"

They joined Luci, Paulina and Sebastián.

"Come on, and let's forget it ever happened."

"Why not call Tito?" asked Luci.

"Leave him alone. He won't come. He's offended."

"But not with all of us."

"Yes, with all of us, more or less."

"Poor Tito!" said Lucita. "We shouldn't have let him go off like that."

She looked up and down the bank, searching for him. Now the fat Buddha was down there with his daughter, and they were soaping the dog Oro, who was struggling to get away.

Fernando and Mely waded downstream to join Miguel and his fiancée. But the water was already up to their shoulders, and Mely hadn't the courage to go any further.

"Ali!" she shouted. "Alicia!"

Alicia replied with a cheerful shout and a wave of the hand.

"Are you in your depth out there?"

"No, not quite," answered Alicia. "Stay where you are if you're frightened."

"Don't listen to her, Mely," said Miguel. "Come on. Just let yourself go."

Mely shook her head and said to Fernando: "No, I'm not going. I'm afraid I might get tired."

Then she shouted back to Alicia and Miguel: "Come back, you two. We've got something to tell you."

"Idiot!" said Fernando. "You're not going to tell them all that story, are you? They won't find it very interesting you know."

"I only said that to make them come, silly."

Fernando smiled: "Yes, yes, to make them come ... You really are an odd girl. You wouldn't mind stirring up half humanity if you felt like it. And, what's more, my girl, you've got the gift of getting away with it. People don't seem to mind. They'll forgive you anything you do."

"Indeed?" she said, with affected modesty. "And have you got many things to forgive me?"

[55]

"Wouldn't you like to know, eh? It flatters you to hear this sort of thing."

"Flatters me?"

"Come on, don't pretend. We've seen you at work."

"What a beast you are!" she said, a little hurt, but putting on a smile. "What a filthy swine you are when you snigger like that, with that rabbit grin of yours. Oh! it makes me so angry I could kill you!" She thrust her head into his face and shook it, clenching her teeth and fluttering her eyes. "Oh, that rabbit grin!" And she laughed herself, amused at her own anger. "Fool! Beast! But here come the others ..."

Now Santos was laughing at Carmen's terror, having dragged her to a place where the water was almost over her shoulders.

"Just look at her, what a panic she's in!" he shouted gaily to the others.

The girl was clinging to him with both hands, and craning her neck as if trying to get as far away from the water as possible.

"You're a bully, that's what you are, a bully! Oh, I'm out of my depth, Santos. Don't let go of me, I'm out of my depth."

She doubled herself up, and clung round Santos' shoulders.

"Of course you are if you pull up your legs. Put your feet down girl, and you'll be able to stand all right. You're digging your nails into me. There's nothing to be afraid of."

"You're a bully. You're making fun of me, and now you're calling the others to make them laugh at me too," she protested sulkily. "I want to go out."

The other three were now coming up behind them. Sebastián was swimming in clumsy circles, kicking up a great deal of foam, and continually bumping into the swarm of people in the river. There was a child in his father's arms, weeping and threshing his legs with howls of terror at his proximity to the water. The father did no more than damp his head, and kept on repeating: "There, there, boy! It's all right."

Paulina and Luci looked at him.

"Oh, these kids! I don't know why people will make them swim."

"I'm beginning to feel cold," said Luci. "We've been in a long time. Shall we go out?"

"Wait and see what Sebas is doing."

She looked everywhere for him among the crowd.

"There he is," said Luci. "Look. He's going downstream after the others."

He was swimming away towards Miguel and the rest.

"You can always tell where he is by the splash he makes," remarked Paulina. "There isn't anybody in the whole of the river who throws up a quarter of the foam that he does. More than the *Queen Mary*, girl. Come on."

They found Tito lying in the sun in a clearing, and went up to him.

"What are you doing?"

"Sunning myself. Had enough already?"

"Yes, we have," said Luci. "Do you mind if we lie down near you?"

"Mind, Lucita? Don't be so absurd."

"I don't know . . . You might rather be alone."

She had blushed.

"Oh, don't be such an idiot."

Paulina and Luci lay down beside him.

"Now the sun's really nice," said Paulina.

"It won't be for long. I'm beginning to burn already. It's only nice when you've just come out."

"What's Dani up to? Have you been to have a look?"

"He's still where he was. I went to get my tobacco. He's boozed. He didn't even stir."

"Why come to the river for that?" asked Paulina.

*　*　*

A little yellow dog ran in, brushed the trousers of the man in white shoes, and began to make a fuss of everybody. He was a lively, sportive little dog, and seemed to be saying good morning. He then lay down on the threshold, looking restlessly outside. His tail thumped against the bottom plank of the counter.

"Now look at that dog," said Mauricio. "How restless he is."

[57]

"Just like his master," observed the butcher. "He's the living spit of El Chamarís."

"All dogs end up by resembling their masters," stated Lucio. "I've still got the scar of a bite I had from a black dog that belonged to my sister-in-law."

The butcher burst into a loud laugh: "That's a good one!" he said.

The little dog got up again as two men came in. He thrust his nose against the trousers of White Shoes and began to sniff.

"Morning everyone!"

The man in white shoes had turned round when he felt the dog's nose on his leg.

"Down, Azufre," cried his master.

And the dog lay down.

"Well?" said Mauricio.

"Very hot. Got any beer up?"

"It's been on the ice since early this morning."

"Splendid."

"You have to wait till Sunday to get beer here."

"Oh, I could get beer up every day if you wanted it. Only you'd have to promise to drink a crate a day. Otherwise nothing doing. After one day it isn't air-tight any more, and no one will drink it."

"Whose is that motor-bike outside?" asked the man who had come in with the owner of the dog.

"It belongs to one of the boys from Madrid who've come here for the day."

"I thought it was the doctor's from Torrejón. It's the same make."

"I don't know one bike from another," said Mauricio. "They all look alike to me. It's the sort of crock . . ."

"A motor-bike's a fine thing," put in the butcher, "for anyone who wants to get moving on the road. It's a marvellous thing. You travel quickly and you travel comfortably. If they could only make it go cross-country, your humble servant would swap his horse for one. I wouldn't think twice."

"You'd have to pay quite a bit extra."

Mauricio winked as he pronounced: "He's got the money."

"Tell me, Aniano, what would a machine like that cost?"

"Let me think. A DKW of that model, five horse-power, chainless drive. It'd certainly be dear."

"How much roughly?"

"Thirty-five to forty thousand. Depends on its condition."

"That works out right," said the butcher. "Five times the cost of a horse. You did say that it was five horse-power, didn't you?"

"Yes, five horse-power."

"So you see," said Lucio, "horses cost the same price whether they're flesh or steel. They're horses just the same either way."

Aniano corrected him: "It goes by internal combustion. Now look, you can't talk about steel horses."

"All right, combustion horses if you prefer it. It's all the same thing."

"It's as if a motor-bike had five horses shut up in its engine," interrupted the constable with an excited laugh. "That's why it makes so much noise on the road. And the bigger the horse-power the more noise it makes. Just imagine one of a hundred horse-power." He shook his fingers. "That'd make an awful din."

Aniano loosened his tie. He wore a light suit, frayed at the cuffs, and a yellow pencil case with a cap stuck out of his pocket. The skin of his neck was sweating, and he dabbed it with his fingers. El Chamarís wore a kind of pale-grey windbreaker with a zip in front. The zip was open to the bottom, and his shirt to the third button. He had a leather watch strap on his right wrist and a wedding ring on his ring finger. "Roll yourselves one, gentlemen," he exclaimed suddenly. He offered Lucio a black tobacco pouch. Aniano, who was smaller, leant back on the counter with his elbows. He was looking at the white-wood cupboard at the end of the room and at a coloured print behind the constable's head, of rabbits, melons and a dead pigeon lying on a tablecloth. The constable, thinking that Aniano was looking at him, hesitated, took a step to one side, and then seeing that Aniano did not shift his gaze, also looked towards the end of the room. He might have made some remark about the prints, but Aniano shifted his position and picked up his beer from the counter.

The two women came in loaded, just back from San Fernando. Justina went to Lucio and gave him his tobacco.

"Here's your packet."

"Doesn't *cazalla* make you hot?" Aniano asked the butcher.

"No, beer's much more heating, although you mightn't think so. The more you drink the more your body asks for, and you end up in a sweat."

He passed the butcher his pouch. "Have some?"

"You may be right," said El Chamarís. "It's the same with bathing. Sometimes I feel like having a swim in the river, more for cleanness' sake than for anything else. At first it seems to make you cooler, but afterwards you're sweating more than you did before, I'd say."

The constable followed the pouch with his eyes as it passed from hand to hand. Now Aniano was giving it to Mauricio.

"No thanks, I've just put a cigarette out." He nodded at the floor. "Give it to Carmelo."

The constable took the pouch rather excitedly, like a child that had just been given a sweet.

"Thanks, I'll roll myself one," he said, clicking his tongue.

"Things fight against themselves," said Lucio. "Cold dislikes cold, and heat dislikes heat. You've only got to think how you rub your face with snow in winter and it burns at once, and goes as red as a beetroot. There's nothing so likely to stimulate a reaction. It's the same with him and his *cazalla*. It immunizes him from the heat, you see."

"Why don't you follow his example, and drink it yourself?"

Lucio tapped his belly.

"Me? My health won't let me. Pussy in here doesn't like *cazalla*. She says no. It makes her cross, and then she starts clawing and biting, as if I'd stepped on her tail."

El Charamís smiled: "You as well?" he said. "So you've got an ulcer too?"

Lucio nodded.

"Shake on it," said El Chamarís, and they did so. "Listen, we were discussing this same subject the other evening at Coslada, and we counted up, out of curiosity, to see how many men we knew in the village who had stomach ulcers. Well there were only four of us talking, and how many do you think we reckoned? Reckon up for yourself, and guess the number."

He was just absent-mindedly closing the pouch that Carmelo had returned to him. But Carmelo pulled his sleeve and called his attention with a lift of the eyebrows to the man in white shoes who was still standing with his back to them, watching the vultures from the doorway. El Chamarís went up behind him and tapped him on the shoulder with his pouch. "Roll yourself one . . ."

White Shoes turned round.

"I don't know what's wrong with you today. You don't seem to be in a mood for conversation. Now stop looking out of the door, and listen to what we're saying. Take a grip of yourself. A chat will take you out of yourself."

The barber merely twisted his mouth in a vague smile and took the pouch.

"Thank you," he said. "Don't imagine that we're . . . Yes, I should like a cigarette."

El Chamarís returned to the centre of the group.

"Well now, Señor Lucio," he said. "How many ulcers do you think we counted that evening in Coslada?"

"Perhaps a dozen? I don't know."

El Chamarís smacked him on the shoulder and pronouncing each word separately, announced: "Seventeen. No less than seventeen stomach ulcers. What do you think of that, eh?"

He became almost aggressive.

"That's not bad, not bad at all. Not a bad proportion. And don't you suppose there are just as many, if not more, in San Fernando?"

The butcher burst out laughing. "Splendid!" he exclaimed. "We ought to have a competition between the two villages, to see which has the most. It's an idea! And Aniano here can draw up the regulations as he does for festivals. Well, what do you say?"

"You can laugh," said El Chamarís. "No danger in watching the bulls from behind the barricade, is there? But if you had an ulcer, or a pussy-cat as Lucio here so rightly calls it, gnawing at your inside, you'd sing a different tune. You wouldn't find it such a joke. And you wouldn't care for *cazalla*, no sir!"

"You can live a long time with an ulcer. Plenty of things are worse."

"True enough, so long as you take care," said Lucio. "But one day you get a perforation, and then you go pushing up the daisies. You can't play tricks with the pussy-cat. It's not a playful animal."

"And there's so much you have to give up. And you get discomfort and pains too, and it ruins your temper."

"It's very unpleasant, I can tell you, very unpleasant," Lucio agreed.

"Now then, Lucio, don't pitch us a tale . . . When have you ever given anything up? You drink more in a day than any of us in this room. And now you're asking for sympathy."

"You're right there. Because I don't care whether I live another ten years or five. That's how things are when you get to my age. My sister-in-law will be relieved and I don't care how soon." He gave a stifled laugh. "It would never occur to her to say to me, even out of politeness: 'Take care of yourself, Lucio.' The idea would never even come into her head. Not on your life!"

"Back to the old subject!" said Mauricio. "You hadn't mentioned your sister-in-law for a long while. She was due for a turn. But fancy you keeping so quiet about her all this time. You've quite surprised me."

The others laughed.

*   *   *

The dam echoed with the splash of divers. Their bodies could be seen for a moment on the concrete edge, and then the spray rose as they cut the water. Every voice had a clear ring, like an echo refracted by metal. Miguel and Alicia had joined Fernando and Mely, and all four were laughing at Sebas, who was swimming towards them.

"What does he look like? The effort he puts into it!"

"Yes, he kicks up a fuss all right. Even more than his motor-bike."

Sebas arrived, panting.

"What's up?"

"Nothing. You seem to imagine swimming's a sort of wrestling match. Anyone'd think you were fighting the water."

"Everybody has his own style," said Sebas with a laugh.

"Yes, yes, of course."

"But what are you all doing?"

"They've been telling us about the row."

"I thought they would. But I say, isn't Daniel coming in?"

"Goodness knows what Daniel's doing."

"Look at him there," said Fernando, pointing at the trees.

"Daniel's having a doze, that's what. He doesn't intend to swim."

"Let's call him."

"Come on, all together, when I say three. Ready? One, two, three!"

"Danieeel!!"

"Louder!"

"Daanieeel!"

"No good. Why didn't you shout, Mely?"

"Oh, let him have his sleep. If that's what he wants it's his business."

"He's probably drunk all the other bottle. I wouldn't put it past him."

"I shouldn't be surprised if he had."

"What shall we do now? Go out?"

A great number of people had now come back to the shore and were lying in the sun. The clearings were crammed with people in swimsuits, lying on towels and beach-robes on the dusty ground. You could see a line of heads all along the edge of the dam, but their bodies were invisible, lying on the sloping concrete of the farther side. All that could be seen were heads, or arms hanging down to the water and dabbling and splashing with their fingertips.

"Let's creep up," suggested Fernando, "and catch him by surprise, all together. Then we can bump him, or chuck him in in his clothes, just as he is."

"No, not that, or he may turn nasty."

"He'd come off worst. He'd have two of us to deal with."

"Leave him alone," said Miguel. "Better not to try any jokes. They always turn out badly. You've just seen it happen."

They touched the bank and all began to run, shouting as they went. Only Mely lagged behind, walking slowly. When they came to Daniel they began to dance round him crying: "Daniel! Danielito. It's eight o'clock. Wake up, old boy, or you'll be late! The cobbler's opened his shop. Daniel, breakfast! Your coffee's getting cold . . ."

He opened his dazzled eyes and forced a smile. He flourished his arms in the air, to chase them off as if they were wasps.

"Pull yourself together!"

"Let me alone! Go away. You're dripping over me. Get away from here, the whole lot of you, and take a running jump at yourselves . . ."

"Aren't you thinking of bathing?" asked Miguel.

"No, I'm all right as I am. Go for a nice long walk . . ."

"All right, old son."

Miguel felt a tap on his shoulder and swung round.

"Look! What did I tell you?" said Fernando pointing to an empty bottle. "You see?"

Daniel had now turned over and hidden his head in his arms.

"Yes, I see. We'd better leave him alone."

They took out their towels and dried themselves. There were now fewer people in the river. From one spot came the smell of food, and in another encampment not far off they were beating their spoons on dish-covers and aluminium plates to the general annoyance of their neighbours.

"Look at my fingers," said Carmen to her fiancé. "They look like raisins."

And she showed him her fingertips shrivelled by the long bathe. He seized her hands and squeezed them saying: "Poor little hands! But, darling, you're shivering like a puppy."

"I know I am," she answered in a spoilt voice.

"Let's go off for a bit. You don't seem very fond of the water. But you shouldn't be so frightened of it really, darling."

They went down to the bank with their arms around each other's waists, and waded heavily through the water.

"It's your fault. You just try and frighten me. You enjoy doing it."

"I only want you to get used to the water, Carmela, and not feel so scared of it and anxious."

They fell playfully into step, gazing at the water, where their feet emerged as they neared the bank.

"How beautifully soft the mud is here!" said Carmela. "Don't you like walking in it? It feels so nice."

"It's just like gelatine."

Santos leant down and plunged a hand in the water, bringing up a fistful of reddish mud which slipped through his fingers. He dripped some of it on the girl's back.

"That feels funny. Now I shall have to rinse myself." As she stopped to rinse her shoulder, she asked: "Tell me, Santos, swimmers cover themselves with grease all over, don't they, so as not to feel the cold?"

"Yes, when they're out to beat a record, like swimming the Channel for instance."

"What a business!"

They clasped each other round the waist once more. Santos looked behind him.

"I can't see the others."

"What do you want them for? They've been pretty awful this morning."

"Yes, you're right. It's nicest, isn't it, love, when you and I are on our own? We don't need anybody else."

They paused on the bank, and she looked into his eyes, smiled and nodded.

"Darling," she said.

"Now you can wash that skirt of yours and spread it in the sun to dry."

The others called to them, inviting them to play leap-frog, and Santos went over to them, leaving Carmen to wash the mud off her skirt, which was stained from her fall that morning. Paulina had joined the players too, but Tito and Lucita stayed in the sun. Sebastián volunteered to crouch first, and then the rest formed a line along the river. Immediately after jumping, each one bent down in front of the leader, till he was at the end of the row and it was his turn to jump again. Whenever it was Mely's turn someone always shouted "Up!" and lifted his back just as she was jumping. But in the end she got her revenge on Fernando and bowled him over. The others burst out laughing.

"Serve you right, boy! That'll teach you not to tease Mely."

Afterwards they all banded against Miguel.

"Down with old flat-feet. Let's chuck him down!" they cried.

The line was dropping downhill towards the bank, and Miguel was not easy to overturn. The girls gave up the game, protesting that it was too rough and no fun at all. In the end Miguel and Sebas fell in a heap, and all the rest piled on top of them. They tried to drag Miguel down to the water, but they could not beat him, and all four fell in. They came out dripping and laughing.

"Good for Miguel! He's a damned ox!"

"He's a strong man. You can't get him down."

The girls looked on.

"Why has there always got to be so much rough stuff?" complained Paulina. "It's the only thing they like."

"Miguel's the strongest," said Mely. "It was three to one and they couldn't manage him."

Paulina gave her a sidelong glance.

Carmen had now slipped her blouse over her swimsuit and tied it round her waist. She was stretching out her skirt to dry when she heard Daniel calling her. Daniel looked very odd. He was scratching his neck, his face was flushed from sleep and the marks of the ground were patterned on his cheeks like the smallpox. His voice sounded scared. "Where have they all gone?"

Carmen smiled at his appearance.

"They're down there, man," she said. "Down there. Can't you see them?"

Daniel had not recovered from his stupor.

"You do look a bit bleary-eyed. You really do."

He raised his hands to his eyes and rubbed them. Then he looked vaguely into the blinding light on the river. There were few bathers. Over among the trees he saw two little naked boys with big bellies and white cloth hats. Lower down he saw Mely in the sun. He turned back towards Carmen, but she had gone. He lay down on his stomach.

"Fernando played you a dirty trick . . ." said Lucita.

"I don't know," said Tito. "Just forget about Fernando."

"But the whole thing was Mely's fault, wasn't it?"

They were both lying on their stomachs and supporting themselves on their elbows. Tito shrugged his shoulders. "What's it matter whose fault it was, anyway?" he asked.

"Tell me, Tito, what do you think of Mely?"

"How d'you mean?"

"I don't know. Do you find her attractive, I mean, and all that?"

"Sometimes."

"She's very pretty."

"Yes, she is."

"But she thinks far too much of herself. Don't you agree?"

"I don't know, I'm sure. Why do you want to talk about Mely at this moment? It's boring."

"But you have to have something to talk about . . ."

She spoke in a mournful voice, as if thrown back on herself. Tito turned and looked at her with an apologetic smile. "I'm sorry, girl. It just made me cross that we should be talking about Mely. You ask so many questions."

"We girls like to know what you think about us. If you think we're conceited and so on . . ."

"Well you aren't."

"Aren't I?"

She paused as if waiting for Tito to continue, and then added: "But I am, sometimes I am, even if you don't think so."

There was a few minutes silence, broken by another question from Luci: "Tito, do you think it's right for a girl to wear trousers, like Mely?"

"Never thought about it. Why should I? Trousers are clothes, I suppose, like any others."

"But do you like a girl to wear them?"

"I don't know. Depends whether they suit her, I reckon."

"I thought about wearing them once, you know, but I didn't dare. The time we went to the Escorial on Corpus Christi, I very nearly went and bought a pair. I hadn't the nerve."

"Silly of you to be frightened. After all, what could anyone have done to you?"

"I might have looked a fright. Isn't that a good enough reason?"

"There are so many ways of looking a fright. But I can't see why you would have looked a fright, not you!"

"Oh, but I'm not tall enough, you see, to wear trousers."

"But you're not a dwarf, honey, either. You've got a good figure. You don't have to be all that tall to be nice-looking."

"Do you think I'm nice-looking then?"

"Yes, of course. Any man would find you attractive, believe me."

Lucita reflected for a few minutes and said: "Yes. But if you thought the opposite you wouldn't say so."

"But I don't think the opposite. See?" He looked at her with a smile. "Now let's go out of the sun or we shall be boiled alive."

They got up.

* * *

The butcher spoke again in a tentative voice: "I really don't know why you talk about yourself as old. You could still get a job if you really set about it."

Lucio shrugged his shoulders: "Where? There's really more or less nothing I can do now. After everything that's happened, how could I?"

"What was your trade in the old days?" asked Aniano.

"I was a baker. I had a shop in Colmenar. My partner sold it and kept the cash. Of course he didn't reckon I'd ever come out of that place, you see. They said afterwards that he'd gone to Corunna and was in business there or something like that. The bastard walked off with the lot, as cool as a cucumber. To go and look for him . . ."

"But it's not possible! Didn't you have any papers? Wasn't the partnership registered somewhere? Wasn't there any document in your name?"

White Shoes was now interested.

"Papers? What papers?" asked Lucio. "Do you imagine that in those days of chaos it was possible to find papers or prove anything. Everyone seized hold of what he could, and afterwards . . . who'd know how he got it? It didn't leave me very keen to start up again."

"I should think not," agreed White Shoes. "A man meets with nothing but troubles, you might say. It's better to stay just where you fell when they shot you down. You know what life is, you do."

"It's cost me something to find out, I can tell you. I'd rather have remained in ignorance. You have to pay so much for experience that

[68]

when you finally get it you might as well not have it. It's no use to you."

"I don't agree," said Aniano. "I don't agree with you. The worst thing in the world is to give yourself up for beaten. Never do that. You've got to pick yourself up and go on."

"D'you think so?" asked Lucio fixing him with his eyes, and adopting a new, patient tone. "Now, let's see. How old are you, my friend? I doubt if you're old enough to know anything about those days. You and your lot might just have been old enough to be playing nine-pins."

Aniano flushed and frowned. Lucio went on: "So you mustn't give yourself up for beaten? You'll find out one day, or perhaps you won't, that it doesn't depend on you to decide whether you're beaten or not . . . You'll see. But for the present, you'd do better to keep quiet, my friend."

"You seem to be a bit of a know-all. And what's more, nobody gave you permission to call me 'your friend'. To hell with you and your greybeard wisdom!"

El Chamarís grasped his arm to calm him, and Lucio said coldly: "It's not that I'm an old man, but you're a child, an ignorant, presumptuous young pup. That's how it is, neither more nor less."

Aniano was getting very excited.

"That's enough, Aniano, don't get worked up," said Mauricio.

"I'm not getting worked up. It's this man here who thinks he knows more than anybody, he's insulting me. I'm not a child and I'm not ignorant. I've been to the grammar school, which is more than he ever has. And I've got a perfectly good diploma. He's got no business to talk to me like that and call me 'my friend'."

El Chamarís was getting restive. The butcher winked and said quietly, with some amusement: "Now, you see . . . now he's started parading his education."

"I'll take this gentlemen on whenever he likes," continued Aniano, red with vexation, "at mathematics, grammar, geography, the lot! We'll soon find out whether he knows as much as he says he does. You don't spend seven years rubbing your elbows thin on a school desk to have a retired baker come and tell you you're ignorant and read you a lecture."

[69]

"For goodness' sake, man! For goodness' sake!" exclaimed somebody.

Mauricio waved both his hands at Aniano as a sign to calm down, and hissed: "Shhhh! Quietly! Nobody's trying to deny your merits. Nobody denies you the merit of your schooling and your knowledge. Everybody respects you for them. We all know what these things are worth and what it costs to get them. Nobody here is questioning your education or trying to deny it."

"Well who does he think he is then to call me 'my friend' before he knows me?" Come on. I've got myself a position and it's thanks to my education that I'm doing the work I am, and I've earned the right to be treated decently and with proper respect ... Do you understand?"

The tears almost sprang to his eyes in his fury. But everyone was quietly laughing at him.

"Of course," said Mauricio, "of course we respect you for it. Of course you have our respect."

"How much do I owe you, please?"

He had the money already in his hand.

"Eleven pesetas."

He put the money down on the table, leaving a glass of beer that he had hardly begun.

"Aren't you going to drink it?"

"No. The gentleman can have it. Good day to you."

He rushed out so precipitately that he almost knocked down White Shoes who dodged to one side with his arms extended, as if he were being charged by a bull. "There he goes," he said when the young man had already vanished through the door.

"What an idiot!" exclaimed Mauricio. "Once these youngsters have a little bit of schooling they think they've got the right to tell anybody his business."

"Oh he's a good lad," replied El Chamarís. "I hate to see this sort of thing, and I know he'll be sorry it all happened for a long time to come. He likes to be on good terms with everybody, and to feel they appreciate him. If he sees that anyone doesn't like him it hurts him quite a lot."

"Let it hurt him then," said Mauricio. "Who asked him to interfere in other people's business? I should like to hear him airing his conceit in Madrid, I should indeed."

"He's not a bad youngster, I tell you. Once you know him and can take him, you even come to like him. I respect him, honestly. Think about him a minute. He's got a generous nature. There's not an ounce of malice in him."

"Well, he put his foot in it all right this morning," remarked the butcher.

"Yes, of course he did. But Señor Lucio was also partly to blame. He went a bit too far with him."

"I wanted to see how far he'd go with his criticisms and his bits of advice. I wanted to see how he'd like it if somebody talked to him in the way he talks to other people. If you don't use the right word and say 'horse-power', then this lad'll come and tell you what you should have said. What stuff you have to listen to!"

"But you shouldn't have talked to him like a child, Señor Lucio. That wounded his pride."

"Why not? I'm old enough to be his father. In the old days everybody talked to boys of his age like that. I don't know what things are coming to now, but here suddenly a fellow like that's somebody. Is it because he works in the Town Hall that he thinks he ought to be treated as a big-shot? I should never talk to a boy of that age otherwise as if he were a grown man. He got on my nerves, and I gave him the treatment he deserved. That's all."

"I agree with you. Working at a typewriter flies to the heads of these whipper-snappers, and that's a fact. We all treat them as if they were the lords of the earth every time we have to go and ask them for some wretched form, or to comply with some regulation. And what use do they serve except to make life more complicated all the time? Do they produce anything of value? What have they got to be so idiotically conceited about then, when they bring you a batch of papers? Luckily for them people are inventing new complications and devising new forms every day. Otherwise they would have nothing to eat. And what'd happen then? A lot of useless unemployables would be wandering the streets and starving to death."

[71]

"Now, Señor Mauricio, you're really working yourself up against the poor boy. I tell you there's not a speck of malice in him."

"Of course there's no malice in him," said the butcher. "Just a bit of pride, which is a bad thing in a lad of his age. How old can Aniano be now? Not more than twenty-three or twenty-four ..."

White Shoes listened in silence, and Carmelo brushed the dust from his cap with his sleeve, rubbing up the letters of his badge until they shone.

"Pride is something you've got to learn about," said Lucio.

"It's bad not to have enough. Then everyone orders you about and treats you like a dummy. But it's worse to have too much, because then you make trouble for yourself. What you need in this life is self-possession. If you've got that no one will make fun of you, and you won't be tripped up by your own arrogance."

"It was the same thing with that idiot and his shop," said Mauricio. "You know what happened to him. Bursting with pride he was. And why was the fellow so proud? Because he had his name in great big letters above the door. And what good did it do? All that pride just led to his own ruin, and what's more it showed everybody he was a fool."

"And he wasn't a bad fellow either," put in White Shoes. "He treated his staff well. Of course he kept them at a distance, that was his nature. But he was very generous to them. I've shaved him hundreds of times, and he could be a very friendly soul when he wanted to be. Whenever he made a joke, I remember, or told a dirty story, he'd lift his head from the cushion and look all round with the soap still on his face, to see how it had gone down and whether people were laughing. He always did that, I remember."

"Have you heard anything more about him," asked Mauricio.

"Hardly anything. I think they went to his wife's village afterwards ... It was somewhere near Caceres. What is its name now ...? Navalmoral, that's it. Navalmoral de la Mata. It's a big village, I know."

★　★　★

The branch of a tree was washed down the river.

"Look. It's just like an animal, the way it moves!" said Fernando. "An alligator."

It was a green branch that had only just broken off. Every now and then it grounded on a sandbank, swung round on itself and floated off again slowly, just sticking up from the red water. They enjoyed watching it.

"I'm hungry," said Alicia: "It's time we thought about eating." Now some children, who were just coming out of the water, went back to see the branch, caught it by one end and brought it ashore. They dragged it up the bank, trotting like the mules that drag the dead bull out of the ring. Now the whole band made for the encampment where Daniel was, and Carmen came to meet them.

"What's he doing?" asked Santos. "Is he still asleep?"

"He just opened his eyes a minute ago. I did laugh ... He's as sozzled as can be. He's got a real thick head."

Tito and Lucita had now come up. Tito stretched his limbs, extending his arms wide and lifting his chest to the sun.

"Now," said Miguel when they arrived. "How'd you like to arrange things? Would you rather eat here, or shall we go up the hill?"

"I think it would be nicer to eat up there," said Fernando.

"Oh no it wouldn't," said Mely. "Why drag all the way up the hill in this frightful heat? What a hopeless idea."

"Of course we must eat here. Has anyone got the strength to move? It's quite a long way, you know, and we should have to get dressed and all that."

"I only suggested it because we should have a table in the garden, and chairs to sit on, and a table-cloth too if we wanted it."

"Not worth it, old fellow. What's the fun? If we'd wanted to eat like that we could have stayed at home. What do we come to the country for? We're out for the day, and we'll have a picnic. Otherwise count me out. We know all about eating at table."

"Of course. Variety's the spice of life, as the saying goes."

"Not on your life. We stay here. That's all there is to it. We've made up our minds."

"Well then, let's decide who's to go up for the tins."

"We'll have to draw lots."

"The Chinese way, by straws, eh?"

"You're crazy, boy," said Alicia. "Drawing straws takes ages and we shall drop with hunger in the meantime."

"Straws are more exciting."

"Oh, forget about the excitement. Let's do it any way, and get it over with."

"All right. We'll be as quick as setting cement," said Miguel. "You'll see. We'll do it with bits of paper. Anybody got a pencil? Hasn't anybody got a pencil?"

"Who would think of bringing a pencil into the country? What on earth'd we want it for?"

"Will a lipstick do?" asked Mely. "You can have mine if it will."

"That's fine. Chuck it over."

"Pass me my bag, if you don't mind."

"Coming over."

Mely caught it in the air, and while she was searching inside she said: "Don't mess it up will you? They're very expensive."

"Of course I won't. Now, where are we going to find the paper?"

"Here, take it," said Mely to Miguel, as she handed him her lipstick. "You'll hardly have to press it at all. It need only touch the paper and it'll make a mark."

"There's plenty of paper here, look."

Tito picked up a newspaper from the ground and tore a strip from the edge. Mely had taken her packet of Bisontes from her bag.

"Like one, Ali."

"Thanks. Chuck it over."

"One of us won't be enough to carry all that stuff. Two of us will have to go up, I think."

Miguel was now distributing the papers.

"Yes, two. There must be two."

"We mustn't leave Daniel out of the draw," said Fernando. "Put one in for him. He may be sozzled, but we won't let him off. That'd be a cheat."

"He's in his seventh heaven at the moment, the poor devil."

"Then he'll have to come down."

"We've got four blanks and two marked with a cross. Whoever

gets a cross puts his clothes on and goes up to get the food. Agreed?"

"Agreed."

Mely and Alicia had lit their cigarettes, and Santos who was watching them said with a laugh: "Seeing women smoking takes away all my taste for tobacco."

"Don't be so beastly. Do you want to keep all the pleasures for yourselves? You men have got enough advantages already."

"Tell me one."

They had finished folding the papers, and Fernando called to the girls: "Now I want one innocent hand! Come on. One innocent hand to draw the lots."

The girls looked at one another and laughed.

"There aren't any innocent hands here. What ideas you fellows do get!"

"Well then," said Santos, "which of you ladies is the most innocent?"

Mely said with a spiteful expression: "Lucita! Lucita is the most innocent of us all."

"Yes, Luci of course," they insisted, laughing. "Let her do it."

"Come on, Lucita. They've seen through you." said Fernando.

"Come over here. You've got to draw the lots."

"What exactly have I got to do?" asked Lucita, who had gone quite red.

"We're going to tell you in a minute. It's very easy. Now Mely, my beautiful, you can lend us something else. That cap of yours would just do for us to put the papers in."

"You come down on me for everything. All right, here's my cap. Catch."

Sebas caught her cap, put the papers into it and mixed them up, saying: "Three fingers of vermouth, two of gin, a drop or two of peppermint, a little bit of ice, shake and serve immediately. Take it, Lucita, darling."

"Look, you stand here with your back to us and take out the papers one by one, and each time you take one out, you ask me, 'Who's this one for?' Then I name somebody, and whatever is on the paper you've drawn applies to him. Is that all right?"

Luci nodded.

"Come on then."

"Within a few brief moments," began Sebas in the voice of a quack at a fair, "we shall proceed to the draw. Now silence for the winning card."

Lucita had taken up her position.

"Who's going to get the booby prize?"

"No more bets, gentlemen," said Miguel. "Draw, Luci. Draw the first lot."

"Here now. Who's it for?"

Miguel looked at everyone with a smile.

"Foooor . . . for Santos."

"And now what do I do? Do I have to open it?"

"Yes, of course, to see what's on it."

There was a silence as Luci unfolded the paper.

"There's nothing on it. It's a blank."

"That let's him out then."

"As good as a rupture, boy."

"What? Let's see it. Let her show it to us."

"Suspicious, eh? Don't you trust Luci then?"

"Come on. Draw another, and on with the fair."

"Right away?"

"Yes, yes. We're in a hurry."

"Here you are. Who's it for?"

"This is for Tito."

Tito was also let off. He said nothing. But having been on his feet, he now sat down.

"Put it there," he said to Santos. "We two aren't going up."

The next lot was for Fernando, and it had a cross.

"The fifteen million prize at Arguelles," shouted Sebastian.

"That's fine," said Mely. "Wasn't it you that wanted us to go up. Now you can put your clothes on."

"Wait a minute, girl, till we find out who else it's to be. Let's see who will be my partner. Go on, Luci."

"Who's this for?" asked Luci.

"For me," Miguel replied.

It was a blank, and Sebastián protested: "You're too clever. He's a cunning devil, he is. He knows the same lot hardly ever comes up twice running. So he waits for a cross to turn up, and then he says the next one's for him. That's sharp practice."

"Send for the complaints-book then. Next, Luci."

The next one was for Daniel and it had a cross. They gave him a cheer.

"Daniel's in luck."

"Put it there, boy. This'll wake you up a bit."

Daniel lifted his head and frowned at their jokes. Fernando went up to him and smacked him on the back.

"There you are, old fellow. It's you."

Daniel pushed his hand away.

"I'm not going."

"What do you mean?"

"I mean what I say. I'm not going."

"Not going? What's all this about?" He turned to the others: "Did you hear what he said? He says he won't go. You'll come up the same as I will. I'm telling you. If you don't like it you can lump it. Do you think I'm overjoyed myself? I don't want to go at all, but I shall all the same."

Sebastián tried to make peace.

"Now, Daniel, please don't be a bore. You're the only man here who's dressed, so it's less trouble for you. Now don't put everyone else out. The girls are dying of hunger."

"But I'm not. I'm not at all hungry, you see. I couldn't eat a mouthful. So I've no reason to go up the hill."

"You should have said that at the beginning. Now it's been decided on the draw, and you're going. I tell you you're going. And if you don't eat anything yourself, that's your affair," shouted Fernando. And when he saw that Daniel was not moving he seized him by his vest.

"Did you hear me? Get up now! Get up, I tell you."

Daniel tore himself free and faced up to Fernando. "Take your hands off me, you. I've already told you I'm not going. I haven't any intention of going. Do you get it?"

"This is ridiculous. If you can't persuade him . . ."

"You're a prize one, you are. You ought to be ashamed of yourself. Why should you be treated differently from anyone else? Who do you think you are?"

"Chuck it, Fernando, let him be," said Miguel. "Much better let him be. What can you do? We can't drag him up there. I'll go up myself instead, so that settles it. We'll go up together. But we'll leave his tin up there, since he claims he's not hungry, and that's flat."

"But it's all wrong, Miguel! He drew a cross. So why doesn't he go? Why should we let him get away with it just because he says no. He's behaving like a spoilt child."

"Well, what do you expect me to do about it? You can't drag him there by force."

"If Daniel won't go, then I won't either, and that's flat. Send the office-boy."

"What a bunch you are! Always quarrelling," said Paulina. "Look at the time."

"Settle it amongst yourselves. The draw lets me out. Let's stick to it."

"If I were Fernando I wouldn't go," said Mely. "He'd be a fool if he did."

"Daniel's a selfish brute."

"He's got no team spirit," agreed Alicia. "You'd be a fool to go."

"Be quiet, you."

"Why should I be quiet? Aren't I standing up for you? And don't talk to me like that anyway."

"Right," cut in Miguel. "I shall go. If anyone else volunteers, he can come too. Otherwise I shall go alone."

Tito got up.

"Wait a minute and I'll be with you."

Sebas, who had laid his head on Paulina's lap, remarked: "Look, if you are going, you might take these three bottles back and get them refilled."

Silently they picked up their clothes and the bottles, and made for the bushes, where they got dressed.

[78]

"What a day!" said Tito. "Did they tell you about my row with Fernando?"

"Yes, Mely told us about it."

"Mely's a mischief maker. The whole thing was her fault. And then she goes and blabs about it. Now we've got Daniel refusing to go up. Not a moment's peace. One damn thing after another."

"Don't let it worry you. There are always frictions. But you mustn't take too much notice of them."

"Yes, but what have we come here for? To quarrel or to enjoy ourselves? It makes me sick. It's a hell of a nuisance to have these rows all the time. A nice look-out."

"Rubbish, man. You must take them for what they are, just silly nonsense."

"Listen. You may think I'm joking. But just now, I don't mind telling you, I was on the point of getting on my bicycle and clearing right off back to Madrid. That's the truth. And if I stayed here it was for your sake, for you and Alicia, and two or three others."

"That would have been really absurd. It wasn't as bad as all that."

"Fernando's a good pal. But just look what he does. If he had been anyone else I'd have laid him out when he went for me in the water. And it was all because of Mely. She's to blame for the whole thing."

"So you find Mely attractive too, do you?"

"Me? Lord, no. She leaves me absolutely cold. And after today even colder than that. After today's affair you can have her. I want nothing more to do with Mely. In future it'll be 'hello' and 'good-bye.' That's all she'll get out of me, not another word."

"That's a big resolution, chum. You're getting quite the strong man."

"Yes, I've made up my mind. You'll see. She really is a silly girl. Wherever she is there's always trouble. She's a mischief maker, a trouble maker, and nothing else."

Miguel smiled as he buckled his belt.

"She's got you rattled and no mistake, chum. I'm ready now when you are."

"Let's go."

They started off.

"Who did you say found Mely attractive," asked Tito.

"I? Nobody. I don't know."

"You *did* say something about it just now."

"No, I didn't. I didn't say anything. She's a girl with a lot of good in her, you know."

They climbed on to the embankment by the twisting steps that were cut into the bank.

"I don't know about anybody in particular."

The job of climbing reduced them to silence. On reaching the top they stopped, out of breath, and looked back. The tops of the trees still towered above their heads. They could see the sluice and the stretch of water contained by the dam. On the other bank there were only clumps of willows and holly bushes with a few groups picnicking among them wherever there was some shade. Beyond, a flock of sheep covered the flat ground like a little moving sea. The shepherd in his white cap had come down to the bank and was looking curiously at the people, resting his weight on his stick.

"What do you think? Is Fernando after Mely?" asked Tito.

"Possibly."

The railway track ran high on an artificial embankment which cut the flat ground in two. Bushes climbed the bank and even brushed the train wheels. Further off, where the hills began, the straight line of the track was broken. It ran underground into a narrow tunnel. From where they were they could see the outlet of the sluice on the other side. Now hundreds of people in swimsuits were sunning themselves on the concrete dam. Packed tight together and scorching on the overheated slope, their little shapes melted into a multi-coloured agglomeration of human limbs. Arms, legs, heads, chests, swimsuits formed an anarchic and indistinguishable mass.

"Let's get a move on, Tito. They're waiting for us. If they knew we'd got no farther than here . . ."

The water ran more swiftly below the dam where the sluice gates emptied out. Swift and shallow, it ran among rounded stones and lumps of red earth crowned with tufts of grass. Close by there were *merenderos* places, one after the other, along the course of the river; single-storey shacks. The nearest of them were perched on a bluff which had been formed by erosion. But those beside the dam were at water-level, and they could look down on their roofs. They could see people picnicking there and swarming beneath the arbours, and distinguish voices and laughter, the sound of fists and crockery on the wooden tables, the smoke and smell of frying, and the coming and going of trays in the hands of waitresses or of some part-time waiter in a black bow tie and white jacket: all of which came up through the gaps between the leafy branches of a giant mulberry tree. Tito and Miguel passed two *merenderos* on the hill, which were full of rather quieter people who were talking discreetly over their food. They took the path that led on to the road, which was flanked on the right by a wire fence screening a vineyard. But the vineyard on the left was unprotected and subjected to the constant depredations of crowds of children who invaded it from every side. Powerless to prevent them, the old watchman threw stones and cursed them.

"God-awful Sunday he's having!"

When they came to the road there were other properties divided from it by walls crowned with bottle-glass.

"I call that really vile," said Miguel, pointing to the walls. "You'd have to have a nasty mind even to think of a thing like that."

"Some people are frightened to death of being robbed."

"Nobody likes it, you know. But that's not the way to prevent it. It's not so much the thing itself, though, as what it represents. What do they think they're doing? Merely showing their selfishness and how anxious they are about their possessions."

"True enough. It's a beastly trick."

"The fellow who invented the idea of putting broken glass on walls must have needed a nice long rest after that brainwave. He must have been the meanest-minded skinflint this world has ever known. The perfect son-of-a-bitch."

"Couldn't agree more."

They arrived at Mauricio's.

"Afternoon!"

"How is it going, lads? Was it nice in the water?"

"Pretty good."

"Are you going to eat up here?"

"No down, by the water. We've come to fetch the grub."

"Sounds a good idea. So you want some more wine, eh? I see the lot I drew for you this morning hasn't laid you out."

Mauricio lifted the bottles from the top of the counter.

"Come on," said Lucio, "and give them a glass each on me. You can fill ours up too at the same time."

Miguel turned round.

"Thank you very much."

"Not at all."

The constable came forward and, pointing at Miguel, asked Mauricio: "Is this the gentleman you said was such a good singer?"

Mauricio rebuked him with a glance: "Yes. What do you want with him?"

He turned to the others. "Now you watch. You just watch. He can't leave anybody in peace."

The constable paid no attention to Mauricio. He talked excitedly to Miguel: "Excuse me. Allow me to shake you by the hand? Carmelo Gil García's my name. I'm crazy about singing." He addressed Miguel as if he was a famous singer.

"It's a pleasure."

"The pleasure's mine. And what I specially like," went on the constable, "what I particularly like is flamenco. Not last winter but the winter before I had to pull in my belt. I bought a radio. Or you might say I gave it myself for a Christmas present. And all for the singing. You can guess what sacrifices I had to make. But it was worth it, I can tell you. Yes sir, Pepe Pinto and Juanito Valderrama, the stars of song, I know all their names, yes sir, yes sir . . .'

He was still grasping Miguel's hand, and Miguel was smiling at him.

"But you mustn't take me for a professional, really you mustn't," he said. "I sing a little, only a little. Just for my friends."

"I'm sure you must be very good. Perhaps I'll have the pleasure of hearing you give us a song. We should really enjoy that."

Mauricio lost his temper.

"Let go of his hand, you fool. As if we weren't sweating enough on our own in this weather without holding hands into the bargain!"

Carmelo did as he was asked.

"Leave him alone," said Miguel. "He's a good fellow . . ."

"You're wrong there. When he's drunk a couple of glasses, he starts clinging to anybody he can lay his hands on. And I'll tell you what he's after. He wants you to start singing flamenco with him, this very moment without so much as a bite or sup."

"That's a lie," the constable protested. "I know you can't start a man singing as easily as all that. Don't imagine I don't. You can't ask anyone to strike up on the spur of the moment. A man's got to get into the mood and warm up a bit. Isn't that right? You don't get fine singing any other way, do you now?"

"Look here. Will you leave this lad in peace once and for all? What's all this nonsense you're talking got to do with him? Can't you see that you're boring the company?"

"What's got into you, man? I've been pleased to meet this young man and exchange ideas about a subject that's very dear to us both. Tell me, young man. I haven't been boring you, have I?"

"Not at all. Quite the opposite."

The butcher and El Chamarís were dying of laughter.

"Fine chap Carmelo! He's got a way with him!"

Tito had to restrain his inclination to smile, and soon Carmelo joined in the general laughter. There was a surprised and happy look on his face, as if he were delighted at having been the cause of it all. Only White Shoes was not laughing. A little girl in a red dress appeared in the doorway and said from there: "Father . . ." She stopped short on noticing the presence of White Shoes.

"Come in, my dear," said Mauricio. "Don't stand out there in the sun."

The girl was scared, but El Chamarís insisted: "Come in, Marita. Don't be so silly. Nobody's going to eat you."

She rushed in, crossed the room like lightning, and clasped El Chamarís round the legs. El Chamarís kissed her on the head and said: "But darling, why are you so shy today? Generally she's a cheeky girl, believe me. Tell me, what do you want?"

The child answered in a whisper: "Mummy says will you come to dinner."

"Good. We'll go this very minute."

The girl squeezed her father's leg more tightly every moment, turning her back on all the others. Now White Shoes went up to her and crouched beside her, saying with a smile: "So it is the same little girl as I saw this morning. Don't imagine I can't recognize you, you sly puss."

She hid her face between El Chamarís' legs and White Shoes persisted: "Turn round, young lady. Look over here for a moment. Are you afraid you've made me cross?"

Half the child's face appeared and she began to smile. Then she hid her face again. White Shoes still persisted: "Don't you want to be my sweetheart?"

Now the child smiled more broadly, and suddenly showed her whole face.

"What secrets have you got with the barber?" asked her father.

"That's our business," said White Shoes. "Isn't that true, my pretty? What's your name?"

"Mari."

El Chamarís drained his glass.

"You two are up to some mischief," he said. "Come on, darling. Home we go."

"You've got a very charming little girl," said White Shoes as he got to his feet. "See you again soon, Mari, my sweet, eh?"

"Come, darling. Answer the barber, do, seeing you're such friends."

"Goodbye, mister barber."

"Won't you give me a little kiss?"

He bent down his head, and she gave him a perfunctory kiss, which scarcely touched his cheek.

"There. See you soon, dear."

"So long, gentlemen. Here, Azufre . . . ."

The dog leapt up and rushed through the door ahead of his master.

"See you this evening."

"She's quite a big girl for a father as young as that," remarked White Shoes. "How old is she?"

"She must be six or seven."

"Tell me," said Miguel to Mauricio. "You couldn't let us have a jug by any chance, and a few pieces of ice, so that we can make a *sangría*?"*

"I'm not very well off for ice, I'm afraid. What I have here has to last till tonight. But we'll see what we can do. I can let you have a jug. Faustina! You'll want lemonade too for a *sangría*."

"Yes. And a lemon, if possible," said Tito.

"I think we can find you a lemon."

Faustina entered.

"What do you want?"

"See if you can find a jug for these young men, and a lemon."

His wife nodded and went out again.

"That's a very fine idea," said Lucio. "A good *sangría* goes down well in this heat. And if I were you, you know what I should put in? Two or three tots of gin. Then you get back, so to speak, the alcohol that you lose by putting in the lemonade. What do you think of that recipe?"

"Grand. But it's enough of a mixture as it is. It flies to the girls' heads in no time."

"Yes, of course. In that case . . . If you are considering the ladies, I say no more. But let me tell you in my day we weren't too considerate. Anything we could we did. But in these days, I know . . ."

Faustina came in and put the jug on the counter. She then went out again, but stopped in the door, addressing Tito and pointing to the jug: "And don't you break it for me. It's the only jug I've got. So take good care of it."

"Don't worry, Señora. We'll guard it with our lives." Faustina disappeared down the passage.

"And the lemon," Mauricio shouted after her, raising his head from the icebox. He took out a few lumps of ice and put them in the jug.

"You'll have to do what you can with these bits. I can't spare any more."

* A cup made of red wine, lemonade, lemon and ice.

"That's plenty. Thank you very much."

"How many lemonade do you want?"

"How many do you think, Miguel? How many ought we to take?"

Miguel was busy stowing the wine bottles and food tins into the haversacks.

"Let me see . . . I think we could do with eight. Eight ought to be enough. And another big bottle of wine. They'll have about finished all that we've got down there, by this time."

"Eight then."

Faustina came in.

"The lemon," she said. She put it down beside the jug with a little thud, and went out. Miguel and Tito were stowing away the crockery.

"Tidy few of you come today," observed the butcher.

"Eleven of us altogether." He turned to Mauricio. "Another glass for everybody, and score it up to us please."

"Thank you very much, young man."

"Don't mention it!"

"It's a bad thing not to be equal numbers when you go out for the day," said Lucio. "There's always one left out."

"Don't you worry. The odd man out today has drunk himself silly and he's been sleeping like a log. He didn't even have a swim." said Miguel.

"What about Dani's box?" asked Tito. "Are we really going to leave it up here, or shall we take it down after all?"

"Take it down of course. You don't want us to play a dirty trick like that on him, do you?"

"Well, he played one on us first, didn't he?"

"You want to pay him out for being stupid then?"

"No, of course not. I couldn't care less. It was your idea. So far as I'm concerned we take his box and that's that."

Miguel had finished his packing, and said goodbye to the others.

"Right. So long, everybody."

"See you later. Have a good afternoon."

"You've got plenty on your backs. Mind you don't stumble."

"Thanks a lot. Don't you worry. So long."

The two young men went out with the sacks slung on their backs.

Miguel was carrying three bottles in his hands, and Tito carried the fourth bottle, and the jug that Faustina had lent them.

"What's the time?" asked the butcher.

"Time for dinner. It's after half past two."

The constable had taken off his cap again and was scratching his head.

"Something itching?" asked the butcher.

"Yes, his brain's beginning to work," explained Mauricio.

The butcher yawned and went to the doorway. There was a sound of distant music.

"You can hear the row they're making on the river even up here."

"There must be a big crowd down there, sure enough!"

"In the old days," said White Shoes, "it used to be us from the villages who went to spend our Sundays in Madrid. Now things have changed and the Madrid people come out in the country."

"Nobody's content with his lot," said Lucio. "He always wants the other thing."

"Yes, that's right," observed Carmelo. "But if I could live in Madrid I'd give all this up without a damned thought. Better be your own master in Madrid, even if you're nobody there, than be mayor of Torrejón, though it's quite a place. What do people say? 'Madrid's half-way to heaven.' They're right. It's a fact."

"Well now," said the butcher, turning to him with a smile. "What would you do in Madrid? Tell me that. Let's hear?"

"Me? What should I do?" His face went red. "What should I do in Madrid?" He clicked his tongue as if about to make an exciting statement. "Well first of all . . . I should go to a tailor, and let him make me a suit, a good suit. Really well made. A three-piece suit for five hundred pesetas."

He rubbed his hand over his worn jacket as if to effect a transformation.

"For five hundred pesetas?" interrupted Mauricio. "But what do you think it costs to have a suit cut for you in Madrid? For five hundred pesetas you wouldn't even get the waistcoat, man."

"Never mind the cost," said Carmelo. "Five hundred or seven hundred, it's all the same to me . . ."

"All right then, go on. Let's take it that for seven hundred you'll get something that's not too bad. What would you do then? Go on. Let's hear."

"After that then, I'd go out in my smart suit, all dressed up, with a silk handkerchief here in my top pocket. See? And a wrist-watch – one of those chronometers, and I'd take a stroll down the Gran Vía. Only a short one, just up and down. Next thing, when I was tired I'd sit myself down on the terrace of that café. What is it called? The Zahara. On the terrace of the Zahara. Then when I was good and comfortable, I'd clap my hands." He mimicked the action. "And up comes the waiter. I'd have a large beer, as much as the glass would hold, and . . . and a decent portion of chips with it. Yes, and the bootblack. I'd call for the bootblack to put a good shine on my shoes . . ."

White Shoes looked at his uppers.

"Just as I thought, my friend," said Lucio. "That was exactly what I expected."

"What was?"

"That the first thing you'd do would be to call the bootblack. I was sure you would."

"And why were you so sure about it?"

"Because I was. I couldn't be wrong. I'm an old man, you see. It's a sure thing. The first thing that occurs to anybody when he's thinking about the good life is that he'll send for some fellow to clean his shoes."

* * *

"What about starting on this fourth bottle, right away?"

"Without any eats?" asked Alicia. "The right thing now would be something for an appetizer."

"All right," said Fernando. "There are little crayfish in this river. See if you can catch us some."

"Ha! Ha!"

"Didn't the peanut man come by a minute or two ago?" suggested Sebastián. "We could get a couple of pesetas worth. They'd make a snack."

"Not a bad idea. Did you see where he went?"

"He went down towards the water. He's only just gone. A man in a white coat with a hat made out of newspaper like the kids in the comic strip."

"Look if you can see him."

"If anyone mentions food to you, honey . . ." said Mely to Alicia.

"There he is all right. Just down there . . . Look! That's the fellow, isn't it?"

She pointed him out among the trees, stopping at another group; a patch of sunlight shone on his white coat. Fernando put both his little fingers in his mouth and gave a long whistle to call him. He was taking some money, but he signed to them with his other hand to wait a minute and he'd be with them.

"You spotted him pretty quick," said Fernando.

"If it's got anything to do with food, that girl . . ."

"Stop teasing me, do. Anyone'd think I ate like an ox."

"There's nothing bad about that. It's a sign of good health." Sebas got up for a moment to look past Paulina at a nearby party.

"Talking of food," he said, "there's a fine smell coming from that pan. Haven't you smelt it?"

"I've been sniffing it for a long time, boy," answered Santos.

"I didn't like to say anything in case it made you hungry. I'd like to go over and visit them, I should, just to see if they'd make a little room for me."

Over there in the Buddha's family they were all dipping their spoons into the pan and eating straight from it. "If you stop to blow you miss your turn," the Buddha had said, shaking with laughter at his own words. He laughed so much that he coughed, choked noisily, and went red in the face. Now the noises had died down everywhere in the trees, and music could be heard from the picnickers' radios. "Oh Portugal, why do I love you so . . . ?" The shadows of the trees pointed north towards the Somosierra. There was nobody in the river.

"Hand over that bottle," said Santos.

The peanut man arrived.

"A very good day to you!" He lowered his basket to show them his wares. "What can I give you?"

"Peanuts."

"They're one peseta a portion." He held out a little wooden scoop bound with iron. "How much do you want?"

"Five pesetas worth."

"Shut up, Fernando," said Alicia. "This is my business. Miguel will pay."

Fernando felt for his money: "What an idea!" he answered. "Don't be so ridiculous."

"But I asked for them, didn't I? I've got Miguel's purse here."

"Nonsense, Alicia. I really can't take that. We're all going to eat them, aren't we? Come off it now."

"Well we do stand on ceremony, don't we?" said Mely. "Nobody can treat you to anything these days except your fiancé!"

"It isn't that, silly. It's because it was me that asked for the peanuts."

"So what?"

Fernando took the peanuts in a cone of newspaper from the man's hands and gave him five pesetas.

"Mind they don't drop out," said he. "Enjoy yourselves." He went off through the trees. "Fine roasted peanuts!"

Sebas turned over in Pauli's lap and said to her: "Just scratch my back a bit, Pauli darling."

"Listen to him!"

"It's really itching, girl."

"You shouldn't have lain in the sun. It'll only be worse if I scratch it. The best thing I can do is to put some Nivea on it. I'll do that."

"No, I don't want any cream, or all the dust'll stick to it."

"Then there's nothing I can do. Sorry. I'm certainly not going to scratch you."

They were all dipping into the cone of peanuts. The cracking of the shells made Paulina turn round.

"You've got to be on your toes here," said Mely. "They're like a pack of wolves."

"We're too hungry to mind our manners."

The cracking was continuous, like the sound of a little grinder.

The cone lay on the ground between them. The shells fell on their bare thighs.

"In forty and forty-one they used to make coffee out of these things," said Fernando.

"Who told you that?"

"I know. They used carob beans too and worse things than that. It was foul stuff."

"That wasn't coffee or anything else," said Santos.

"Call it what you like. The fact is they made it with peanut shells and they called it coffee in the shops."

Paulina went over to the bag and took out a good handful of nuts.

"Well I'll be damned," said Alicia. "What are you up to now?"

"Equal shares, girl. Take it in turn."

"This is for both of us, Sebastián and me, because he doesn't want to move. I shan't take any more."

Then the snatching started again. They all fell on the bag, struggling with shouts and laughter over the booty. Only the torn twist of newspaper remained on the ground, together with a few nuts that had been trampled on.

"That's not fair," said Mely, "I only got two."

"You've got to keep awake," said Fernando.

Mely turned to Alicia: "How many did you get, Ali?"

"A good handful. Have some of mine if you like."

Daniel squinted up at them all, his cheek on the ground. When she saw he had opened his eyes Lucita offered him some nuts.

"Like some?"

Dani shook his head, clasped his hands behind his neck and looked up into the tree-tops.

"That's the way this sort of thing always ends," said Carmen.

"How."

"Like this, with a scrimmage. The roughest always gets the most. It's like at a village wedding when they throw pennies at the church door, to see the kids struggle for them."

"Have you ever been to a village wedding?"

"Yes, the year before last."

"Was it fun?"

"It's fun if you've got someone to laugh with. But if you get stuck the way I did at the dinner, between two dummies who did nothing but ask me whether I went to the Casablanca or the Pasapoga when I went out dancing, it's pure murder, I can tell you. I was bored so stiff that it took me two weeks to recover."

"What's wrong with them asking you that sort of thing? I can't see . . ."

"Oh, but they're so dull and awkward. They've no idea how to talk to a girl. It makes you feel like a hen in the wrong farmyard. You want to get away as quickly as you can. You know they want to amuse you and don't know how. You go on getting more and more exasperated, that's all. You're irritated, and sorry for them at the same time. Because they've got no sense of humour, poor devils, and they try so hard to make you laugh. I've never hated a party more in all my life, and I don't expect I ever shall."

"In a case like that there's only one thing you can do," said Mely, "go for them and make them look fools."

"I'm sure that's what you'd do. But I'm no good at making people feel fools, and I don't like doing it. You can do it all right, no doubt. That sort of thing amuses you, I know."

"What do you mean by that, Carmen? I don't understand you, really I don't."

Alicia broke in before Carmen had time to answer: "I don't mind the country at all. It's a quiet life . . ." She reflected a moment. "And everybody knows everybody else."

"I can't stand the quiet," said Mely. "It makes me restless. Quiet always gives me the creeps. As for everybody knowing everybody else, that's fine! But where's the attraction if you know everybody already. I don't fall for village life, I'm afraid. It must be a real bore."

"I'm with you, Mely," said Fernando. "There can't be anything to look forward to if you know that you're going to do the same thing tomorrow and the next day and the next and the next, right through the year. Same faces, same places, everything the same. There's no spice in life. It's just like your job. You have to be there every day doing the same things and in the end all you can think of is how to get away. Village life is like that, exactly like that."

"But you don't have so many complications, or so much heartbreak. You've got everything right here."

"I don't find that at all attractive," said Mely. "You know what I mean? That kind of life has got no kick. What can there be to look forward to?"

"Oh, nothing! But do you have to have something to look forward to? You just live quietly and are happy with what you've got, and that's that."

"Yes, you just sit on your backside and gaze up at the flat ceiling. It's ideal."

"It's not like that, Mely. Don't exaggerate. There are amusements in a village too. You've never heard about village festivals, I suppose. Everybody enjoys them wherever they are."

"Well, if that's true they've got all the luck. I get bored often enough even though I live in Madrid and all. But what would it be like if I didn't, I'd like to know."

"Depends on a person's nature and what he's used to."

"Talking about being bored, I'm sick of waiting for those two to come down with the food. Everybody else is eating now all round us, and we're still sitting here, laughing ourselves to death."

"It's nearly three o'clock," said Fernando.

They looked through the trees to the hillside steps beyond which they expected their friends to appear at any moment.

"What on earth can they be doing to take so long?"

"It was nice enough of them to go, poor boys," said Paulina.

"They didn't have to. We've got nothing to complain about and that's a fact."

"Nobody's complaining, nobody at all," said Santos. "The only objector is my stomach."

"How right you are! And you can't silence that. Your stomach always tells you the truth."

"And it tells you the time too. It works by the sun."

Sebastián lifted his head and said, turning to the others: "What I like best about the country is the prickly pears."

Everyone laughed.

"We're awfully late," said Miguel. "They must be cursing us."

"It's your fault," said Tito, "with all your admirers . . ."

"That's fame, my boy," said he with a laugh. "What do you expect me to do? One has a duty to one's public."

"Who's been doing all the propaganda for you?"

"Must have been the boss, surely. He knows me from last summer and the one before you see."

"And the other fellow, he must have thought you were practically Fleta himself."

"Yes, I expect he did."

They were walking down the stretch of road between the vineyards alongside the wire fence. Someone had brought the keeper of the unfenced vineyard his dinner, and he was chewing it with his eyes on the grapes. There was nobody about now. Suddenly they heard the panting throb of a motor, and an old Madrid taxi appeared on the road to the *merenderos*, making straight for Tito and Miguel, who stepped aside to allow it to pass. It was loaded with people, and the driver shifted down and turned into the track, raising a cloud of dust. The old vineyard keeper cursed the taxi, and the cloud of dust that fell on his spoon – and on a Sunday too! He quickly lifted his food tin from the ground, to cover it and protect his dinner. Then he looked up and saw Tito and Miguel, whom he had not noticed before.

"You can't even eat in peace," he shouted to them. "They don't even let you eat your dinner in peace, bugger them!"

And finding that he had an audience he grew more heated.

"Goddamn these blasted Sundays, I say!"

He flourished his food tin in the air and sent it crashing to the ground. Beans and sauce were spilled on the broken earth and spattered the grape clusters. Then the old man sat down again, and clumsily took out his pouch and cigarette papers. His fingers trembled violently as he rolled himself a cigarette. Tito and Miguel continued on their way.

"He's cracked," said Tito, "throwing his food about like that . . ."

"The old boy's just having one of his tempers."

"It's never any good flying off the handle. It doesn't get you anywhere. You only do yourself harm, that's all."

"Yes, but nobody on earth can remember to think like that when he's in a foul mood. It'd save a lot of trouble if only we could control ourselves in time."

They had come to the edge of the hill. The voices coming up from the trees suddenly grew clearer as the picnickers became visible. Somewhere there was a sound of cheering. Tito looked into the jug. "The ice won't last. It's almost melted already." They began cautiously to go down the little earth steps.

"Look, there they are! They've come at last!"

The whole group swung round, shouting: "Miguel! Miguel!" and Miguel laughed in answer to their applause. They helped to unload all the things.

"What have you got in this jug, eh?"

"Sure you haven't forgotten anything?"

They all fumbled in the sacks to find their own tins.

"This red one's mine."

"But they've got ice in here. What's the ice for?"

"Have you brought any more wine?"

"Here it is. Can't you see it?"

"They seem to have brought plenty!"

"And where did you steal the lemons?"

"If you go on tugging at the strap you'll bring the sack down."

"A little method, if you don't mind!"

"Say, who's this lemon for?"

"For His Royal Highness, the . . ."

"Very nice. Whoever . . ."

"Really, ice and the whole works."

"Just take a look . . . But it's half melted already."

"They've been long enough bringing it. Anything would have melted in that time."

"Dinner is served."

"Come on, take your partners now."

"Who's my partner?"

"I'm your little partner," said Mely to Fernando.

"Take a seat here . . . beautiful! Your Majesty!"

"If you'd been much longer we'd have set about roasting Daniel," said Santos.

"He'd be pretty tough."

"He'd have laid you out flat for a week. Daniel's flesh must be ninety per cent pure alcohol."

"And the other ten per cent pure nastiness," added Fernando.

"You can't talk," cut in Alicia. "You've got him to thank that you didn't have to go up and fetch the food."

"Aren't they being nasty?" said Carmen.

Daniel raised his head and looked at Fernando.

"It looks to me as if you're trying to mess everything up today, Fernando. My advice is lay off it. Don't say I didn't warn you."

"Oh, you're waking up now, are you?" answered Fernando. "It was about time. You didn't bring Daniel's tin down, did you?"

"Here it is. This last one must be his."

"But we said that you were to leave it behind."

Miguel raised his voice: "Never mind what we said. You could have gone up yourself, and then you could have left it behind if you'd wanted to."

"All right, Miguel, all right. Keep your hair on!"

"Miguel's quite right," interrupted Carmen. They brought yours down, didn't they? Say thank you and be quiet."

"That's what I call being a pal."

"Let's leave it at that," remarked Mely. "Are we going to eat or not? Sit down, Fernando."

"There's a lot too much bad feeling here."

"Now here's someone else wading in. I think I shall have to sing you a song," said Miguel. "Perhaps that'll keep you quiet. What are you standing up for, Tito? You look like the town crier."

"Let's get down to it," urged Santos, "or it'll get cold."

"Come on, Miguel," said Mely. "*Do* give us a song. Come on. Cheer us up now."

Tito stripped off his shirt and sat down beside Miguel.

"Aren't you going to strip? It'll make you cooler."

Miguel shook his head. He was taking the lid off a red casserole that had been tied up with string, and was investigating the contents.

"Half a sec," exclaimed Tito. "What about the *sangría*?"

"Good Lord, I'd forgotten it! Quick now, before the ice melts!"

"The lemon. Where's the lemon?"

"Has anyone seen the lemon?"

"In with the ice, to keep it cool."

"Whistle for it. Perhaps it'll come."

"Don't be so funny or you won't get any *sangría*. The ice won't last much longer.

"I bet Mely's got it inside her swimsuit," said Fernando. "Let's. see, Mely."

"Come and look for it, boy," answered Mely. "And mind it doesn't burn you. You'll get such a slap from me if you try."

"Look, here it is! Hasn't anybody got eyes in his head? It's got a little squashed but it's still whole."

"Give it to me."

Miguel interlaced his fingers over the mouth of the jug and strained away all the ice water on to the dust. Tito sliced the lemon.

"How do we open the lemonade?"

Sebas had one of those knives with gadgets for everything. He wiped the blade on his towel and passed the knife to Miguel.

"Leave a couple of bottles," said Carmen, "for those who don't want *sangría*."

"Everybody here wants *sangría*."

"Leave a bottle of lemonade for me," put in Paulina. "I can't drink *sangría*."

"Let's have the lemon," said Miguel, with the jug in his hand.

Tito threw the slices on to the ice at the bottom. Then he picked up the jug, and Miguel opened the bottles and added the lemonade.

"Now the wine."

Tito looked at Daniel as he held up the jug into which Miguel was pouring the wine.

"That's done," said Miguel. "It's a whale of a *sangría*." He brought over the jug and Tito sat down beside Daniel.

"What's the trouble, Dani? Aren't you going to eat? There's a place for you here."

"I don't want to be in the way."

"Don't be such a fool. Take your tin, and eat your food."

Santos had turned to see what Sebas had in his box.

"What have they given you?"

"Nothing much. Hash and hard peas."

He covered his own food with his aluminium lid.

"Come now, I'll swap you blind."

"Go on, scram!"

"You'd come off best, you know."

Tito continued to press Daniel.

"Have we got to go down on our knees to you? Come on, don't be an ass."

Sebastián and Santos joined in: "If you go on like this, we'll share your grub between us. Make up your mind."

Daniel got up and fetched his tin. He and Mely exchanged glances. Looking on the ground and pulling up one strap of her swimsuit, she said to Alicia: "He's got no cause to behave like this . . ."

Daniel had sat down.

Sebastián gave him a rather serious look, took him by the back of the neck and shook him: "Come on now, Daniel. I'll tell you what's the matter with you. The drink."

"It's a good thing to eat something every now and then," said Santos to Daniel admonishingly. "Just a little snack every now and then. We know that wine is the mainstay of life, but a little food never did a man any harm. So long as you don't take too much, of course. Don't be put off by it, just try a little. You'll find you get used to the stuff, bit by bit . . ."

He smiled as he spoke, at the same time systematically separating the chips in his box from the rest of his food. He looked up at Daniel and Daniel smiled back at him. "Stop pulling my leg . . ."

Santos gave him a quick wink and smacked him on the knee.

"Oh, Daniel," he cried. "What an ass you are! If you didn't have old uncle here to look after you and give you good advice, you would be in a mess!"

Sebas had taken some cutlets out of his tin; the fat had congealed. He looked at his sticky fingers and put them in his mouth.

"Licking your fingers, eh?" said Santos.

"What did I tell you?" answered Sebastian. "Didn't I say you'd have come off best? Will you have one now?"

He took a cutlet out of his tin and offered it to him. Santos took the cutlet and, lifting it by the skewer, let it fall into his mouth like a flag from its pole.

Luci was hardly eating. She looked from one to another, wanting to offer something to somebody. "I've got turnovers. Try one. They're stuffed with pimento. They're very good."

"I don't like pimentos," said Paulina.

"What about you, Carmen?"

Opposite them were Alicia, Mely and Fernando. Alicia had stopped eating, and was rubbing at a spot of grease on her swimsuit with a handkerchief soaked in lemonade. Luci was eating her turnover, which she held in a paper napkin. On the napkin was written ILSA.

"I suppose you nick those serviettes at your job, don't you," Daniel asked.

"Well, you must get something out of it. I've got lots of them. Take one if you like."

"Thank you. I've been there pretty often but I've never seen you serving. What hours do you work?"

"Always in the mornings."

"Which stall is it then? Isn't it the one behind the Metro steps?"

"Yes, that's the one. I'm stuck there every day from ten onwards."

"It's very odd . . ."

He shrugged his shoulders.

"Ah, here's the *sangría*. Who wants a drink?"

Mely's brown arms stretched out towards the jug above everyone's head: "Some for me." She seized it, shook back her hair and lifted the drink to her lips. A drop ran down her chin and trickled down between her breasts.

"Oh, it is cold! Do you want some, Ali?"

The jug passed from one to another.

"Is it good?" asked Lucita.

Carmen had taken a bite from her turnover. "Very good."

Luci held her tin out to Daniel. "Won't you try one of my turnovers, Daniel," she asked.

*　*　*

White Shoes said from the door: "You don't often see a Madrid taxi in these parts, a crate like that in the middle of the country."

"Is it coming here?" asked Mauricio from inside.

"Looks like it."

"It must be Ocaña. He said he'd be coming one Sunday."

The taxi had turned across the road and was coming up the track to the bar, raising a large billowing column of dust behind it. Mauricio had gone to the door to see it arrive. The cloud of dust was slowly dispersing and finally settled among the leaves of the olive trees.

"When are you going to swap that old rattler for a decent car?" cried Mauricio through the taxi window, while the driver backed his car into the shade.

Mauricio followed it with both hands on the top of the window. Ocaña laughed but said nothing. When his hand was on the brake, he answered: "When I've got as much cash as you have."

Mauricio opened the car door and they embraced in front of it, smacking one another violently on the back. A stout woman got out, with a big girl and several small children, as well as Ocaña's brother and his wife. The stout woman said to Mauricio: "Getting at my husband again, eh? It's always the same. How's Faustina? Well I hope? And your daughter?"

"All well, thank you. And I can see you are too, all of you."

Mauricio put his hand on one of the small fair heads. Then he looked at the girl.

"Well, she's quite a little woman. It won't be long before she starts giving you trouble."

"She does already," answered the stout woman. "Meet my brother-in-law and his lady."

She stressed the last word as if to deny her the title.

"Delighted. How are you all?"

Both man and wife were thin. Ocaña, the driver, mopped up his sweat with a handkerchief.

"This is Mauricio, the great Mauricio."

And the stout woman said: "They know you already. They've heard us mention you a hundred times. Felipe's always talking about you. He'd as soon forget you as forget his own children. Look alive now! Have you all gone to sleep? Go and help Father get the things out of the back!"

She then turned to the girl: "You look after the bottles, Felisa dear, and see you don't break them."

After that she addressed Mauricio once more: "They're so careless. No glass or china's ever safe with them." She shook her head.

"It's only their age," said Mauricio. "Wouldn't you like to come in? It's very hot in the sun."

White Shoes watched them approach from the door.

"What a lovely river you have," she went on. "You've nothing to complain of."

White Shoes stepped back for them, and squinted down at her figure.

"Watch your step," warned Mauricio.

The woman gave them a quick greeting: "How do you do."

The couple followed her. The constable left the counter and clasped his hands behind his back. Mauricio offered them chairs.

"You get such a crowd," she said as she sat down. "It gets bigger every year. It makes our river look stupid. It's the size of a basin, and the water's so filthy it's a disgrace to the city."

"I thought they were going to do something about it."

"No one could do anything about that river. The papers say Churchill's a genius. But if they made him mayor of Madrid, even he wouldn't be able to get anything done, with all his talents."

"It's just a question of money."

"Unless they were to shift Madrid, lock, stock and barrel. . . . What a place to have chosen to build the capital of Spain! I suppose they did it a very long time ago, in ancient times." With a wave of her hand she indicated the far distance. "They must have been an ignorant lot. They might at least have chosen something a bit more like a river. With all the lovely spots there are."

Felipe Ocaña had stuck his head inside the car. He had lowered the back of the rear seat, and was taking things from behind, which he passed to his children who were standing at the car door to receive them. Sometimes there was no hand ready. Then his voice sounded from inside: "Come on! Don't keep me stuck here!"

Finally he heaved his body out and said: "Now take the things in and be quick about it."

They divided the load among the four, and Felisa said: "Mum said I was to take the bottles."

Felipe wound up the windows, and the four children entered Mauricio's place, carrying all the bundles. The two boys, who were very fair, wore gym shoes, and were already in swimming-trunks. They looked all round them. The doors of the taxi banged to behind them. Felipe locked it, and as he was walking away turned round to take a quick sideways glance at the tyres. He whistled as he walked. The children were already going in.

"Put everything up here for the moment," said their mother. "Juan, darling, do be careful!" She turned to the boss: "Which way to the garden? Is it shady like last year?"

"Shadier, I put in another ten vines in the winter, and now there's quite a bit more shade. You'll be more comfortable out there."

Faustina was coming down the passage and had just reached the door. On seeing the visitor's back however, she turned sharply away. Ocaña's brother was saying: "How nice it is here, with the garden at the back and all. You must do pretty well here in the summer."

"Don't you believe it," answered Mauricio. "The ones that do the trade are the ones close to the river and the road. Not many people come up here. It's a bad position."

Felisa drew up a chair and sat very close to her mother in a studied position. One of the boys looked at Lucio, surveying him from his feet to his head.

"But there's an easy remedy for that. You've only got to put up a few arrows and notices on the road to guide them up, and you'll get the people."

Mauricio went behind the bar.

"They won't let me put them up. Besides, there's a state tax on that sort of thing."

"Yes, of course. There's nothing you don't pay taxes on. But it'd be profitable."

Felipe had appeared on the doorstep, with a bunch of keys on his finger which jangled as he swung them.

"Here we all are," he said.

At that moment Faustina came out through the inside door. She had taken off her apron and was still arranging her comb.

"What a welcome sight!"

Felipe's wife turned round. Carmelo and the butcher stared at the bottles on the shelves. Faustina shook hands with Señora Ocaña and stepped back as if to admire her. "But you get better looking every year!"

The other woman half shut her eyes and shook her head, assuming a modest and deprecatory smile. "Don't you believe it, Faustina, don't you believe it. Appearances are deceptive. Time treats me just the same as it does every other human being. You're wrong, I'm afraid . . .'

Lucio stared unashamedly at them all.

"I had rather a poor winter. If only you'd seen . . . I'm not the woman I was, indeed I'm not."

The butcher spat and trod out a burning cigarette stump. He took advantage of the moment to look furtively behind him.

"Things leave their mark." She changed her expression. "Meet my brother-in-law and his wife."

Faustina stretched her arm out to them across the table.

"Delighted," said the other woman.

They noticed her Catalan accent.

"Make yourselves at home. Consider yourselves part of the family, like you did last year."

"Thank you very much." It was Felipe's wife who spoke up for her brother-in-law. Faustina greeted Felipe while Carmelo and the butcher were paying Mauricio. White Shoes went up and down on the tips of his toes, gazing at the ceiling.

"Do be quiet, Juan dear," said Felisa to her little brother.

The boy was going round and round the table, sliding one hand along the marble and making a noise like a steamboat. Then his hand became an aeroplane and took off from the table. It skimmed over Felisa's hair. She tried to give him a smack, but her hand hit the empty air.

"Mum, look what Juan's doing."

"Enjoy yourselves," said the butcher as he went out.

The constable touched the peak of his cap with his forefinger to say goodbye, and White Shoes tilted his chin by way of farewell.

"Are you staying?" the butcher asked him.

"Just for a minute," and he pointed to his wrist-watch without looking at the time.

Carmelo and his companion went out into the sun, and took the road to San Fernando. Justi had just come in in her Sunday clothes.

"Well isn't she a pretty girl?" said Felipe's wife to Mauricio. Justi laughed not at all shyly. She stood beside the stout woman, who had put her hand on the girl's thigh as if to make sure that she was solid.

"I suppose she's got a young man," she said, looking up at Justi.

"Yes, she's got a young man," answered her mother. She put her hands together and smiled.

Felisa looked at Justi with interest. White Shoes had gone up to Lucio, but they were not talking. Ocaña said to his wife: "Petra, my girl, it's half past three already. I think it's time we went out in the garden."

"All right," she agreed, beginning to move. "I'm ready whenever you are."

They all got up and Justi began to gather their things.

"Don't you worry, my dear. Put those things down. We're not short of hands, thank goodness, to carry all this stuff and a lot more. Don't you bother. Let the children do the carrying. They've nothing better to do."

"It's no trouble at all," said Justina.

And she disappeared down the passage with a basket. Mauricio came out from behind the bar and went in front as if to clear the way. When they reached the garden he picked out the best table.

"Don't leave anything behind," said Petra.

He drove his children ahead down the passage. His wife, his brother and sister-in-law went next, and he brought up the rear. Nodding his head towards the door through which they had disappeared, Lucio remarked to White Shoes: "That chap must have to keep his eyes on the road, with those four young wolves at home waiting to be fed."

"And wearing out shoe leather," added White Shoes.

* * *

Trickles of sweat that were grey with dust rolled down Sebas' neck to disappear in the hair on his chest. He had well-built shoulders and strong forearms. His hands, which were hard as iron, let little shreds of omelette fall on his thighs. Santos, pale and hairless beside him, stretched out his hand to Lucita's tin.

"May I?"

"Take one, of course."

"You *are* letting yourself go."

"You'll leave the poor girl without a turnover for herself."

"They're there for eating. I've got plenty. Do have one, Santos."

The sun above them drenched the tree-tops, shining through the variegated green of the foliage. Its metallic light flashed between the leaves and struck the lower branches diagonally in shafts of shining dust, which made a pattern of fish-scales on the ground. It formed little round blobs like gold coins on Alicia's and Mely's backs and on Miguel's shirt. It speckled the white metal tins, the red casserole, and the jug of *sangria*, all of which lay on the blue and white check serviettes spread on the dusty ground.

"Santos is doing well. He's tucking in all right. What an appetite!"

"We've got to keep ourselves nourished, man. And you're not doing too badly yourself."

"I haven't eaten half as much as you have. You're non-stop. You get right into it."

"It's a pleasure to watch him," said Carmen.

"It is, is it? Listen now, did you hear that? It's a pleasure to watch him eat. That's what I call a fiancée, see!"

"Yes, you're right. But he doesn't appreciate her. Really, he doesn't."

"You don't find a girl like that every day. He's a lucky fellow. He doesn't deserve to have such luck."

"Yes, he does," protested Carmen. "He deserves all that and more.

Don't you say nasty things about him or I'll get annoyed. Poor darling!"

"Well! It's like that, is it?" laughed Sebastián. "What did I say?" They all laughed as they looked at Santos and Carmen.

"What now?" said Santos. "What's all this about? Do you want to take her from me?" He threw his arm around Carmen's shoulder's and pressed her ardently to his side, threateningly flourishing a fork in his other hand.

"Anyone coming for her?" he asked with a smile.

"You can put on your act now," said Sebastián, "but you usually keep the poor girl waiting for you on the street corner till she's quite worn out."

"That's a lie. There's not a word of truth in it."

"Let's hear what she says."

"I'll throw this at you!" threatened Santos, picking up a tin of sardines.

"Pipe down!"

"Hi, just a moment," interrupted Miguel. "Let's see that tin."

"This tin?"

"Yes, you see . . ."

"Catch!"

Santos threw the tin, and Miguel caught it in the air and looked at it.

"Well, I'll be jiggered," he exclaimed. "Just as I thought. Sardines! This fellow's got sardines and he doesn't say a word, the sly devil. Why it's criminal!" He rocked his head from side to side.

"He's got sardines," said Fernando. "The old thief! What were you keeping them for? Afters?"

"I hadn't thought about it. I was just keeping them for my dinner."

"That's enough. You had a tin of sardines, and like an idiot you never thought how damned good they'd be to start on. They're in oil, what's more. That deserves a penalty, my boy. Silence in a case like this deserves a penalty!"

"Yes, I'm sticking to these," said Fernando. "It's never too late to use a tin-opener. Chuck me over your knife, Sebas. It's got an opener on it, hasn't it?"

"Sebas' knife. What a question! It's got more gadgets than a surgeon's kit."

"We'll have it open in no time," said Fernando, catching the knife.

"You won't splash me, will you?" warned Mely. "Careful you don't get any oil on me."

She moved away. Miguel watched Fernando making clumsy efforts to pierce the tin.

"Give it to me. I'll do it. Just you see."

"No, let me alone." He pushed him off with his shoulder. "But this opener's no good at all in any case."

"Go and drown yourself," protested Sebastián. "Clumsy workmen always blame their tools."

"Well, let's see one of you do it then."

Miguel took the tin from him. "Give it here, boy, give it here."

A very dark man passed in the sunlight, carrying a roll of cork on his back: "Fresh ice-cream!" he cried. He had a very piercing voice like a dry biscuit. "Fresh ice-cream!" His dark face stood out beneath his white cap. The sardines came out in pieces. Sebas put one on his bread and spread it like butter with his knife. He licked the blade clean.

"Pig!" scolded Paulina.

"We don't waste anything here."

"What about having ices?" suggested Carmen.

The ice-cream man had stopped in the shade and was serving a girl in a swimsuit. Other children from various groups crowded round him.

"Tell him he can come back here in about five minutes."

"Do you suppose he'll come back for you?"

"Oh, all right. Let's buy them now," said Carmen. "I can't resist an ice. Who else wants one?"

Fernando had gone up to Tito with the sardine tin.

"Do you want a sardine, Tito?"

Tito lifted his head and gave him a look. Fernando smiled.

"Yes, I would like one."

Fernando held the tin, while Tito pushed bits of sardine on to a slice of bread that he had put alongside it. Then Fernando slightly tipped the tin and let some drops of oil fall on the bread.

"Thanks, Fernando."

"Don't mention it. Don't mention it," answered Fernando, and flipped him on the chin.

Tito looked up and they exchanged smiles. A little bit of sardine fell on Tito's trousers.

"It doesn't matter," he said quickly, "it doesn't matter a bit."

"So you two have made it up. That's a good thing."

"I want an ice too."

"So do I."

"And me too."

"And over here."

Santos and Sebastián got up to fetch the ices. Lucita tried to give Sebas a peseta in small change. "Here, Sebas, bring me one too."

"Don't be so silly, Lucita, put your money away."

"No . . ."

But Sebas went off towards the ice-cream man without answering. Sebas hopped theatrically on his bare feet, because the ground burnt the soles as he walked.

"How thin Santos is," said Paulina. "You ought to take better care of him."

"He was made like that," replied Carmen. "He's never any fatter than he is now."

Fernando was still standing in the middle of the group with the sardine tin in his hand. He watched Santos and Sebastián walking towards the ice-cream man.

"What do you think ice-cream would be like," he said, "mixed with sardine oil?"

"What odd ideas you do get," protested Mely. "Enough to spoil a girl's appetite. Don't be so horrid."

Fernando laughed. He threw the sardine tin away.

The ice-cream man had put his roll of cork on the ground, and was making ices continuously in his little tarnished ice-machine. A dog was sniffing round it. He had found a wafer. "Get out of it!" The dog withdrew two steps and immediately went back to the wafer.

"Make a line! Make a line!" shouted the children.

They got into a close line, one behind the other.

"You're out of turn. I came first."

"Rubbish! I've been waiting here ten days, squirt."

"Don't push. There's enough room for everybody," said the ice-cream man, making the peace. Santos and Sebastián stood out by their height among the crowd of youngsters.

Paulina laughed at them from afar: "What a pair of drones!"

"It would be easier if you came down here," said Sebastián to the ice-cream man.

"How can I? Can't you see all the customers I've got? Unless of course you'd rather wait till I've finished . . ."

"No, all right. Serve us and we'll take them over."

"How many?"

Sebastián turned to Santos: "Did Daniel say if he wanted one?"

"I don't know."

"Ask him then, and find out."

The children in the queue protested: "Hurry up now, it's melting. Don't talk so much!"

"Daniel!" shouted Santos.

Daniel stood up among the group, and made a questioning sign.

"Do you want an ice?"

Everyone in the queue waited for Daniel's answer. He nodded his head.

"Yes, he wants one," said one of the children.

The ice-cream man had already handed Sebastián three ices.

"Eleven, please," said Santos.

A dark boy looked up at him and waggled his fingers.

"Oh Lord! Eleven!"

Then he stuck his head into the little well of the ice-machine to see how much was left. Sebas' hands were now full. He had five ices.

"I'll carry this lot over before they melt," he said. "Take the money."

He nodded with his chin towards the belt of his swimming-trunks into which he had put three five-peseta notes. Santos took them out. Two youngsters were fighting. They had left the line and were rolling about in the sun. The rest watched the fight from their places in the line. Santos went off holding the ices, and turned back every now and then to see the fight. The smaller of the two had caught the bigger by his lip and was digging in his nails. Voices from the line cheered them on. They were covered with dust and were tearing at one another, but neither uttered a word. Both were panting and sweating. Both were in swimming-trunks.

"Good for you, midget, you win." Now the little one had his face in the dust, and the bigger was holding him there. But the little one had his feet free, and was grasping his enemy by the waist. Santos had paid, but still stayed watching the fight, while his friends shouted to him from the distance: "Come on, it's all melting."

"It's disgraceful," shouted a woman to the children in the line. "Letting them hurt one another like that, it's disgraceful! They're just like animals. Fancy allowing that sort of thing to happen."

She went over to the fight, and, dragging one of them by the arm, tried to separate them.

"Come on, you little beast, let go! Fighting like this . . ." They took no notice of her.

"Let them alone, lady," said the ice-cream man. "Let them fight. It's good for them. It gives them spirit."

"And you're as bad as they are! Just a beast like them!"

The ice-cream man did not take offence, but went on making ices. "We're all animals if it comes to that, lady. Now perhaps you understand?"

Santos advanced a few yards and then turned again to look. His friends went on shouting at him. The fighters were covered with dust. Their backs were streaked with scratches and fingermarks. The ice-cream man was grinning at the retreating lady's back.

Santos joined his friends.

"Slow, aren't you, boy? The ices'll be in a fine state."

He lowered his collection of ices into the middle of the circle.

"Where did you think you were? At the Stadium or what?" Yellow trickles of melted ice ran down Santos' fingers. Paulina sucked her ice and laughed. The others relieved Santos of his load.

"They're half melted," protested Fernando. "And the wafer's damned well soaked through."

"It was highly exciting," said Santos, licking his ice. "They were giving one another a thorough pasting. That little boy's a real genius."

"What did I tell you? He thought he was at a wrestling match."

Then suddenly Sebastián grasped his jaw with a look of pain. "Oh, my teeth!" He threw his ice away and writhed, still holding his jaw.

"There's nothing worse than an ice for the toothache," said Lucita. "Does it hurt you much?"

Sebastián nodded. An unexpected gust of wind raised dust and paper among the trees. They all closed their eyes and shielded their ices with their hands.

"What's this?" asked somebody.

The ice-cream man quickly tied up his cork roll. The wind had only lasted half a minute, and already it could be seen moving across the plain in front, blowing up the dust from the ground ahead of it. It had passed the unblinking eyes of the shepherd.

"Autumn's coming," said Fernando.

Everything was once more as it had been, and the ice-cream man was serving again.

"Yes, autumn," said Mely. "And very welcome too. If only it could be autumn for good and all!"

She pointed up to the tree-tops which had rustled in the wind. Miguel was lying beside Alicia and playing with her feet.

"No, not on my feet. You're tickling me. Don't!"

One man was shouting to another from the opposite side of the river.

"Why are you so keen on the autumn, Mely? What makes you in such a hurry for it to come?"

Only Luci was still sucking the last remains of her ice.

"I'm always in a hurry for time to pass," said Mely. "What I like is a change. I'm bored by anything that lasts too long."

She lay down with her hands under her head. She had shaved the hair from her armpits.

* * *

"You and me," said White Shoes to Lucio, "each in our own way, we've both been left with the dud ace in this life. But he's had a raw deal as well. Four children to provide for must give you a headache."

Lucio agreed. "When we die," he said, "at least we know that no one will miss us. Quite the opposite, in fact; they'll be pleased to have us out of the way."

"Yes, I'm pretty well out of touch with my family. It's more than fifteen years since I've been to see them, and I don't intend to. A postcard to my sister at Christmas, at least in those years I remember to send it, and that's as far as our relationship goes. That's the only trouble I cause them, always supposing that they read it."

"What have you got? Mother and father?"

"Mother and brothers and sister. My father's dead, and my mother married again."

"Is it long since you lost your father?"

"Yes, a long time. He died in '35. I was seventeen and I was the eldest. At nineteen I had to join up. When I got back from the war I found that the house had another master."

Lucio took a sip of wine and said: "That can't be pleasant for anybody."

"You bet it isn't. They made a great fuss of me, to see if I could swallow the dose. I didn't. What would you expect? A woman of thirty-nine with three grown-up sons in the house, and no shortage of money or anything, and she takes it into her head to marry again."

Lucio agreed with an understanding nod.

"I hadn't the courage to get out of doors, or meet my friends in the town. I was too ashamed, and they all damned well knew it. But none of the lads, not even my best friend, had the courage to tell me, about the turn they'd played them. It was my little sister who told me, and not till I'd been back a fortnight. I couldn't hold up my head for shame. And then what do you think I did? I got up very early one morning and packed my bag. And when I had it ready, I went out to the cowshed and took a bell from one of our oxen, just as they'd done." He was breathing deeply and his face darkened. He looked at the door and wiped his mouth with his hand. "They were still in bed. I went and stood in the doorway of their room with my bag in one hand and the bell in the other, and I rang and rang, a rare peal of bells for the happy pair. That was my farewell. There was a fine row.

They woke up. My brothers didn't interfere because I was the eldest. After all they must have been on my side although they didn't like to say so. The old boy came out and tried to hit me. 'How dare you do that to your mother,' he said. 'I'm not doing it to my mother,' I answered. 'It's for your benefit more than for hers.' He went at me like a wild animal. But I didn't let him touch me. And I went on ringing the bell under their very noses. My mother was screaming at me from the bedroom, and saying things about my dead father and how I wasn't worthy to be his son. She couldn't get herself out of bed. So finally I took the bell and chucked it into the bedroom, and went away. Only my sister came and saw me off on the bus. Practically everyone in the place had heard about the row by then. Imagine how it must have upset the poor kid. She was only fifteen."

Lucio looked down at the ground and scraped with one foot.

"They're sad things family rows. How did you get along after that?"

"Well, at my age and with my experience in the war, I didn't find the world very frightening. I had learnt my trade as a barber at the front. First you shave one man, then another, and you end up as the company barber. So I went to Burgos. A sergeant major lived there who had been a buddy of mine in the Army, and he found me a job. There I learnt how to give a proper haircut. But in the end I had a little trouble and I left. I've been wandering about ever since, from one place to another. I'm a rolling stone. Here in Coslada I've set up on my own for the first time. But, as you can see, the struggles and botherations are just the same. That's why I say I've been left with the dud ace in this life. What's your opinion? Am I right or am I wrong?"

"You're right and that's a fact. When a man leaves home twisted, whether it's his own fault or not, he'll take a twisted path wherever he goes. Nothing can get him straight. Once you start on the wrong foot, you can never change step. Whether the wrong was on your family's side, or whether it was on yours, it's all the same. The thing's got inside you and nothing can get it out, however long ago it was, and however many miles you've put between them and you."

"Yes, I expect you're right."

"I'm sure I am. What is it that forms a man's character? The treatment and the frictions he's met with at home. If you're used to quarrels and regrets and that's what you've left behind you, quarrels and regrets will follow you right through your life. You may make your pile, or sweat your guts out after success, but still there'll be no escape. The way you leave home, you stay for life, never mind what happens afterwards."

"The dud ace or the ace of trumps, that's what I say."

"It may be any card; you might pick any one of the fifty-two. But you'll never be rid of it. You can't cheat at this game. I know that from experience. I may not have the dud ace, but I've got a pretty foul hand, I can tell you . . ."

"Yes, I was listening to what you said about your bakery just now."

"That's the way things have always been. I've been hit on the same cheek. But there's one difference between you and me. I have less to complain about. My family didn't behave badly to me, I behaved badly to them. At least that's how I look at it. So I have to keep quiet and take what comes to me. All that's come in the past, and all that's still to come."

White Shoes passed his hand over his face. There was a silence. Then he said: "That's why a man doesn't feel like marrying. I almost got married two years ago, but I stopped in time. I think it was better for me, and better for her, and better for those that would have come after us. Don't you agree?"

* * *

Petra lifted aside the hanging branches of honeysuckle and American vine.

"First class!" said Ocaña as she sat down.

Justi was splashing water from a bucket on to the ground. To the left of the table at which they sat there was a hen-house with a little run surrounded by wire. A very fat rabbit was watching the newcomers with ears erect. The three small children stuck their faces and hands against the hexagonal mesh to look at it.

"She's very white," said the little girl.

The rabbit came a little nearer and sniffed, twitching its nose.

[114]

"She doesn't take any notice of the hens," observed Juanito.

"Of course not. They don't understand one another. They aren't the same kind of animal, you see."

"Look how she twitches her nose."

"Of course she does," said the elder boy. "I know a man in our street who twitches his nose just like that."

"She's got red eyes," said the girl in excited surprise.

Amadeo, the elder boy, took a step backwards: "Don't lean on the wire," he warned the others, "or it'll fall down."

A voice called from behind them. Only Amadeo moved.

"Come on, Mum's calling us."

The rabbit had taken fright on seeing Amadeo move.

"Wait till she comes back," said Juanito.

Their mother called again. The rabbit had stopped at the entrance of her burrow. Amadeo insisted: "Come along!"

"Wait and see what she does now."

Justina came up behind them without their noticing her approach.

"Your mother's calling you."

They turned round, surprised to hear a voice. Justina smiled.

"Well, did you like the rabbit. She's a beauty, isn't she? Do you know what she's called?"

"Has she got a name?"

"Of course she's got a name. She's called Gilda."

The little girl looked disappointed.

"Gilda? I don't like that name. It's very ugly."

Justina burst out laughing.

"Now, listen, Mauricio," Petra was saying, "I'm sure you can tell me. What's the name of that place just on the main road, on the left as you come here. The one with the pretty garden. You know the one I mean?"

"Yes, I know. It used to belong to Cocherito of Bilbao, the famous bullfighter. It was his country place. You've heard of him, I expect."

"Yes, but he's dead," said Felipe.

"Yes, he died years ago. When he bought the land nothing of all this was here. There wouldn't have been as much as four houses along the river."

"Yes, we noticed it this morning, didn't we, Felipe? The avenue leading up to the house and the clumps of trees. To judge by what you see through the railings, it must be a marvellous place."

"Yes, it is. Now some new people have taken it."

"It's a big place. Must be worth a lot of money," said Ocaña.

"They knew how to live in the old days. They didn't build the silly little houses they do today.'

Mauricio was standing beside their table. Through the window, on the other side of the garden, Faustina could be seen cooking.

"Now what are those children up to? Amadeo, come here at once!" shouted Petra.

"In Barcelona," said Ocaña's sister-in-law, "we've got some very fine villas, on the Bonanova. Really tasteful, you know, with magnificent gardens that are worth a fortune, and fountains and tiles and all that. The people they belong to have got . . . you know what I mean." She made a show of counting banknotes with her thumb and first finger.

"Yes, there's lots of industrialists there," said Mauricio.

Petra called again: "Here, children! Petrita! Come here at once." She lowered her voice. "Oh, those children! It must be nearly four o'clock." The children came. Felisa sat down beside her mother, and looked in her face as if she were on the side of the grown-ups.

Justina excused them with a smile: "They were looking at the rabbit. Don't be cross with them. They never get the chance of seeing one in Madrid."

"She's white," said Petrita getting excited. "She has red eyes, you know, Mummy!"

"Be quiet and eat your food," answered her mother.

They ate with a cheerful appetite. Their arms stretched across the table in all directions to take one thing or another, despite the fact that now and then they got a good slap from their mother.

"Ask for what you want. Haven't you got a tongue in your head? You're behaving like a bunch of savages."

"There's never been a bullfighter as good as Juan Belmonte was," said Felipe Ocaña. "Not even Manolete. Has there now?"

Mauricio agreed: "No, he was the man. You got the impression that he did it all with his chin. It was the same when he made a *veronica*, as when he came in to kill or to get the applause. I believe he really laid them out with his chin and not with his sword at all."

"And the way he had of playing his bulls, carefully and slowly without getting excited. Just like a carpenter working in his shed, or a barber in his shop, or a watchmaker, just the same thing."

His brother spoke:

"I was once lucky enough to see him at Caceres, at a festival about eight years ago, playing his bull on horseback and then killing him on foot. What a horse he had! A marvellous beast!"

"Mauricio," said Petra, "we haven't offered you anything to eat. Will you try a cake?"

"No thank you. We haven't had dinner yet."

"Really?"

"No. Excuse me, please. I'll have one later." He turned to Ocaña. "Who's fighting at Las Ventas this afternoon? Do you happen to know?"

"Rafael Ortega. He's fighting all six bulls. It's a charity event."

"He's got some nerve. There aren't many today who would do that. And certainly not for nothing as he's doing."

"Ortega's one of the old brigade. He knows how to make the bull feel his weight when he draws him into his cape. He makes you realize what weight and power there is in that mountain of flesh. I'd rather have his real integrity than all the capers of all the others who get twice the money he does."

Mauricio was still standing, but leaning slightly over the table with his hand on the back of Petrita's and Amadeo's chairs.

"I don't know him," he said, "except from reading about him in the papers. It's nearly four years since I saw a bullfight."

His wife called to him through the kitchen window. There was the sound of a blow and a cat shot out into the garden. Another shout from the window: "Get out! I won't have these animals in my kitchen."

The cat jumped into a bed of dry leaves under the arbour.

"What do you want?" Mauricio shouted back.

"Come in and have your dinner."

[117]

Justina was in the chicken-run. She came out with an egg in her hand. When she came into the house her father asked her: "Which one laid it?"

"The speckled one. It's four days since she laid the last one."

Ocaña's sister-in-law was saying to her husband: "Don't take so much of that salad, Sergio. You know pimentos don't agree with you. You'll make yourself ill."

"Oh, let him be," interrupted Petra. "Sunday's Sunday and he can't always be thinking about his health. Let him be."

Felisita looked from her mother to her aunt as if to see which of them was right. Juanito was beckoning and coaxing the cat.

"Give him this," said Petrita.

It was a bit of meat. But the cat did not come.

"At least we must order some drinks and coffee," said Ocaña to his wife. "We must spend some money here seeing that we've brought our own food."

"Whatever you think. He's so generous he may not let you pay."

"Of course he'll let me pay. Why shouldn't he let me pay?"

"You've done him so many favours ... !"

"But he's done me favours too. You are a funny woman. If he refuses, I'll shove the money down his throat. I do feel rather ashamed though that we've brought our own wine instead of buying his."

"You never said anything to me about it," answered his wife. "And now you start talking this way."

The white rabbit had come up to the wire, and was leaning against it with both forepaws, showing her belly.

"Look, look! She's standing up," shouted Juanito.

They all looked at the rabbit.

"Isn't she lovely?" cried the little girl. "Isn't she lovely?"

"She'd be lovelier still in a stew," said Ocaña's brother with a laugh.

His sister-in-law scolded him: "What a dreadful thing to say before a child. Can't you see she's fascinated with the bunny. Aren't you, darling? Your uncle's a cruel man. Nobody's going to kill the bunny. When we come again next year we'll bring her some lettuce and you shall go and feed her. Won't you, darling?"

[118]

"Yes, Mummy," answered Petrita, without taking her eyes off the rabbit.

* * *

"We'll take our food outside tomorrow," said Mauricio. "We shall boil alive here with the heat of the stove."

His wife didn't answer. She was busy with her pots.

"What a chap Ocaña is! He knows how to live," Mauricio went on, pointing his spoon towards the window through which the visitors could be seen at table. "He never saves anything. Any time he's got a couple of notes, he brings his family for a Sunday in the country like he's doing today." He sucked up the soup from his spoon. "You know on Sundays a taxi gets passengers all the blessed day, and they charge five pesetas extra for every trip to a football match or a bullfight. He loses all that, and he doesn't mind."

"Why doesn't he come on a weekday then?" asked Justi. "He wouldn't lose so much."

"Because of his brother, I suppose. Obviously he's only free on Sundays. Cheerful and open-handed as the day's long. That's the way to live. Otherwise it's like the tale of the man who lost pounds and pounds looking for a chemist's shop to weigh himself."

"Well, if that system appeals to you," replied Faustina, "why not apply it to yourself, starting from tomorrow? Tomorrow you can shut up shop and give yourself over to the gay life. Well, why don't you?"

A voice called down the passage from the bar.

"Why do you think? Don't you imagine there aren't times when I'd like to? Just not to have to listen to you . . . Look in and see what they want. Tell them I'm having my dinner."

Faustina went out, and Mauricio glanced at his daughter with his spoon in the air. Then he looked down at his soup and asked: "What time's your young man coming?"

"He'll be here at half past four or five, I expect. It depends whether he takes the bus or the train."

"You're going to the pictures?"

"I suppose so."

Mauricio paused. He looked out at the garden through the open window. Ocaña's sister-in-law was laughing.

"Come on, now, let's have the meat."

Justina got up. Her father followed.

"You don't know what film you're going to?"

"Oh, Father, why do you ask such a lot of questions? We'll go to one of the films. What does it matter to you which? Why do you suppose I should know now?" She changed her tone. "Anyone would think there was something you wanted to find out with all your questions. I don't like this at all."

"I'm not trying to find out anything. Only what you're doing."

Another burst of laughter came from the garden.

"What the two of you do on Sundays."

"And don't you know now? What do you expect we do? . . . No, no, nothing like that about it."

"Good! But what's all this about your not thinking it right to help your father serve here in the garden on a Sunday? What put that into your head?"

"What? Whoever told you such a thing?"

"Your mother, this morning. It seems that Manolo doesn't care for your serving people. He thinks it's unrefined or vulgar, and she agrees with him."

"Oh, Mother! Well, that's the first time I've heard this story. A fine state of things!"

"But didn't you know? Come now, tell me the truth."

"It is the truth, Father."

"All right. That's enough, darling. You don't mind doing it?"

"No. Just wait till he comes, though. He'll hear something this afternoon!"

The dog Azufre appeared, sniffing.

"Go away! Horrid dog! If there's one thing that really infuriates me it's to have arrangements made behind my back. Now when did all this happen? I know, of course. It was one day last week, when he caught Mother alone. That was the day, I'm certain. They must have put their heads together about this. Why did you beat about the bush so much before you told me?"

"Oh, I don't know. Very often people don't understand what you mean ..."

He shrugged his shoulders.

*　*　*

Faustina put away the money that White Shoes had given her. She wrinkled her nose as she looked at Lucio, and said with a nod of her head in the direction of the door through which he had gone out: "What do you make of him?"

"A good man. One of the best."

"I don't understand his sort of life. He may be a good fellow. I've no doubt he is. But I don't understand him, I can't make him out ..."

El Chamarís came in with Azufre, his yellow dog. Behind him came the constable, the butcher who had been there in the morning and another butcher from San Fernando. Azufre was whining and wagging his tail.

"How do!"

"Faustiná." The other butcher accented the last syllable of her name by way of greeting.

The dog went down the passage sniffing for strangers. Just as he was about to make a fuss of the Ocaña family he met the cat in the middle of the garden. A fight threatened. But the cat faced up to him and Azufre retreated, followed by the voice of Justina, who had shooed him away when he appeared in the kitchen.

"Can you give us some coffee?"

"It's just beginning to boil."

The other butcher was taller and thinner than his mate, but had the same healthy air. He hunched his shoulders like a cat or a cyclist, and lowered his head when he talked. He read from the shelf: "Ojén Morales. An old-time drink. It'll suit you. You like *cazalla*." He poked his friend with his elbow.

"Ojén isn't a thing to drink every day."

Faustina went to see to the coffee.

"I hear you put that puppy from the Town Hall in his place this morning. Who does he think he is?"

Lucio glanced at the others and said: "Don't talk about it please." Mauricio came in.

"Afternoon."

"Got visitors, have we?"

He nodded. "The owner of the taxi you saw when you came in. He's a very old friend of mine."

"Well, if you've known him as long as he's had that broken-down taxi, you must be old friends."

"Come now, no friendship in the world could last as long as that old bus," said El Chamarís with a laugh.

"There are some older than that still on the roads."

"If you were to give his bus a pair of glasses and throw a sheet over its head, it'd be Gandhi to the life."

"Now stop insulting his car," interrupted Mauricio. "You've said enough."

The others laughed. Justina came in with the coffee.

"Here you are, Father." Then, turning to the tall man. "Hullo Señor Claudio, not gone fishing today?"

"No, my dear. It's no good trying to fish with all this crowd about. And that sort of catch is too heavy for my line."

Faustina's voice sounded from the passage.

"You give them their coffee, my dear," Mauricio said. "I must go for a minute," and he went out.

"Your father can't stay still today with all these people here from Madrid. He hasn't even got a moment for us."

"He's happy all right. He's enjoying himself. We haven't seen them since last summer, you see."

She put down the glasses and poured the coffee.

"When did you get to know one another?"

"When he was in the Provincial with his broken leg. The other fellow was in the next bed after a car crash. Mother and I got to know him at the same time, and his family too, when we used to visit Father on Thursdays and Saturdays. They fixed it up between them that the first to get well should lay on a dinner and invite both families. And they kept their agreement."

"Which of them was better first?"

"Ocaña was. So one Sunday we all went off to Madrid to celebrate. My father was still in plaster."

"Yes, I remember when your father was in plaster. That must be a good six years ago."

"It was in April. So it must be six and a bit. Their little girl was still being breast fed . . ."

"Your father doesn't limp at all after his fracture," said the tall butcher. "He hasn't the slightest limp."

"He always feels it when it's going to rain. His leg pains him then."

"But he's never right," interrupted Lucio. "Or if he ever is, it's just a fluke. If we had no better instrument to go by than your father's leg, it'd be all up with meteorology."

The others laughed. "Meeting people like that," said Claudio, "when you take to one another, makes you friends for life. But it doesn't often happen. At least, when I was in hospital for my operation I never wanted to see the fellows in the next beds again. I couldn't get away from them fast enough."

"But these two, Ocaña and my father, were like brothers. It used to make us laugh. They were always giving one another presents. So much so that Mother used to make a joke that if we brought anything for Father we ought to give it to Ocaña, and vice versa, his family ought to give their presents to Father, and then they wouldn't need to swap everything they got."

"Your father's a generous man. He's on good terms with everybody. If the other fellow's carved out of the same block that explains everything," observed El Chamarís.

Justina had folded her arms on the counter and was swinging one leg. The tall butcher went up to her and said with his head on one side: "Well, my dear, are you going to give us the pleasure today?"

Justina raised her head: "What are you talking about?"

"What do you think, my dear," answered the butcher, pointing with his thumb and nodding towards the garden.

"Get along with you!" said Justina with a laugh. "You're always the same. Can't you do without me?"

"No, my dear. You're the champion. Who else gives spice and excitement to the game? Without you 'Frog' would be a stew without meat. And who have I got to compete with if you don't play?"

"Come on now, don't brag!" protested El Chamarís.

"I warn you my young man's coming to pick me up at five."

"Let's get along then or it'll be too late. The sooner we start the better. We've just got time for a couple of games."

"Come on, Justina," said El Chamarís. "You and I against the meat department. We'll give them a hiding, you see if we don't."

"Only . . ." She broke off. "Come on then."

★ ★ ★

"No more business here. Let's go." The ice-cream man had swung his cork roll on to his shoulder and departed for the point. A small splash was heard from the river. Someone had thrown a dog in. Then there was a lot of shouting from some family because the dog had come and shaken itself over them. Everyone turned round to see what it was all about. " . . . Can't a man have his forty winks," grumbled Daniel. Now the sun had crossed over to the right bank of the Jarama. In the distance the Vicálvaro cement plant sent a long streak of smoke across the sky in the direction of Madrid. In the silence, only a rumbling was heard in the group. "Somebody's guts are singing," one of them remarked.

"Mine," admitted Sebastián with a laugh. "It's the sardines. They're reciting their rosary already."

Alicia lay on her stomach supporting herself on her elbows, and holding her head just above Miguel's face. Now Mely was looking at them through her sun-glasses. Miguel was stroking Alicia and blowing on her neck. Mely was watching them.

"I say, Ali, wouldn't you like me to put a comb through your hair?"

"No thank you, Mely. Not now. Perhaps a little later if you will."

"Now's the time. Before it's finished drying. It'll lose all its wave otherwise, you'll see . . ."

"Finished drying. Why, it's been bone dry for two hours and more!"

"All right. Just as you like."

Mely looked in the other direction. She began to scrape in the dust with a little stick. She drew letters and rubbed them out, and then some lines and crosses, all very quickly. Finally she broke her stick on the ground and turned towards Fernando. She could not see his face since she had put his forearm across his eyes to protect them from the light.

"Well I'm damned, the man's gone to sleep!"

A voice from the picnicker's loudspeakers refracted by the still water of the pool and sounded up in the trees. Mely looked at Miguel and Alicia.

"You'll get your shirt in an awful mess," she observed.

"What? Me?"

"Yes, you of course! You'll get yourself covered with earth. You're both sprawling anyhow . . ."

Miguel shrugged his shoulders.

"Who cares?" he said. "I shall throw it in the wash-basket when I get home tonight anyway."

Mely did not answer. She turned on her back with her hands clasped under her head.

"It's revoltingly hot," she sighed.

As they lay in the shade of the trees, their eyes were blinded by the dazzling glare of the opposite bank, which was in the sun. A heavy sheet of light struck the empty untilled fields, making the sheep of the little flock indistinguishable from the whitish plain.

"I *have* scorched my shoulder badly!" said Lucita, "I can't bear it to touch the ground."

She had raised her body in a sitting position.

"Do you mind rubbing it with a bit of Nivea?" she asked, looking towards Tito.

Tito was lying beside her. He glanced in her direction.

"Do you mind?" Luci went on. "It *would* be so kind of you, Tito, if you would."

"Yes, Luci, of course I'll rub you."

"Thank you. I am scorched rather badly, I'm afraid."

Mely had turned her head and was once more watching Alicia and Miguel.

"Would you like a cigarette, Miguel," she asked. "I'll give you one of my Americans."

"What ? A smoke ? Yes, please."

"I'll get them then."

"Reach me my bag if you don't mind," said Lucita. "It's got my cream in it." She stretched out her hand to take it from Tito.

"I'll get it out for you," he said.

"No, don't pry into my things." She caught him by the arm. "Give me that bag, Tito."

Tito held the bag out of her reach.

"I like being inquisitive. Got any secrets, Luci ?"

"That's my business. I don't want you going through my things. And you say it's us girls that are curious. Come on, give it to me."

Tito handed it over.

"All right, honey. Take your bag. We'll respect your secrets."

"I haven't got any secrets. Don't worry, there aren't any secrets in it. You'd have been badly disappointed. Tell you what, I'll show you everything that's there if you like. I'm not a very interesting character. But I can't help that, I'm afraid."

She rummaged in the bag looking for the tin of Nivea.

"Well, why didn't you want me to see ?"

"Because I prefer to keep it to myself. I'd rather show you what's in it myself, and not have someone poking his nose in. Here's the tin."

She lay down on her stomach.

"On my shoulders, especially," she instructed him.

Someone was shouting down the river, his voice echoing under the arches of the bridge. Paulina turned round. At the approach to the bridge, the sun struck the blue and yellow of a railway signal disk. Sebas' head rested on Paulina's legs. He stretched out his hand and touched a small mark on Santos' ankle. "How did you do that ?" he asked.

"Don't touch it. It hurts. I did it at football."

"When ?"

"Last Sunday, on the Elipa ground, playing against the F.E.R.S.A."

"Oh yes. What was the result ?"

"Oh, it ended in a free fight half-way through the first half."

Sebastián laughed.

"Why was that?"

"Oh, the usual reason. They were a bit rough. So we beat them up. We gave them a good licking." He swung his right arm in the air to suggest a beating.

"It always ends like that, unless there's a couple of Civil Guards there to keep order."

"Yes, force is the only thing that commands respect in these parts."

"And then, only when people respect it, and that's not always either. Even force is liable to fail at times. So your match ended in a pitched battle, did it?"

"Yes, it did. Afterwards we had a friendly game, us against us. We picked up two teams with some of our own members who had come to watch. The F.E.R.S.A. lot had cleared off by that time," said Santos.

He kept the back of his hands over his eyes to shield them from the glare. Paulina was now scratching Sebas' back.

"Tell me," she asked, "have you got girls working in your factory, Santos?"

"Only as packers. Not in our department. We hardly ever see them."

"You'd better not," said Carmen.

"No, dearest," he answered with a laugh.

He stretched out his arm to try and touch her chin.

"Treasure!"

"Now then, no flattery!"

"Can someone like that make you feel jealous?" asked Paulina.

"Just the normal amount," answered Carmen with a shrug of the shoulders.

"The normal amount! God help us," exclaimed Santos. "Why, she's a regular Crazy Jane!"

In the next party they were discussing births and miscarriages, and which of two new babies was the prettier. The talkers were women, and the man with them watched in silence, smoking his cigarette. Before lunch he had been the Buddha, but now he was dressed. Daniel was asleep. The sheep on the hot ground had been frightened by some naked children who were hunting lizards. There

[127]

was a dull sound of stones falling on the soft earth as if on a blanket. The dogs were barking and the shepherd was whistling. Lucita gave a start.

"Not there, Tito. You're tickling me."

There was a sweet smell of Nivea. The ice-cream man passed again; a nearby party called him over. "Sold out!" he called back. Daniel had lifted his head and looked at him for a moment.

"What an ugly brute . . ." he muttered, hiding his face once more in the ground.

"What harm has he done you?" asked Luci.

Mely was examining a pale line on her shoulder left by the strap of her swimsuit. Fernando had opened his eyes and was pointing at the sky in a gap between the tree-tops.

"Look at those birds!"

Clearly outlined above the trees, they were flying an irregular course, gliding with motionless wings and chirping, strangers to the whole scene below.

"What are they called?" asked Mely.

"Bee-eaters."

"What a pretty colour they are!"

"Yes, they're very lovely. I've held a live one in my hand," said Miguel. "You remember, Alicia? It had broken a wing against the telegraph wires. It was at Los Molinos, on one of our trips. It couldn't fly at all."

"They must be marvellous close to," said Mely.

"You're right. Alicia had the idea that we ought to take it home and look after it. But birds of that kind always die the moment they're in a cage, especially if they've got a broken wing like that one."

"How's the time going on, eh?"

"Quarter to six."

"Is that all?" asked Mely.

Down in the sun, against the rusty colour of the waters, was a woman in a black silk slip, rubbing some enamelled pots and aluminium plates with sand from the river bank. The plates emitted momentary glints like a photographers' flash lamp when they caught the rays of the sun.

"I don't let this man of mine go out dancing either," said Paulina. She pushed Sebastián out of her lap.

"There you are, dear. That's all right."

"Boy! I'd like to have ten backs so that I need never stop having them scratched. No kidding. As soon as they'd finished with back number ten, then number one would be tickling again . . ."

"I mean I don't let him go to dances," continued Paulina, "but if he goes to a wedding or somewhere he's promised to go and I'm not invited, I don't like him to look a fool. I'd hate him to be uncomfortable on my account. So I let him have just two or three dances, if you know what I mean."

"I can't see that anyone looks foolish, for sitting in his chair and not getting up," replied Carmen. "I can't see that there's anything to be ashamed of in that, however you look at it."

"But you must admit, dear, that the situation is a bit more awkward for a man. There he is, with everybody enjoying themselves, miserably clinging to his seat. Everyone will say it's his fiancée, and she must be mad, and things like that."

"Well, on that subject we must agree to differ. If people are officially engaged, the man must agree to behave exactly the way he expects his fiancée to. There's no reason why it should be different for him because he's a man. That's how I think things ought to be. I can't see any reason why they should get away with things when we aren't allowed to."

"How they natter!" said Sebas. "Come on, Santos, we're not wanted here. Let's take a stroll, and see if we can't pick something up."

He laughed, but Santos answered in a weary voice: "I'm so comfortable I wouldn't budge from here, if Marilyn Monroe herself went by. I swear I wouldn't."

He turned over on his back and stretched his arms towards the sky.

"I'd like to see it happen. If that blonde piece were to pass and walk right by here, you'd change your tune all right. You'd wake up pretty quickly! Why, you'd be up on your feet in a jiffy!"

"That's a nice way of talking," said Paulina. "So you don't think much of us any more?"

"Don't be silly. It's just talk for talk's sake," said Sebas with a laugh. "Just for the sake of talking you know."

He tried to make up to her, but she drew back.

"Let me alone, you mean beast. You and your fine tastes!"

"I'll tell you something funny," said Sebas. "It's about Marilyn Monroe. Do you know what it said in one of the papers?"

"No. What? Tell us."

"Well, in one of those interviews they have with film stars, she said, 'I should like to be blonde all over.' That's not bad, is it?"

"I can't see the joke, really," said Paulina.

"Oh no," protested Santos. "She couldn't have said that. Don't be silly."

"It was in America, you idiot. She did. Do you think I made the story up?"

"I don't know. I don't know. Perhaps she did say it."

"It's not very funny in any case," said Paulina, sticking to her point.

They looked up. A plane was flying very low. It passed immediately above them, and looked as if it were going to brush the tree-tops with its wings. The noise of it drowned all the sounds in the copse.

"How close they come!" said Mely.

"It's a four-engine plane."

"It must be coming down," explained Fernando, "to judge by its direction. They're on to the Barajas runway as soon as they've crossed the main road."

"Oh, how I wish I was in it!"

"Not in that one, girl. In one that's taking off."

"Would you like to go to Rio de Janeiro?"

"I believe they have marvellous carnivals . . ."

"The Rio Carnivals. . . ."

"The Fallas at Valencia don't hold a candle to them."

"They don't burn anything there."

"No, but they're good and noisy."

"Why don't they let people wear masks here?"

"Because of pickpockets. It'd give them a great opportunity, don't you see?"

"And aren't there any in Rio?"

"There's plenty of money there! Just think of the coffee they sell. Every country buys coffee from Brazil."

"Yes, it's a bad habit."

"Cuba's the same with its tobacco. Bad habits always bring in money."

"If on the other hand you grow wheat . . . just look at us."

"Well, let us plant coffee, and we'll see whether after a year or two they don't let us wear masks."

"What's wrong with our faces?"

"We wear them in the street every day," said Sebas.

"Then why talk about Rio? Our faces are a carnival in themselves!"

"Yes, a non-stop carnival. The Rio Carnival's got nothing on us, Mely."

"Hasn't it really? But you'd get in the queue to go there."

"Me? Yes, out of curiosity."

"We all would. To see Rio de Janeiro and the Rio Carnival."

"Yes, but there'd be a little more in it for us than that. We wouldn't go simply and solely for the sights."

"Yes, we might win a wooden whistle there in a tombola."

"Is that all, eh?"

"What about Bahía?"

"Yes, Bahía too. Bahía can't be too bad either."

"Astorga's the place."

"Don't make me laugh, brother!"

"It wasn't a joke."

"No?"

"No."

"What was it then?"

"It's as far as I can afford a ticket."

"Yes, I see, and third class at that."

"Quite right. So Rio de Janeiro's a joke. And so's Bahía. And . . ."

"Well, what have you got to say now?"

"Easy, Santos. I've got my tenth share in a lottery ticket at home. Perhaps it's not just a joke for me."

"More for you than for anybody else."

"Why?"

"The stronger your imagination, you see, the funnier it is. Astorga's the place for me. Give me a ticket there. How much? There you are. That's the place for me. Astorga's my limit, you can really have fun there. I've got a ticket, a pretty little ticket – and Astorga's the place for me . . ."

"Imagination doesn't buy tickets."

"No, that's the good thing about it," said Santos. "It pays for nothing. It's colossal. It's stupendous – " He made a pause – "like my appetite. And like an appetite, you get it for nothing."

Hardly anyone was walking in the sun, out of the shadow of the trees. At river level the heat was dancing, the minute and transparent dance of evaporating water. Mely looked all round her. The bee-eaters floated once more over the tree-tops. You could hear them twittering.

"What shall we do?"

"What time did we arrange with Samuel, Zacarías and the others?" asked Alicia.

"We told them to meet us at the *merendo*, between seven and half past for certain."

"What about going to the dance at Torrejón?" proposed Fernando.

Sebastián agreed: "Yes, sir, a wonderful idea, a stupendous idea!"

"H'm, more pedal pushing? Pedal pushing for me . . ."

"But it's nothing. We're almost there."

"Chuck it! Torrejón? Not on your life. Get that idea out of your head!"

Sebas was singing: "She isn't more than thirty – her name's Adelaída – and when she goes out dancing – she lifts her petticoats – she lifts her petticoats – she lifts her petticoats."

"Just listen to him!"

"Are you often taken like that?"

Sebastián had got up and was doing a grotesque dance with his arms in the air.

"She isn't more than thirty – her name is Adelaída."

"This'll bring the rain down."

"You're raising dust, you brute!"

Sebastián suddenly fell back on the ground, bursting with laughter.

"Crazy like a fox I am! And that's the truth."

"Well, if you admit it . . ."

Come on now. Dancing at Torrejón! Those in favour, raise the right hand!"

"Chuck that idiot in the water! He's a damned bore."

"Quiet now! Shall we make up our minds, yes or no?"

"There's nothing to make up our minds about. Nobody's going to Torrejón. You're just getting excited for no reason at all."

"She isn't more than thirty – her name's Adelaída . . ."

"Put him out! Now, Sebastián, please . . ."

"We were going to Torrejón, to kick up a real row. We should have had a whale of a time . . ."

"If you go on like this, I shall leave for one. Let me warn you now."

"Don't upset yourself, Mely. You needn't worry about this crazy lunatic."

"That's true enough . . . He gets attacks sometimes."

"Can't you see that you're being a nuisance, Sebas?" scolded Paulina. "Don't you understand? Or do you like annoying people?"

"Everybody's dead. You must put some spirit into them."

"Yes, but not that way. All you do is infuriate everyone."

"Hear, hear!" said Mely.

"You always want everyone to do what suits you."

"No, I don't. I don't want anybody to do anything. All I say is that I'm not going to Torrejón. Everyone else can do as they like."

"Thank you very much for making that clear."

"What a nasty man you are!"

"Well, we're not doing anything at present. Now what I propose . . ."

"Where have you put the wine?" interrupted Fernando. "We've got to wet our throats first."

"I'll start it going round."

"What were you going to say, Tito?" asked Miguel.

"Me? Nothing."

He lay down again. Santos picked up the bottle.

"Who wants a drop?"

"I do. Chuck it over."

Fernando clapped his hands and signed to Santos to throw him the bottle right across the whole party. He blocked it with his body, pretending to have stopped a goal. Some drops of wine spattered his naked chest.

"That was a good save!"

"No joking about serious matters."

Fernando poured the wine down his throat. The sun gleamed on the bottle and on his raised arms. The wine gurgled in his mouth.

"Don't forget tomorrow's Monday," said Miguel, to hurry him up.

Fernando put down the bottle and panted: "It's marvellous. Here you are."

"Aren't you drinking, Tito?" asked Miguel.

"Drink, man, while you've got the chance. The best thing you can do."

"Don't make so much fuss, boy. It's bad manners."

Luci was sitting in silence between Tito and Daniel, sitting in a huddled position, her arms clasping her legs and her chin resting on her knees. She was rocking slightly from side to side. Miguel took a drink.

"Could one of you oblige me with a light," asked a man who had come across. He was wearing a blue sports shirt and pointed to his cigarette.

"Yes, of course."

While Miguel was searching for some matches, the stranger was busy eyeing the girls. He looked them over one by one.

"That fellow's got a nerve!" said Alicia when the man had gone.

"Some people don't mind staring."

"What did he do?"

"He looked us all up and down, the bastard, and no disguise about it."

"No harm in that," said Fernando.

"It's not nice," answered Mely.

"Come off it. You know you like men to look at you."

"Ugh, believe me, it tickles us to death! We thrive on it! The damned cheek!"

"All right, girl. All right!"

Mely gave a sign of impatience, and looked down the river past the shade of the trees. There were some mules on the sand below the bridge. A little man in dark clothes had brought them down to the water and was waiting in the sun while they drank. The first to finish lay down on the ground worried by the flies. He threw himself violently on his back, kicking his legs in the air and raising a great cloud of dust as he rubbed his painful stings against the ground. Sebastián had lain down again. Paulina and he had now moved away. They had their backs to the others. Daniel gave a start when Lucita touched his arm with the wet glass of the bottle. "What is it?"

"Did I give you a fright? What did you imagine it was?"

"I don't know. A snake. A boa-constrictor at the very least." Lucita laughed and pointed to the bottle: "Well, well! Do you want some of this?"

"Hand over the remedy! Where's the joke?"

Carmen was leaning against a tree-trunk, and Santos was resting his head on her breast. She was breathing into his hair and combing his temples with her nails.

"Darling, what you want is a haircut."

She pulled some strands of his hair away from his head so that he could see how long they were.

"I should like to go for a walk," said Mely. "Will you come with me, Fernando?"

"Delighted, I'm sure."

"Well, let's go. Are you coming with us?" she added, turning to Alicia and Miguel.

"It's much too hot, girl. Where are you going at this time of day?"

"Somewhere or other. I can't stay here any more. I'm fed up with this idea of never doing anything, and that's a fact. Do you mind?"

"Goodness no! Go for a walk if you want to," said Alicia. "But you'll come back here, won't you?"

"Yes, of course. We're only going for a stroll."

Fernando and Mely were on their feet.

"Just as we are?" asked Fernando.

Amelia rubbed her hands down her body to get rid of the dust, and pulled up her swimsuit. "What do you say?" She looked at Fernando.

"No, I shall put on my trousers and sandals. Come as you like, though. Chuck my things over, Ali, if you would."

"I'll put my things on too then. The sun's still beating down like hell. You daren't expose your back."

Lucita watched Mely putting on her trousers over her swimsuit. There was a clatter of a freight train crossing the bridge. Paulina watched trucks the colour of dried blood coming on to the bridge, one after another. They stood out against the flat ground, moving in the sunshine along the top of the embankment.

"Are you counting the trucks?" Sebastián asked.

"No, no. I was looking at that hill over there."

She pointed into the distance at the Cerro del Viso, near Alcalá de Henares, white and dark in the air dusky with August heat. The freight train was now entirely clear of the bridge and was moving in that direction, to lose itself in the plain ahead, panting and rattling dully. Mely was tying up her sandals.

"Try and be back before seven," said Alicia, "so that we can all go up together."

"Don't you worry. Are you others going to swim again?"

"I don't think so. What do you say, Miguel?"

"Difficult question."

"It would be a good idea. Because afterwards we're to join the others and all that. Aren't you going to put on your blouse?"

"No, a skirt and swimsuit top looks smart."

Fernando returned from the bushes dressed.

"Ready when you are," he said to Mely, who was looking at her face in her pocket mirror.

"Here already?" she asked, tilting her powder compact to catch his face in the glass.

Fernando laughed.

"The things you girls learn from the films!"

"What, for instance?"

"Talking to a fellow's face in the mirror. You learnt that from Hedy Lamarr."

"Don't be ridiculous. Can't a girl do anything without having learnt it off somebody or other? I don't need to copy anything from anybody. So there!"

"See! That stung her, didn't it?" said Fernando. "Come on, Mely. I didn't mean to annoy you. We all know that you're O.K. as you are, and then some. So now we're agreed."

Mely put on her glasses.

"Good. Thank you for the apology. I'm ready when you are."

Fernando smiled and offered her his arm, with a wink and a chivalrous gesture. Mely took it, and they kept up the pantomime for a few steps. Then Mely turned round. "How's that?" she asked Alicia and Miguel with a laugh. Miguel was laughing also.

"Very fine, girl. To the manner born. You two could get parts on the stage. Off you go, and don't be late."

"See you soon," said Mely. "And now let me go, kind sir. It's much too hot."

They departed. Daniel watched Mely's brown shoulders and the naked sweep of her back in her swimsuit. Fernando was hardly taller than she. She had put her hands in her trouser pockets. The two of them were talking as they walked.

Santos crept over to Alicia and Miguel.

"I'm going to pinch one of those cigarettes of hers," he said.

"That's a dirty trick," said Alicia. "If she knows you've been rummaging in her bag, she'll be furious. But it's up to you."

"She'll never know. Do you want one, Miguel?"

"Not on your life! What's more you'll get us all in the cart. No thank you, I'm not looking for trouble."

Santos took the packet from the bag, and went back to Carmen. A sharp smell, like thin smoke, drifted in, as if someone were burning leaves and undergrowth near by. The smoke was invisible; only the smell could be detected.

"Who said you could pinch her cigarettes?" asked Carmen. "You know what she's like. The fat'll be in the fire if she notices it. You'll catch it if she finds out."

"She won't miss one, darling. She can't have counted them."

"I wouldn't put it past her."

"Don't exaggerate now. I know you can't stand the poor girl. But why do you suppose she'd count her cigarettes? It's mean even to think of such a thing. You aren't getting jealous of Mely as well, are you?"

She put her hands on either side of Santos' head, and rocked it from side to side, whispering into his hair: "You always think I'm jealous of everyone. Who do you think you are, silly?"

She brushed his forehead with her lips, and blew behind his ear. Long whistles could be heard from the river. Miguel and Alicia had got up and moved over beside Paulina and Sebastián.

"You don't mind if we come over near you? The sun's beating down where we were. We're not disturbing you, are we?'

"No, of course not. Quite the opposite. We're delighted to see you," said Sebastián, briefly raising his head.

They settled down. Daniel had taken a look at the three couples, and turned towards Tito and Lucita.

"Let's have some fun, kids," he said. "The afternoon's rushing by, and we must have some fun. What else is there we can do when all's said and done? So pass me that wine which you're keeping to yourselves over there."

Tito gave him a disgusted look and passed him the bottle.

"You're quite right, Daniel," said Lucita. "There's not much life about us."

"What sort of a trio do we look like? The last three teams at the bottom of the league, a sure case for relegation. I can't think of anything else to call us."

"Now then Tito, no groaning here! That's point number one. Luci, we'll chuck him out if he's stupid, now won't we?"

"I think we're quite all right here, the three of us . . . We could have a marvellous time."

She raised her eyes to Tito's face as if expecting to see him cheer up.

"Tito," she went on, "lift up your head, Tito!"

"Come on! Can't you hear when you're spoken to? We don't have to say everything twice, do we?"

"All right, boy, there's nothing the matter. Why are you so worried about me? I'm fine."

"We'll soon see if that's true," said Daniel. "We don't want any moaning here."

He then turned to Lucita. "Let's see, Lucita, how are we off for wine? That's the first thing."

Luci looked all round before replying: "There's a drop in here and two full ones." She waved the almost empty bottle in the air, shaking up the small amount left in the bottom.

"We're well off!" said Daniel. "Millionaires almost! We can go a long way on that. Quite a long way. Send it over."

"Yes," said Tito, "now we shall see . . ."

Daniel had taken the bottle and drawn the cork. He offered it to Lucita.

"Have a drink!"

"You first."

"No, you. The first drink of the evening."

Lucita put her lips to the bottle, and Daniel touched her arm.

"No sipping, girl."

"I can't drink any other way. It runs down . . ."

When she had finished she rubbed a patch of lipstick off the mouth of the bottle and passed it to Daniel. "Here you are, nervous! I haven't anything catching."

* * *

"The advantages of living in the country," said Ocaña, "here they are. From the hen-house to the stove."

His wife agreed: "That's the way to get the good out of things."

"Naturally. Without any of those middle men. They just complicate matters and make everything more expensive, and they don't do anything for you."

"By the time we get an egg," continued Petra, "two thirds of the good has been lost on the way."

"Fine, that's fine," protested her brother-in-law with a smile. "That's very fine. So poor us, who earn our livings by trade have no right to stay alive. Is that it?"

"Yes, that's it. It's you who rocket up the prices. Poor women get the headaches, going down to the market every blessed day of the year. And who's the cause of it all? You are."

"But leave us our little corner, dear. Everyone has a right to live."

"You're very well provided for. And what can we do about it? It's only when we see something like this that we notice anything and know what it's costing us."

"You're quite right," admitted her brother-in-law. "It's quite true. That's the way things are, I agree. A fine state of affairs! Why a laying hen must bring a man a small fortune judging by the price eggs are today. Must be worth its weight in gold."

"Now, you see," interrupted his wife, "instead of breeding canaries, you might have kept nine or ten fowls at home, and it'd have paid you better." She spoke with great emphasis.

"At home? On top of the cupboard? Obviously you don't know how expensive hens are to feed or how hard it is to keep them laying."

"Well, if it's a question of work, the canary cages keep you pretty busy . . . But what do we get out of your pretty little birds? What profit is there in keeping canaries?"

"They sing."

Petra was handing cakes round to her children in order of age, from youngest to oldest. The little girl had taken hers and was now looking at those her brothers were getting.

"Here," said Juanito to her, "I'll swap yours with mine."

"Don't want to." The little girl shook her head and went away, holding her cake jealously in her hand. It was a long time before she started to eat it.

"It's a nice thing to have pets in the house," said Felipe. "Any sort of pets. They keep you company, you get fond of them, and they take you out of yourself."

"As for us," said Petra, "with these four in the house, I don't think we want any more to look after. They take us out of ourselves enough, and to spare. Anyone who wants distraction is welcome to a load or two of ours. We'd be only too willing to let them have it."

"But that doesn't stop people. I have a married friend in Barcelona, who has three children, but that doesn't prevent her from keeping cats. She's got five in the house."

"How revolting! And five of them too!"

"Yes, it depends on your point of view. If you don't like them, it'd be wrong to keep them of course."

"Indeed it would," said Petra. "Holy Virgin, how they must stink! And you could never keep up with the cleaning. They'd mess your things up quicker than you could get them washed. What a penance to follow them round from morning till night with a cloth and a shovel. Give me a little peace! No animals for me! No cats or dogs or anything else! What's the good of them?"

Ocaña's sister-in-law burst out laughing.

"Excuse me Petra, but you do make me laugh. Don't take it so much to heart! But you say such funny things that I can't help laughing at you." She slapped Petra's arm and went on laughing. "There's nobody like you. You're such a laugh."

Petra had looked at her mistrustfully at first. But then she burst out laughing also, and they looked at one another, laughing together, neither of them able to stop.

"What a crazy couple you are!" said Sergio. "You make me die!"

Nobody else at the table was laughing, and everyone was watching those two.

"What are they laughing about, Papa?" asked Petrita, alarmed. She pulled at her father's sleeve to attract his attention. "Tell me, what are they laughing about?"

"Nothing, darling, nothing," replied Felipe gaily. "Your mother's a little strange in the head."

"Oh, my goodness, I do feel bad . . ." said Petra, quite exhausted with laughing. "I almost died . . ."

"Nobody ever died of happiness. It's healthy."

"Oh, she's marvellous, she is!" exclaimed her sister-in-law. "Absolutely marvellous."

Their laughter died down. The children looked at the faces of the grown-ups and did not know what to say.

"Now what about a little cigar, Sergio," said Felipe to his brother. "Shall we light up?"

"I'm with you. Go ahead," replied his brother, flexing his arm muscles as if preparing to do an important job of work.

He shook the crumbs out of his lap. Felipe passed him a Farias.

"Here you are. They're not a bad brand these, as you'll see."

Felipe Ocaña put the cigar to his nose and ran his hands over his trousers and his jacket, which was hanging on the back of his chair, hoping to hear the sound of matches in some pocket.

"The light's on me," said his brother.

"Papa, do you enjoy smoking that cigar very much?" asked Petrita.

"Yes, darling, just as much as you enjoyed that cake you just gobbled up."

"And you too, Uncle?"

Sergio was lighting up, and his wife answered for him.

"Your uncle always enjoys anything that's bad for him, you see."

Sergio looked up from his cigar and his match to give her a look. Then he took a deep breath, and Petrita watched the comet trail and the smoke of the match, which fell extinguished in the garden soil.

"How's the tummy feeling?" asked Felipe.

"Very comfortable."

"Don't worry, Nineta, a good thing never does anyone any harm. Your husband isn't going to suffer for today's little excesses. I've never heard of anyone dying of anything like this."

"What you're saying isn't quite true, Felipe. There's healthy food and indigestible food. Sergio's always having trouble with his stomach. But I don't interfere, you see. He knows all about it, and it's up to him . . ."

Juanita got up from his chair.

"Where are you going, boy?" asked Petra.

Juanito said nothing but sat down again.

"Can we go and see the rabbit, Mother?" asked Amadeo.

"Have you finished? Let's see your faces . . ."

The three children automatically assumed expressions of goodness and looked up into their mother's face.

"All right. But mind you don't go anywhere else. I shall be watching you, see. And be very good. Off you go!"

They all leapt up and rushed to the chicken-run.

"Don't you want to go with them, Felisita?"

Felisita blushed.

"Don't want to," she said, giving nothing away.

Tears could be heard from Petrita, who had fallen flat in the middle of the garden. She was crying with her face to the ground, and did not get up. Sergio was on the point of rising to go and fetch her, but her mother prevented him.

"Leave her alone, Sergio. Don't you go . . . Listen, darling, just you pick yourself up if you don't want me to come and do it for you."

Petrita redoubled her weeping.

"I can see I shall have to come and slap you. What did I say, now?"

"Perhaps she's really hurt herself," suggested the brother-in-law.

"What! I know that child as well as if she were my own. And she is, let me remind you. She's as cunning as a monkey, and that's a fact."

Petrita had got up and was still crying, with her face to the creeper on the wall. Amadeo went up to her, and pulled at one arm to get her away. But the girl resisted and continued to weep into the leaves of the American vine.

"Don't you want to see the rabbit?" asked Amadeo. "Look at the crybaby . . ."

Felisita was sitting beside her mother, with her arms folded across her chest, and her eyes downcast and motionless, looking at nothing: enigmatic, and far away, and apparently completely cut off from her surroundings. Felipe took a great puff at his Farias: "What do you think of it?"

Holding the smoke in his mouth, his brother gave a nod. Nineta looked at him. Sergio contemplated the ash at the end of his cigar. His right arm rested on the knob of the chair and dangled over the back. His fingers played idly with the leaves of the honeysuckle. Petra heaved a sigh: "Oh dear, dear . . ." and her ample bust rose and fell with her breath. She looked at her children. Petrita, now quiet, had gone to join her brothers. The three of them were leaning against the wire, with their backs to everyone. The Great White Rabbit was nibbling a lettuce leaf with her sharp incisors. She then looked up and gazed at the children, still chewing, moving her little nose, her whiskers and her round furry chops very fast.

"She has her dinner first," said Juanita. "Supposing a hen was to come along, she'd nip it on the crest and make it bleed, poor thing."

"That isn't true. She wouldn't do that," protested Petrita.

Then Felipe Ocaña said: "We ought to go and ask for our coffee and brandy now that we've started the cigars. We ought to take our pleasures all together."

"Do you think your friend will have finished his dinner?"

Felipe looked towards the house, and in at the kitchen window. Neither Mauricio nor Justi was visible. All he could see was Faustina standing there eating. She held her soup plate in her left hand and was pushing back the hair on her forehead with her right arm, still holding her spoon.

"I can't see him in the kitchen."

Faustina had seen him, and came to the window. "Were you looking for my husband?" she shouted. "I'll call him this moment."

"Don't bother him, don't bother him. Just as soon as he's ready." But she had already disappeared inside.

"Lucky I've got another cigar on me that I can offer him. I know he likes them."

"I've saved these three cakes for them," said Petra. "We must at least show him that politeness. We must do that at least."

Mauricio appeared in the doorway.

"Did you enjoy your dinner?"

"Yes, thank you, Mauricio," answered Petra. "How could we have helped enjoying it in this marvellous spot you chose for us, right here in the shade?"

"But it's the appetite that counts. You must have had a swim to get such a good appetite. That's what it must have been."

"Get along with you! It's this marvellous place. Look, Mauricio, we've kept some little cakes for you. Here, take them."

She offered him the cardboard box.

"Oh, why did you bother about us? You must have robbed the children of their cakes, and they enjoy things like that twice as much as we do . . ."

"Please take them and don't worry about the children. If they eat more than one they get upset inside and diarrhoea, and I don't want that sort of thing. Besides, I wanted you to have them. They're not much, but *do* take them and say no more about it. If you don't they'll go straight back to Madrid as they are. So there's no point in making any more compliments."

"No, of course not. I didn't mean to hurt your feelings . . ." Petra handed across the table the box, at the bottom of which lay the three sticky cakes. He took it back to the kitchen window so that Faustina could put it in the shade.

"Thank you very much," she shouted to Felipe.

Petra answered her with a smile and a wave of the hand. Mauricio returned to the table, eating his cake.

"These are very good," he said emphatically. "We've nothing to touch them here. We don't know anything about cakes here, absolutely nothing. All we have are ordinary little things, and little doughnuts, that lie here." He pointed to his stomach. "We don't know anything about fine confectionery here, nothing at all."

"Oh, I really can't agree with that," said Petra. "You have your own things in the country. Every place has its local speciality. There are all sorts of dainties, you know, each made in its own district. There are Astorga biscuits, for instance, and Toledo marzipan, and tarts from Alcázar de San Juan." She counted them on her fingers, attributing to Mauricio as a countryman the products of every town and village in Spain. "There are Soria buttercakes and almond paste from Cádiz, and hundreds of different specialities, every one of them delicious. Aren't I right now?"

"Yes, I know all that. But all we have hereabouts are sugared almonds from Alcalá de Henares."

"My goodness, yes! Sugared almonds. Now they're famous if you like. They've got titles of nobility. Alcalá almonds. A real local speciality."

"And tipsy-cakes from Guadalajara," added Felipe.

"That's a bit farther off," answered Mauricio. "That's in Alcarría." As he said Alcarría, he made a gesture of exclusion as if wishing to push the district away.

Felipe took a puff at his cigar and laughed. Then he took out the third Farias.

"Here, Mauricio, I brought this for you."

"I shan't make any compliments with you about that, I'm sorry to say," said Mauricio, putting his head on one side. "I'm very fond of a cigar. Thanks, pal."

"Don't mention it. Now could you bring us a drop of coffee and some liqueurs?"

Mauricio squeezed his cigar and looked up.

"The coffee's not very good, I'm afraid. I can't recommend it."

"Never mind. Don't worry about that. We're not fussy. So long as you bring us something black . . ."

"Well, you'll see. I've given you fair warning."

"Let's have it. Let's have it. It can't be worse than you get in many bars in Madrid where they call it a 'special', and charge you three pesetas for the drippings off a priest's cassock."

"Now the liqueurs. What's it to be?"

Felipe turned to the party and raised his brows interrogatively.

"Brandy for me," said Nineta.

"The same," said her husband.

"A sweet *anís* for yours truly."

"Three brandies and one *anís* then," said Felipe.

"Right you are. And four coffees. I'll be back with it all in a minute," and he walked off.

As he entered the passage he bumped into Justina, who was coming out with Carmelo, El Chamarís and the two butchers. He squeezed himself against the wall to let them by.

"We're going to play a game of 'Frog' with your daughter," shouted the butcher Claudio. "Mind if she comes?"

Mauricio shrugged his shoulders: "So far as I'm concerned . . ."

As he came into the bar he added for Lucio's benefit: "They can play knucklebones if they like. What's it got to do with me?"

Justi had stopped at the kitchen door. "I must get the disks."

The disks were in the drawer of a whitewood table, among the spoons and forks and tin-openers.

"Carmelo's not playing," said El Chamarís, and turning towards the Ocañas' table: "Good health to you, and good afternoon!"

"Thank you, and good afternoon to you."

"I shall watch. I like it just as well."

Justina returned.

"Now who's to have first throw?"

"You," said Claudio. "You of course. Ladies first."

"Very clever!" she answered. "You know that will be to your advantage."

"Not a bit of it. We'll start first if you like. There's nothing in it."

Justina passed him the disks. El Chamarís counted five steps from the box of the frog and drew a line in the dust with the toe of his shoe. Claudio took his stand on the line, leaning forward from the waist and preparing to throw. He stopped short, however, and said: "Wait while I move these bikes. They're spoiling my aim."

"What a fairy-tale!"

Carmelo helped him move the bikes, and El Chamarís said to Justina: "Look now, I shall throw first. I'm the weaker of us two. You provide the strength of our partnership. So you'll throw second, and do anything I haven't done to beat them. All right?" He gave her a wink.

"All right," answered Justina.

"Planning your game, are you?"

"Yes, we are," answered Justina.

Carmelo and Claudio had got the bikes out of the way.

"Come on, the butchers' team takes the field."

Claudio, standing on the line, stepped back on his left foot and leaned forward from the waist. He swung his arm several times with the disk in his hand, and described an arc in the air from his forehead to his knees, with careful precision. Then he threw the first disk. It bounced off the lip of the frog and fell in the dust. The other nine struck the wood or the metal, one after another, and bounced off without entering any of the holes. The seventh scored a *frog*, but the ninth only *molinillo*. Two fell on the ground.

"We're beginning badly," said the butcher.

"It's the first game. Let me get my hand in. I shall warm to it all right."

El Chamarís counted the score and picked up the disks.

"You've made three thousand, four hundred and fifty. My turn now."

"Mind how you throw," advised Justina.

"I'm throwing in your honour," said El Chamarís, raising his arm.

He stretched his arm almost to full length level with his right eye and on a line with the frog's mouth, closing his other eye. Then he slowly lowered his arm, drawing it back to an exact point in the pit of his stomach. Finally arm and disk shot forward. The disk went down the frog's throat, and he turned to Justina.

"Dead true first time." Lowering his arm for the second time he said slowly: "And this one . . . to draw even."

But he did nothing much more. The other nine disks scored low.

"If only you wouldn't talk after you've taken aim," scolded Justina.

The other butcher raised much amusement by his spirited way of throwing the disks. One of them struck a bicycle bell and raised a ring. His throw was erratic and he was often off the line, but he scored two *frogs*, each of which he celebrated with "Olé!" So Justina was left with a difficult task in the first round.

"Now you'll see some play," said Carmelo.

He stared down at Justina's blouse as she bent her body. She kissed the first disk and kept her eyes fixed on the frog. Dropping her arm to her waist and putting out her tongue, she quickly lifted her arm. The disk shot away, and she remained after each throw with her left foot off the ground as if just about to lose her balance. She scored two *frogs*, but this still made them behind the others, who were now about 2,000 ahead. Claudio increased this advantage still more in the second round by scoring four *frogs*, and El Chamarís did not succeed in improving on his former achievement. But the other butcher hardly got anything from his turn either, and just managed to pull off two *molinillos*.

"Now let's see if you can improve things, Justina," said El Chamarís when it was her turn.

[148]

Justi scored three *frogs* and made a gesture of annoyance when her last disk actually bounded off the frog's bronze lips and fell to the ground.

"Rotten luck!" she exclaimed.

Claudio maintained his average in the third round, but at the same time El Chamarís made a considerable improvement, scoring two *frogs* and two *molinillos*.

"We'll beat them yet," he said as he threw his second *frog*.

The short butcher was a little better than last time, but did not make much difference to the score.

"This girl will show them," said Carmelo as Justina was about to have her turn.

Ocaña's children had come to watch the game.

"Good luck, Justi," said El Chamarís. "It's in your hands."

She looked all round, scraped her foot in the dust to steady her stance, and bent towards the frog with a smile. Her first disk missed, but the second and third fell into the bronze mouth. El Chamarís clenched his fists.

"Attagirl, my beauty," he whispered.

The fourth disk rolled on to the ground. "You've lost your aim," and neither of the next two got in. El Chamarís shook his head. Azufre looked at his master with his ears erect. Then one after another, four clean *frogs* skimmed into the bronze mouth and fell to the bottom of the wooden box.

★　★　★

"Goot tay," he had said, pronouncing his d's as t's. A little round basket hung from his forearm.

"May I see the lady?" he added, giving Mauricio a ceremonious smile. When he took off his worn panama, he revealed his scanty white hair which stood up like a thin smoke from his bald, sunburnt head. The contents of his basket were wrapped in a napkin.

"Come in, Esnáider. I expect she's in the kitchen. You know the way." The visitor made a slight bow and departed in the direction indicated. Lucio stuck out his head towards the basket as it passed him and pretended to sniff at it.

"You must have something very good in there."

Old Schneider stopped at the door, and answered, raising his arm with the little basket on it: "It is the finest fruit that I have growed in my garden. I take it as a present to Señora Faustita. The Christian catechism says: 'Give tenths and firstfruits to the Church of Got.' Faustita is goot like the Church to my wife and me. So I bring zis to her."

He gave a short guffaw.

"May I gum in?" he asked at the door, smiling again.

Faustina turned from the sink. "Come in, Esnáider. This is nice."

Schneider bowed again as he entered. He held his panama against his stomach, grasping it with the tips of his fingers. He put his basket down on the cloth-covered table. Faustina was drying her hands. Outside in the garden the frog disks sounded against the bronze and the wood.

"But what have you brought today? What's the latest crazy idea? You make me quite shy, you do really, with all your attentions."

Schneider laughed.

"Figs," he said, glowing with satisfaction. "You try Schneider's figs."

"No, I won't," interrupted Faustina. "You shouldn't have taken all this trouble. This time, let me tell you, I really can't accept them. I don't care what you think, but do me a favour and take that basket back. Come now, you'll be giving us your house next. Are you going to bring everything here that grows on your trees?"

"Now please, you do me the honour and try Schneider's figs. My wife prepare this basket espezially for you."

"You won't persuade me, I promise you."

Schneider began to laugh again.

"If I gum back to the house wid those figs my wife beat me. A dreatful woman!" he laughed. "And I shall be offended if you do not take the figs of my garten."

But Faustina picked up the basket and tried to hang it back on his arm.

"Now do me a favour and take this away, Esnáider. If you don't you'll make me very cross."

Schneider continued to laugh in the same deliberate way. He took the basket in his hand, but instead of hanging it on his arm, he lifted the napkin and showed her the figs, all of even sizes and beautifully arranged in concentric circles. He picked up the middle one with two fingers and offered it ceremonially to Faustina.

"Now try, Faustita, this succulent fig that I have much pleasure in offering to you."

He made a knightly gesture as if wearing gloves, and moved the fig up and down in time to his words.

"Now stop this Faustita business," said she. "You really oughtn't to do this, but I shall take your fig so that you don't feel offended. But only on one condition, though, that you don't worry about any more presents. Understand?"

"You eat the fig and say how it is goot."

"I don't have to taste it to know that it is very good. I know that it'll be a lovely fig, pure syrup, like everything you grow in your garden. I know that in advance."

She looked at the fig as she peeled it, and added: "You've only got to look at its skin and see the way it peels. But what's the good of your having these fine trees and keeping them so well, if all you do is give away everything that grows on them."

"The goot is that they keep us goot friends, goot people like Señor Mauricio and Señora Faustina. That is worth more than fruit or trees or garten or all together."

And he laughed again. Then Faustina raised the fig to her mouth and he watched her spell-bound.

*   *   *

"That old fellow's very attentive," said Lucio, nodding towards the passage.

"You're telling me. He's taken it into his head to be grateful to us ever since that lawsuit about his house, and now he's for ever turning up with some present or another."

"He's an odd customer!"

[151]

"There are people like that. Goodness knows why. Perhaps it's the way they educate them in their country. I've no idea. They think themselves obliged to be everlastingly grateful to you if you've taken the slightest trouble to help them. They're very nice people, poor things, both him and his wife. After all the terrible thing that happened to that only daughter of theirs, they might easily have been embittered for good and loathed our whole nation."

"I heard something about it. What actually happened?"

"It was criminal. It doesn't bear talking about. Some scoundrel from Madrid took her away, did an abortion on her, and it killed her. A terrible thing! Just think, their only daughter."

"I can imagine."

"Just suppose they had done that to my Justi, God forbid! No one can imagine it who hasn't got a daughter, an only daughter, like him and me. You know what I mean? That's why I can understand what that poor German must have suffered. I can understand it entirely. And it calls for the patience of a saint to bear it like that couple!"

Lucio looked down on the floor and agreed. There was a silence. Mauricio spoke again.

"And now they've got an orchard that's a real wonder. The old boy knows an awful lot about grafting and all that. You must have seen it if you've been past there this summer. The marvellous trees they've got! All so well looked after, all with that sticky paper round their trunks to stop the ants climbing up and eating the fruit, you know."

"That old boy gets up before anybody. However early you go by you'll always find him there, inspecting his trees. You can imagine the condition they're in. Trees repay the trouble you take with them. These people – the Germans I mean – must be very hard workers, all of them. The old boy must be sixty-five or even around seventy. That sort of thing explains why Germany's been the country it was – and looks like being again now they've got their hands a bit freer."

"Yes, just like us!"

"How right you are! Only just the opposite! We could take a leaf out of their book, though we mustn't go in for comparisons. In just what you've been talking about, gratitude, for instance."

"That's nothing. Their customs are different. It's nothing to make a fuss about! They're educated in quite a different way. And they're so thorough in everything too. With us things are all done anyhow, according to the whim of the moment. And the next day we're absolutely exhausted."

"Yes, they're solid and they hold on in a way we can't imagine. We've got other qualities, you can't deny that, but this way of going on day after day, plod, plod, plod . . . we haven't a notion of that. We know nothing about it . . . with us the wind changes and the boat turns."

"Yes, and they're the same about their friendships as they are about their work. Just as single track. It seems really funny to us, his coming every day and giving us presents just because we gave evidence for him in his lawsuit when they tried to take away his house. We couldn't have done anything else. We didn't try to twist the facts one way or the other – so don't you get any ideas. But one fine day, you'll see, the people round here will start saying we were bribed or something of the sort."

"But that's just the sort he is. He must have imagined – it was only reasonable – that, being in a foreign country, he'd have very-one against him, and on the side of his opponent – who's a native of the place. And when he discovered that wasn't so, that there was someone who stood up for him despite everything, he felt very grateful. It's natural that he should."

"But don't you imagine I was a friend of his before this case. I knew him, of course, from seeing him about the district. He's been in San Fernando quite a few years. But only to pass the time of day, that was all. Otherwise we hardly knew each other. So when I had to give evidence it was simply a matter of justice, not friendship."

Lucio looked hard at the boss, and said: "But you knew all about his daughter at the time of the case. I'm sure you'd heard about that."

"Yes, of course. But that all happened at least eight years ago. What are you driving at?"

"Nothing. Perhaps that was what really made you decide to take Esnáider's part, though you didn't know it yourself, or so I should think from what you said a minute ago."

Mauricio pinched his lower lip and reflected. "So you think that, do you? But I didn't even remember about it." Then he looked towards the door and added: "I couldn't tell you for certain one way or the other. You may be right. Who on earth can tell what our reasons are for doing things?"

Lucio spoke slowly: "I've never believed in this business of people acting out of pure justice. When it comes to it, the only justice there is is the justice you have in here." – He pointed to his chest – "And even men who act disinterestedly, let me tell you even they, though you may find it difficult to believe, always have a hidden motive of one kind or another, which makes them act in one way rather than another."

"But that's a thing that none of us can know," answered Mauricio, looking in his face, "not you, or me nor anyone else."

"Then I see you agree with me."

* * *

They were walking downstream between the groups of people.

"I don't know what's come over them today," said Mely. "They're more disgusting."

Fernando kicked back a ball that had rolled towards his feet. It bounced against a tree, and a child protested: "Watch out. You might have lost it for us, you might!" Fernando came back to Mely's side.

"I'm in form," he said. "Were you saying something?"

"No, nothing."

Mely kept her hands in her trouser pockets and inspected the groups.

"Where can the others have gone?"

"What others?"

"Samuel and company."

"You'll soon know. We're all to meet later at the *merendero*. Why are you in such a hurry?"

"I'm in no hurry."

"Why do you want to know, then?"

They came to the end of the peninsula and crossed the narrow plank that spanned the blocked channel. There was an arm of still and dirty water which stopped a little farther on, the last remains of the branch that in winter separated the wooded island from the mainland. Now the channel was dry along most of its length, and so the island was joined to the land except in this final place where it formed a peninsula which was reached by the little wooden bridge.

"It's not very safe," said Mely, looking down at the murky greenish water.

On the other side were bushes and yet more bushes, and dirty patches consisting of tufts of rough grass and slime, and dried water-weed, like decayed festoons: a scum of rotten vegetation, left behind by floodings in the distant past. They crossed the bridge quickly.

Suddenly they were greeted by a gust of noisy music. They saw tables spread with red and white tablecloths in the shade of a huge tree, and a crowd of people seated at them. They heard the clatter of glasses and crockery, and above it the sound of a radio at full blast. The terrace filled the rectangle bounded on the river side by the mole of the dam, and on the other three by the hillside and the fronts of the *merenderos*, which were L-shaped, and painted white, with their trellises and lettering picked out in blue. There were geraniums. When you looked up, the great tree formed a green dome that covered everything. You could see the toothed wheels of the sluice-gates at the end of the embankment, and the deep orange-coloured water eddied as it washed and probed the concrete wall which broke the current, guiding it into the narrow outlet. Here the water roared on finding itself free once more and escaping from confinement. They walked along the embankment, beside the tables, and some men stared at Mely, following her with their eyes as she passed. Mely stopped at the sluice-gates and looked at the people who were still lying on the concrete slope below the dam.

"Can you see them?" asked Fernando.

Mely did not answer. She stopped looking and resumed her walk. The river widened again below the dam, and the newly freed water washed once more around red islands hardly touched with green. They walked for a while along the little canal which drew its water from the pool and then turned away to the right, leaving the roar of the sluice-gates, the voices and the music behind them. Here the river bank on both sides was flat and level with the water.

"Oh, it's wonderful!" said Mely. "How pretty it is here!"

On their right a line of poplars ran along the little canal and veered away with it across the fields. There were less people; only a few scattered groups of youngsters throwing stones into the water, hunting or fishing for goodness knows what. At the end could be seen the tall black poplars that bounded the orchards, and on the right, further off, the walls and houses of San Fernando. Now the tune of "Siboney" came clearly across the fields. Mely started to dance in the middle of the flat expanse, singing: "As the palm-trees softly sway I think of you . . ."

"You're crazy!"

"That tune gets into my feet."

"You're crazy, girl!"

Mely laughed, and they looked at the place from which the music was coming. It was another *merendero*, on its own in the middle of the flat expanse and about a hundred yards from the river. It had a large sign: GRAN MERENDERO NUEVA YORK, written in black letters with paint which had run a little. It looked like an inn frequented by fishermen or farm workers. There were very few people at the tables outside. Mely started dancing again.

"Siboney, I-I-I love you, I'm dying for love of yo-o-ou . . ."

There was a serving bar made of old planks with a smoke patch on the whitewash above the window. Now the poplars were beginning to throw their long shadows eastwards, but the sun above was still describing its own dazzling arc, scorching the dirty wool of the untilled fields and the thin backs of the hills. It gleamed for a moment on the zinc of a new pail and the splash of water which someone was spilling on the dust. It was caught by another person's glass which flushed a bright red as it was raised and quickly emptied. It struck a woman's hair and back and ear-rings like a magic hand. It buzzed dully across the land like a legendary swarm, with the dense, weary, ill-defined drone of persistent light-vibrations, and fell opaquely on the clean and the dirty, the new and the old, on all things alike. They saw seven cypresses peering over a yellowish wall.

"This must be the cemetery."

It was near a farmhouse, on an old road that dropped from the village to a ford, sheer down to the Jarama.

"How very odd!" said Mely. "Most villages have their cemeteries on a hill, but here it's different. The village is on a hill, and they've got their cemetery near the river."

"They're original, that's all. With a bit of luck, they'll get a cloud-burst one fine day, and all their dead will be washed away."

"Better have the dead washed away, boy, than the living."

"That's true. I expect that's how they look at it too. Life's very odd. And they tell you people aren't very wide-awake in the country!"

You could see the iron crosses through the fence. Scarcely one of them was upright. They stood among the tall grass that was en-croaching on the paths between the lines of graves. At the end were hive-shaped niches and the dull white of cheap marble showed up oddly here and there among the rusty iron and bricks, the weeds and the rubble. You could see indistinctly against the white stones of the uniformly square tombs, inscriptions, faded crêpe, wreaths, photographs and slim glass vases containing dried flowers. The music of the radio reached even here, "Siboney" and the shouts of the boys by the river. It stopped suddenly and fell deadened like snow on the crosses and the field of the dead. A man passed them, leading a donkey loaded with green maize. As the leaves rubbed together they made a cool sound that contrasted with the beast's rapid trot. The man wore dark clothes and was driving the donkey fast. He took a fleeting look at Mely's arms and shooed the creature on. He looked quickly back along the road and increased his pace.

"How very lonely the dead are," quoted Fernando in an emphatic and mocking voice.

"We're getting quite romantic," said Mely with a laugh, as she freed her cheeks from between the iron bars. "We might choose a rather more cheerful spot."

The little canal that came from the dam crossed the road under an old brick bridge, and flowed into a very careful irrigation system on the other side. Two small boys and a girl were pounding something on the parapet. They gave Mely an impudent look. Then they rushed home, dancing as they went, and hissing some obscure insult over their shoulder.

"They're shocked to see a girl wearing trousers."

"Well they'll get used to them soon enough when the Yankees start working at Torrejón," said Fernando.

They turned slowly back.

"What Yankees?"

"The ones that are going to build the airfield. They're going to build it somewhere over there," he pointed. "Didn't you know?"

"Me? No. I don't read about politics. Only what films are showing."

"You ought to keep a little more up-to-date, Mely."

"More up-to-date. Listen to him! And why?"

The music had ceased. A high, clear voice was coming over the open country announcing the next record, with a list of the three or four persons for whose benefit it was being played, as if they were listening to it from some distance, hiding or lost somewhere on the river, or crouching behind some thicket on the flat ground.

"Perhaps you'll take a space on the radio one day and choose a record for me," said Mely.

"When I've got thirty pesetas to spare, I will. That's a promise." The music sounded again and a slow voice began to sing.

"And when the new year comes . . ."

Someone called "Psst" behind them. They turned round.

"Me?" asked Fernando, pointing at his own chest.

They were two Civil Guards, who had appeared from behind the cemetery and were coming towards them. The taller of the two nodded, making a gesture with his hands as if to say: "Who else would it be?" Fernando advanced to meet them, but Mely stayed behind, watching. However, the taller Guard beckoned to her.

"You too, miss, if you please."

"Me?" she said in a disagreeable voice.

Fernando and the Guards came over to her. "What's the matter?" Fernando asked politely. But the Guard spoke to Mely: "Don't you know you're not allowed here dressed like that?"

"Like what?"

"The way you're dressed."

He pointed at her bust, covered only by her swimsuit.

"Oh, I'm very sorry. But I didn't know really."

"You didn't know?" put in the other Guard, who was older, nodding his head with the smile of one full of years and wisdom. "But we saw you from the hill, peering through the bars of the cemetery. You're not going to tell me you didn't know it was disrespectful. That isn't the proper way to behave in a place like this. You're not going to tell me you didn't know that? Everybody knows that."

"Everybody knows that sort of thing," the taller Guard went on. "You must show proper respect in a cemetery, like in a church. It's the same thing. You have to observe the decencies. What's more you mustn't go about dressed the way you are in this place we are in now either."

"No, but just a minute," Fernando interrupted very politely. "All that happened was just that we went for a stroll looking for some friends, and we came here without noticing it. That's what happened."

"Another time you must be more careful," the old Guard answered. "You must watch out better where you're going. Our orders are that no one must leave the river bank without dressing completely, as is proper." He turned to Mely. "Kindly put something over your shoulders, if you have anything with you. Otherwise, go back to where you came from. Get along with you, you're not a child."

"Yes, yes, we were on our way back anyhow," Mely answered dryly.

"Excuse us," said Fernando. "We'll know another time."

"Right. Off with you. You can go now," said the elder Guard, with a movement of his chin.

"Thank you," said Fernando. "Good evening."

Mely turned on her heel without a word.

"Good evening," said the elder Guard in a weary voice.

Mely and Fernando walked for some yards in silence. When they were sufficiently far away Fernando said: "A fine pair of snoopers! I thought they were going to give us a huge great fine. And that would have cost me all the money I'd have spent on that record I was going to get them to play for you. You very nearly lost your record, girl!"

"I'd much rather pay the money," she said in an irritated tone, "and lose my record than talk to them in the mealy-mouthed way you did."

"What do you mean? How did I talk to them?"

"I'll tell you. As if you were scared. You let them humiliate you ..."

"Oh, and how do you think I ought to have spoken to them? You're full of ideas. I suppose you think I ought to have answered them back."

"It's not necessary to answer back. You just have to know how to hold your ground, and not bow and scrape, putting on that sugary voice, and giving them soft soap. Besides you needn't have worried, because you wouldn't have had to pay the fine yourself anyway. I'd never let anyone pay a fine for me."

Mely looked back. The two Civil Guards were still standing there, looking at something farther back. She put out her tongue at them. Fernando gave a bitter smile.

"Now look here, Mely. I've got something to say to you. You're spoiling for trouble! See! You know precious little about the world, it seems to me."

"More than you do, I can tell you!"

Fernando shook his head.

"You don't know what sort of customers you're dealing with, girl. They treat other people the same way as their chiefs treat them. They're only waiting for somebody to blow his top and get nasty with them and they'll let him have it, same as their superiors do to them if they have the nerve to answer them back. Every underdog is always looking for someone just below him. Didn't you hear the way he said: 'You can go now,' just as if we were in barracks?"

"All right, Fernando. But I won't be bossed about by anybody. I'd rather come out with a fine, if I've got to, than lower myself before anybody. That's the way I live, and that's the way I like living."

"I see. It wouldn't be as easy as that, I assure you, if you were a man. Because you're a woman you can get away with it. Be glad you are then. If you suddenly turned into a man you'd see how quickly you'd have to change your way of thinking, or you'd have got a real pasting just now. I've known men a great deal prouder than you, but after they'd been knocked down a couple of times, they've calmed down in double quick time. You pay attention to what I'm telling you."

"Yes, Fernando, yes. I accept everything you say. You win."

Fernando looked at her and said, tapping his forehead: "You're obstinate, you are. What you need is a fiancé who'll keep you under control."

"Under control?" said Mely. "That's fine. Only perhaps I'll keep him under control."

★ ★ ★

The brass bell clanged against the blackened brick of the station, beneath the large sign that read: San Fernando de Henares-Coslada. It was three stations from Madrid: Vallecas, Vicálvaro, San Fernando de Henares-Coslada. Then the train from Madrid creaked in between the platforms. In the almost empty third-class coach, an old man and a girl in a yellow blouse with a black and brown chequered bag at their feet were saying goodbye to the man in a white jacket who had travelled in the opposite seat. "Have a good journey," he said. He stood on the step until the train stopped. Ten or a dozen people got out and dispersed in different directions. The station was open to the fields and the scattered houses. Behind them the train started up again. The man stopped in front of the shed and looked round. The girl and the old man were watching him from the moving carriage. Then he went out between the two buildings, lifting a couple of sheets that were stretched across the way. There were three trucks lined up in front of the station. Hens were picking in the dust beside their wheels. From the back it was a house like any other, with the living quarters of the railway employees, their hen-runs, the parsley in their windows, their wooden tubs and their washing boards. Someone shouted at him from the distance: "Come to see the girl, eh?"

It was a familiar voice. He turned round.

"Hullo, Lucas! What do you think?"

"Cheerio! Enjoy yourself!"

He took the main road, and passed three little weekend villas, almost new. Their small fenced gardens were very exposed. At the gate of one was a shining blue and yellow Buick two-seater. He stopped for a moment to examine the upholstery and the control panel on the dashboard. It had a radio. Then he glanced over its gleaming roof at the half-closed blinds of the villa. The sun was blistering. He started walking again, running his fingers under the collar of his shirt which had stuck to his neck with sweat. He loosened his tie. He looked on the ground; pointed stones were working loose from the road. Wire fences, green shutters, almond trees, "Eggs for sale" it said on one wall, and "Haberdashery" on another. He came to the little bridge where the road began to climb a little; to the left he saw a reddish stretch of river, the beginnings of the wood and the coloured shapes of people. Then the large estate of Cocherito of Bilbao with its leafy trees cut off his view of the river. The sunlight, reflected from a very white wall, was blinding. He appeared on the threshold.

"Good evening to you."

"Good evening, Manolo," said Lucio.

Mauricio looked at him for a bare moment.

"Hullo, how are you?" he muttered, glancing down into the bowl of the sink. He started washing glasses. The newcomer had stopped beside Lucio. He passed his hand over his forehead and puffed. Lucio looked at him. "What do you expect . . . with that tie," he said. "It stands to reason you sweat."

Manolo took a white handkerchief from the top pocket of his jacket and passed it under the neck of his shirt. He observed Mauricio.

"It gives me a pain to look at it," Lucio went on. "The most useless article of clothing. You can't even hang yourself with it, it's too short."

"Everyone wears them."

"The exigencies of city life. Formalities that ought to be abolished."

"Yes." He turned to Mauricio. "Would you be so kind as to give me a large glass of cold water?"

Mauricio looked up: "Cold? It'll be at room temperature."

"All right. Just as it comes . . ."

Mauricio filled a glass. "It's what we all drink," he muttered, putting it down on the counter.

"Eh? What did you say, Señor Mauricio? I didn't hear what you said. What was it?"

"I said it was the same water as everybody drinks here. It's at room temperature. You asked for cold water, but we haven't got any. Unless you were thinking of the water in the jar, but there isn't much difference. Anyhow the third jar I've bought this summer cracked last week, and frankly I'm not going to spend the whole summer buying water-jars. I think three is quite enough."

"Yes, of course, Señor Mauricio, nobody's complaining."

"No. Only as you asked for cold water I'm telling you, so that you know what we've got. As I've told you we drink it here at room temperature. That's how things are. Cold water we haven't got."

Manolo gave a forced smile.

"But, Señor Mauricio, if I asked for cold water it was only a matter of words. A ready-made phrase, if you know what I mean, that comes to your tongue. Only that, that was all it was."

"Well, I don't call things by their wrong names, I can tell you. What's the sense in it? Call it a ready-made phrase or anything you like, but when I ask for cold water it's cold water I mean. That's the only way to talk, and any other way's just plain silly, in my opinion."

"All right! All right! You're just trying to trip me up. I can see that."

"Me? God forbid! What gives you that idea?"

Manolo looked at him with a pale smile.

"I can see it. It's no good saying you're not."

"Don't be ridiculous. That's not the sort of man I am."

"You are this afternoon."

"What? Oh, for God's sake. Anyhow it's not as simple as all that."

"Oh, but I believe . . ."

"That's enough. Drop the subject. Don't go on so."

"Very well. But I warn you, you can't get at me like that. I mean that sort of joke leaves me quite cold. I don't mind having my leg pulled, so long as it doesn't hurt. I like a joke as well as the next man let me tell you."

"I'm delighted to hear it, boy. That's the only way in life. You've got to have a little humour to get over the difficult patches when you've got other people to deal with. It makes everything a lot easier. Because sometimes you need a bit of patience, don't you now? A great deal of patience in fact. You have to have a hell of a lot of patience."

Manolo suddenly looked suspicious. He took some time in replying.

"Listen now, I haven't any use for this patience of yours. I don't take any notice of difficult situations, I just ignore them. I just let them flow over my head . . ."

"Yes, but you have to take care not to think yourself superior to things, or you may find that things have suddenly got on top of you."

"That's always possible if a man's careless."

"Or for a fellow who doesn't think he's careless. It could happen to him too. Because there are some people who think themselves very clever, and they're the stupidest of the lot. And they get splashed full in the face all of a sudden, you know . . ."

"Here, give me a hand!" exclaimed a peremptory voice outside. There was a sharp rap at the door.

"What's up?"

They looked towards the doorway. It was a man in a wheel-chair, and another, dressed in black, whose hand was pushing it from the back. They had stopped in front of the door.

"Isn't anybody coming out, or what?" persisted the man in the chair, continuing to knock at the door.

"It's Coca and Don Marcial," said Lucio.

Manolo went out to give them a hand. They pushed the wheel-chair round outside, and the man in black came in carrying the cripple, a little deformed mass.

"Where am I to leave this?" asked Manolo from outside.

The cripple, in Don Marcial's arms, turned his head towards the door.

"Leave it in front, it doesn't matter where. Anywhere you leave it will do."

He addressed the men in the bar as Don Marcial sat him down.

"Well, what's the matter? Isn't there a game this evening? Not very lively today considering it's Sunday. Give me a glass of *anís* now. What will you have, Marcial? No one to play against us this evening?"

Don Marcial pushed the chair on which he had placed his companion close to the table.

"A brandy for me. What were you talking about?"

"The heat."

Don Marcial slipped his hand into his coat pocket and chinked some coins, and the cripple said to Manolo: "I suppose we can't ask you to sit down for a bit and have a game of dominoes. You're bound to be engaged now, aren't you? And you, Don Lucio, aren't available either, eh?"

"You won't need them," said Mauricio. "Your great friend Carmelo's outside and so are Claudio and the others."

"Oh, good! But why don't they come in? What are they doing? Go and call them, won't you?"

"They're playing Frog in the garden."

"Playing Frog, eh? Well if they want a frog to play with, they can play with me. I'm the only real frog here. There isn't another, and you couldn't want any improvement on me. Why I might only have been out of the pond a couple of minutes." He laughed.

"What a row this excuse for a man does make!" said Don Marcial, lifting the glass that Mauricio had just poured out for him. "Ever seen anyone like him? Come on, drink that, and see if you can't be quiet a minute and let us have time to breathe."

"You're a cruel swine," answered the cripple giving him a pinch on the backside.

"You're as spiteful as a weasel, Coca-Coña. And because we can't hit you . . ." He pretended to raise his hand against the cripple. "You take advantage of the fact you're only half a man. Nobody would have the heart to hit a frog, as you've been calling yourself."

"That's enough of your Coca-Coña. Just forget it for a bit."

Don Marcial laughed as he hung his jacket on the back of a chair.

"That's him all over. He gives himself a nickname, and then he gets nasty if you use it. Did you ever see anything like it?"

Don Marcial sat down opposite the cripple, and Manolo asked:

[165]

"Oh but did he invent the name himself? Whatever made him think of it?"

"Don't you know? It's just like him. One day, it was last summer, I think, about the beginning of last summer, our friend was on the main road in the little vehicle he uses for getting around and he found himself next to another little car marked 'Coca-Cola'. You know the one I mean, with the name in big red letters. Well, it was one of them, and the two cars drew up side by side, almost bumping into one another. Then he comes out with the remark: 'Well, if that's the Coca-Cola, then I suppose that I must be the Coca-Coña!'* Laugh? Why that evening I thought we should have died . . . ! You see Coca's his surname. A coincidence both ways, don't you think?"

"That's funny, really funny," said Manolo.

"Yes, but for several days now, he's been telling us not to use that name, d'you see? So really you don't know where you are."

"The joke's stale. Either give me another nickname or use my christian name. Now call Carmelo, and quickly. Tell him to come here, to this table at once. Hurry now and don't keep me waiting. Pull him by the ear and make him come."

He pushed the table into Don Marcial, to force him to get up.

"All right, I'm going, I'm going. You know I'm here to look after you. You give the orders and I obey."

He got up, drained his glass, and went into the garden. "And bring in anyone you find out there!" Coca-Coña called after him.

"Yes, Señor Esnáider must be out there too," said Mauricio. "He's very fond of a game as well. Perhaps he'll join us."

"What? Oh that one! He's a good player. I like playing with Señor Esnáider, indeed I do. You might ask him. Then we shall have our game."

★   ★   ★

The little Ocañas looked at Justina's face, then at the tall butcher's.

"She's won," said Juanito.

Justina turned to Petrita and leaned down to kiss her.

* An indelicacy. *Coña* means not only the female sexual organ, but also a stale joke.

"Do you like the game too, darling? Would you like to play?"

"You always win, don't you?" said the girl.

Justina adjusted the collar of the little girl's dress and took a withered honeysuckle leaf out of her hair.

"No, darling," she said. "I lose too sometimes."

Juanito and Amadeo were fighting for the disks that lay about the ground. They brushed the trellis with their naked, sunburnt backs. Azufre was leaping about, wagging his tail. He wanted to romp with them.

"She plays like an angel, that girl," said Petra from the table.

"Magnificently," Sergio agreed.

Mauricio had brought the liqueur glasses and the coffees.

"That game's existed since the beginning of time," observed Felipe. "It's never out of date."

"Yes, it's not like miniature football and those other modern inventions that are all the craze with the youngsters and then disappear overnight and you never notice it."

"Yes, they're a dreadful waste of time, and bad for the children," said Petra. "They lead children into bad ways."

"Do you remember, Sergio, the time of yo-yo? It was just before the beginning of the war," Felipe asked his brother.

"Remember it? Yes, of course I do."

"Now that was an absolutely crazy invention if ever there was one. Everybody going about with one of those wretched toys and jerking it up and down from morning till night."

"Society's clean off the rails," said Sergio. "People are caught by the first silly idea that comes along, and then they all copy one another like sheep."

"The public in the towns is spoilt by having too much. So when anything slightly new comes along, they all rush after it and they're very soon bored by it too."

"Yes, but come to think of it, d'you know who was very keen on this game of Frog?" said Sergio. "Remember that friend of mine, the fair fellow I used to go around with in my bachelor days, when you and your family were still living in the Calle el Águila?"

"Yes, I know who you mean. He was a traveller in something or other. Wait a minute . . . Eau de Cologne, wasn't it, or something?"

"Perfumery. That's him. Natalio was his name. That boy used to play a marvellous game. He said – I never saw it – that he'd once got all ten disks into the frog's mouth. Maybe he was telling a tall story. But he'd actually swear it was true. I've seen him playing, and he may not have got all ten in, but at least no one could beat him at the game, no sir."

"I remember. I passed the time of day with that chap Natalio not long ago. In fact I've bumped into him more than once. The last time was in Holy Week, when you and the wife were in Barcelona."

"I should like to know what he's doing these days, and how things are going with him. Did you have any conversation?"

"No, just passed the time of day. But by the way he was rigged out he looked like at least a marquis."

"Well-dressed?"

"Fit to kill. But the impression I got, if you want to know, was that he was the sort of man who went hungry at home so as to cut a figure in the street. Just to look at him you got that feeling."

"But come off it, he must have done well for himself."

"No, man, that's something you see straight away. You can tell at a glance the difference between a man who goes about well-dressed because he's comfortably off, if you know what I mean, and one who has to make real sacrifices so that he can dress beyond his income."

"Come now. You're another of those who think they can see everything at a glance," said Sergio. "How can you know people's private lives by just saying hello to them in the street?"

"When you drive a taxi, you know, and see fresh people all day long, you come to know the game in the end. It gives you a sharp eye for the fine points. Believe me, that chap Natalio doesn't earn even a quarter of what he wants you to think he does."

"All right. Things may be as you say. But the poor lad must have his reasons for behaving that way. He's no fool. Far from it. He's not doing it out of false pride or because he likes dressing up. The fact is that he must know that you can't get ahead in life without a good appearance. And more in our profession than in any other."

"A good appearance . . . ?"

"Yes. Make no mistake. It may seem funny, but if you go any-where in good clothes and well turned out, with a good manner, and something to say for yourself, if you know what I mean, they'll take infinitely more notice of you and you'll sell a lot more goods than if you turn up looking anyhow and start talking business at once."

"Well if what you say's true, it's not much consolation. There must be some connection between . . ."

"But that's how business is today, Felipe. What's to be done about it? Neither you nor I can put things right. The only thing to do is to accept the realities of life and act accordingly.

"But it's quite wrong . . ."

"I know that, Felipe. I agree with you entirely. Of course we all know you're the same person and worth neither more nor less in one suit of clothes than in another. We also know that the goods are the same too, and if they're all right you don't improve them by going about well-dressed, nor if they're bad either. You and I can say this off the record, sitting here quietly smoking our cigars. But neglect your appearance when you're out on business, and see if you aren't sunk in three days. Don't kid yourself. That's the truth, neither more nor less. At the present day it's appearances that count; and what's true in business is just as true in any other walk of life."

"Come now, don't let's exaggerate. There are plenty of fields in which a man is judged by his real worth. In business it may be as you say; you know better than I do. But in other places – come off it, don't tell me tales! You really can't fit everything into the same system."

"Yes you can, man. Into the same system, more or less. On the whole, yes. I don't know what your ideas are. But if you were to go slack for a couple of days and forget to rub your leather every now and then over the paintwork of your cab, you wouldn't get a quarter of your usual passengers, would you? Or, for example, compare yourself to a fellow who's got one of those new cars. Find out from one of them who has the most fares."

Petra now broke in in support of her brother-in-law.

"There, you see! He's quite right. But it's no good, Sergio, it's no good. It's useless to talk to him. You won't budge him. Haven't

I said the same thing a hundred times or more! It's a good five years since I first said to him: 'Felipe, we must make an effort, and save a bit. Then you can put in for another car, now that you can get these wonderful new Renaults on such easy terms that you can pay your instalments on them without noticing it.' I don't know how many times I've said that to him. I've got tired of repeating it. But it's no good. He'll go on driving his present bus until one day it falls to bits on the Gran Vía. And then, my dear Sergio, tell me what we shall do. What'll the kids live on the day when your engine finally refuses to go? When it says: 'Here I stop, and not an inch farther.' And all this is just obstinacy let me tell you. What you need . . . No savings and nothing put by for the future . . ."

"All right, dear, but this has nothing to do with what we were talking about. I really don't know why you've got to bring all this up now."

"Never mind why! No one would believe that a man with four children could have so little sense of responsibility and not even give a glance to the future. And I'm not the only one to tell you so. You can't say that I'm just making all this up. Here's your brother who supports me in what I say."

"But dear, how's my brother supporting what you say if I may ask? Sergio hasn't said a word on the subject. If only you'd listen a little to the conversation. You're always trying to make grist for your own mill. You were just waiting for the first possible excuse to jump in on your own account and turn our conversation."

"Well, that's cool . . .! You'll have the nerve to tell me to my face that your brother never mentioned the new Renaults, next. You're impossible! Can't you see how impossible you are? It's you not me that only listens to as much as it suits you to hear. And when I tell you home truths, it's me that turns the conversation. But that's an old story. I know you, I know you!"

"But don't get annoyed now over anything so silly," interrupted Sergio.

"It's not silly, Sergio, unfortunately it's not a silly thing at all. If only you knew! He's got me really worried over this business. I can't rest at night for thinking of the day when that old bus of his will pack up for good. I can't bear to think about it . . .!" She covered her eyes with her hands, striking a sibylline attitude as if to shut out some ill-omened vision of the future. "If only we'd saved what he spends on repairs, what he spends on repairs alone, you know, on daily repairs, that Renault could be ours already, and that's a fact."

"But what do you know about cars, woman, talking like that? Is there anything you know about them, tell me? Are you going to start teaching me my trade next?"

"Your trade, no. I wouldn't dare. But a sense of responsibility for your children and an eye for the future, yes. You ought to have both, and you haven't either."

Felipe turned to his brother.

"Now what do you say? Twelve years I've been struggling with that same car, and now I have to be told what I ought to do with it."

"Can't you see it's you that turns the conversation? Can't you see it now? Can't you see how you dodge and change the subject immediately someone says something to you that you don't want to hear? It's silly, Sergio, you can see that. There's no way of dealing with this husband of mine, no way at all . . . You can't get anything straight with him. Now tell me, Nineta, is it right?" – she rolled her head from side to side – "With four children to support . . . I – I . . ."

"Now it's true what Petra's saying, isn't it Felipe?" said Nineta. "Anyone needs a little security for the future. You ought to buy a new car, and just see if you aren't pleased when you've done it. You won't be sorry . . ."

The voice of Felisita piped up: "Don't cry, Mummy. What are you crying for? Stop now . . ."

Petra wiped her eyes with her handkerchief, and raised her head.

"I'm not crying, darling. What should I be crying about? It's your father . . . But it's nothing. It doesn't matter."

She turned her tear-stained eyes towards the garden.

"O good heavens!" exclaimed Sergio in a low voice.

Ocaña shifted in his chair and looked bored. Nineta had taken her sister-in-law's hand, which was lying on the table, and squeezed it between her own.

Don Marcial now appeared through the passage door. He greeted the party at the table with a brief nod of the head. Ocaña's children were rolling on the ground, picking up the disks.

"I'm Daddy's favourite," said Petrita to Justina, clasping her round the legs. "Did you know?"

Justina laughed.

"And who told you that?"

"Daddy did."

Don Marcial had grasped Carmelo by the collar and was dragging him towards the house. He paused a moment as he passed Justina, and whispered in her ear in a semi-confidential tone: "Your fiancé has arrived. I don't know whether you know."

Justina cast a rapid glance towards the passage door.

"He can wait," she answered.

Felipe Ocaña was toying with his empty glass, moving it to the right and then back again. He stubbed out his cigar against the chair-leg. Azufre was friskily jumping about, inviting Ocaña's children to play with him, but they took no notice. Finally the dog put both his forepaws on Amadeo's bare back.

"Go 'way!"

The two boys went rushing off after the dog, which ran off. Petrita stamped on the ground, grasping Justina's skirt, and begged her: "Pick me up! Pick me up!..."

Justina took the child in her arms, and Petrita looked down at her two brothers running about the garden. She peeped quickly first over one of Justina's shoulders, then over the other, and laughed as she followed Azufre's turns and twists and capers in his game with Juanito and Amadeo.

"You'll bump my head in a minute, darling."

"We haven't chosen a bad day," said Sergio, "and this vine really does keep the sun off."

No one answered him. Nineta touched the edge of her sister-in-law's dress.

"Is this the skirt you made yourself?"

"Yes, this is it."

"It has turned out well, hasn't it?"

The butcher Claudio was throwing the disks. The dog and the children got in his way and he had to interrupt his throw.

"Call this dog of yours off. Don't spoil our game now with that dog of yours."

"Azufre, here! Azufre, lie down!" called El Chamarís.

"Can't you see they're playing?" called Ocaña's wife from the table.

"Don't be a nuisance. Why have you always got to be in the way? Come here this instant!"

Amadeo and Juanito obeyed their mother, and Azufre obeyed his master. They were now watching the dog, who was lying against the trellis on the other side of the garden.

* * *

Faustina was standing at the table drying the dishes with a cloth, and putting them down on the American cloth, beside Schneider's hands. He was sitting down, with his filthy panama on his knees.

"This week, without fail," said Faustina. "By Thursday at the latest I'll come and see her, I promise. As soon as I catch up with myself a bit."

The skins of three or four figs still lay on the table top.

"Frau Berta very old, poor dear," said Schneider. "She cannot go out much. I am the stronger."

"You're still a young man."

"I eat my fruits and that is good for the body." He gave his little mechanical laugh. "That is why I bring them to you."

"Yes, Señor Esnáider. I don't mean to say your fruits aren't good, but there's nothing that will ever give me back my health. It's three years since I've known what it is to be a healthy woman."

She had stopped with her cloth clutched to her side, to nod her head piteously and heave a sigh. Then she picked up another plate from the pile.

"You'll live to the age of ninety, Señora Fausta," said Schneider, extending all the fingers of both hands. "If you would be so kind as to permit me, I would smoke a cigarette, eh?"

"No need to ask. I don't mind at all."

"Goot, thank you very much."

He searched for his pouch in the inner pocket of his coat.

"I know it's on Sundays that she's always at home on her own. But it's just Sundays, I'm sorry to say, when I have most to do. Otherwise I should be delighted to go and spend an hour with her."

"Oh, she sews and reads and thinks." He rolled his cigarette carefully. "She sits quietly in her chair sewing. All mendings." He lifted his arm from the table top to show the worn and mended sleeve of his jacket. "Buy nothing new now till death. Only sew, sew, sew." He made imaginary stitches in the air. "Old clothes like old Schneider, like old wife. Clothes to last till death. Now she spends no money; only sew, sew, sew."

Faustina picked up the fig skins from the table, and threw them through a little window above the stove. There was a great cackling of hens outside.

"Yes, old people like us don't have to look smart."

She lifted the lid of a little pot that was on the stove and poured the contents through a coffee strainer, into a glass. Then she put it down on the cloth in front of Schneider with a saucer, the sugar and a little spoon.

"Portuguese coffee," she said. "See if you like it."

"*Danke schön*," he answered quickly, "Señora Faustina's coffee always succulent."

He put some sugar in and laughed. Faustina sat opposite him, with her arms folded on the cloth. Schneider stirred the sugar and lifted a spoonful of coffee to his lips.

"What's it like?"

Schneider sipped it. He waved the little spoon three times in the air like a conductor's baton, as he said: "Goot. Goot. Goot!"

"I'm glad you like it. Don't mention it to my husband, though. He doesn't know I bought it, and if he finds out it will be gone in two days."

She looked up. Carmelo and Don Marcial were entering the kitchen.

"Good evening."

Schneider turned in his chair, and looked towards the door.

"Oh, these are my friends. I am very glat. Are you well? Are you well?"

He greeted both with a smile and a slight nod of the head.

"How are you, Señor Esnáider?" asked Don Marcial. "Sitting here drinking your coffee, eh? They treat you well in this establishment, it seems. Any complaints?"

"Oh, no, no. Absolutely none," and he laughed.

Then he put his forefinger on Don Marcial's chest and added, tapping him gently: "I can guess the cause why you have come here." And laughing again, he looked down at his steaming cup.

"Yes, he knows well enough. And look at him – if he isn't pleased! But don't hurry. Drink your coffee slowly or you'll scald yourself."

Carmelo smiled but said nothing.

"Why did you have to come and bother him with your wretched game?" said Faustina. "Can't you let him drink his coffee in peace?"

Schneider drained his glass and got up, saying: "And that cause is for a game of dominoes. I am disposed when you are ready." He picked up his hat and turned to bow to Faustina. "Señora Faustina, I am very grateful for your coffee."

He pointed to the door with arm outstretched, ceremoniously giving way to the others.

"After you," said Don Marcial. And they all left the kitchen.

When Coca-Coña saw them coming he shouted: "The dominoes! Where are the dominoes? Here comes our game. How's life, Señor Esnáider? Are you ready for a battle?"

"The very thing," he answered.

The edge of the marble table came up to the top of Coca-Coña's chest, and his shoulders hardly appeared above it, with that neckless head of his sunk into his thorax. His two arms floated above the marble, turning over the dominoes.

"The two tallest play together," he said.

An individual entered in greasy blue overalls with sweat on his forehead. He greeted everybody.

"Today too?" Lucio asked him.

"Today too, Señor Lucio. No Sundays off. I've only this moment left my truck."

Schneider got Don Marcial for partner.

"Sit down there, Carmelo," said Coca-Coña. "Now you'll see what we'll do to them."

Manolo scraped his shoe on the concrete floor, and said to Mauricio: "I'll go through now if you don't mind."

"All right, old fellow, do as you like."

"Odd customer!" said Mauricio after Manolo had departed.

"Now you've got your knife into the lad. Nothing strange about that of course. Nobody accepts a son-in-law very easily, even if he's a real St Anthony."

"St Anthony my foot! That fellow stinks. He's as snobbish as they come. I can't stand the sight of the bastard, I tell you flat, with that fat white face of his."

"But just how fond of him you'll be," said the truck driver, "when they present you with a grandson and you see him running about the place."

Mauricio poured him a glass.

"Around this place? If the kid turned out anything like his father, his grandfather wouldn't see much of him. He'd be a precious specimen. Quite a picture."

"I call that really nasty, disliking the poor little thing in advance when he hasn't even been thought of."

Don Marcial had drawn the double-six.

"Here you are," he said, putting it on the table with an air of disgust, as if he were depositing a cockroach. Coca-Coña looked at his hand. "Here's a quick answer to that." Schneider put his dominoes down very carefully, but Coca-Coña thumped them as if he were shooting them from a gun.

"That's good and solid!" he shouted after that.

"Good and solid," answered Don Marcial. "But that's more than this place will be if you thump your pieces down like that. Wouldn't it be just as good if you played a bit more gently?"

"Just as good? No, a well-laid piece is worth twice as much. We're shaking your morale. That's why you're complaining."

Schneider laughed and laid his domino down quietly.

"And wipe that smile off your face, because you won't be able to go next time. Next hand you won't be able to."

"I doubt that," answered Schneider, rearranging his hand. "I don't think I'm going to pass."

"Just you wait and see."

Carmelo enjoyed Coca-Coña's sallies, and watched his play, very glad to have him for a partner. But suddenly as the hand was finishing, Coca-Coña began to shout: "Hell and damnation! You made a fine balls of that, my friend! What the hell were you thinking of? Don't you understand the game? When you saw that they couldn't play, you should have put down your double, you cunt, instead of letting them into the game again. What could you have been keeping the double-four for at this stage? If you hadn't kept it for the next round ... And you think you're a clever player. You've excelled yourself, you fool! You silly bungler! ..."

"That's enough of that, you," cut in Don Marcial. "You're a very bad loser. Why start abusing Carmelo? You're like a woman. Always taking advantage of being the weaker sex and attacking everyone else. That's the way they get their strength. You're just like a woman. You're up to cussing Carmelo as you know he can't knock your block off, because you're a great puffed up frog and one blow would knock you out."

"A frog, a frog! Mix the pieces and shut up, your Lordship. I'm a frog on dry land, but you're a wet frog let me tell you!"

"That's enough! No professional allusions. You know that I don't care for jokes on that subject."

"That's enough – my play," cut in Coca-Coña. "Double-five."

His piece made a sharp tap on the table.

* * *

"What's the news about your wedding, Miguel?" asked Sebastián.

Miguel was lying with his right forearm over his closed eyes.

"I don't know," he said. "Don't talk to me about my wedding now. Today's a holiday."

"That's fine. But I don't know what's standing in your way. I only wish we were in the same position as you and your girl."

"Oh! Don't imagine it's so simple."

"But your position ..."

"That doesn't mean a thing, Sebas. There are plenty of other snags to be reckoned with. If you don't live alone, and when they're used to an extra wage in the house, they're not prepared to lose it just like that. There's quite a difficulty there apart from anything else."

"Naturally I don't like to interfere in anyone's affairs, but to tell you the truth, boy, I think the time comes when a man has a right to get married, even if there are complications. Unless of course he has serious responsibilities, an invalid to support or something of that sort. But if it's just a case of them going a little short, I think you've got to forget the money side of it and push off. Of course you take away a wage packet that they've been counting on up to now. But what else can you do? Everyone has a right to live. And besides when you go there's one less mouth to feed. So, if I were you – of course I don't like to interfere – I shouldn't worry about the family but put on my hat and coat and let them moan. That's my point of view, at least. Well? That's what I say."

"That's easy enough to say. But things aren't all that simple, Sebastián. No outsider knows what a lot of fuss and argument there is in a home, even when people are all fond of one another. The terrific number of little things that go on, on one side and another, all day long, when you live in a family of more than four or five people. Don't you imagine it's easy."

"Of course we know that. But you have to face up to that sort of thing."

"No, man, not at all. It's better to swallow your impatience and wait for the right opportunity."

Alicia yawned, put her hand to her mouth, and looked away towards the river. Then she said to Sebastián with a shake of the head: "Don't listen to him, Sebastián. It isn't a matter of argument, this reason or that. The real point is that somebody must know for himself what's the right thing to do. People are always ready to offer the first excuse that comes to hand. Everything they say amounts to that, more or less. They can always find an explanation for everything."

"That's one for you, boy," said Sebastián, slapping Miguel on the arm. "They shoot to kill. A hit! The bullet struck home all right. And they tell us women believe all we say!"

Miguel gave a wry smile. He looked over his fiancée's head and became serious.

"You're talking about something you know nothing about. Better not have introduced the subject at all. I've told you that before."

"But it was you took it up, Miguel. Don't start blaming me. I told you at the beginning that I wasn't trying to interfere in anyone's affairs. If what your fiancée said annoyed you, it's got nothing to do with me."

"Just go and take a walk, if you would, and leave me alone. You've put your great foot in it this time, and that's a fact."

"What a fellow!" exclaimed Sebastián. He says I've put my foot in it. You should be ashamed of yourself. Attacking me. But you just leave him alone."

Miguel did not answer. But Paulina intervened.

"He's quite right. You'd no business to start arranging other people's lives for them. You've got enough to do with your own before you set up as anyone else's saviour. If they answered you, it was just out of politeness. But it was very rude of you all the same, although they don't like to say so."

"So you're against me too? It's a nice thing to attack a person from two sides! I don't understand it, really I don't."

"It's plain enough," said Miguel. "I couldn't have said it better myself. And if your fiancée says the same thing, there must be something in it, Sebastián."

"Look here, Miguel," said Alicia. "You can't take me in. I know you too well."

"I wasn't talking to you, Alicia. You've said too much already. Just you pipe down."

"But look, Miguel," said Sebastián. "I've only one thing to ask you. Are we friends or aren't we? If we are, and I've always believed we were, I really can't understand what all the fuss is about. Isn't it possible for us to discuss one another's affairs?"

"You can't understand, eh?" Miguel paused, took a deep breath and snorted. He raised himself on his elbows and looked in all directions, towards the river and the bridges. "And I can't either, Sebastián, if you want to know. The heat's pretty scorching today and that's all there is to it. Nobody likes other people to mention the thing that's on his mind . . ." He passed one hand over his forehead, and turned his eyes to the sun, above the trees. "But nobody wants complications. You're right, she's right and I'm right, and so is the other fellow. But at the same time none of us is right, and that's a fact. That's why it's unpleasant to talk about. But don't be cross with me. You know I've always been . . ."

He gave a frank smile.

"Really, boy," answered Sebastián, "you've got some tricks that leave me flabbergasted. You get so terribly serious, it's very irritating. As far as I'm concerned, well, imagine for yourself. You ought to know. As far as I'm concerned, I just ignore it, of course, and beside . . ."

"Stop it," interrupted Miguel. "You make me sick. But don't let's talk any more. Hand round your tobacco. Come on!"

"I wonder where the others have got to," said Paulina.

Sebastián went over to the other tree to offer Santos his pouch. Carmen and Santos were quietly petting.

"Here!" said Sebas. "You're not going to give us a public performance, are you? Have a smoke."

"Talking to me?"

"No. Must be to someone else."

"Thanks, old man. But I don't want a smoke at the moment."

"All right. See you later, eh? Enjoy yourselves." Sebastián returned to his group.

"What was it you were saying to them?" Alicia asked him.

"Nothing. They're in love's sweet dream."

"Let them alone then. The kids have their own lives to lead."

"How right you are! But you needn't worry. They'll look after that."

"And quite right too," said Miguel. "I've never seen an engaged couple so keen on one another in all my life."

"Life today doesn't encourage that very much," observed Paulina.

"If people don't let themselves go a bit from time to time, darling," replied Miguel, "you jump from Saturday to Monday without even knowing you're alive."

"But he never seems to me a solid type. One of these days he'll crack up."

"Bah! They gave him an X-ray last winter, he's as sound as a bell," said Sebas. "They found nothing wrong with him except dirty feet. It's just his constitution that prevents him putting on fat."

"What I can never understand," said Paulina, "is the way they live without ever thinking of the future. They've been engaged for a couple of years at least, and they'd rather die than save a peseta."

"That's a bad thing," commented Alicia.

"The girl's right," said Sebastián. "Money burns a hole in his pockets. He's always taking her dancing at expensive places, or buying her presents, or wandering round the bars with the boys."

"But listen now, if he reckons he can afford it, that's good enough. You can't throw it in his face as a sin," said Miguel.

"Stop kidding. We all just about know what it is to have fifty pesetas in our wallets, and we know the temptation to spend them. All the same, that doesn't prevent us giving some thought for tomorrow," replied Sebastián.

"For tomorrow," said Miguel, throwing back his head. "We're always worrying our heads so much about tomorrow. What about today? Nobody bothers about today. But one day before you've got time to look around a truck hits you, and leaves you flat in the middle of the street. All your life's gone for nothing. You've let everything go by. That wouldn't be much of a joke would it? So why calculate and make plans for the blessed morrow? A hundred years from now we shall all have lost our hair. That's what life is, just that. It's obvious."

Sebastián gave him a thoughtful look.

"Now on that point," he said, "I don't agree with you. The real trick is to take the risk and do things with no idea of what is coming to you. Of course I know you're running a bigger risk that way. But the other way's too easy, anyone can manage it."

"Do you really think so? Don't we run a risk when we live life just as it comes, without trying to protect our backs? Isn't there any risk in that? You've got to have courage to do things that way, and you don't need any for the other."

Some picnickers passed singing. Sebastián did not know what to answer.

"Well if it comes to that," he resumed, "there are always risks in life, however you look at it."

"Right. Then it all comes to the same thing, and you can't escape it anyhow. So it's better not to worry or take things to heart."

"Yes, to take things less to heart. But you have to have . . ."

"A serious view of life is quite ridiculous . . ." hummed Alicia.

Paulina and Alicia both burst out laughing.

"Women are cruel!" exclaimed Sebastián.

Then he stretched out his arm and drew Paulina to him.

"Come to my arms, my love."

Paulina sprang away.

"Don't dig your claws into my back, man. It hurts. My back's all scorched with the sun."

She rubbed her naked shoulders to stop the pain.

"Shouldn't have stayed exposed for so long. So don't start weeping now. Anyone would think you were paid to get brown. You'll feel it tonight."

"I always sleep on my stomach. See?"

"On your stomach? You must look enchanting when you're asleep.

Miguel began to sing mockingly in Sebas' ear: "To see her – to see her – to see her when she sleeps. Ha ha!" he went on. "The romantic life for me! Don't get me wrong."

Sebas stroked the back of Paulina's neck.

"Go away and take your hands off me! Can't you behave yourself? Behave yourself! . . ."

Alicia looked impatiently behind her.

"They aren't coming," she said.

Miguel looked at the time. Sebastián put his head back on Paulina's feet.

"Why are we in a hurry?" he asked. "I don't mind waiting a year like this."

He got comfortable and relaxed his limbs. A freight train passed in the direction of Madrid. Paulina glanced towards the bridge. Calves' muzzles could be seen between the planks of some of the trucks.

"Beautiful animals," she muttered to herself..

★ ★ ★

Drops of wine ran down Lucita's neck and fell in the dust.

"Lucita's not doing too badly this evening."

"No, she's all right. She's keeping up with us."

Luci shook her hair.

"I shouldn't like you to say . . ."

"You're quite right, honey. You have to prepare yourself for life today. Pass me the bottle, if you would."

"Easy now," said Tito. "Nobody's in a hurry."

"I am."

"Oh then, I say no more. Take the bottle, take the little bottle! And what's the hurry, if I may ask?"

Daniel smiled as he looked at Tito, and shrugged his shoulders.

"Life and all that."

He took a long gulp. Tito and Lucita watched him.

"Here," she said, "we all live our own film life."

"True enough. But what I could eat now is a meat sandwich, a monstrous meat sandwich. I should fall on it like a tiger."

"If you're hungry see if you can find anything at the bottom of the food tins."

"What a hope! I've had a good look. Anyway, mine is as clean as the day it left the shop window."

"I think I might have a turnover or two left," said Lucita. "Pass me mine from over there."

"Delighted, Lucita. But which one is it?"

"The one farthest away. That one. But I'm afraid they must be all crumbs by now."

"That doesn't matter. Just see how quickly I'll put them together again."

They opened the food tin. The turnovers were at the bottom. They had crumbled a little.

"Terrific!" cried Tito. "Absolute mountains of pastry. I shall console myself with these."

"That's what they're for. You're in luck."

"I should say! Thank you, your Ladyship."

"Not at all, fair sir."

"There's something of everything here, like a chemist's shop," remarked Daniel.

"Do you want a bit?"

"Take it away! I'm not eating now."

"You live on air, Daniel," said Lucita. "I don't know why you aren't thinner than you are."

"Don't you want any either, Lucita?"

"No, Tito, thank you very much."

"The pleasure's mine."

He put in his fingers and stuffed lumps of pastry into his mouth.

"They're first-rate," he said with his mouth full and scattering crumbs.

"You like them, eh?"

"They're not at all bad, not bad at all."

"There's no need for you to tell us," said Daniel.

"Pass me the wine, please. This requires liquid to wash it down."

"They must be so dry in this heat that you can hardly swallow them. You look as if you're eating powder cakes. Come on, Luci, shall we make him laugh?"

"Leave him alone, poor boy. Let him at least eat in peace."

They gave him the bottle. Tito went on picking up one pasty after another. "Not even Charlie Chaplin would make me laugh now," he said.

Daniel turned over on the ground. "Boy, I can't bear to watch you. I can't stand the sight of food today. Just to see anyone eating in front of me makes me want to throw up, it really does."

"You must be ill," said Lucita, looking into his face.

"Maybe I am."

"No, you're not," said Tito. "I tell you you're not. Because the wine goes down your throat all right. It's a pleasure to see it."

"No, I don't enjoy the wine either."

"So that's the trouble. But if you manage to get it down . . ."

"No, I've told you how I feel."

"Then I don't understand you, boy. If you say that wine makes you feel so sick, I don't know who's compelling you to drink it. See what's the matter, Lucita? This fellow's wrong in the head."

Lucita shrugged her shoulders.

"Nobody's compelling me. I don't need that. What is there to do here except drink?"

"There is such a thing as eating." said Tito. "I can't understand this fellow. Have you just come to the river, boy, to have a miserable day? You don't swim, you don't eat, and now you start talking like this. If that's all you're going to do, you might as well have stayed in Madrid. It would have been over quicker."

"Perhaps he's love-sick," suggested Lucita with a smile.

"Ah, yes. It might very well be something like that. Come on, now, we've found you out. Own up at once."

Daniel was lying on his back, looking up into the trees. He turned his gaze towards them.

"What?" He smiled. "There's nothing to confess."

"Oh yes, there is. Don't try to get away like that, you sly devil. Tell us what you're hiding in that little heart of yours. We'll keep your secret."

"What a couple you are! What do you expect me to tell you?"

"You're drinking to forget."

"I'm drinking because I've got the chance to, because I must have got up feeling like that this morning."

"Feeling like what?"

"With a special feeling."

"Oh, shut up! You're an idiot."

"Who knows which of us is the bigger idiot?"

"Anybody could tell that."

"Could they? All right. It's me then. Pass the wine over this way."

"Here it is, brother. See if it doesn't make you feel a bit worse."

"Or better. You can't tell which."

Tito nodded.

"Yes, possibly better. Later we shall see. It does some people good."

"Let's get drinking. Your health!"

He tilted the bottle till its bottom pointed to the sky, and took a long series of gulps.

"A good thing he isn't thirsty," said Tito to Lucita, prodding her with his elbow.

Daniel put down the bottle and took a deep breath. A smile spread over his whole face, as he looked at them and said: "Next!"

"Your turn, Lucita. Now we'll see how well you do."

She grasped the bottle and said before drinking: "Either this cures all three of us or we all go nuts."

Tito and Daniel cheered her as she drank.

"Keep it up, girl! That's the stuff!"

Lucita put down the bottle and said: "All right. But you promise to take me home, don't you?"

"We shall see. We shall see who takes who home."

Now they were all close together, with Lucita in the middle. Tito took his turn at the bottle and Daniel said: "Now things are warming up." They put their heads together and clasped their arms round each others' shoulders. They looked at one another and laughed. And Daniel went on:

"You know you're a marvellous girl, Luci. I didn't appreciate you properly until today, word of honour I didn't. You're the best of the whole crowd, you know. I mean what I say. But don't you agree, Tito? Isn't she now? You do agree with me, don't you, that Luci is by far and away . . . yes, by far and away . . ."

The three of them rocked, clasped closely together with their heads joined.

"And sympathetic," continued Daniel, "and pretty . . ."

"Oh, pretty? Me pretty? He's seeing double. What did I say now? You must be suffering from delusions, boy, saying that I'm pretty."

"Shut up, you! Nobody asked you your opinion. I said pretty, and that's final. I've just had an idea, another idea. We're going to call you . . . wait a minute . . . we're going to call you our . . . we're going to call you . . . But it doesn't matter. Something or other."

★   ★   ★

Justina put Petrita down.

"Let me go now, darling. It's my turn."

The little girl ran to her parents' table. Claudio was reckoning the points and picking up the disks. He passed them to Justina.

"Now then, champion, see if you can do as well as last time."

Felipe Ocaña was examining his nails. Petrita wanted to sit on the same chair as Amadeo.

"Don't you see there isn't room for two of us, silly?"

Petrita grasped Amadeo's fingers and began to play with them.

"Let your hand go," she said.

Sergio was silent.

"My Singer, the one my mother left me, God rest her soul," Nineta was saying, "is still lying at my sister's in Barcelona. She thinks she's going to keep it, you see. But she's made a mistake there, I can tell you."

"Haven't you asked her to send it to you?"

"Yes, I've written to ask her twice, and I asked her when we were there, but she pretends not to understand. But I'm not standing for that, I promise you. I'm not standing for that. In September, if we go there for our two weeks' holiday, I shall bring it back with me. You see if I don't."

"A sewing machine, especially a Singer, is a godsend in any house. Don't you stand on ceremony. Just you bring it away."

"I certainly shall. You see if that precious machine doesn't come to Madrid in September. It will, I promise you."

"It's useful in the house and for other things, no doubt of that," pursued Petra. "You can't give up a sewing machine just like that. Things might go badly with the family one day, and then you've got something to bring you in a few pesetas, sewing for your neighbours. You can look after yourself then for a while until things clear up a little. That's obvious. With a machine in the house a set-back doesn't catch you so unawares, and you can always get a set-back."

She put some pins into her untidy hair.

"Yes, it's good for that sort of emergency too," her sister-in-law agreed. "Like a machine for printing bank-notes. Think of all the pesetas my sister has made in the two years she has had it, just by doing her own sewing."

"You're right. Don't you be a fool. You get it away from her while you can. Why should anyone make money with what's yours? Think what you would have made in dressmaking, my dear. And machines don't last for ever even if they are Singers. Everything wears out, and

[187]

the later she gives it back to you the worse condition it'll be in. Don't you forget that."

"Mummy, I'm bored," said Juanito, throwing himself on his chair.

"Go and see the rabbit now, do!"

"We've seen her."

Petra took no notice. She was listening to her sister-in-law.

"She's selfish, you see. That's why we've never got on very well. You see she's younger than me, but she had to marry before me. That's one example. But there are other things, if you know what I mean. She married first but I was going out with Sergio before she even met her husband."

"Yes, younger children are always more selfish than older ones."

"And there's another thing." Petra put her hand on her sister-in-law's knee. "For every fortnight my brother Ramonet spends with her in Barcelona, he spends at least a month here with us."

Petra looked for a moment at her children who were still swivelling round on their chairs.

"I understand, Nineta," she said with a sigh. "But mine's a Sigma, dear, and that's not nearly as well-known a make. The name Singer carries its own guarantee. But mine hasn't let me down. It's never let me down so far, and I can't tell you how much work I get out of it. You won't see my kids wearing many clothes that I haven't made on it, without help and with my own hands."

"You're a clever woman, Petra. There's nothing you don't know how to do. You sew and you cut out, and you take it in your stride. You're a really good housewife, you are."

"Oh, don't flatter me, Nineta. Don't over-praise me," said Petra with a deep laugh. "It's quite true of course – and naturally I don't want to boast – that if I had to sew for strangers at any time, I don't think I should be too bad at the job. Look . . ."

She turned to Felisita, and lifted her from her chair to show her sister-in-law.

"You see this. Turn round, darling. And this, d'you see? That's not a bad little dress, is it? Nothing out-of-the-way, of course, but the kid could wear it anywhere without looking out of place. But do stay still, darling. Well, Nineta, what do you think?"

"Oh Mummy, don't mess me about! . . ."

"Be quiet. Do you see these, Nineta, these pleats? . . . You see I gathered it in a bit here to get the shape – the little puffs, you see. Do you notice how I did it? And this little pleat at the back, I . . ."

"But Mummy, don't lift up my skirt," muttered the little girl, looking uncomfortably across the garden.

"Will you keep still now! Can't you see I'm showing your dress to your aunt?"

Manolo had greeted the Ocañas at their table with a slight nod. Felisita blushed.

"Leave me alone, Mummy. Leave me alone!" she begged in a plaintive whisper.

"That must be the girl's fiancé," said Sergio, turning to the two women. They both looked at the same time across the garden, and Felisita found herself free. Manolo had come up to Justina.

"I'm sure that's him," said Nineta.

All except Felipe Ocaña watched the engaged couple.

El Chamarís was picking up the disks. The two butchers were bringing out their tobacco.

El Chamarís hissed to them: "Now there's going to be trouble." He raised his eyebrows to Manolo's back. "He's in a real fury . . ."

The big butcher smiled.

"Sh! We'll talk about it later."

"I don't like this behaviour of yours at all, Justina," said Manolo to his fiancée.

"You don't?"

"And what's more you've known it a long time."

"Yes? All right." She shrugged her shoulders. "Anything else to say?"

"Now look, don't act like a fool . . . I don't want a lot of discussion here in front of everybody."

"Me? I'm not acting like a fool. You are though."

"Very well. But listen now, Justina. Hadn't you better go and get tidy, and then . . ."

El Chamarís had come up.

"Excuse me a moment," he said to Manolo with a suppressed

smile, pretending to feel uncomfortable. "The disks, Justina . . . You know where you keep them."

He put them into her hand.

"Sorry to bother you. See you another time," he added retiring.

"It's no bother," said Manolo quickly, and went on bitterly in a quiet voice: "You expect me to stand your playing Frog with three men and making an exhibition of yourself before the whole garden, and the gentlemen at that table. Tell me, do you expect I'm going to put up with that?"

"Do just what you please, boy."

"Don't answer me like that if you please, or I shall lose my temper . . ."

He gave a quick look behind him to see if they were being watched. El Chamarís and the butchers were lighting their cigarettes.

"That's no way to answer – get me?"

"Really? Oh you do terrify me. Are you going to get cross? You really frightened me!"

Manolo clenched his teeth, and growled softly: "Look here, Justi, we're making an exhibition of ourselves, I warn you. Don't, don't . . .!" He caught her arm and squeezed it, digging his nails into her flesh.

"D'you hear me?"

Justina swung round.

"Let me go, idiot. You're hurting me. Take your hand off me this moment, you fool, or you'll see which of us two gets cross."

She broke loose from Manolo and went on: "You talk and plot with my mother behind my back. You butter her up and tell her that you don't like me helping Father in his business, and that it's not the right thing for a girl, and all sorts of snobbish nonsense. Who do you imagine you are, to arrange for me as you think fit?"

He went red.

"Don't talk so loud. Those gentlemen are listening to you!"

"You're ashamed, are you?" She passed the disks from one hand to the other, making them chink. "So you're ashamed, are you?" she said curtly. "But I'm going to do the same now as I've done all my life. Don't think that I'm suddenly going to decide something's wrong that has always seemed perfectly right to me up till now. Don't you imagine that, my dear Manolo."

Manolo was getting impatient. He glanced back once more.

"All right. That's enough for now. We'll talk about this subject later. Now will you please get tidy, and we can discuss it all later on."

"No, I won't get tidy! What do you think I am? I'm not going out today. I can't go out. I've got to help my father, if you want to know. I'm not going in to get tidy, and you needn't expect me to."

"No? So you're not coming out with me today, eh? You've thought this matter out, I suppose?"

"Of course I have."

"You have, have you? Well, you won't play this trick on me twice, I can promise you. You won't get a second chance. So you won't get tidy?"

"I thought I'd told you already."

"You'll be sorry. You'll be so sorry that you'll bite your nails to the quick." He raised his fingers to his lips by way of demonstration. "You'll pay for this. I swear by my mother, God rest her soul, you'll never set eyes on me again."

"Come, don't swear so much. It's a sin. And don't bring your mother into it, it's not her fault. Stop swearing now and do something. Do anything you like."

"Very well. But you'll be sorry later. Have a good time."

"Don't you worry about that," smiled Justina. "If I'm sorry I'll drop you a postcard."

Manolo was about to answer, but half-turned and went into the passage.

Justina stared at his back and nodded her head. Then she raised her hand to her mouth and nibbled her first finger, staring reflectively at the ground. El Chamarís and the two butchers watched her as they smoked. Justina lifted her head and went over to them.

"Did you see? That idiot! That blockhead!" she said. "What a fool the man is!"

"What?" said Claudio. "Have we been having a tiff?"

"For goodness sake shut up. He's more than any woman could stand."

"Bu-ut . . . ? For good and all?" asked El Chamarís, bringing down his hand like a knife. "For ever?"

Justina nodded.

"For all your life," he said in a mocking tone.

"You mustn't say that, my dear," the short butcher put in. "You mustn't say that. Things are always changing. You can't be as drastic as all that."

"So far as I'm concerned, I assure you there won't be any change."

"Say no more. Say no more. You're still worked up. Let it all cool off and we'll talk about it again. You don't know about a thing like this until you've slept on it."

"Nonsense. If there wasn't another man in the world I wouldn't change my mind, I promise you."

"It's easy to say that." said Claudio the butcher. "You know very well you'll never be left an old maid unless you want to be. But, if you hadn't got your youth and good looks, you'd come round to my opinion. Still, as you are, you're all right."

"Good," cut in Justina, giving herself a jerk. "We're all square at present. Now for the deciding game."

She threw the disks up in her hand and walked very quickly towards the frog to continue the game. Claudio, however, said to her with a smile: "No, look here, my dear, not now. We don't want to take advantage of the situation. We should beat you hands down, don't you see? You couldn't throw a disk now even through that window. Another day, another day."

"What!" protested Justina. "Because of that silly fool? What's the idea?"

"You'd see what I mean, if I let you go on playing. I promise you we'll come tomorrow and play you as many games as you like. Besides it's late now, and we must go and see what your father and Señor Lucio and company are up to."

He trod out his stub in the dust.

"Just as you like then. We'll leave it for another day."

They all walked across to the passage door.

"But I'm not upset, am I? Look and see."

"No, you're not upset. Only a very little bit," said Claudio, bursting into laughter. "Oh Justina, we're not so young as we used to be." He nodded his head once or twice. "Justina! Justina . . .!"

Sergio, at the table, was remarking: "It couldn't have pleased him very much of course to find her playing Frog. He doesn't think it at all funny."

"That's natural enough, you know what a fiancé is."

"Shall we play this game?" Petrita asked her brother, catching him by the wrists.

"No, I don't want to. Let me alone . . ." answered Amadeo, and he put his elbows on the table, with his head in his hands. He looked at one thing and another in a bored way between his half-closed fingers: leaves, shadows, stalks, spots of light on the wire and honeysuckle flowers. Felipe Ocaña stifled a large yawn with his hand. Juanito had leant forward across the table, and stretched out his arm to reach a fork. He jerked the handle up and down in his teeth, using the tips of his fingers as a lever.

"Sit properly," said the mother to her children. "I hate to see you behaving so badly."

Juanito obeyed her slowly, as if he were tired.

"They're sleepy," said Nineta.

Sergio relit his cigar.

"Leave the match for me, Uncle," said Petrita. "Don't blow it out, will you?"

Felipe looked at his brother.

"Still got your cigar?"

"I'm smoking it gradually."

"And each time you relight it," said Nineta, "it smells worse."

Sergio threw his niece the match.

"See if you can catch it. But don't burn yourself, will you?"

She put it out with the fingers of both hands.

"Light me another."

"No more matches," interrupted Petra. "Or you'll wet your bed tonight."

The little girl made a peevish grimace and grumbled: "I'm bored . . ." She squeezed behind her parents' chairs, brushing her side against the leaves of the vine. Felisita stared at the garden without moving her eyes.

"Mummy, what shall I do?" asked Juanito.

"Keep still. When the sun's gone down a bit we'll pack up our things and go home."

Sergio looked down on the ground and smoothed the earth with his foot.

"Now," said Nineta. "Don't start thinking of going back already. Once you start thinking of that you stop enjoying yourself."

"But, dear, we must go back sooner or later."

"Naturally, but don't think about it now, not until the time comes to go."

"On an evening like this ... I get an odd sort of feeling, you know."

Felipe suddenly seized Petrita who was passing behind his chair, and shouted: "Get away from here, child. Come along, all of you, now. Amadeo, Juanito! Now, out into the road with you! Get right away and play out there! Amuse yourselves. Off with you, off with you! Run away. Into the road! You Petri, give your Dad a little kiss and off you go!"

Juanito and Amadeo very gladly jumped down from their chairs and rushed off with a great shout of "Hurrah".

"Wait for me! Wait for me!" Petrita called after them.

Amadeo stopped at the door into the house.

"Come on!" he said, and the little girl caught him up. The pair disappeared, hand in hand.

"I was tired of seeing the kids hanging around here. They were getting on my nerves. Let them run about and get a bit of exercise. On the one day they come into the country in the whole blessed year!"

Petra looked askance at her husband, and turned to say to Nineta: "A fine way their father brings them up, if he can't think of anything better than that. To send them off on their own, like little hooligans, with no one to keep an eye on them. Why, anything might happen to them. Just so that they shan't bother him, you see?"

"I don't know why you've got to say that," observed her husband. "You always think the worst. I sent them off because you can't keep

[194]

children by you like slaves all day long, the way you like to do. It's bad enough that they spend the whole year shut up on the fourth floor, without you insisting on keeping them like prisoners tied to your apron-strings on the one day that they can enjoy a bit of liberty."

"I don't agree. Little children ought always to be under their parents' eye. That's what parents are for. They learn obedience that way, and one can look out in case anything happens to them."

"But what do you suppose can possibly happen to them? The sooner they're used to being on their own, the sooner they'll learn to shift for themselves in this world, and to take care of themselves. Otherwise all you do is to make them timid, and always in need of a grown-up at their heels."

"But that's exactly what mothers and fathers are for – to know what their children are up to."

"Very well. And then when they're twenty, it'll be a fine kettle of fish. They'll be incapable of taking a single step on their own!"

"But must you go on arguing?" put in Sergio.

"No, Sergio, you're quite right. But he has no idea how to deal with his children . . . Now tell me . . ."

"My dear girl," said Sergio, "I really don't think anything dreadful is going to happen to the children in just half an hour. Particularly here in the country, where there are no cars or any other kind of danger. You see how very good and obedient they've been all day."

"All right. Just as you like. I've said my say. If their father insists on bringing them up badly, it won't be my fault. That's his business. Still it's lucky they're in their swimsuits. Otherwise you'd see what a mess they'd come back in. Still, if I had my way . . ." She suggested her veto with a wave of her hand.

"Look at this girl now," said Felipe, putting his hand on Felisita's head. "We've seen plenty of her today. You've had her absolutely tied to your apron-strings. A fine Sunday she's had! Seriously now. She may like being bored, but you mustn't make her . . ."

Felisita said nothing, and her father continued, his hand still on her head: "Really this is the most ridiculous nonsense."

"Why do you have to humiliate the child? That's really too much." Don't pay any attention to him, darling. Come over to me."

She drew Felisita to her, but already the child was sniffing, and hiding her great silent tears against her mother's stout, naked arm. Suddenly, however, she raised her head with snakelike violence and in a burst of anger, hissed at her father through her tears: "I'm not doing you any harm, am I? I'm not doing you any harm. If I am silly, that's my business. If I am silly, all right, I am. All right, I am."

She hid her head once more in her mother's arm, and burst into fits of sobbing.

"Now you see," said Petra maliciously. "Of course you had to . . ."
Felipe said nothing, but got up shortly afterwards.
"I'm going to have a word with Mauricio."
He stopped as he passed the kitchen door, and put his hands on the door-frame. Mauricio's wife and daughter were inside.

"I'm going to have a word with your husband," he said. "I want to hear all the news."

"Yes, of course. The customers are keeping him busy at present. But if he had his way, he'd spend the whole evening out in the garden talking to you."

"Yes, that's what I came for. If the mountain doesn't come to Mahomet . . . See you in a minute."

★   ★   ★

Manolo had departed without stopping in the bar, and hardly greeting the customers as he went through.

"There he goes," said Lucio.
Mauricio had shrugged his shoulders.
"There must have been a row," he said with a smile.
When El Chamarís came in with the two butchers, Mauricio asked them: "Well, was it amusing?"
"Amusing? Was what amusing?"
"The scene with my daughter's young man."
The tall butcher put his head on one side.
"Oh! So you'd like to know. Well, I suppose there was a bit of trouble. Has he gone?"
"He went out like a fury."
"It must have been quite a row."

"Did either of you overhear anything?"

"No, we didn't hear anything. They were very discreet. They didn't talk above a whisper. But we saw his face and that was enough."

"Yes," said Mauricio. "But tell me in a few words what happened."

"You do want to know a lot. There's no satisfying you," protested the tall butcher with a laugh. "Well from what she said to us, she told him to go to hell. Does that satisfy you?"

Mauricio took out the glasses.

"The snobbish bastard! Now what will you have?"

Claudio dug his elbow into the other butcher's side, and said, pointing to Mauricio: "Well, if he isn't pleased! Just look at him. You'd expect him to be upset that his daughter has quarrelled with her fiancé."

"He never had much use for the chap," said El Chamarís. "There wasn't much love lost between them. I wonder who his choice was for a son-in-law."

"I haven't got a choice. I don't mind who it is so long as it isn't that commercial chap. He makes my stomach heave every time I set eyes on him. Just think what he does for a job!"

"Well, what does he do?" asked the truck-driver.

"What does he do? Why I'm almost ashamed to tell you. He travels in buttons! He's the representative of a firm that makes plastic buttons. Doesn't that tell you everything?"

They all laughed.

"Yes, you can't help laughing. That's really a joke!"

"Come on, pour us our wine. Well, he is in a state!" said Claudio.

"He seems to have practically poisoned your life, this fellow."

"No, don't you believe it," resumed Mauricio as he filled the glasses. "A traveller in buttons! He turned up here one evening, the fellow did, with his samples under his arm. That was a sight. A bit of cardboard, about the size of that calendar hanging on the wall, with a lot of little buttons sewn on it. They were all shapes and sizes, and there was quite a choice, believe me. The most ridiculous thing you ever saw. I couldn't have looked anyone in the face if my daughter had married a fellow like that! Well, you see things in life!"

They laughed long and loudly.

"Seems to be a joke in here." interrupted Felipe Ocaña as he came in.

"Hullo, Ocaña, how's things?"

They opened their circle a little to let him come up to the counter.

"But you're very comfortable as you are. Don't disturb yourselves."

"Come and have a drink," said Lucio.

"Thank you."

They were silent for a moment. Then Lucio opened the conversation.

"Will you smoke?" He offered his pouch.

"Well," asked Mauricio, "had enough of your family?"

"Yes, that's it, more or less."

"Now let me introduce you to these gentlemen. They're the pick of my customers, you see. The cream of the company that frequents this place."

"Thank you very much. Delighted to meet them."

"How are you?"

"Very well, thank you."

They did not know whether to shake hands, and the truck-driver said: "Come to spend Sunday in the country then? To avoid the heat in Madrid."

"Quite right."

"Cars like that must run pretty well I should say, even though they are old. The model you've got, I mean."

"Yes, true enough."

"Tell me now, with that little car of yours," the truck-driver went on, "you must be able to go anywhere, more or less, without it costing you much?"

"Yes, you're right there. I've had no reason to complain of my car up to now. I couldn't have had better service in the twelve years I've had it."

"You see now! Very different from the Chevrolet of the same year. Where would you be with one of those?"

"Nearly all the Chevrolets of that year have been taken off the road, and quite half of the next model too. But there are still a good few cars like mine about. And yet they're beginning to bother us now with the new ones . . ."

They had drawn apart from the others.

"What'll you have, eh?" interrupted Mauricio.

"What? Oh, brandy. And another here."

"No thank you. I'm drinking wine."

"Won't you have a little glass, really?"

"Thank you very much, but I won't. Liqueurs don't agree with me very well, you know. You were talking about the new models. What's happening today is that they're manufacturing a great quantity of cars, but the quality's getting worse and worse. A great deal worse, don't you think? Very smart cars with a very nice line, and some good details. All the trappings. They're good enough to look at, but nothing else. As for durability ... and it's durability that counts in a car when all's said and done, they haven't got it. None at all. You have to look things in the face. When it comes to it, what they're manufacturing today is nothing but scrap."

"You're right. But what can you do about it? That is the modern standard of production all over. What matters to the manufacturers is for their product to last as short a time as possible, and for the models they send out on to the streets to be worn out in X years, if you see what I mean. And so they continue to increase their sales. It's easy enough to explain."

El Chamarís and the two butchers had retired to join Lucio, leaving Ocaña with his fellow driver.

"Where's the dog?" asked El Chamarís.

"He's out in the front with the youngsters. This gentleman's kids."

"He goes quite mad when there are children about. There's no controlling him."

"He must get bored with you. Until the close season's over, and you can take him out shooting again."

There was a sound of dominoes on marble. The other driver agreed with Ocaña.

"Till the time comes when a man buys a car, eh?" he observed.

"It's brand new, and he starts off to drive to Puerta de Hierro, let's say. A short run. But when he's been there and back the car's fit for the junk-heap. Next evening he goes to the dealer to buy another. Take another example. You have a letter to register. You get in your car and drive to the post office. When you get back, same thing. Off with it to the junk-heap. That's how it is. One trip and you chuck it out. Like a paper serviette, if you see what I mean. No difference at all. People will do just the same with cars one day, at the pace we're going . . ."

"Yes, yes, I shouldn't be surprised. I shouldn't indeed. Now this car of mine, on the other hand, rattles like a tin-can, and there's no way of keeping it quiet because nothing fits properly any more. Well, it's still going all the same. And it's done quite a mileage, I can tell you."

The constable put down a piece and smilingly watched the others pass, one after another. His turn came round again.

"Very funny!" protested Don Marcial. "You silly old sod, if you've got the piece put it down, and don't waste time keeping us guessing."

Coca-Coña was amused.

"Don't listen to them, Carmelo. That's all right. Let 'em curse."

"Not generous," said Schneider. "Don't tease your opponent. That is ugly. Teasing at games is very ugly. Don't do it again."

"I didn't mean to annoy you, Señor Esnáider . . ."

"I was not annoyed. I only wanted you to play seriously."

"Don't you worry, Carmelo. Take no notice. Go on."

"Very well, Herr Coña. But you'd be annoyed yourself. You wouldn't like that joke played on you."

"Perhaps he took it badly. But it was just a harmless joke. You know Carmelo's not spiteful. He's as innocent as a new-born babe."

"I know that all right. But it is not right to make fun of your opponent."

"Okay. Your lead," cut in Don Marcial with a smile.

Two men entered, and one of them said from the doorway: "Take a look at those kids outside. One of them's messing about with your invalid-carriage." He pointed to Coca-Coña. "They'll be running it down the slope in a minute. If you don't stop them quickly the thing will be destroyed. They've no respect for anything."

Everyone looked at the speaker. He had one eye.

"That must be your kids, Ocaña," said Mauricio. "Go and see."

Ocaña suddenly came to himself.

"You're right. It will be them, right enough. Tell me, which way did they go?"

The one-eyed man pointed from the door.

"There in the stubble, straight in front. They've just crossed the field pushing it full steam ahead, with a little girl riding inside."

"Oh my God!" cried Ocaña. "They'll smash it up!" and he rushed out to find his children.

"That way! That way! Behind the little hill!" called the one-eyed man, still signalling to him from the doorway.

The two butchers had come out of the door, and so had Mauricio and El Chamarís.

"So those kids who went by just now are the cabman's children?" asked the truck-driver.

Mauricio nodded assent, but kept his eyes firmly fixed on the stubble.

Ocaña had disappeared into a little dip between the two tilled fields.

"At least," said Coca-Coña in the bar, "at least somebody's getting some pleasure from the wretched machine."

The wheel-chair had got stuck in a dip between two fields beside the door of an old shed which was now inhabited.

"Amadeo!"

The three children turned round, surprised by their father's voice.

"You must be mad! Quite mad!" he said in a panting voice.

Petrita got down, and her brothers waited motionless till their father came up.

"Couldn't you find anything better to do than that, you destructive little hooligans."

He looked to the side where something was moving. From behind the sacking that covered the door of the shed, a woman in black had emerged. She looked at them in silence with her arms folded.

"Good evening," said Ocaña.

She did not answer.

"What a disgrace!" Ocaña continued, addressing his children. "Didn't you know that carriage belongs to a poor cripple who can't

[201]

even walk? You must learn to respect other people's things. You're old enough, Amadeo, to have a little sense. Why you might have thrown your little sister against the wall. What a thing to do! Now come and help me get the thing away."

They got rapidly to work. Ocaña pushed the chair from the back and the two boys helped its wheels over the rough places. They passed in front of the shed. The woman had not moved but looked at them fixedly.

"Oh, children! Children!" groaned Ocaña. "They don't give you a peaceful moment."

The woman slightly moved her head. They climbed the little slope and came in sight of Mauricio's place once more.

"You've put me in a very awkward position with that fellow. What am I to say to him now? Do you see what you've done? Now you go straight off to your mother in the garden, and don't stir from there till it's time to go home. Understand?"

"Yes, Father," answered Amadeo.

Ocaña reflected for a few moments;

"No, all right. Stay about here if you like. But don't you do anything silly. Promise?"

"Yes, Papa, we won't do anything else."

"What little monkeys children are!" exclaimed Mauricio. "The things they get up to!"

"They haven't got two-pennyworth of sense, the little devils. That's the reason," replied Ocaña as he put the wheel-chair against the wall.

"It's only their age," observed the tall butcher. "There's no spite in them really."

"Yes, but the eldest is old enough to know better than to do a thing like that."

Ocaña dried his sweat with a handkerchief. As soon as he went in the children gave a bound and rushed off towards the back of the house. Ocaña went up to the cripple's table.

"Please excuse all this," he said. "I'm very sorry indeed. But children don't realize what they're doing. Please forgive them."

Coca-Coña lifted his head.

[202]

"Me? I can see you don't know me. I shouldn't care if they rode about in it all the blessed day. It's a useless object. Why, I was only saying just now, how glad I was that someone was getting some amusement out of the thing. It's not the same damned miserable contraption as when your's truly is riding in it. So don't worry or come to me making excuses, because there's no need for it."

"It's very kind of you to take it like that, and I'm very grateful..."

"Don't talk rot! It's I that ought to be grateful to your children, although this may surprise you, for having made some use of that damned tricycle. I'm thankful they had some fun with it. When did that ever happen before?... Right. I play a four!"

He banged the domino down on the marble.

"Will you let me stand you a glass of brandy?" enquired Ocaña. "You and your friends here."

"Yes, I'll accept that," exclaimed Coca-Coña, raising his head once more from the game. "I'll accept that, and as many more as you like."

Ocaña smiled.

"If a man will stay miserable in this world," said the one-eyed man, "it's because he wants to."

Coca-Coña turned round and shouted at him: "What did you say, you Alcarrenian hen-thief? You with one eye in your head, that looks like a poached egg!"

"There he is picking a quarrel again," put in Don Marcial. "Attend to the game, man, attend to your hand, or else you'll lose and then you'll start pitching into poor Carmelo."

At this point five young people from Madrid came in, three boys and two girls. After a word with Mauricio they went through into the garden.

"I said it and I'll say it again," answered the one-eyed man, "if a man won't take comfort it's because he doesn't want to, and I've got my reasons for saying it too."

"As for you, I don't know what comfort you can take for that poached eye of yours," retorted Coca-Coña, "except perhaps that you don't have to shut it when you go shooting. But if you were to have the thing out it might at least be useful to you in a game of skittles."

[203]

The Alcarrenian burst out laughing.

"Well, you've certainly got a spiteful tongue, whatever else you're short of. No doubt about that. It runs away with you, if your legs don't. And faster! Whatever is missing on one side, I say, is generally made up for on another, and that's certainly the case with men who have disabilities like you and me. We develop in the most unexpected places. Shall I tell you how it's taken me?"

"No need to mention it," answered Coca-Coña. "You've got a dirty mind, you have. No doubt about your coming from Alcarría!"

Coca-Coña turned his attention once more to the game.

"Yes, sir, from Alcarría," said the little man who had come in with him, and who carried a shepherd's game-bag, "from Alcarría, like all our other troubles, the foxes and the wolves, for instance, that kill our cattle."

"You too?" said the Alcarrenian. "You'd do better to have a shave on a Sunday instead of butting into other people's arguments."

Then, turning to El Chamarís and the two butchers, he went on: "Yes, it's quite true that if a man doesn't take comfort it's because he doesn't want to. Do you know what they said to me when I lost this eye at the age of eighteen?"

"Something stupid, no doubt," said Claudio. "Let's hear it."

The Alcarrenian wiped his mouth with the back of his hand and said:

"One of the villagers said to me two or three days after it happened . . . It was with a box of percussion-caps, you know, the regulation kind that have a little acorn at the bottom. You don't see them today. But, as I was saying, this old man comes up to me and says, as bold as brass: 'Don't get upset. That'll let you out of your military service all right.' Damn the man! I took that pretty hard I can tell you. But the time went by, and in the end the day came when my class was called up. And believe me I was damned well pleased when they sent me back home and all the rest of them had to do their service. What do you say to that?"

"Yes, everything has its advantages and disadvantages."

"Yes, that's why I say that if a man won't take comfort it's because he doesn't want to. Even bad luck has some advantages. So far as looks were concerned I had nothing to lose; it was no worse being ugly with one eye than ugly with two. It was merely a question of sight. But there I should say, if you ask me, that a man can come to have more sight in one eye than he had in both. Don't think I'm talking nonsense. What happens is that when you've only got one eye, when you know that you've only got that one, you take care to keep it very wide open from night till morning and from morning till night. And it begins to be pretty sharp, that eye does," and he put his forefinger to his cheek below his sound eye. "So that in the end you come to see a lot of things with one eye that can't be seen with two."

Ocaña was again talking to the truck-driver.

"The best of the cars they're producing today are the Peugeots. Though they have one fault, I must say, they're rather low-slung."

* * *

The sun was going down. It was the size of a waiter's tray and still about twenty or twenty-five feet above the horizon. The heights of Paracuellos in the east turned red from the setting sun. The high ground fell in abrupt terraces to the Jarama, forming ravines, table-lands, clefts, abrasions, piles and whitish mounds in disorderly array without geological unity, like the debris after a landslide, or like excavations made by the picks and shovels of giants. Beneath the long rays of the evening, which threw them into higher relief, they did not seem to obey the heavy laws of earth, but the ancient whims of Titans.

"That's Paracuellos over there, isn't it, Fernando?"

"Yes, Paracuellos del Jarama. You can see the tower. Come on. Don't stop now."

"Have you ever been there?"

"To Paracuellos? No, girl. What reason could I ever have had for going there?"

"Some reason or another. I don't know. D'you know where I should like to be now? I should like to be sitting on the edge of that precipice. It must be very nice over there."

They started walking again.

"Oh, we all know you, Mely. You've always been a bit fanciful."

[205]

They heard the music of the *merenderos* again and the noise of their customers. Now their two long shadows, Mely's and Fernando's, ran ahead of them, perpendicular to the river. The terraces with their drink-stalls all round them were now completely in the shade, and people were moving about in the cool of the greenery and the nearby water. The sluice was roaring, Mely and Fernando passed once more in front of the tables, walking on the very edge of the concrete embankment. She watched the eddies, and the pressure of the current towards that place where all the water was made to converge at the sluice head. She watched the increasing violence of the water in the narrow channel.

"What would happen if I fell in?"

"You wouldn't be there to tell the tale."

"It makes me frightened, Fernando." She shook her shoulders, pretending to shiver.

Then they recrossed the little plank bridge and climbed up through the trees, to the place where they had picnicked.

"What have you been doing?" asked Alicia when they got back. "Do you know what the time is?"

"It can't be late."

"It's after seven all right."

Miguel got up.

"Time to gather our bits and pieces together and go up the hill."

"You'll never guess what an adventure we've had."

"What happened to you?"

"The Civil Guards stopped us over there," recounted Mely. "Apparently you can't go about dressed as you like. They told me to put something on my shoulders, the couple of old scarecrows."

"Did they? That's funny. Can't be the same there as it is here?"

"Obviously not."

"Nonsense. They just take a pleasure in going around to stop people living their own lives."

"That must be it," said Alicia. "Come on now and let's get dressed. Get up, Paulina."

"But I don't want to go at all. We could always stay here a bit longer and all join up later, couldn't we?"

"What's all this? Come on, girl, we've got to meet the others now. You see, we shall have a good time."

"I don't know what to say."

"Well, whichever it's to be, make your minds up quickly."

"We stay," decided Sebastián.

"What a pity! Everyone going a different way!"

"What I should have liked to do was to go to Torrejón and dance."

"You've said that once," said Mely. "What a man! Once he gets an idea in his head the devil himself can't get it out again."

"What are the others going to do?"

Miguel went over to Tito's group. They were singing.

"Come on up the hill, eh?"

"What did you say? We didn't hear," replied Daniel. Lucita laughed.

"Come on. Less funny business. It's getting late. Make up your minds."

"What have we got to make up our minds about?"

"To do something, instead of just talking. Stop fooling and say whether you're coming or not."

"But, old chap, that depends where ..."

"All right. It's clear we can't count on you. I've wasted enough time already. Do just whatever you like."

Miguel turned his back on them and walked over to the others. Carmen and Santos had got up. She was stretching her arms to loosen her muscles, and gazing up into the sky. She looked down.

"Why are you looking at me?"

Santos stood in front of her, leaning against a tree. He steadied himself against it and rubbed his cheek across her face.

"Darling," he said.

"Coming to get dressed, Carmela?"

"Yes, Mely. Just coming. I'm collecting my clothes." She bent down to pick them up. Santos was still leaning against the tree.

"Tell me, Carmen."

"What, darling?" She looked in his eyes.

"Do you very much want to go up?"

"Me? I really don't know. Why?"

"No reason. If you were tired...I thought perhaps you were tired."

Alicia came over again. "We're going on. If you're coming, come." She was carrying her clothes, and a pair of green sandals.

"Ready!"

"Come on and get dressed then," said Alicia. "Why don't you get moving? What are you waiting for?"

"Coming! I'm coming..."

Miguel was already putting on his clothes. Santos moved away. Mely was going off with Alicia and Carmen. They passed near Daniel's group.

"Three prize fools," said Alicia.

Mely did not look at them, but Carmen said: "What a lovely day we've had! The best Sunday afternoon ever."

"Do you think so?" asked Mely. "You'd know."

Sebastián's head was propped on Paulina's legs. She was looking at the bricks of the bridge stained deeper by the sun, and the shadow of the arches on the muddy waters of the river.

"Tomorrow will be Monday again," said Sebas. "We've a rush of work these days..."

"In the garage?"

"Where else do you think?"

Fernando had passed in front of them, and was now rinsing something in the river.

"More work every day. It makes you sick. The boss is pleased enough, but it's absolutely killing us."

"Don't think about anything."

"How can I help it?"

"Don't think about that now, anyway."

"You can't stop thinking altogether unless you go to sleep. Nobody can stop having thoughts all the time."

"Go to sleep then." She put her hands over his eyes.

"Don't. You don't come out on a trip to go to sleep."

"Well, what is it you want then?"

Fernando returned twisting his swimsuit to squeeze out the water.

"Not to have so much work. Not to spoil my Sundays by remembering all the other days of the week."

"What's up?" asked Fernando. "What a lazy lot we are! Flat on your back! Lucky for you that you've only got to get on the motorbike and press the accelerator, and you're back in Madrid without doing a thing."

"Real princes, eh?"

Carmen was dressing in the bushes on the bank while Mely and Alicia held out the cloak.

"I'm as red as a lobster." She looked at her shoulders. She slipped her body into her clothes. Under her blouse she undid the straps of her swimsuit.

"Just finishing, girls. Don't look." She laughed.

"What an idiot you are!" said Mely. "Anyone would think you were Scheherazade."

Carmen had got her arms into her blouse and was hooking up her skirt. Then she dropped her swimsuit and stepped out of it. Fernando's voice was heard, telling them to be quick.

"Don't go to sleep. Everyone else is ready."

There was a sound in the bushes as Alicia was dressing. She jumped. Someone was throwing down earth from the top of the hill.

"How disgusting!" said Mely, looking up the slope. She had caught sight of two heads ducking.

"Guttersnipes," said Carmen.

"It's not funny."

A shower of earth fell even more heavily on the leaves of the bushes. Alicia looked up also.

"They've got some cheek, they have. I call it a damned nuisance."

"It takes all sorts to make a world," said Mely. "Finished, Alicia?"

"Ready when you are."

The others had now started shouting at them.

"The place isn't on fire, is it?"

They joined the men.

"Got everything?" asked Miguel.

"Don't worry. Let's go."

Miguel turned to Paulina and Sebastián.

"Right now. Try to be up at the top before ten. If you aren't you know, we'll leave you all the tins and stuff to bring back on the motor-bike. That all right?"

"Yes, man, you needn't worry. We shall be up before you go."

"See you later."

"Have a good time."

Daniel, Tito and Lucita had got into a huddle. You could hear them laughing.

"What a trio!"

"Seeing that you're staying," Miguel called to them, "there's nothing more to be said, only that we're pushing off at ten. But do just what you like.'

Tito had lifted his head and waved them away with one hand.

"You go off. Go off. It doesn't worry us. We're independent."

"The Independence of Cuba!" Daniel shouted after them.

"See you later," said Lucita.

The others were moving away.

"They're going to get thoroughly stewed," said Miguel as they went off. "I'm sorry for Lucita's sake."

Santos and Carmen had gone ahead. They were now beginning to climb the earth staircase, holding one another by the waist and looking at their feet as if counting the steps.

"The pair of turtle-doves," said Mely.

Fernando was talking to Miguel.

"It's half past seven now, boy. They must be more than tired of waiting for us."

Gradually they mounted the steps, leaving the people on the bank far below them. There were still many groups scattered among the trees and on the other bank, among the bushes on the edge of the yellowish rough land. There were naked bodies on the concrete dam almost colourless now against the light. The shadows of the poplars beside the channel were very long and delicate.

"It's hard work."

Fernando was panting. They had reached the top. Mely had stopped half-way.

"Wait for me," she shouted to them from below. "You've got to take this slowly."

The music of the radios came up, aggressive and out of tune, with the noise of the people and the roaring water, from the drink-stalls hidden in the trees. It came up out of the foliage like the hot dust of a fair.

"How feeble, you are, Mely!"

She climbed very slowly, helping herself by resting her hands on her thighs. She looked up towards the others, to see how much more she had still to do.

"It's my heart. I can't," she sighed.

Then they turned away, leaving the trees, the rough land, and the bridge out of sight behind them. The crest of the rise hid the river, the water that was the colour of dirty flames, the turbid vein that ran almost invisibly through the distant countryside, under the orange sun which was level with the earth. They passed once more between the vineyards. Alicia was hanging with both hands on Miguel's arm. She leaned her cheek against his shoulder. Miguel was humming.

"Do you think they'll have remembered to bring the gramophone?"

"We'll kill them if they haven't."

"Are you all that keen on dancing?"

"Oh, what a life!" said Mely. "All day long I've been trying to have a bit of fun. But nothing doing. I'd hate to go home as browned off as I am now. Why the moment she saw my face in the house, my aunt would ask me if I was ill."

"Oh dear, so you've been bored all the time, I suppose."

"Don't worry," said Fernando. "I know what's the matter with that girl."

"You're very clever."

They were building a factory there on the left of the road which was now constricted between the fence of the building site and the wire around the good vineyard. Long buildings with concrete roofs, and empty scaffoldings. Two pigeons flew over.

"I don't understand," said Miguel. "You're always telling us how bored you are, and my sister does too. But I've never understood it. To tell you the truth I can never tell when I'm being bored and when I'm enjoying myself. I swear I can't. Perhaps I never am bored, or perhaps I always am." He shrugged his shoulders. "Lucky you!"

Just as they were crossing the main road, Santos and Carmen stopped and shouted to somebody who was coming towards them. Santos turned and shouted to the others behind him on the path: "They're here." It was Zacharías, Samuel, Marialuisa, Ricardo, Mariyayo, Lucas, Lolita and Juanita. Zacarías and Miguel were the first to shake hands, like two tribal chiefs, in the middle of the road.

"How's things, you crooks?"

"We've been waiting an hour for you to show up."

"We were here all the time."

"I suppose you've brought the gramophone, or is that too much to hope?"

A fair girl who was with them looked at Mely's trousers.

"In the trees?"

"Yes, down there by the dam."

"And?"

"Nothing. Here we are."

"It's pretty crowded there."

"What about you?"

They had stopped in the road.

"Didn't Daniel come?"

"Oh yes, he came."

Fernando embraced Samuel whom he addressed as "old Sammy-boy," punching him on the arm. You could see the lines of Zacarías' ribs through his open shirt.

"Tito came and Sebastián and his fiancée, and Lucita, and that's all, I think . . ."

"Well, how modern we're getting!"

"What, me?"

"They've stayed down on the river. I don't know . . ."

"Come on, or we shall still be here by the time it gets dark."

"What don't you know?"

"How they'll end up."

"Here comes a car. Out of the way!"

"What about the records?"

"He's got them."

"What a dust!"

"Let's get moving . . ."

Three of them had sat down in the ditch.

"You don't know Mariyayo, do you? She's a new acquisition."

She had a Chinese look and straight black hair. They shook hands, and Fernando took a look at her bust and thighs, and then he gave her his hand also.

"Yes, sir, and a good acquisition, what's more," he commented with a laugh.

Mariyayo stood up to his look with a mischievous smile.

"Delighted . . ."

"We had six records. But that idiot Ricardo broke one this morning."

"What are we hanging about for?" said Mely. "Let's get going, eh?"

"Where have you been hiding all day? We couldn't get a sight of you anywhere."

"We go to the good spots," said the fair girl. "What do you suppose?"

"We're posh, we are."

The man who was carrying the gramophone had put it down in the ditch and was examining a scratch on his instep.

"I say, Dentifrice," said the man who was carrying a haversack, "is that the proper place to leave the gramophone?"

The man raised his head. "My name's Ricardo."

He had very white perfect teeth. The man with the haversack laughed.

"There'll be quite a crowd of us," said Miguel. "How many are you?"

"Eight and the dog."

"What dog?"

"No dog. You swallow anything."

"You must always have your joke. Now what are we waiting for? Let's go."

Santos and Carmen had already gone ahead towards the bar. The others started walking slowly, straggling and waiting for one another. Fernando placed himself on the right of Mariyayo.

"What part of Madrid do you come from?" he asked. "If you don't mind my asking?"

"Curio-city, if you happen to know it, nosy?" answered Mariyayo with a laugh.

Miguel and Zacarías were walking together, and Mely had taken Alicia's arm.

"She's pretty. She looks like a Chinese."

"They used to call her the Korean at the dressmaking school, which was where we met."

Zacarías turned round to shout to the party carrying the gramophone, who were still lagging behind near the main road.

"Come on Ricardo, tomorrow'll be too late!"

Samuel was walking with the fair girl; his right arm was clasped round her shoulders. The sun was staring at them now, at the end of the road, over the hills of Coslada. The two other girls in the party were waiting for Ricardo and the man with the haversack.

"What time does your train go?" Miguel asked Zacarías.

"Half past ten."

"Regular time-table, aren't you?"

"It says ten-thirty at the station."

"Well, we've plenty of time. We can have quite a lot of fun before ten-twenty."

"Yes, perhaps, unless one of the girls spoils everything by wanting to go home earlier."

Santos and Carmen had stopped in front of Mauricio's.

"Miguel," said Santos. "Come here a moment. I want to tell you something."

Carmen was leaning against the wall.

"What is it?"

"Listen. Carmela doesn't feel too well. She's tired, you know, and all that. So we think we'll start back for Madrid. Because we shouldn't be doing anything here if we stayed, you see. And it would be better for her to go home and get to bed earlyish."

"Yes, yes, just as you like. If she's tired, move off by all means.

Just as you like. I'm sorry you're going so early, man. But if she's tired, that'll be best."

"I'll go and get out the bike then, and we'll push off right away."

He took a side glance at Zacarías and added: "You'll forgive us not waiting for you, eh?"

"Don't be silly!"

"She isn't used to river bathing, you see. I'm sure it's the bathing that has made her tired."

"Yes, of course, boy, of course. You don t need to apologize. Get the bike and off you go."

They had now all come up to the bar.

"Do we go in or what?"

The tall butcher was looking at them from the doorway. Santos said: "Well, if you're passing Machina, we'll have a reckoning to-night and see what everybody owes. If not, in the morning."

"Right you are," said Miguel.

They all went in. The men in the bar looked at the girls as they passed through.

"Here we are again!"

"Right," said Mauricio. "You'll be going into the garden, won't you?"

"Yes, sir."

"Go ahead then. Go ahead. You know the way."

They went into the passage, Mely at the rear.

"Hats off to the modern style," muttered the Alcarrenian after taking a look at Mely's trousers.

"You don't see things like that back in Alcarría, do you?" said the shepherd.

"Not likely. There were some people once who got out of a car, with a woman in trousers. They were talking foreign. Down at the inn they wouldn't give them anything to eat because everyone said they were Protestants."

"That's the sort of thing that could only happen in Alcarría," said the shepherd. "I ask you, what's the connexion between a person's religion and the clothes he wears."

"None at all, of course. But the woman who kept the inn at the time was a pious idiot, and she wouldn't give them food because she was afraid the priest would tell her off."

The Alcarrenian laughed and went on: "Yes, they said they'd come to see the monastery. 'What monastery?' the boys asked them. Then somebody pointed out four rickety stones perched up on a hillside, which is all that's left of this monastery they wanted. There's so little there that nobody thinks of calling it a monastery. But they were quite crazy about this damned monastery. The more modern people seem to be, the keener they are on antiquities. You can understand it. That's where the widow at the inn got her great disappointment. She was livid with fury when she saw the Father himself go and show these people over this bit of ruin. And from that day on she stopped haunting the church, and her piety was over and done with."

The butchers were very amused and the shepherd said with a laugh: "He's a wit, he is."

"That's the way things are in the country," said the Alcarrenian.

"It's very different there from what it is near Madrid, where people are more spiteful and know a thing or two."

"Very much too spiteful," agreed the shepherd, nodding his head.

Don Marcial sucked the point of his little copying pencil and scribbled on the marble. The truck-driver in greasy overalls said: "You've only got to see where the headlights are placed in this model and compare it to the way they're placed in the Peugeot '46. A tremendous difference." He turned to Mauricio. "Let's have another glass, now, for me and this gentleman. It's just that there are some firms always trying to make technical improvements in every model they put on the road."

"Yes, while others only change the fabric. Just the outside that makes the impression. The façade as we might say. But Peugeot's, they're a solid concern."

"You're right. Here!" He put the glass, which Mauricio had just poured out, into his hand. "It's the same in the car business as in everything else, it's the inside that counts in the long run. The same as in everything else. Why should cars be any different, anyway?"

Carmen and Santos passed them, carrying their bicycle by the handlebars.

"Off already?" enquired Mauricio.

"Yes. We're in a bit of a hurry, you know. The others will be staying later."

"That's all right. Perhaps I'll see you again next Sunday."

He wiped his right hand dry on the cloth and held it out.

"The tall fellow who's staying on will settle with you for what we've had today," said Santos, gripping his hand across the counter. "To save us having to reckon up now, you see."

"Very good. See you young people again soon, I hope."

"Goodbye. Keep the party going," said Santos, as he lifted the front wheel of the bike to get it up the little step at the door.

★ ★ ★

"Have you given the order?"

The gramophone rested on a chair. The Ocañas were watching in silence from the opposite corner of the garden.

"They're going to bring us a drop of wine."

"I drink absinthe," said Zacarías with a laugh.

He tipped his chair backwards, plunging the back of his head into the vine. The gramophone shook violently as its owner wound the handle.

"And what's that?" asked Mely.

"An Eastern drink."

Zacarías laughed; he had a face like a greyhound, with sharp features.

"Eastern like you!"

"I was born in Baghdad. Didn't you know?"

"Anyone could see it."

"What? I shan't show you my birth certificate, because it's in Arabic and you wouldn't understand it."

"Your word's good enough for me, darling."

They all sat down at a large table on the left of the passage door, and alongside the main wall of the house. The man with fine teeth was standing beside the man who was winding the gramophone.

"What about some music?"

"A little patience, please."

"What records have you got?" asked Alicia.

"Some records from before the flood."

"They're good enough to dance to," said Samuel. "We've even got a samba."

"That's nice."

"And a Gardel tango – 'The Pirate'."

Samuel's fair girl leaned back, resting her elbows on a window ledge behind her. Her breasts stood out boldly. She wore a scarlet blouse.

"Don't sit like that," said Samuel.

"Why?"

"Put down your chair, or you'll break it."

"Who's got the needles?"

"You have."

He tapped his pockets and heard them chink.

"You're right. What shall we put on?"

"Is it working? Then put on a rumba."

"The first one that comes," said Ricardo thrusting his hand into his haversack. "Here it is."

"Tell us which it is."

"No. A surprise."

The other five youngsters from Madrid who had come in half-way through the afternoon occupied a table in front of them, near the hen-run.

Petra looked at her watch.

"Oh, these kids, these kids! . . . It's nearly time."

Sergio had turned in his chair towards the middle of the garden, to watch the dancing.

"They'll be back."

"And what about him? In there filling himself up with wine, without so much as a thought."

"We shall have to light the fire and cook the supper," said Felisita in a judicious tone, supporting her mother.

"As if nothing mattered. Some people never think of anything," said Petra.

All four looked at the gramophone, and at Miguel and Zacarías' party.

"Give the kids a little peace, Petra."

A ray of sun which had shone on the bricks of a patch of wall that was free from creeper between the Ocañas' table and that of the gang of five, had shrunk and finally disappeared. Now the whole garden was in darkness. Juanito's head appeared above the wall. The music began.

"Cuckoo, Mummy! Look at me, Mummy!"

The *pasodoble* of the Canaries sounded on the gramophone.

"Now, Juanito! Come down from there immediately! Come back here, all three of you, at once. And quick about it."

Juanito's face disappeared.

"Oh lord, what a pest children are!"

A girl in black came forward to dance with Ricardo. Fernando was laughing in a corner with Mariyayo. She was displaying the manifold resources of her Chinese eyes.

"What a girl!" said Fernando. "Darling you've got eyes, like a film, each one of them. A double feature, and what's more, continuous. Shall we dance?"

Mariyayo consented with a laugh.

"Let us come by, you."

Zacarías shifted his chair and the others passed behind it, brushing the foliage of the honeysuckle with their backs. Mauricio appeared with the wine.

"Put it down here, please."

"Well now," said Mauricio. "You've come well equipped this time." He took the glasses from the tray four by four in his fingers, and put them down on the table.

"Why do you say that?"

"That instrument." He tilted his chin in the direction of the gramophone.

"Oh yes," said Samuel. "Tell me, do you charge anything for dancing here?"

Mauricio looked at him with his tray dangling in his hand, and already half-way back to the house door.

"Charge anything?" he said. "Come! What would you expect me to charge for? The dust you raise shuffling your feet? That wouldn't be a bad thing, you know." He went into the house.

"It wasn't such a silly question," said Samuel, looking at the others. "If you just think . . ."

"Yes, you're right."

Mariyayo's laugh rang out from the middle of the garden. Miguel had filled himself a glass and emptied it at a gulp. He led his fiancée out to dance. The owner of the gramophone was still standing beside the chair.

"Let it be, Lucas," said one of the girls. "It's going on its own." He lifted his head and went over to her. Zacarías was filling the glasses.

"What? Don't you trust your contraption?" he asked.

"The record's almost finished. But I will all the same."

Samuel and the fair girl had put their arms round each other's shoulders and swinging in their chairs. The girl was humming the *pasodoble* in time to the gramophone. Mariyayo laughed again. Zacarías gave Mely a dig with his elbow.

"There now!" He tilted his sharp chin towards the dancers. They've taken away the partner I brought for the day."

"Mariyayo?"

He nodded.

"You let them take her," said Mely. "Do you mind?"

"I prefer the substitute."

"What substitute?"

Zacarías tilted his chair back once more and buried the back of his neck in the honeysuckle.

"You'll tip the chair over and fall on the ground, Zacarías. Tell me, what substitute?"

"You. Who else would it be?"

"Me?" She turned towards him. "Ah, boy, now I understand. But what if she comes back?"

Zacarías smiled, putting his hands behind his head. "She's lost her job."

The Ocañas' children made their way through the dancers. Juanito bumped into Mariyayo.

"Watch out, child! . . ."

"You might go round instead of disturbing everybody," scolded his mother. "Come here! Come on! Look at your faces."

She caught Petrita and wiped her nose. Then she wet her handkerchief with saliva and rubbed the child's face. Petrita complained that she was doing it too hard, and her mother then showed her the black marks on her white handkerchief: "Look! Do you see?"

When they passed the gramophone, Fernando and Mariyayo stopped dancing for a moment, while he stretched out his hand to put the needle back almost to the beginning of the record. Lucas looked up when he heard the break in the music.

"Leave it alone, you! Don't touch the instrument."

"What's wrong? Does it need a technician?"

Lucas had hurried to the gramophone.

"It's delicate. The least thing will make it stop." He listened to the working of the gramophone for a few seconds and they began to dance again.

"It's more fun like that, don't you think? We get twice the dancing to the same tune."

"And do you suppose that makes the time pass any slower?"

"What's your father doing?" Petra was asking.

"He's with some people in there."

"Because if he says that his headlights are out of order, it'd be better to get back to Madrid before the light goes, or else we'll get fined by the gentlemen in black hats and that would be too bad."

She caught sight of Mauricio beside the table of the five; he had brought them another bottle of wine.

"Mauricio! My husband's with you in the bar, isn't he?"

"Felipe? Yes he's up at the counter. Hasn't stirred an inch."

"Well, go and ask him from me, please, what he's up to, and whether he's watching the time."

"Do you want to go back?"

Fernando picked up a glass of wine as he passed the table. He did not stop dancing.

"Too old?" he shouted at the friends who were still sitting.

"Wait for the rumba and I'll show you," answered Samuel. "He's never seen me dancing, has he, Zacar? Do you remember at the Palmeras, the winter before last?"

"Did you often go to the Palmeras?" asked Mely.

"Yes, with that creature. We went four or five times."

"More, more," said Samuel. "More often than that."

"And you let him?" Mely asked the fair girl.

"He wasn't going out with me then. If I caught him going there now," she threatened him with her fist, "I'd teach him a lesson."

"They keep you in your place, eh Samuel?" smiled Zacarías. "Don't you deny it."

"This girl? Bah!"

"Just you try and you'll see," said the fair girl. She took Samuel's hand, and added for Mely's benefit: "But he's a nice boy, you know."

"Of course he is," said Mely.

Fernando passed again and put his empty glass on the table. Zacarías refilled them.

"Yes, it was marvellous at the Palmeras," he commented. "It was terrific. It's certainly gone down a lot since then."

"What do you know about it?" asked the fair girl. "How do you know?" She squeezed herself against Samuel pettishly.

"Pff! Not a patch on what it was, darling! Nothing like it."

"You're opening your big mouth, Zacarías," said the fair girl. "I don't have to say more, do I?"

"Let him be," said Samuel.

Zacarías laughed.

"That was nasty of you," said Mely. "You were trying to make trouble for him with his fiancée."

"Me? It's in one ear and out of the other. What's past is past. Do you think I should quarrel with Samuel at this time of day, about what Zacarías says or doesn't say?"

Zacarías drank some wine and said: "Marialuisa, you've taken away the best pal I had in the world, and you've taken him for ever. That's how things are. So don't think I forgive you all that easily."

"But look, it's quite possible to put that right, and easy too. If you miss Samuel so much, find yourself a girl-friend, and we can all four go out. Why not?"

"It's not as easy as all that," answered Zacarías.

"Don't you think so?" asked the fair girl. "I think it is."

"I'm going to produce my Bisontes," said Mely. "Would you all like a smoke?" Her bag was hanging from the back of her chair.

Miguel and Alicia were dancing in silence.

"Put a bit more life into it," said the girl in black to Ricardo.

"We're crawling round."

"A man would have to have legs like an acrobat to dance with you, girl."

"You're exaggerating a bit."

"Well, shall we put it back again?" asked Fernando as he danced past them.

"You'll come to a bad end if you do. I'll kill you if you touch that gramophone again!"

Fernando laughed.

"We'll let it stop then . . ."

And he danced off with Mariyayo, quickening his step. They went round more often than the others, laughing and spoiling the others' more contrived effects.

"So that's the famous Mely?"

"Have you heard of her?" he answered.

"Who hasn't?" she said. "She has quite a reputation."

"I didn't know it was as big as that."

"Well, I've heard a lot about her. Alicia has talked about her, especially. Obviously she thinks she's terrific. But after all that talk, I'd expected more. The famous Mely!"

"A lot more what?"

"I'd expected a bombshell, somebody quite out of the ordinary."

"So you're disappointed in Mely?"

"Well, she's pretty of course. But after all. She's not . . ."

"What?"

"She's not all that."

During this discussion, they glanced quickly in her direction each time they went past the table. They stopped talking, but Mariyayo continued to look at Mely, who had now lit a cigarette.

The music stopped. The gramophone needle continued on its spiral course. Lucas hurried over to pick it up.

"Good?"

"Absolutely grand."

They went back to the table. Alicia had sat down on the left of Mely. "And you so fond of dancing?" she said.

Mely made a vague gesture and shrugged her shoulders.

"Would you like a cigarette?" she asked.

"Thank you, Mely, later." said Alicia, examining her arms.

Mely opened her mouth and blew the smoke out slowly without inhaling.

Petra spoke to her children: "Get dressed now, darlings. Go and get the things you aren't wearing. We'll move off just as soon as Dad comes. Don't put them on top, Amadeo. What are you thinking about?"

He was putting his trousers over his swimsuit.

"But they're dry, Mummy," he said. "Feel them! Look, feel them!"

"Oh, how genteel you are. Go and change behind that chair, if that's what worries you. And mind you don't let anybody see you. Hide yourself, or everybody may be shocked and run away! Anyone would think you had some reason to be so bashful . . ."

Juanito had come up to Petra and was slipping the straps from his shoulders.

At the table of the five a girl could be heard singing softly.

"Have you finished then?"

Amadeo did not answer. He did not stir from the shadows behind the chairs; he was crying.

*   *   *

There was a beggar on the main road just by the level-crossing. He had exposed the stumps of his legs, and was lying on the great sheets of an unfolded newspaper. The sky was a greenish yellow behind the ruined factory of San Fernando de Henares.

Faustina was sieving lentils on the cloth table top, in the light that was still coming through the window. She could hear voices from the garden.

The bricks of the bridge had gradually darkened, and the sun's rays were far away on the other bank. Paulina's eyes followed them beyond the stubble fields towards the tableland of Alcalá, where the last whitish hills were taking on a copper stain, roasted in an opaque and dusty fire.

"What are you looking at?"

"Nothing."

Sebastián lifted his hand to touch Paulina's face.

"Are you happy?" she asked.

He ran his fingers through her hair.

"I've done some journeys on that truck . . . Listen now: Santander, Valladolid, Medinalcampo, Palencia . . ." He counted the towns on his fingers – "Burgos, Astorga, Toro, Corunna, all over Galicia, Ponferrada, the port of Pajares, Oviedo. I've done them all in this Peugeot, and Zamora, and Peñaranda and Salamanca . . . All over Spain. I could mention no end of places. The world held no terror for me by night or by day, when I was doing those trips. It was when I was twenty or twenty-five, you know. That's an age when you bite off more than you can chew, and you think the world's too small for you. It didn't matter to me then what time somebody came and offered me a journey. I didn't ask any questions. I got out of bed, splashed some cold water on my face, and I was at the wheel. It might be to Zamora for garlic or to Vascongadas for a load of iron. I didn't care which. I put on my leather jacket and went. Fill us up, Mauricio, please. I had an Alsatian you know, a perfect picture. He was a picture, that dog! A treasure! I shall never forget that dog of mine. And his teeth! But as I was saying, nobody can teach me anything about a Peugeot."

Beside the level-crossing the beggar was rubbing his stumps, and intoning for the benefit of those who were coming up from the river to the bus-stop and the station.

The shadows were growing among the leaves of the honeysuckle and the American vine.

"Oh lord, what can he be thinking of? It's getting so late!"

Felisita was gazing at Miguel and Zacarías' table. She observed them all, and hung on their every word and movement.

"Come on! It doesn't matter which. One's as good as another so long as we dance . . .!"

The girls displayed their arms, moved their arms this way and that, looked at their arms, and passed their hands over the skin of their arms. A moment ago someone had closed the shutters of the window behind the fair girl's head. Now you could hardly distinguish the expressions of those who were sitting in the shadow, under the creepers. The cat was lying in ambush in a corner of the garden.

"And always trespassing on people's kindness! The poor cripple who is always exhausting your generosity! May you never lack oars to row you through life. A little money for those who cannot look after themselves! Christians, a small coin, if you please, to buy bread for a cripple who can't earn his living . . ."

The poles of the level-crossing were being lowered. Some coins fell on the newspaper, beside his amputated thighs.

"I'm sure I've got a bit of cheese," said the shepherd, "left over from my dinner."

He rummaged among the paper in his haversack. He extracted a triangle of pink cheese from its wrapping.

"There. Ewe's milk. It's a good cheese. Lucky I remembered to put aside a bit for my friend when I was having my dinner."

The game went on under its own angry impetus, with brief exclamations and long silences, punctuated by Coca-Coña's implacable banging down of his dominoes. At the end of each round conversation broke out, and comments.

"It's not too good in the fields at midday under the full force of the sun."

He had put it down on the wooden counter top, and was cutting it into small pieces with his clasp-knife.

"Here you are," he said, closing the blade. "Take a bite. It's not much . . . but it's all I've got."

"There's plenty of bars, plenty of smart places in Madrid where they offer you cheese like this for a snack."

"I wouldn't doubt it," said the Alcarrenian. "Won't you have a bit?"

"Thank you very much, but I'm just going."

The shepherd insisted.

"Wouldn't you like some cheese? Just this little bit, so as to say you've tasted it." He shook his head. "Oh, Señor Lucio, I think you're turning into a real intellectual. Otherwise . . ."

Azufre had smelt the cheese and was wagging his tail in expectation of the rinds.

"Yes I think he is," said Mauricio. "He didn't eat anything at midday at all . . ."

"That can't be good."

"That was sly!" cried Coca-Coña. "You'd counted them up very well. That was a fine bit of defence, yes sir! We've scored off them properly this time. Eh, Marcial, what do you say? Reckon up, reckon up!"

"Reckon up for yourself, they're your points," replied Don Marcial.

Azufre was catching the scraps of cheese that El Chamarís threw him, before they reached the ground.

"Will he remember that I've still to get the supper? Will he remember that the children have still to be put to bed?"

She folded and unfolded her serviette again and again.

"And apparently we've no lights, or so he says. With the daylight that's left . . ."

She looked up at the sky.

"We'd have a bite and a fag at Alba de Tornes and we'd be at Zamora at six. We went over the passes like a flash. No harder to climb than to come down. Everything might have been flat for that bus. Drink up. There's another one coming."

Ocaña obeyed automatically.

Paulina looked across the flat ground, and at the railway running along its embankment. The main train from Guadalajara was coming in on the righthand track. Sebastián raised his wrist and looked at his watch. With a lazy sigh he changed his position. In the far distance on the Levante tableland the sunlight had left the last hills.

"May the charitable find their reward! God bless the young couple! May they have the good luck that this poor cripple has never had! Always trespassing on people's generosity! Always pestering everyone! Christians, spare a small coin for this miserable creature!"

They had shut the level-crossing. Some women were running.

"What about going through Vicálvaro?"

Carmen did not hear; she was listening to the noise of the train that grew louder as it came on to the bridge. She was leaning her arms on the red and white pole of the level-crossing. "Plenty of time! Plenty of time!" cried one woman to another. "Don't run." But they ran all the same. The ground trembled. Santos held his bike by the saddle.

"Listen, Mely. I'll keep your seat for you. You're coming back, I suppose. Aren't you?"

As she moved past, to dance with Fernando, she turned her head.

"Yes, Zacarías, keep it for me." They exchanged glances. "Thank you very much."

The gramophone played a tango.

The train passed blowing out steam in a succession of furious Fs, followed by the long reverberating clatter of its iron wheels. It was grinding to a halt in the station. The last coach stopped only sixty feet away from the level-crossing. Large numbers of people gathered round the carriage doors.

"What are we waiting for?"

The poles were lifted again and people crossed the lines.

"I was saying, what about going through Vicálvaro? Then we should strike the Valencia road and come into Madrid through Vallecas."

"Isn't it a long way round?"

"Not really. We avoid all the congestion of cars coming in from a day in the country. There's no traffic on that road. It's all fields."

"All right, if you know the way. Isn't it getting late?" He took the bicycle off the road, stopped and put his leg over the saddle. Then he steadied himself with both legs on the ground.

"Get on."

Carmen climbed on the cross-bar and gripped the handlebars.

"Leave me in peace! I don't want anything to do with you."

It was all very grey in the shadow of the trees.

"But what have we done to you? Come here, Daniel . . ."

"Nothing. You haven't done anything to me. You're in my way."

He walked a few yards away from Lucita and Tito and fell flat on his face in the dust. Now you could scarcely distinguish the waters of the Jarama from the soil.

"In a cottage – by the sea – where the bold waves roared – the fisher's wife – lived happily – with her little family – "

The almanacks were getting dark on the back wall; their details were becoming confused.

"Dad, let's go."

"Yes, my boy, tell Mummy we're going now. Last round, Mauricio, the last one for the road. Tell her I'm just coming . . ."

Two couples had come out to dance from the table of five.

"Who invited them to dance to our music?" commented Fernando.

"Let them be," said Mely. "What can it matter to you?"

"Well they've got a nerve."

"Do you think they ought to have asked your permission?" she retorted.

Zacarías was observing them from his seat. The ancient voice of Gardel wailed nasally from the gramophone.

Nineta wanted Sergio to dance with her.

"Our dancing days are over, dear. Besides, Petra's in a hurry."

"If that's the only reason," said Petra, "you've time to dance a whole ballet. Well, darling, what did he say to you?"

"He said he's just coming."

They had left the main road and the whining beggar behind them. Santos was pedalling, bent over with his cheek close to Carmen's.

"Supposing we get lost," she said.

"Do you mind if we do?"

"No, not much," she smiled, rubbing her face against Santos' chin. "So long as I'm with you, nothing matters, not even drowning."

Now the road ran between orchards on the outskirts of Coslada. The little trees stood out black against the red twilight. Coslada lay behind them.

"Damn it, the man's deserted," said Tito.

"That's his affair. Don't you worry."

"I do worry. I don't like him going off like that." He felt Lucita's arm against his own.

"Well, there's nothing wrong about that," she said. "It's just as nice as we are. He isn't indispensable, is he?"

"We were all three together."

"And now we're two. The fewer the people the lighter the room."

"Lighter. I see. Everything's very hazy to me, darling. Nothing looks very light to me with all this wine inside me."

"Nor to me either," said she with a laugh.

She put her face close to his and added: "I'm rather lit up, you know." Her eyes shone. "You leave Dani alone. If he wants a bit of a snooze, let him have it. He said we were in his way. Listen, Tito!"

"What is it?"

You could see the towers of Vicálvaro against the dim light of the water and the chimney of the Valderribas cement-works. Everything was blotched with smoke. The bike made no noise on the dust; only the joint in the chain creaked gently at regular intervals. Carmen felt Santos' breath on her cheek. They had to dismount at Arganda to cross the railway track. Someone was calling to someone else across the fields.

"Lend us a hand, Carmela."

They hauled the bike up the bank. They stopped at the top, beside the railway lines.

"Give me a kiss."

They could see the shadow of Almodóvar, a solitary flat hill that stood up ahead, dark and near, standing out against the low greenish light of the western sky.

"Music belongs to everybody. A gramophone may be private property, but music can't be. Music belongs to anyone who listens!"

The bottles had ceased to shine on the shelves. Mauricio yawned.

"If you hadn't been so caught up with your friend you'd have tasted the cheese," said the Alcarrenian. "Ewe's milk cheese is really something special. It was his." He pointed to the shepherd. "He can make cheese even though there's nothing else he's good for."

The shepherd confirmed his judgement. "Yes, I wish you'd had a taste. So that you could see what we make round here. Some of our things aren't bad. But I didn't dare disturb your conversation to ask you."

"Don't you worry, man," said the truck-driver. "This gentleman's bound to come back. He'll come back another day. He's sure to. And he'll come alone without his family on top of him. If he tells us in time we'll kill him a goat, eh Señor Claudio, and dress it properly for him? With a car there's no difficulty about the journey. You'll see, you'll see. Madrid isn't the only place where a man can enjoy himself." He touched Ocaña cordially on the shoulder for a brief moment.

Faustina suddenly noticed that she could no longer see the lentils on the table top. She looked up at the window; the garden was still light but the colours had now disappeared; one by one they had grown dim and cold and melted into the grey of their ashes. Faustina took off her glasses and put them down on the table.

"In the stormy waters – the sea wolf drowned."

Her glasses had black celluloid frames. She got up from her chair to switch on the electric light.

"Pick any day you like for a visit. You've only got to drop me a postcard a couple of days before, and we'll get the whole show going for you in no time. You'll enjoy it."

"Yes, but it would be difficult at the moment. Mauricio knows that, don't you Mauricio? Don't imagine it's because I don't want to come. Because if I could I should be really delighted. But thank you all the same for the invitation."

"What's all this about thanks? Nothing to thank me for. Nothing at all. Just come, that's all. Otherwise, nothing . . ."

"You can't see a thing now," interrupted Coca-Coña. "I couldn't pick out three priests on a mound of plaster! Think a little bit more about your customers, Mauricio, and less about saving on your electricity bills. Here's poor Señor Esnáider lifting the dominoes up to the light before he can see to play them. Soon he won't know the difference between the double-one and Carmelo's little eyes."

"Be quiet," scolded Don Marcial. "You're nothing but a freak from a fair-booth, with one flat foot pointing towards France and the other towards Portugal!"

"Listen to the nasty little squirt! He's a fine one to pick out his neighbour's faults. It must have cost your mother and father a lot of trouble to bring anything as difficult as you into the world. They made us a grand present! . . ."

Mauricio had switched on the light.

The kitchen light fell from the square window on to the garden, but was lost in the diffuse evening twilight.

"It'll be quite dark in a minute," said Petra. "It's almost night already."

Felipe Ocaña appeared in the garden door and walked over to his family's table.

"I hope you don't mind our taking advantage of your gramophone. It doesn't cost you anything, after all. No extra wear and tear, and it gives a better service, so to speak."

"Of course. I only said that to add to the noise. Who on earth would want to stop you?"

"Thank you. We'll wind it up next time. Then the labour will be halved, and we'll have done our share. Wouldn't that be a good arrangement?"

Samuel had brought out a pipe of marijuana, which he handed to Zacarías ready lit.

"A fine pair of Moors," said Loli. "I wonder what pleasure you get out of it."

"Look at Fernando. He's got to know those people already."

"He sticks his nose into everything . . ."

"And do you let him smoke that poison?"

Marialuisa shrugged her shoulders. "Why not?"

"Perhaps you even like it. It makes you feel you're going around with more of a he-man, because he smokes that hemp stuff."

"Not a bit of it. But if he likes it why should I take it away from him?"

"It can't do his health any good."

"So what? Won't you put on another record?"

"Wait and have a minute's rest. We've only got five. You're not going to put them on one after the other, are you?"

"Five? No, there are ten."

"They're not all double-sided. I think at least two of them have nothing on the back."

"Even if there are only eight, we shan't have time to put them all on. We shan't have time."

"All right, Mariyayo, so now we know. Don't say it again or the time will seem shorter than ever. Don't spoil things for us, girl."

[232]

"But why should we pretend what isn't true?"

"All right. Turn the knife in the wound, if you want to."

"What's it like to smoke that stuff?" Mely asked Zacarías.

"Try it. Ask Samuel to fill you a pipe."

"I wouldn't dare. I don't like the idea. What's it like?"

"Well, you float off."

"What do you mean?"

The road ran parallel to the shadow of Almodóvar. There was only the silent trace of the bicycle wheel on the darkening dust. The nickelled handlebars still shone faintly beside Carmen's hands, also the dirty straw of the stubble fields, and the white porcelain insulators on the tops of the pylons which looked out westwards to the last red and purple light beyond the flat top of Almodóvar. Behind them high smoke from the Valderribas cement-factory's chimney stretched across the slate-grey windless sky. It hung motionless above the black buildings of the works, at the solitary edge of Vicálvaro village with its tower and its confused mass of houses. Carmen shuddered, because they could now hear above the thrumming of the long-distance cables the buzzing of the electric wires that crossed the road above their heads.

Santos looked into the almost complete darkness to their right, where the bare slopes of Almodóvar rose above the stubble; the whitish marly sides of the hill, spotted black by the round shapes of bushes, were clear in the diffuse shadow. He stopped the bicycle.

"Let's make a halt."

Carmen stretched her limbs in the middle of the road. Santos looked all round without letting go of the bicycle.

"Shall we climb the hill?" he asked.

"Which? All that way up?"

"It's nothing, darling. Just across that field and then two hundred or two hundred and fifty feet to climb, at the most."

"And a bit more."

"Don't you want to see Madrid?"

"Can you?"

"Yes, you get a perfect view."

He had taken the bicycle off the road.

"Coming or not?" he added.

"How do you know you can see Madrid? Who did you climb it with?"

She too went on to the stubble and they began to walk together.

"One afternoon with my Uncle Javier and another sergeant, when my uncle was posted to Vicálvaro. They wanted to see if there were any partridges. Hang on to me if you stumble. Just keep in the furrow, one foot in front of the other. Then you won't stumble, see?"

"I'm frightened of walking in the furrows. There may be animals in them."

"Yes, there are crocodiles, I think, and leopards."

The stalks of the stubble creaked beneath their feet. They left the bicycle at the foot of the flat-topped Almodóvar, lying on the broken soil. Then Santos took his fiancée by the hand and helped her to climb the slope. Behind them, far away on the Valencia road, cars were cruising with their headlights on.

* * *

"Tell me, what do you do when you're a bit drunk?"

"Wait until it wears off."

"And in the meantime?"

"Nothing. You just try and stop your head from going where the wine wants it to go."

Lucita dug her hands into the ground, and with her arms stiff behind her, tilted her neck and hair backwards.

"But you feel very good . . . " she said slowly, closing her lids.

She lifted her body upright again and added: "I don't want it to pass off. I feel very good . . . What about you?"

"Me too."

Lucita tilted her head to the side, bringing her eyes close to Tito's, as if looking for them in the half darkness.

"I can hardly see you, honey, I'm so seasick."

"Don't move about so much then, if you're seasick. The less you shake the wine about the better."

"All right, I'll keep still a bit." She turned her gaze back to the river and the trees. "It's almost completely dark."

"Yes, almost."

Then she looked behind her.

"Can't see Daniel. No signs of life. He must be sleeping like a log."

"He's well away by now, most probably."

"Do you think so? He's certainly taken enough for it to last a good time. No fear of his waking up. It's funny."

"He's full. He's taken almost as much as the two of us put together. Being between us, he took a swig each time it passed him. That's how it happened."

"Poor chap. We've only drunk half as much, so here we are, floating on air. Only it's like when you're aboard ship, isn't it? And the swell, can't you feel the swell?" she laughed. "Just imagine that we're together in a boat. That would be fun now. You'd be doing the rowing; the sea's very rough, very rough. It's a terrible night. We strain our eyes but still we can't see the shore. I'm very frightened, and then you . . . I'm talking nonsense, awful nonsense. I bet you're laughing at me. I'm talking awful nonsense, aren't I, Tito?"

"No, honey. It's funny, what you were saying, not nonsense at all."

"Don't you think I'm an idiot? You must think I'm like a child, who imagines she's riding on horseback, and thinks up all sorts of adventures. I bet that's just what you think. You do, don't you? I seem quite crazy, don't I?"

"Stop it now! Say whatever you like, girl. It doesn't matter. Wine makes everybody invent stories. Why do you go on worrying about it?"

"But I was talking about me. Forget all about the wine. I mean me, me myself."

"What about you?"

"Me as I am. I mean what do you think about me?"

"Eh? I shouldn't be here with you if I didn't find you nice. But you oughtn't to ask things like that. You care too much about people's opinion of you."

"Not everybody's. But all right, it's silly of me. Why should I care? It's a question of taste: fair or dark . . . When I want to laugh, I laugh. I've got a wardrobe with a mirror in my room. What do you think? . . . It's not really your opinion I want. As for being what I am, I know what I am . . . I'm half-tight, Tito."

"All right. Lie down for a bit then and rest."

"Yes, Tito, thank you." She lay back on the ground. "You won't take any notice of the things I say, will you? It's almost none of it true. I try and talk straight, but the thread of what I'm saying get's twisted. I'm giving you a fine performance!" She smiled. "But all right, it doesn't matter so long as we enjoy it. But it's all rubbish, isn't it? What do you think about it?"

"Nothing, honey, I think you're terrific this evening."

"We're in luck, that's good. Except that now I don't seem to be in a boat but on a horse in a merry-go-round."

She laid her head on a pile of clothes and turned over on her side.

"Now it's getting really dark," she added. "Night's come right down." From the ground she could see the other bank, the flat hill in the distance and the black ravines, in which the shadows grew and from which they spread, invading the land and climbing the hills bush by bush, until everything was completely dark. A grey, impalpable, feline darkness, in which wild animals seemed to be lying in wait. They began to fear the slash of concealed claws, of talons and lurking jaws. A voracious and bloody night that had scented defenceless coveys: a black field in which the cyclops eye of a train shone like the eye of a wild beast.

"Come on, tell me something."

There were still groups of people among the trees; the soft music of a harmonica could be heard in the darkness. It was a march they were playing, a German march of the Nazi epoch.

"Come on, tell me something, Tito."

"What do you want me to tell you?"

"Just something, anything that comes into your head. It doesn't matter if it's not true. Anything so long as it's interesting."

"Interesting? What an idea! I can't tell stories. But what kind of thing? Tell me what kind of thing you find interesting."

"An adventure story, for instance, or one about love."

"Ooh, love!" He smiled and wagged his finger at her. "Now you're talking! What sort of love? There are plenty of different kinds of love."

"Any kind you like. So long as it's exciting."

"But I'm no good at telling romantic stories, girl. Where do you expect me to get them from? If you want that, you'd better buy a novel."

"Novels. I'm fed up with novels, Tito. Don't talk to me about novels, I've read too many. But what's that got to do with it? What I want you to do is to tell me an exciting story now, here, at this moment."

Tito was sitting with his back against the tree. He looked at the ground, at Lucita's body lying to the left of him. He could scarcely distinguish the white of her shoulders from the black wool of her swimsuit or the arms clasped behind her neck.

"And do you expect me to tell you something that isn't in any novel?" he asked. "That's asking something. So you reckon I've got more imagination than the people who write them, eh? If I had I shouldn't be selling goods in a shop, believe me."

"I only wanted to get you talking. It doesn't matter. Don't tell me a story. Because they're all the same when it comes to it. Novelists don't bother themselves any more than anybody else. Sometimes they make her fair and him dark, and sometimes she's dark and he's fair. That's almost all the variety there is . . ."

Tito laughed. "No redheads? Don't they ever have redheads?"

"Don't be ridiculous. Imagine a novel whose hero has red hair. That would be dreadful. But if she had red hair, it might be all right."

"It's a very nice colour," he said, laughing again. "Carroty hair!"

"Yes, but don't laugh. Stop laughing. Stop it, I said. Now listen a minute. Will you listen to me?"

"But don't you like it if I laugh, honey?"

Lucita sat up. She was still very close to Tito.

"No, it's not that," she said. "You've done enough laughing. Now let's have a change. I didn't want to interrupt you. I only wanted to have a change. Let's talk about something else."

"About what?"

"I don't know. Something else, Tito, whatever else comes into our heads, anything you like. But leave me a bit of tree, do, so that I can lean back too. No, don't move away. There's room for two, room for us both. I only want a little room."

She leaned against the tree on Tito's left, her shoulder touching his.

"Are you comfortable like that?" he asked.

"Yes, Tito, very comfortable. I think I felt more seasick when I was lying down. It's much better like this." She tapped his arm gently several times. "Hello!"

Tito turned round. "What is it?"

"I was saying good evening . . . Here I am."

"I can see you."

"Yes, and you haven't told me anything, Tito. No one would believe you were that sort, really. You haven't been able to tell me a single tale, and I haven't had a thing to listen to. I love listening to tales that go on and on. Men always tell very long stories. I envy men for telling such good stories. But not you, of course. Oh, but I do though. Because I believe you know how to tell marvellous stories when you want to. I can tell it from your voice."

"What are you talking about?"

"You've got the voice for it. You've got the voice of a man who tells long stories. You've got a very nice voice. Even if you were to talk Chinese and I didn't understand a word, I should love to hear you telling a story. Really I should."

"You do say some very funny things, Lucita." He looked at her with a smile.

"Funny? Well, if you say so . . . I feel very funny this evening, and everything around me looks funny. So I'm not surprised if what I say's funny too. Everybody does as best they can, don't you think? And I'm doing what I can with this merry-go-round going round in my head . . ."

"You're doing very well, you know. You're very brilliant this evening."

"This evening? Yes, of course, being half-tight – temporary charm. When the drink passes, the charm's departed. Once the drink's gone, we're back where we were, no doubt about that. Oh, Tito, I do feel seasick! Of course it's only the merry-go-round starting up again. What were we saying just now . . . It's dreadful the way it goes round. Oh, I suddenly feel so giddy!"

"Very bad?" Tito had leaned over towards her and clasped her round the back. His arm was on her shoulders. "Now come and lean against me."

"No, no, leave me alone, Tito. It's going off. It's going off quite quickly. Don't bother. It's like the waves. It comes and goes, comes and goes . . ."

"Sit up, girl. Don't worry about me. Come on."

"Let me alone. I'm all right here. It's going off on its own. Why do you bother me? I'm all right as I am . . .!"

She put her hands over her eyes and forehead.

"I was only suggesting it for your own good," Tito said. "Nothing to get cross about, Lucita. Come on, is the seasickness wearing off yet? Would you like me to wet your handkerchief in the river? Would that help? Shall I go?"

Lucita shook her head.

"All right. Just as you like. Do you feel better?"

She said nothing, but turned her head and rubbed her cheek against his caressing hand, like a cat. Then she slid her face all the way up Tito's arm and buried it in his neck. She pressed her face against his chest, put both her arms round his neck and made him kiss her.

"Aren't I a naughty girl, Tito? You must think I'm brazen. I'm sure you do."

"Don't ask questions."

"But after all, what were you asking for? You said: 'Lean against me,' and you said it again just now. Well, you see? You know how I am tonight. Well, here I am leaning against you, and you see what happens . . . What did you want to do to me? Tell me now."

They kissed again. Then suddenly Lucita wrenched herself free, pushed him violently away and fell on the ground. She began to cry.

"But, Lucita, what's the matter now? What's suddenly come over you?"

Her face was hidden in her hands. Tito had leaned over her and taken her by the shoulder. He tried to uncover her face.

"Go away! Leave me alone! Leave me alone!"

"Tell me what's the matter, girl. What's wrong with you. What's come over you so suddenly?"

"Leave me alone. It's not your fault. You didn't do anything wrong. It was me. It was me that started all this. I'm the only one to blame. I behaved like a fool, like a fool." Her voice sounded fierce between her sobs.

"But I don't understand you, girl. What's all this about being a fool. What's that got to do with it?"

"Do you want me to be more of a fool? Do you think I don't know what you think of me?..." Her words were punctuated by tears. "Of course I know. Oh, I'm so ashamed of myself, so terribly ashamed. Forget all about it, Tito, please do ... I should like to disappear, I should like to sink through the ground..."

She said no more, but went on sobbing, lying on her breast with her face hidden in the ground. Tito said nothing, but kept one hand on her shoulder.

★ ★ ★

"Floating? Yes, that's the word they use in Morocco. It means not exactly drunk. It's different from that. How can I describe it? You see ..."

"Drowsy you mean?"

"Something like that, but that isn't it either. Wait a minute. It's more like being concentrated, you see? Taken up and steeped in yourself, that's it, steeped in your own being. We used to make long speeches – Samuel will tell you about them – when we were recruits, he and me and a lot of other fellows. We used to meet at a café ..."

"In Morocco?"

"Yes, at Larache. We used to talk. I can't tell you what a lot of stuff we talked! There's one thing about it, you know. You start talking, and you get excited all on your own about this, that, or the other. Once you're off, then you're well away, and before you know where you are you've been holding forth for half an hour, an hour, or even two hours on end. That's what people call floating, floating on marijuana. It's very peaceful, you understand, like a drunk but in a peaceful, pleasant way, that's to say just the opposite of a drunk, of having a binge on wine. Because over there, you know, the Moors have to do without alcohol on account of their religion."

"Yes, I know that. I've heard about that."

"Well, that's how it is. So their form of drunk is to float off, that's what they do. A few of them gather together, they sit in a circle on their mats, and there you are. One pipe of marijuana after another, and they drink tea and more tea, smoking all the time, and gossiping. The way they talk, you can't understand a word they say; the women are shut up at home, and then they haven't another thought in the world. That's the kind of night out they go in for; it's a usual thing with the Moors. That's why in the end half of them don't work, you know. Because it's the same as with everything else. If you indulge in it too much it attacks the brain. The smoke's very powerful, you see. So some of them become complete nervous wrecks, and suffer from delusions, and crazy things like that. And over there, you know, they look on a lunatic as holy. That's the way in Morocco. If a man's off his nut they're very respectful to him, girl. They let him do any stupid thing that comes into his head. It doesn't matter how crazily he behaves, no one dares call attention to it or do anything to stop him. They treat him just like a saint. Things like that are different in different countries, of course, and the view of life they have there. Whatever country you go to you find the people reasoning in their own peculiar way."

"Well, you be careful of yourself, anyhow, and don't indulge in this stuff too much. Because we don't call nut-cases holy men here like they do there. Here we put you away good and quick the first time your mind gives way. We give you a comfortable room in a madhouse whether you like it or not. You can make any complaints you like afterwards, but they won't take much notice of you."

"Don't you worry about that. It'd be a splendid way of getting your food without having to work for it. And it would be fun too."

"Try it as an amusement, and you'll see."

"Tell me, Mely, would you be sorry if they shut me up?"

"Me? I should be as sorry for you as for anybody else."

"Oh, that's not much! I shan't play, it's not worth it. Only as sorry as you'd be for anybody else?"

"What do you expect me to say?"

"The truth."

"And what would you like it to be?"

"Do you really want to know?"

"Answer me."

"A little interest does cheer a man up, darling."

"Why? What good would it be to you?"

"It's pleasant, if it's no more than that."

"I understand."

"Don't talk like that Mely, please."

"Like what?"

"In that silly way you do sometimes."

"Oh, so I'm silly, am I? Thanks for the compliment."

"You see? That's what I mean. You're doing it again. What do you think you gain by your nasty, stuck-up tone? Tell me that now."

"Charming as ever, Zacarías!"

"Who began it? All of a sudden you start on me in that nagging voice. Or perhaps I'm imagining it?"

"What a tactful fellow you are! Do you take me for a radio set, with adjustable tone to suit the listener?"

"No, but you'll be sorry in the end, I can tell you. Just go on. You're a spiteful little devil, but the day I get you you'll pay for it, I promise you."

"Are you serious? You make me laugh."

"You can laugh. But just wait till I catch you one of these days."

"Catch me today. What would you do to me, I should like to know."

"Nothing."

"Come on, tell me. What would you do to me? Do I make you so furious?"

"Yes, I could tear you to pieces. If you're trying to infuriate me, you're going about it the right way. You'll see just how furious I can be, the day I get my teeth into you – that's a promise. You needn't expect to be let off lightly."

"Little Red Riding Hood and the Big Bad Wolf! How exciting! Go on, go on! What next? Go on with the story . . ."

"That's all. And it isn't a story either."

"What is it?"

"It's a fact."

"That's cool. So you take me for a Little Red Riding Hood?"

"No, but rather like her. Not very different. I'll find a way to get you just the same, and I'll bury my teeth in you."

"Where?"

"I don't know. Your mouth, perhaps."

"That wasn't a nice thing to say, Zacarías."

"Why? You're asking for it and the wolf's telling you. That's how I feel. Do you mind?"

"No."

"Then why don't you like me telling you?"

"I do like it. I like to hear you say it."

"You are a devil, you know."

"A devil?"

"Not a wicked devil, the other kind. Another kind of devil that I can't describe. All I can tell you is that I like that sort, I go for them."

"Don't talk so loud, or they'll hear you . . ."

"If all devils were like you, St Peter would be out of business."

"Why do you call me a devil now? I can't see the point."

"There is a point, girl. There's a point, all right."

"You rather frighten me, Zacarías. But I like being with you, you know. I wonder if it isn't because you do frighten me."

"Have a drop of wine. Where's your glass?"

"No, don't move from where you are, don't move. I don't want the others to see my face. Stay where you are."

"All right, till my elbow's worn a hole in the table. I'll stay at attention, like a soldier."

"Go on talking to me, Zacarías."

* * *

Carmen looked behind her and was suddenly frightened. Hastily she clung to Santos' side. The red moon, close, immense and newly risen above the horizon, had surprised them on the hillside, coming up behind their backs.

"What is it, darling?"

[243]

Carmen began to laugh.

"Nothing dear. Oh dear me! It was the moon. It came up so quickly, it gave me quite a shock! All of a sudden it was there, and I didn't know what it was. I can't imagine what I took it for."

"But, pet, you gave me a fright too. It was a miracle that it didn't send us both rolling down the hill."

She laughed with her face against Santos' chest.

"Just think, darling. Fancy being frightened by the moon . . . How silly! But it was there so suddenly, a huge great red thing . . ."

They both looked at it, halfway up the hill. It was climbing well above the horizon beyond the black fields, heavily raising its great red face. Carmen nestled against Santos and looked at it sideways.

"How big it is!"

"Do you know what it looks like?" said Santos.

"What?"

"A gong."

Moving her face away from Santos' shirt, she looked straight at the moon.

"Yes, you're right. It does."

"One of those copper gongs. Come on."

They reached the top of Almodóvar. It was flat as a pancake up there, and dropped away precipitously towards the plain; the top must have been about three hundred yards long and a hundred across. They went to the other side with the moon behind them, and looked down the opposite slope. They could see Madrid. A great valley of lights down below like a galaxy spread out on the earth; a lake of black oil with innumerable lighted lamps, floating and flickering on it, sending their smoke up into the night to form a diffuse halo above them. This halo hung motionless in the Madrid sky like a purple flagstone, or a roof of luminous smoke. They sat down close together on the edge of the hill, with their feet hanging over the edge. Scattered above the black countryside they saw the other smaller galaxies of nearby towns. Santos pointed them out with his finger.

"Vicálvaro's there on your right," he said. "Vallecas is the one over there . . ."

Vallecas was a little to their left, down, almost at the bottom of the hill. They were sitting two hundred and fifty or three hundred feet above it. They talked quietly without knowing why.

* * *

Paulina tapped Sebastián on the shoulder.

"Look at the moon, Sebas!"

He raised his body.

"Oh yes. It must be full."

"It is. You can tell in a moment. It's like . . . do you know the planets they show you in films about the future? That's what it's like, isn't it?"

"If you say so."

"Yes, it is. Don't you remember that film we saw together?"

"*When Worlds Collide?*"

"That's it. When New York was all swallowed in a tidal wave, you remember?"

"Yes, all fantastic nonsense. Those film people are useless."

"I like that sort of film. I enjoy them."

"Yes, I know, there's nothing but nonsense in your little head."

"All right, there isn't. But supposing we live till then, then you'll tell me."

"Live till when?"

"Oh, the future, when they have all these inventions and that sort of thing. You'll see."

"Will it be a Wednesday or a Thursday?" He laughed. "But darling, don't get so hot about it or you'll run a temperature. You certainly get good value for the eight or ten pesetas it costs to buy your ticket."

Sebas looked behind him and added: "Hadn't we better look and see what's happened to our three casualties?"

Now a reflection from the moon once more revealed the Jarama's waters in the darkness, like a shimmer of phosphorescent scales or the copper back of a fish.

"Shall we go and pay them a visit?"

"Yes, come on."

They got up. Paulina passed her hands over her legs and her swimsuit, to rub off the earth and the little stones that had stuck to her.

"What are you up to now."

"We're there."

They could hear the voices of women among the scattered shacks. Names called in drawling tones from the doorsteps of isolated habitations. Distant voices, whistles answered from roads lost in the darkness. Paulina and Sebastián sat down beside Tito and Lucita.

"We've come to join you. Tell me, where's Daniel?"

"He's completely stewed. He's lying over there, dead to the world. He's completely drunk."

"Some people like making complications. What's to be done with him when it's time to push off?"

"Nobody could possibly move him. The dawn chorus will bring him back to life tomorrow morning."

"No, Tito," said Paulina, "we can't have that. We can't leave him all night on the river. It would be a weight on our consciences."

"This time of year, in summer, you can sleep quite comfortably anywhere."

"No, forget it, he could easily catch a night-chill or worse . . ."

"Unless you send for a crane . . ."

"It isn't funny."

"Don't worry," said Tito. "We'll carry him somehow, on our shoulders if need be, like a wineskin."

"A real wineskin."

Lucita said nothing. There were still people among the trees. You could hear the quiet mumble of conversation among the groups in the darkness. You could see the burning tips of their cigarettes, like a swarm of fiery glow worms.

Somebody's foot stumbled on Daniel's huddled form. A voice said: "Sorry," and the body replied from the ground with an incomprehensible murmur. Very fine parallel streaks high above the blackness, in the narrow opening; flitting bats against the transparent night.

*　*　*

A bottle tipped over, but was caught in time to prevent it falling off the table.

"Two shots a peseta," said someone.

The wine glistened on the wood and Mariyayo channeled it with her finger to the edge of the table, to make it drip off. Fernando felt the drops falling on his sandals.

"Look out, girl, you're wetting me."

"Delighted," she said, and touched his shoulders and forehead with her wine-moist fingertips.

"Just like you. You're a real marvel . . ."

It had got dark. The Ocaña clan was on the move, gathering their things.

"Now kids, do we dance or what?" cried Lolita.

"Why don't you go and wind the thing up?"

Felipe Ocaña was standing beside his family's table. He whistled as he looked at them, twisting and clanking his keys round his first finger.

"And don't let me find anything's missing when we get home," said Petra.

"You'll miss the country," said Felipe. "You'll miss that if nothing else."

"Yes, you're right there. I'll miss it and gladly. The day here is something I wouldn't have minded missing."

"The children have enjoyed it," said Felipe. "What more do you want?"

"Yes, and my husband too. I've simply mouldered in my corner, cooling my heels for everybody's else benefit."

She reinforced her words by vigorously putting one thing after another into her basket – plastic mugs, knives and serviettes.

"I promise you that," she continued. "It always has to happen to me. If a pot hits a stone, too bad for the pot. If a stone hits the pot, the pot's broken just the same. That's how it is, and that's how it's always been."

Nineta helped her gather her things.

"What a da-ay!" continued Petra. "I shan't miss the country when I'm back in Madrid, not on your life. Give it to me, Nineta, it goes here. And don't just stand there, you. What are you waiting for? You might go and give that old crate's handle a turn. You can see how late we are."

"It may be a crate, but it's our bread and butter."

"All right. I know that speech by heart. Don't let's have it again. Haven't you told us already that the lights aren't working properly. Look how dark it's got now. You know the traffic cops aren't all that kind-hearted. So if they give us a fine . . ." She put her head on one side.

"Well! You pay up and that's that!"

"Really you make me wild . . ."

"By what arithmetical rule," protested Lucas, "do I have to look after the gramophone? Have you specially appointed me to the post?"

"It's been you who wouldn't let anyone else go near it."

Zacarías waved away another lighted pipe that Samuel offered him.

Samuel prodded his fiancée with his elbow.

"Just take a squint at those two," he whispered, "and see what they're up to in the corner." He tilted his head towards Mely and Zacarías.

Marialuisa nodded.

"I told you so. Don't you remember what I told you?"

"Yes. They can't take their eyes off one another."

"I'd rather not look. Better leave them alone."

Ricardo inclined an ear.

"What are you talking about?" he whispered. "Let me hear too."

"Inquisitive," said Marialuisa. "That's our business."

"State secrets," added Samuel with a laugh.

"Rubbish, I can guess if you want to know. I know very well what you're talking about."

"Well, if you're so clever, don't ask questions, Dentifrice."

Loli, Fernando, Mariyayo and the other girl in their group were kicking up a great row to annoy Lucas, banging the wooden table with their fists and glasses, repeating: "Mu-usic! Mu-usic! Mu-usic! . . ."

Lucas put his fingers to his ears.

[248]

"If you think you're going to persuade me by raising that din," he said, "you're very much mistaken. It just makes me obstinate."

"Mu-usic! Mu-usic! Mu-usic! . . ."

The five at the other table had added their voices. Fernando had got up with a bottle and went over to pour them out a glass of wine.

"With the compliments of our lot," he said, pointing with his bottle at their own table.

The five cheered.

"Now the wine's finished," said Miguel. "We shall have to order some more."

Samuel turned to the wall and blew down his pipe to clear the bowl; a pellet of ash dropped out. The Ocañas were leaving their table and crossing the garden. Petra shepherded her flock.

"This way, children," she said. "Here's the way out. Sure we haven't left anything behind? Nineta dear, please go and look."

"That's all right."

She looked under the seats, in the corners, at the bottom of the trellis. It was almost impossible to see anything. Nineta left last.

"Off already?" exclaimed Mauricio's wife from the kitchen door.

"Yes, Faustina, we're off now," said Petra.

Faustina followed them into the bar. The men around the counter made room for them to pass.

"Well?" said Mauricio. "Well?" He came out from behind the counter.

"The time has come," said Felipe shaking his head.

"Well, you must have had a nice day," pursued the boss, and lowered his gaze to Juanito. "You're in a real mess, you are!" He looked up again. "That's the result of a day in the country."

"Perhaps you're right," said Ocaña.

Petrita had gone over to the domino players and was staring hard at the cripple.

"Thank you very much," said Petra, "for everything you've done for us." She turned to Faustina to include her in her thanks. "And you know very well, I don't have to tell you, that any day you come to Madrid . . ."

The Alcarrenian, the truck-driver, the shepherd, El Chamarís and the two butchers stood slightly apart, discreetly silent. Only Lucio from his chair took part by glancing at them in such a way as to show that he subscribed to all their politenesses.

"Everything I've done for you!" exclaimed Mauricio. "What nonsense! Why, as far as I can see I neglected you for almost the whole afternoon and evening, to look after my trade in here. But believe me, it wasn't because I wanted to. I would much rather have paid you more attention."

"Don't talk nonsense, Mauricio. You did a great deal more than was necessary. Who on earth could have expected you to neglect your customers and look after us? It's quite enough that . . ."

"Never mind," said Mauricio. "What matters is that you come again." He turned to Felipe. "I tell you, Ocaña, you must come again, you must come again. You mustn't let this summer go by without paying us another visit. And I say the same to you two. It's been a pleasure to meet you."

Nineta gave a smile of acknowledgment.

"It's mutual," said Sergio. "You're a marvellous family, and were very grateful to you for everything."

"Thank you very much. But don't mention it. You know that we're at your service here for anything you want. It's enough that you're one of the family, Felipe."

He tapped him on the arm: "It's a damned shame, man, that you came on a day when I was so busy. Otherwise we could have had a real chat."

Every now and then the players looked up from their table, without interest, at the departing guests. Only Carmelo took any notice of them, as he shuffled the dominoes on the marble. "Here, here, pay attention to what you're doing. Don't poke your nose into other people's business. Attend to the game."

"Like we did in there," said Ocaña. "You remember? When shall we get as much talking in again? Barring another accident, of course."

Mauricio laughed.

"And yet . . . And yet . . . Unless you're a rich man you have to wait for some sort of accident, or to break a bone, before you can get the full pleasure of life. That's how it is with us."

"That's the way!" broke in Petra. "You're sorry to be out of hospital now. Oh, men are all alike. Just listen to them! What a pair!"

Faustina agreed. "One's as bad as the other," she said, raising her eyebrows and shaking her head, as if to show she had great need of patience.

The two husbands exchanged glances and laughed.

"But come on, we're interrupting these two gentlemen's conversation," said Petra. "It's getting late though and we won't disturb you any longer."

"You're not disturbing us, señora," said Claudio.

Petra did not hear him but turned to Faustina.

"Well that's all. Keep well." She held out her hand. "And let's see if one of these fine days you don't decide to take a trip to Madrid."

"Oh, I don't think we shall," said Faustina, raising her eyes to heaven. "We've very much enjoyed your visit, Petra."

"Isn't your daughter about? I should be sorry not to say goodbye to her. She's such a nice girl."

"She's about somewhere. She must be in her room. I'm surprised she didn't hear you come through. I'll call her this minute."

"No, no, don't bother her, Faustina. Let her alone."

"Don't be silly," said Faustina, and called up the passage. "Justina! Justina!"

She was in the dark, lying on her bed. She could hear the voices in the garden, and the occasional tap of Marialuisa's or Samuel's hand on the glass behind her closed shutters. They were all there, making a noise outside her window; she could tell one voice from another. She could see on the ceiling, above the plaster Virgin, the little circle of yellowish light thrown up by the pool of oil of the little lamp her mother had lit for her on the Novena of the Virgin in August. It also threw a bright spot on the chromium of her bed; the reflection trembled. Outside they were calling "Music, Music!" because Lucas refused to go and wind up the gramophone. Then they said that the wine was finished, and perhaps it was her job to get up and bring them some more. She relaxed her body. She put her forearm over her closed lids so as to shut out the bright spot on the lath and the reflection on the chromium. Later she heard the Ocañas in the passage. She did not want to get up; the metal bedstead clanged as she changed her position. A dry laurel branch hung from the ceiling almost exactly above the Virgin's head. She dug her nails hard into the plaster of the wall on the left of her bed. She felt miserable and had just turned on to her right side when she heard her mother calling her. She hesitated a moment and then felt for the light switch.

"Coming, Mother!"

She quickly tidied herself before the mirror. Her eyes were still blinking at the light when she went into the bar.

"They didn't want to go, darling, without saying goodbye to you."

"Did you have a good day?" she asked them, without conviction.

"Splendid, thank you, my dear," said Ocaña.

"I'm very glad. And you, darling, won't you give me a kiss?"

The little girl looked away from the cripple and ran into Justina's arms.

"Up you go!" cried Justina lifting her into the air. "Now let's see. What did you enjoy best? Tell me what it was."

"The bunny they've got in there," said Petrita, pointing up the passage. "Is it yours, really?"

"And yours. From today on it's more yours than mine. Come here whenever you like and we'll feed it together. All right?"

"Yes." She nodded her head.

"Now get down, darling, because Father and Uncle are in a hurry and we mustn't keep them waiting." She put her back on the ground. "You'll come back another day, won't you? Give me a kiss."

She put her head down to the child's level to get her kiss. But Petrita put her arms round Justina's neck and hugged her.

"I love you very much," she said.

Felipe Ocaña was saying goodbye to the others.

"Now you know," said the truck-driver in a confidential voice, stretching out his hand, "on your own, without the family or anybody." He gave a wink. "And see if we don't have a lively day."

Ocaña agreed with a smile. "I'll think about it." He turned to the domino players.

"Goodbye, gentlemen."

"A good journey back. See you again soon."

"And listen, if your children have a fancy for another ride in my limousine, you've only got to bring them. Eh? That's what that wretched machine of mine needs, a bit of an airing, and perhaps it'll give it a different look!"

"Very well, I will," agreed Felipe, smiling wryly at Coca-Coña, and looking at Petra out of the corner of his eye.

"Well, as I said before, enjoy the rest of the evening."

"Thank you. We mean to. And the same to you. And come again, come again!"

Schneider, scarcely lifting his bottom from his chair, gave them an automatic bow of the head. As they went out Nineta exclaimed: "Oh, look at the moon, Sergio. Isn't it pretty? And isn't it big?"

There was a copper-coloured reflection on the curve of the mud-guard and on the dusty paintwork of the door.

"Pass me the things," said Ocaña, moving the back of the rear seat.

Mauricio and Justina had come out with them. The truck-driver was watching them from the lit doorway. Felipe stowed the crockery in the space behind the seat. Then the family got in.

"No rushing, children," cried Petra, "no rushing. There's room for everybody."

Justina was standing in front of the car with her arms folded.

"Wait, I must pay you for the brandy and coffees," said Felipe to Mauricio. He took out his pocket-book.

"I wouldn't hear of it."

"But that's impossible." He caught Mauricio by the sleeve. "Please tell me just what I owe you."

"Go on. Go on. Don't be so ridiculous."

"Now listen . . . We shan't come back then, you understand. Don't annoy me now, but let me pay."

"Get away with you."

Petra looked at their shadows from the car window.

"This is really too bad," she exclaimed.

Mauricio pushed Felipe towards the taxi.

"Get in now, do! You're in a hurry, and you're wasting time."

"In a hurry, my foot! This really isn't right, Mauricio."

Mauricio laughed and Petra broke in.

"No, Mauricio, it's really all wrong. My husband wants to pay you for what we ordered, and you ought, out of politeness, to let him pay. You're putting us in an awkward position for the next time we come."

"No, no. You'll have plenty of time and opportunity to stand me drinks in Madrid. Then you'll be the hosts. But I am the host here and that's that. Get in, Ocaña."

"All right. But I'll get even with you, I swear. I won't let you forget it, you see."

He got in, and Petra took her seat in front beside him. Justina had leaned her arms on the edge of the window.

"Hope you get to Madrid without trouble," she said, addressing the shadows crushed together inside. She could not see their faces.

The starter chugged. At the fourth attempt the engine started. Felipe Ocaña put out his head.

"Goodbye, you're a difficult cuss." He smiled. "You know how angry I am with you, don't you?"

"Get along with you," said Mauricio. "But off you go because it's very late.

He waved his hand beside the car windows, addressing a general farewell to those inside. The orange gleam of the lights came on, and the car began to move slowly. "Goodbye, goodbye, goodbye!" Justina removed her arms from the window and the taxi turned towards the road. Father and daughter stood motionless behind it under the splash of light that fell from the house, until the taxi gained the road, leaving behind it a trail of dust that darkened the great rising moon.

* * *

"Quiet, everybody! Listen to me for a moment! I want you to listen to me."

Fernando, standing in the middle of the garden, waved the bottle in the air, and the beam of light that fell from the kitchen lit his face and chest, glistening on the bottle also. He was shouting something at the tables in the shadow, at his friends who had resumed their cry of "Music, music!"

"What's this fellow want now, I should like to know. Be quiet and let him speak. Let's hear what it is."

"The gramophone's died of laughter, poor thing," said Ricardo, "and we've been dragging it about all the afternoon and evening!"

"And now it's passed out."

"Listen, let him say his piece!"

"Rubbish! Let's stop him talking. What d'you say?" proposed Ricardo in a whisper. "As soon as he opens his mouth, we'll shout him down."

From the shadows of the honeysuckle in the dark garden they all looked at Fernando who was exposed to the light.

Mely had just said to Zacarías: "Sundays go so fast that they're over before you notice they've begun."

"But they leave behind a taste," he had answered. "Look at the cat! Look at the cat! . . ."

They were informed of its movements in the foliage by a rustle of dry leaves. They saw its fugitive shadow stalking something among the chair legs.

"Every day's a Sunday for her."

"Or every day's a working day," Zacarías had answered. "We don't know which."

Now the two of them were watching Fernando. Fernando was losing patience.

"Now will you listen to me or not?"

"Explain yourself, Mussolini!" exclaimed Zacarías.

"Give the fellow a peseta and tell him to shut up."

He made a pretence of retiring, to avoid the light, which gleamed for a few moments on the nickel of the gramophone, across the garden.

"Don't be silly. Let the fellow say what he wants to say. Come on!"

"Let's see if the others will let him."

"What's the idea? Are you going to christen an Atlantic liner with that bottle in your hand. Let's hear what you're going to call it then?"

"What? Well perhaps we might call it S.S. Dentifrice, or The Young Ricardo. Which do you prefer?"

"It doesn't matter. Call it what you like. Any name you choose'll be enough to send it to the bottom. But come on now, let's hear your sensational news."

"If you don't mind. All I wanted to say," and he addressed them all including the five at the other table, "all I wanted to say is that we'll have to organize this madhouse a little. Because the way we've been running things so far this evening, there's been nothing but confusion all round . . . Because everybody wants something different, and none of us is getting anywhere . . ."

"Tell us the story of your life! Sit down! He's a fine one! What a speech!"

"Turn your loudspeaker off. You're being a nuisance! . . . What I was going to suggest is that we put our two tables together, and join up with this lot. They are a bit out of the picture, though they're splendid people, I'm sure. Then we shall have one table between us, and there'll only be one group to deal with, and we can do it in an orderly way, by agreement. At the same time the assembled company can be reinforced with new supplies of food and drink and both parties will get more fun. What do you say?"

"Good, I agree for our lot," said Miguel. "If they agree, each of them can pick up a chair and bring it over here, because our position is better."

"Hurray! Hurray!" cried a voice from the other side.

"So that's settled."

The five got up and brought their chairs over to Zacarías and Miguel's table. Fernando had now moved out of the light and sat down again beside Mariyayo. The square of light remained clearly defined on the ground. The five crossed it, bringing over their bags and things.

"So that was the only way he could think of to avoid a row, was it?" Ricardo grumbled.

"What are you criticizing now, Dentifrice?"

"I'm not criticizing. I'm only saying that we'd no reason to get involved with anybody. We could have had a perfectly good time on our own. This is a feeble way of doing things, just feeble. And it'll only lead to trouble."

"Come on. You needn't be so stand-offish."

"No question of being stand-offish. We don't know them. So let's leave them to themselves. Who asked you to make friends with anybody? Once you're in, you're in, you know."

There were two girls and three men. They sat down.

"Now look here," interrupted Samuel in a whisper. "The thing's done now. So you'd better shut your mouth and not interfere, or else it'll be you that starts the trouble."

"All right. Better look as if we're pleased. Or even delighted, perhaps."

"What part of Madrid do you come from?" Miguel had asked them.

"The Slaughterhouse. Legazpi. All except this fellow, I mean. Not him. He lives near Atocha. The rest of us are all from Legazpi."

"I like that district. I know a man called Eduardo from Legazpi, Eduardo Martín Gil. Heard of him?"

"Eduardo . . . Yes, I do know an Eduardo, but that can't be the one. His surname's different. He's called Eduardo all right, but the surname's different. What did you say this chap was called? Martín what?"

"Eduardo Martín Gil."

"No that's not the one, I'm sure it's not. I don't think I've ever heard of your man. I'm pretty sure I haven't. Perhaps he has." He turned to his friend. "Does the name mean anything to you? Just do a bit of thinking."

"Eduardo now," he reflected. "Yes, boy, there's that other fellow they call Dua. Isn't his name Eduardo too?"

"Yes, that's true. There's another one for you. He was christened Eduardo, you know. They call him Dua for short, either his friends, you know, or perhaps his family too. From Eduardo . . . Dua, you see how it happens."

"If it isn't that one I can't think who else it is. What's that chap's surname, do you remember?"

"Dua's surname? Just a minute. Yes, boy. Now what was it? I'll tell you in a minute. But just now on the spur of the moment I can't. Still it doesn't matter because it's not the name he said. I'm sure of that. It was something quite different. If only I could remember. If only I could remember . . ."

"All right. Don't worry yourselves," said Miguel. "It's not important. Don't strain yourself. There's no point."

"No, of course not. But if we did know another Eduardo, even if we didn't know his surname, he might very likely be the man you mean. I'm pretty sure he would be. But I'm afraid the fact is these are the only Eduardos we know. Now if it had been Pepes, there's a whole crowd of them. Every man in Legazpi is called Pepe. We're infested with them. But it's funny about this friend of yours. It's funny that we shouldn't have heard so much as his name. I'm rather surprised we don't know anything about him, especially as he's young. Tell me, are you sure he comes from Legazpi?"

"Yes, yes, quite sure. I mean unless he's moved just lately, because it must be a bit more than a year since I saw him last."

"Good. Now let's forget about these Eduardos and decide what to do. Are we dancing or aren't we?"

"Yes, darling, of course we'll dance. We've finished talking. And what about some more wine?"

"This bottle they've brought over may have some left in it. Have a look."

Miguel lifted the Legazpi group's bottle and held it in the square of light shining from the window.

"Not a drop. Not even a trace on the bottom."

"Let's order some more," said Fernando. "Clap your hands and see if anyone comes."

"Why don't you clap? Haven't you got hands?"

"Now then, Lucas. Be a good chap and put on the gramophone."

Lucas got up from his chair, with a pretence of a sigh and a resigned air, and went over to the gramophone.

"Oh that *is* hard work," observed Juanita. "To look at your face, anyone would think you were going to lift a tram back on the rails. He's so tired," she turned to Lolita, "that looking at him you wonder how he manages to go on living."

Fernando clapped his hands.

"What a clap you've got!" exclaimed Mariyayo. "I've half a mind to take you on, when it comes to waking the *sereno** in our block. He's stone deaf, poor old fellow."

"Now Lucas, do me a favour and put on the rumba," cried Marialuisa.

"Only for you? No, for everybody."

"I can't find the rumba," answered Lucas from beside the gramophone.

"Over here I can't see which I'm holding."

"Come over to the light, then, and let's have a look. It's quite a problem."

Lucas did not answer. They saw his shadow as he knelt beside the gramophone, and a series of metallic glints as he wound the handle.

"Don't interfere with him, or he may give up altogether. You know the sort of fellow he is."

"I want to dance. Why shouldn't we dance? I want to dance."

"Keep your itching feet still a moment. There's no hurry. We've plenty of time."

"No, we haven't got too much time, Samuel."

"Must we start that again?" protested Zacarías.

"Start what?"

"Talking about unpleasant subjects."

"Unpleasant subjects?"

"Yes, time, girl."

He turned back to Mely with a smile.

"Go on."

"Well, by that time it was almost half past ten, and suddenly there's a ring at the bell and it was my father. Was I frightened? Boy, I was scared out of my wits. Without a word I went to open the door. You can imagine the poker face I put on. Then we all sat down round the table; my father here, my grandmother opposite, my aunt at the other end, about as far away as that, and my brother over here, on this side. And how I prodded him with my knees under the table! But I was having kittens. Well, things went on. We started supper, and my father didn't let up for a moment. The soup was

---

* A night watchman who holds all the keys for a block and opens up for late comers.

served, and he didn't open his lips, or give any of us a look even out of the corner of his eye. The next dish was served, whatever it was that came afterwards, and it was just the same. He kept his eyes on his food. Just you imagine it. You could never call him a great talker. But generally over meals he likes to have his say, to ask questions and tell stories. He's quite a friendly person, and lively you know. You can imagine what it was like that night. Even grandmother, as I say, didn't dare utter a word. And of course she didn't know what it was all about. But she isn't such an old silly as we thought. She isn't as dumb as all that, I can tell you. Old though she is, she must suddenly have tumbled to what all the row was about. Well, to cut a long story short, it was a really frightful supper, one of those occasions when you know things might explode at any moment but you can't tell when. That's infinitely worse than the worst rocket you can possibly think of. Well there was my aunt, who loathed and hated the lot of us. She was furious and you could see she was, and she couldn't stand this either. So over the fruit she burst out – you could see she couldn't help it. She burst out and said to my father: 'Haven't you got anything to say to your children?' As if she wanted him to scold us once and for all and get it over. But all my father did was to give her a straight look. Then he got up from the table and went to bed. So that night when we went to bed as well, we still did not know what to expect, since the storm had never broken. Of course that was just what he wanted. He wasn't born yesterday, you know. In fact he couldn't have managed it better. Next day he said two or three things to us, but he didn't give us a dressing down, or anything like it. He just said two or three things seriously and without shouting or swearing, all very calmly. He was a bit more severe with my brother, but with me . . . He knew very well that the difficult moment was over. He knew that all right. And that was all . . ."

Zacarías smiled.

"So you pay the *sereno* as much as that, do you?" Fernando had asked Mariyayo.

"Well, what else can I do?"

"Why? What keeps you out in the streets at night?"

"I work in a café, you see."

"Oh, of course. Now I understand. On the night shift. And the vampires don't eat you?"

"No, lad. Don't you worry, they don't eat me."

They had heard Fernando laugh. And Lucas had gone over to the window with the pile of gramophone records. Inside they could see the kitchen and Mauricio's wife coaxing the fire with the lid of a cardboard shoe-box. The coals crackled and flickered, bursts of sparks leaped up and dispersed. Marialuisa had gone over to join Lucas, and Faustina turned round to listen to them as they searched for the rumba record.

"My daughter's coming out in a moment if you need anything," she said.

"It's a good idea to bring a portable," one of the Legazpi girls had remarked.

"But one in better condition might have been better."

"Failing that . . ."

"The worst thing about this one is its owner, don't you think?" observed Juanita. "He seems to think he's got a treasure."

"Nobody's coming."

Fernando had clapped his hands again.

"That idea of yours about me and the *sereno* isn't so bad after all, girl. I wouldn't mind giving up three hours of my sleep every night so that you shouldn't be out alone. It's a good idea. It would be worth it just to have your company. I accept the job."

Now the music had started. Samuel had gone out to dance with the fair girl, and two of the Legazpi couples were dancing also. Then Miguel got up, and as he led Alicia out to dance he touched Zacarías on the shoulder.

"What's up? You don't seem to want to talk to anybody. There you two sit chattering and holding hands. I wonder what fairy-tales you're trying to make her swallow. It's all one big hoax, girl, and he's a terrible old liar. Take no notice of him."

Mely gave him a smile. "He's telling me about his military service."

"All right. All right. Carry on."

Afterwards, when they were dancing, Alicia scolded him. "What

[261]

do you want to interfere with them for ? Can't you see they've hit it off. Didn't you notice that ?"

"I did it on purpose, just to make them angry."

The last one of the five was still sitting at the table. He looked at Loli in the shadows. They could hear the laughter of Samuel and the fair girl, who were showing off. Ricardo sat in silence.

"This is fun, isn't it, Juani ?" said Lolita, hiding her feelings.

Juanita was just going to answer when Lucas came over from the gramophone and led her out to dance. The couple emerged from the darkness into the small rectangle of light, and returned into the darkness.

"If you haven't got a partner . . ." said the man from Legazpi to Lolita.

"What ?"

"If you'd like to dance with me, I should be very pleased."

Justina appeared in the garden.

"Yes, yes, I should love to."

"What is it you want ?"

Ricardo looked at the man from Legazpi who had caught hold of Lolita. They had begun to dance.

"Oy Fernando, they're asking what you want!"

"Oh, some wine please. Let's say two bottles."

"Got any crayfish ?" he added.

Justina looked at him. "I'll ask the chef," she answered as she went in.

"Well you asked for that," laughed Mariyayo. "That'll teach you a lesson."

The dancers cheered. Suddenly the whole garden had been lit up. The light caught Ricardo's bitter expression, Mariyayo's laughing mouth, Zacarías and Mely very close together and half-covered by vine. The light came from a bulb in the middle which had a white shade and hung from two tarred cables. Marialuisa's and Samuel's lips had quickly sprung apart. You could see the dust kicked up by the dancers' feet, and the yellow blouse of one of the Legazpi girls, the empty tables, the paper on the ground, the bicycles piled against the wall at the back and the dented lips of the bronze frog.

"What bad taste to put on the light at this moment!" said Fernando with a laugh. Zacarías turned towards him.

"What's wrong?" he asked.

Beside him Mely was looking into her handmirror.

"You ought to know."

"Pour us some wine, please."

"Just a minute. They're bringing it."

The nasal sound of a trumpet came over from the rumba record.

★ ★ ★

"Give me two bottles, Father."

"Two? There you are. You've put on the light for those youngsters, haven't you?"

"I've just done it."

"Because if you let youngsters dance in the dark you know what happens. Besides – your mother doesn't like it, and she's right. They behave better with it on."

"They can't have been very pleased though," said Lucio.

"Well, that's their funeral. I don't want my place getting a bad reputation."

"Youth has its desires, as everyone knows," persisted Lucio.

"You can't call that disreputable. Real debauchery is another thing, and that's quite different."

Mauricio filled the two bottles.

"That's all right but not here. There are plenty of fields close by. Here you are, dear."

White Shoes came in.

"Good evening."

"But it's night now. Well, how are things?"

Justina went out through the passage, Señor Schneider raised his head from the game.

"I hope you are well, my friend?" he said, smiling at White Shoes.

"Very well, thank you, Esnáider. How's the game going?"

"It's going just as usual. Sometimes I win, sometimes I lose. Just like life."

"Yes, just like life. But less risky, don't you think?"

"Yes, that's right. That's right too. That's a great truth."

He turned back to the game. White Shoes touched the shepherd on the back.

"Well, Amalio, what about those ewes?"

"Oh, so-so. They're not very good, no." He paused for a moment and went on more emphatically: "You'd hardly expect it. How could they be good?"

"Why?"

"My boss. My boss hasn't mastered the cattle business yet. And you can't say he's learning either. I have little rows with him every day, trying to persuade him to do the right thing. But it's no good. It's like this." He struck the counter with his knuckles. "His head's made of wood."

He drank his wine. No one answered him and he went on: "Look now, these gentlemen deal with cattle," he pointed to the two butchers, "they know all about the subject, these gentlemen can tell you what's going on. Can't you now?"

He was silent again. They all looked at him as he gave his opinion.

"It's ridiculous. If a man doesn't bother to renew his herd, sooner or later the herd's done for. It's as simple as that. It's something we can all see. But it never occurs to him. 'Amalio, how bad the ewes are,' that's as far as he can go." He swallowed saliva. "But goodness me, can ewes live a hundred years? He can give them injections of vitamins or anything he likes, or put them into a sanatorium if there are sanatoriums for sheep. When a sheep's done for and loses its teeth, that sheep dies and you can't stop it. It's no good hoping it won't. No good at all, eh?"

White Shoes absentmindedly agreed.

"Yes, yes, that's a fact.'

"Stands to reason," concluded the shepherd.

"He's just like my father, God rest his soul," said the Alcarrenian, "the same case. In his old age he went on saying: 'I don't feel well, I don't feel well.' And how could he feel well or anything like it. What was wrong with him was only that his turn was coming, just from old age. It would have been odd otherwise, and then he'd have had something to think about. Sometimes I wanted to say to him, you know, not disrespectfully, of course, but with all due respect, I wanted to say to him: 'You're old, Father, that's what you are. No reason to look for any other reasons, you're as old as Methuselah, and even older. Perhaps you'll understand one day that it's like that. You're not ill or anything, but you're approaching your end and that's that.' Poor old chap, he couldn't understand that things come to an end of their own accord, and that you don't look for any other reasons or far-fetched explanations. Human beings wear out bit by bit like everything else, and there comes a moment when they're finished. They can't go on, can't go on. There's no mystery about that, is there? When the mainspring of a watch breaks and the watch stops, nobody thinks of saying that it's met with a misfortune, do they? Same with my father, same with this gentleman and his sheep that Amalio's been telling us about. Just the same. None of us realize the difference between illness and old age."

"You're quite right," agreed the shepherd. "It's just wear and tear. Everything suffers from wear and tear, especially sheep. If a sheep's teeth are worn out, tell me what it's going to eat. Are you going to put it on slops?"

"We all know what's the matter with your boss," said Claudio. "No doubt about that. He's got a tight feeling up here." He touched his chest. "Just meanness and nothing else. That's why he doesn't do things the proper way."

"Now just a minute," interrupted the Alcarrenian, with a scolding laugh. "What right have you got to say things like this in Amalio's presence? You shouldn't show disrespect for a master in front of his servant."

"Servant my foot!" exclaimed the shepherd. "Everybody has to accept the truth when he hears it. Señor Claudio is talking Gospel truth, God's blessed truth, and I'd be the first to agree with every word of it."

"All right then. I shall go and tell Don Emilio that you call him mean behind his back instead of defending him as you ought to. Yes, I've a good mind to go and tell him."

"But that wouldn't alter the facts."

"That man has no cause to be mean, with all his money," interrupted El Chamarís.

"Being close-fisted doesn't depend on having or not having money, but on what sort of man you are."

White Shoes was listening in silence.

"I wish we had as much, all of us put together, as he has on his own," remarked the Alcarrenian. "And he doesn't know how to enjoy it."

"Money doesn't make a man happy," said El Chamarís.

"It can. But not so much if a man's mean."

"Yes, money does bring happiness," said Lucio. "I really believe it brings happiness. What happens is that conscience takes it away."

"What conscience?" asked the truck-driver. "Does anybody bother to have a conscience when he has a good sheaf of notes in the bank?"

"Yes, of course everyone's got a conscience," said Lucio. "Well concealed, but they've got it all the same even though it works against them. It's like a worm hidden inside an apple.

White Shoes nodded and said: "You've said it. You're right. A conscience is a little worm that creeps into everything. A nasty little creature."

He emptied the glass. Mauricio was listening, with his arms folded on his chest, and his back against the shelves. The short butcher went over absentmindedly to the domino table. He was staring at Carmelo's bent back. Carmelo was entirely absorbed in the game. With a wave of his hand the little butcher dislodged Carmelo's peaked cap from the back of the chair on which it hung. It fell on the floor, and he returned quickly to the others. But Carmelo noticed it and said: "No good hiding your hand, you know, I saw you. So don't let's have any jokes." He picked up his cap. "It's not on my own account, or for what the cap's worth," he cleaned the dirty cloth lovingly, wiping it with his sleeve to remove the dust. "It's not because it annoys me at all, for any value the cap has got, but for what it represents. You must respect the Town Hall. You mustn't make fun of the Town Hall.

He replaced the cap on the chair, and was once more absorbed in the game.

* * *

There were some very high steel pylons in the sky above Vicálvaro with white and red lamps at the top, which floated like Bengal-lights in the empty night. Behind them the sky was opaque and black. Only the brightest stars could stand up to the moonlight. The heavy smell of summer, the constant thrumming of the cicadas lay thick in the blackness of the warm furrows. Quite close was a rectangular stone which marked the measured summit of Almodóvar.

* * *

Tito lit Sebas' cigarette, then his own. He took a quick glance at Lucita in the light of the flame. He blew out the match and sat down beside her again.

"What's the matter, Luci?" asked Paulina.

"Nothing. Why?"

"You're not talking."

"I feel sick."

"But you *will* drink . . . Why don't you lie down a minute? Lie down, do!"

"Leave the girl alone," said Sebas.

Downstream in the Jarama valley could be seen the broad fields lying like clouds in the dim light of the moon. Further away were the outlines of successive hills, hunched backs or spines covered with an eerie whiteness like snow. They stood out against the night like receding groups of wandering beasts, the giant rams of a fabulous herd. Tito put one hand on the back of Lucita's neck.

"Do you feel better?" he whispered.

"I'll survive," she answered in a weary voice.

She changed her position. She looked down stream, between the trees, at the water imprisoned by the dam, at the reflected light from the bulbs hanging above the *merenderos*, and the enormous shadow of somebody who had appeared on the dam. The dam itself was out of sight, hidden on the right by the lip of the bank, and so were the

[267]

crowded terraces and the light bulbs dancing on their cables under the great tree. Only the shadows were visible and the reflections of the lights in the water. But the din could be heard – the shouts of the revellers and the incessant music of the radios, and the roar of the sluice downstream under the trees and facing the point of the island.

Then the staring white eye of a train appeared on the farther side of the flats. It approached, running noisily and blowing its whistle, along the straight embankment that crossed the stubble fields. It came on to the bridge over the Jarama, surprising some couples, whose figures appeared for an instant, in the blinding light. Then it disappeared almost instantaneously behind the houses on the right bank in the direction of the level-crossing, the station of Coslada and San Fernando de Henares. Lucita shuddered and passed her hands over her arms and shoulders.

"I'm all uncomfortable, Tito . . . I hate all this dust over me. There's such a lot of earth sticking to my body. We're absolutely thick with it. It's horrible."

"The girl's right," said Sebas. "It's everywhere, even in our hair. We've been lying in it all day long. It might be an idea to have another bathe. I should like to. What do you think? What about having a swim?"

"At this time of night!" exclaimed Paulina. "You're not right in the head. I think . . ."

"It'll be marvellous. You'll see."

"I'm all for it," said Lucita. "I'll join you. It's a good idea."

"Good for Lucita! I'm all for it too. Come on, Tito, you as well. Come on, all of us."

"Not me, darling. I don't want to, really I don't. The rest of you can go, and I'll stay and mind the clothes."

"You'll be missing something."

"I still think it's ridiculous," said Paulina. "Who'd ever think of bathing as late as this?"

"We would. Isn't that enough for you? Come on, darling, come and get wet. Don't make us go down on our knees to you."

"Pull yourself together, girl," said Luci. "You'll see how good you feel afterwards. If you don't come, I shan't either. So there, you see!"

[268]

"But a very short swim, eh? Just get wet and come out again."

"Yes, of course, girl."

"What are we waiting for then? Come on. Before it's too late."

Lucita and Sebastián had got up.

"Pull me up, Sebas."

"Here I am."

He took his fiancée's hands and pulled her to her feet.

"Hurry up, because we've got to go up soon."

"Don't worry. Here, keep this for me please."

Lucita gave a leap.

"To the river! To the river!" she suddenly cried. "To the river, my children. And begone dull care!"

The others looked at her in surprise.

"What bug's biting you now, girl?" asked Paulina with a laugh. "I don't recognize you."

"Well, dear, that's the sort of girl I am. See! Crazy. All of a sudden . . . it takes me like this, you know. Down one moment, up the next. There's something to be said for it, don't you think? Come on, down to the water."

They moved off.

"Oh, you are strange tonight!"

They both laughed, Tito put on his wrist the watch that Sebastián had left him and watched their three shadows among the trees as they went off towards the river. The moon facing him across the river was red no longer. It had turned yellow above the hill of Viso in the lonely Alcalá countryside.

They came down to the river.

"It's rather frightening, don't you think?" asked Paulina at the water's edge.

"It's eerie," said Sebastián. "It's quite eerie. But there's nothing to be frightened of. Come on, girl. Don't stop now. Catch hold of my hand."

Sebas entered the river. He advanced slowly, wading through the water. He felt Paulina's hands on his shoulders, clutching him from behind.

"It looks more like ink than water to me," said she. "Don't go in far."

[269]

Lucita followed them in. She stopped a moment and looked back at the dark mass of the trees. Electric bulbs shone here and there in the night, and the light from open doors lit the river and the fields.

★   ★   ★

"So the house is rising," said Don Marcial.

Old Schneider had consulted his pocket watch. Coca asked to see it. "D'you mind?"

On its steel case was engraved the Imperial German eagle.

"That's the bicephalous eagle," explained Schneider, "the eagle with two heads. An ancient creature. Been dead a long time – pum-pum! – sportsmen have killed the poor eagle. *Getötet*." He waved his hand to signify the end and continued: "Well, time I went. Mustn't keep the old woman waiting."

Don Marcial and Carmelo also got up and went over to join the others at the counter. Coca-Coña was left alone at the domino table; he was piling the dominoes into a castle.

"What was the final result?"

"Same as usual."

"I'll just go for a moment and say goodbye to your wife," said Schneider to Mauricio.

Mauricio nodded.

"Nothing very special about the game," said the truck-driver.

Schneider went down the passage to the kitchen.

"May I come in, Señora Faustina? I'm just going home."

"Of course, Señor Esnáider. Now you know it's settled – I shall come and see her this week without fail and keep her company for an hour or so."

"I shall certainly be most grateful. She'll be very glad of your company."

"And thank you very much for the fruit, of course. Here, take the basket now. And don't you come back with any more figs or with anything else. Get this idea out of your head, see? That's settled, isn't it?"

The old man smiled as he took the basket from Faustina. The figs had been transferred to an earthenware dish which stood on a kitchen shelf, festooned with coloured papers. The noise of the garden came in through the window.

"A great number of people," said Schneider, pointing outside.

"Yes, a useless crowd. They're more trouble than they're worth."

Justina appeared.

"Give me a cloth, Mother. Hello, Señor Esnáider, good evening. They've spilled some wine on the table out there. Where's the cloth?"

"Oh, the goddess of San Fernando has come to fetch a miserable cloth! But at least I've seen my Prinzesa in the end, the prettiest Prinzesa in Spain! I shall have sweet dreams tonight. I'm sure the devils won't visit me in my sleep tonight."

Justina laughed. "Well, you do know how to pay a compliment! Nobody could resist you. Do they say things like that in Berlin? How I should enjoy just walking through the streets there."

"Ach, no. Berlin is sad, ugly, much snow in the streets. Without sun you will not see pretty girls. Only this snow that is trodden and turned all dirty like mud."

"I see you don't like it. But there must be pretty things there too. I'm sure there are. Fine monuments and palaces . . . It's just that you don't notice them any more because you've always known them. But I bet you I should be thrilled with them, whatever you say. Well, I must go now. Goodnight."

She picked up the cloth from beside the sink and went out.

"Don't you bother," they told her. "It's not worth while. One of us will be spilling some more in a minute."

"What's the time?" asked Ricardo.

"Time not to ask the time," answered Zacarías.

Fernando filled the glasses, and Justina left them.

"That's true, boy. Give a man some peace!"

"She's got a good figure, the boss's daughter," observed Mariyayo. "Like Gina Lollobrigida, don't you think?"

The rumba had stopped.

"What do you bet I get her to dance?" asked Fernando.

"I'll take you on."

"Wait till she comes out again and you'll see."

The others went back to the table. The thinnest of the Legazpi lads sat down beside Lolita, who had been dancing with him. He was wearing an army shirt.

"My life's like a film," he told her, "a comic film and a horror film all in one."

"Oh, go on with you!"

"No kidding."

Lolita laughed. The other Legazpi lad had started clapping loudly.

"Another two bottles now and put them down to us."

"But we've still got some left."

"It doesn't matter. You can't have too much."

"Why don't you sing, Miguel?"

"And tell me, what's your name?"

"Loli."

"Short for Dolores?"

Ricardo looked at them.

"No, Loli, man, Loli, for goodness' sake! Don't call me Dolores. I can't stand it. It's got a morbid sound. Troubles come of their own accord without your asking for them."

The lad from Atocha got up and went over to the chicken-run.

"There are plenty of names like that though: Dolores, Angustias, Martirio . . ."

They were singing. The light shone feebly on the cream wall of the house, on the glass of Justina's window, and on the worn bricks of the wall that surrounded Mauricio's place. The rest of the garden seemed to be abandoned and almost wild, full of dark corners choked with honeysuckle that prevented the light from penetrating. Suddenly they all looked in the same direction.

"What's that idiot up to?"

The lad from Atocha was running about the garden.

"This way," he was shouting, "this way the dogs!"

"A rabbit! A rabbit!"

The two Legazpi lads rushed up. The rabbit flashed in rapid zigzags among the legs of the chairs and tables, wildly trying to escape in any direction, and terrified by the shouts and antics of its pursuers.

"There it is, Federigo, coming your way . . ."

They shouted and laughed as they ran like madmen, and they bumped into the chair on which the gramophone stood.

"Watch out, you savages!" shouted Lucas.

They did not hear him.

"Now you'll see, we're in for trouble," said Ricardo.

The terrified rabbit was cornered, but slipped between the legs of its three pursuers. Every now and then it nosed the wire of the closed chicken-run in an endeavour to get back to its burrow.

"Don't move or it'll slip through, it'll slip through . . ."

It suddenly stopped dead; it had taken refuge under the pile of bicycles at the end of the garden.

"Quietly. It can't get away," exclaimed Federigo.

"You go this way, I'll go that. Look out, Pedro, there it is!"

They saw it white, trembling and terrified, a curled up ball of soft bristling hair, under the spokes of a wheel and the coloured skirt-guard of Lucita's bicycle.

"I can see it. Don't move, please don't move, and I've got it . . ." hissed the lad from Atocha.

He crouched down cautiously to get his hand under the wheel and catch the rabbit by its back. The others did not move. His hand reached the spot, and his fingers grasped the living ball of white fur.

"The brute," he shouted, leaping up, "the brute tried to bite me." And he pulled it out by its back paws. "I'll knock your damned head in! . . ."

He lifted the rabbit in the air before them all, and the animal struggled upside down, jerking violently. It was heavy in his hand.

"Now we shall do a conjuring trick," he said with a laugh. "A top-hat! Anyone got a top-hat?"

"You low-down bully." She went across to him. "Give me that animal."

She took the rabbit from his hands.

"You didn't have to snatch it . . ."

"Well, a lot of big boys like you . . .! What harm was the poor little creature doing you where it was? You haven't got an ounce of decency in you."

Schneider had followed Faustina and was standing in the doorway.

She clutched the creature to her breast, feeling all the frightened heat of its small muscles and the surging of its blood accelerated by fear. She went to the chicken-run and put the rabbit down; the white form slipped out of her hands and disappeared into its burrow. Then she turned to Schneider and said: "Now you see the sort of thing we have to put up with. What do you think of them, eh? A lot of ill-bred children! A cruel bunch and not a scrap of shame in any of them!"

Schneider nodded his head and turned to the lad from Atocha, who now joined the others at their table.

"This is not good. Little rabbit also God's creature. Why make her suffer? This is what we call hardheartedness." He drove home his lecture by pointing his finger at his own chest, above the heart.

"Leave them alone! Leave them alone! You're wasting your breath to no purpose. You'll never change people like that. It's no good trying!"

The German shrugged his shoulders and followed Faustina into the house. At the table they were laughing at him behind his back.

"My God, that foreigner, he's a conceited bastard!"

"I should think he is. I almost laughed in his face."

"It wasn't very nice," said Miguel. "What you were doing just now."

"I call it fooling about," said Ricardo to back him up.

"All right. Who cares what you call it?" answered Federigo, turning on him. "Keep your opinion to yourself, and we shall all be better off."

"I shan't keep it to myself, not likely! I call it playing the fool and a mean trick besides. That business with the rabbit was a mean trick."

"Now, look here, boy, whatever your name is," interrupted the lad from Atocha, "we didn't ask you for your opinion, did we? So don't start putting other people in their places, please."

"A mean trick."

The others listened in silence. Fernando laughed. "Tempers are getting a little frayed," he observed.

The lad from Atocha had got up from his chair and went over to

Ricardo. "Listen you! What are you driving at? Have you had your say? Because if you're asking for a row, just say the word and we'll be delighted to oblige."

"I don't particularly want a row with anybody. But I'll speak my mind, whether you like it or not. That business with the rabbit was a mean trick."

"You've made your point."

"So what?"

"I don't like it. But it's finished now . . ."

"Sh! Quieten down," put in Samuel. "You don't have to talk so loud to make yourself heard. Don't let's get excited."

"What is it that's finished now?"

"I've finished listening to you."

"You're wrong there."

"Now look here, just a minute. Will you let me speak for a minute . . ." cut in Zacarías' cheerful voice from the end of the table.

They all looked at him.

"As far as I can see," he went on, "now the rabbit hunt's over, you're offering us a boxing match to follow. Is that how it is? As for me, thanks for the offer but before things warm up I should like to point out that the public is more than satisfied with the performance so far, and that you needn't bother to give them their full money's worth. You are requested therefore to resume your seats and put it off for another day. We've had enough sport for now. Are we all agreed or not?"

They all laughed and shouted.

"Good for Zacarías!"

"Well said!"

The lad from Atocha sat down again beside Lolita, to whom he whispered with a tilt of his head towards Ricardo: "A bit loud-mouthed, that young friend of yours . . ."

The girl turned on him: "And you're an idiot."

Mely whispered in Zacarías ear: "You were terrific."

The others asked Miguel to sing.

★   ★   ★

Don Marcial had taken out a cream-coloured pouch and was offering round tobacco to everyone present. El Chamarís said: "We shall smoke the lot. Another round like the last and you'll have none left."

"That's what it's there for," answered Don Marcial, "to be smoked."

He put his jacket on again.

"By last thing tonight you'll be left without any. What will you do after supper?"

"All to the good. Then I shan't be tempted. The less I smoke the better for my throat."

"As for me," put in the tall butcher, "I can hold off far better when I know I've got a full pouch than when I know it's empty."

"That's true enough," agreed his colleague. "You've only got to be without tobacco to feel desperate for a smoke." He rolled a cigarette.

"Yes," said Claudio. "At least it gets me that way too. When I've got some, I leave my pouch on the table. When you know you can smoke a cigarette at any time you like, you go to bed without smoking at all, as calm as can be. But the night you've got no tobacco then you toss and turn in your bed and can't close your eyes. And there's nothing for it but to get up and make yourself some sort of cigarette even if you have to sweep the bits out of all your pockets. It's damned silly, but that's the way life is."

"The natural cussedness of all human beings," commented El Chamarís.

"You're just like my mother-in-law over your tobacco, a very similar case," said Don Marcial. "She kept a couple of pounds of rice right through the war and never used a grain, only so that she need never feel she was short and could always say to her relatives and friends that she, for one, had some rice. And when in the end she brought it out after the war was over, it was quite mouldy. What do you think of that?"

"But listen to me. That way she never missed it. Because she knew that if she didn't make a *paella* on any particular Sunday it was only because she didn't want to. Or let's say she didn't eat rice but all the same she didn't miss it," replied the tall butcher.

Carmelo's glance followed the black soul of his match mounting towards the ceiling.

"That's the great difference," broke in Lucas, "between being compelled to give something up and giving it up voluntarily, when you know that you can have it again any moment you please. That's why your mother-in-law, with her bare two pounds of rice, probably reckoned she had been eating rice right through the war. It didn't fill her belly, but it gave her almost as much satisfaction as if it had."

"Exactly," said White Shoes. "That's the whole difference between not wanting to and not being able to."

"Good lord," exclaimed the Alcarrenian with a laugh. "That takes a bit of believing. I like this idea of yours that you can live off air, or at least die happily of hunger and not feel the pangs."

"This business of wanting and being able," put in the shepherd, "varies according to people's characters. Some men when they have a hundred pesetas go straight off and spend them immediately, and others prefer to keep them and think what they could buy if they wanted to."

"That's true," said the truck-driver. "Some people enjoy keeping their money and some enjoy spending it."

"You're right," resumed the shepherd. "Some are glad because they've had a bit of a good time, and others because they think they could have a good time any moment. Now this lady or girl or whatever she was, what happened with her was . . ."

"But how could she have been a girl, you idiot?" interrupted the Alcarrenian. "Haven't you heard that she was this man's mother-in-law?"

"Well, this lady. It comes to the same thing. What happened with her was that she preferred to spend her three years thinking that she could eat a *paella*, rather than lay her hands on a couple of pounds of rice one Sunday and have one good blow-out and be done with it. And this incidentally, if you don't mind my saying so, is what I would have done in a similar situation."

Coca-Coña was thumbing through a much folded copy of *ABC* that he had taken from his pocket. He licked his thumb each time he turned over a page. Suddenly, however, he looked up and exclaimed:

"Isn't the pouch coming round to me, Marcial? Isn't it going to get as far as my station?"

"It's not that. You're being punished. You aren't big enough to smoke."

Don Marcial threw him the pouch.

"Come on, take some."

The pouch bounced like a ball off the marble and fell to the ground before Coca-Coña had time to catch it.

"Pick it up for me," he shouted.

Don Marcial went over to pick it up.

"You're more trouble than a crazy child."

"Talking of rice, it goes very well with hare," said Carmelo greedily. "With a good big hare . . ."

Nobody took any notice of him, and he turned back to contemplate the hare illustrated on the coloured print at the end of the room. The prints looked dull and faded under the yellowish light.

"With a good hare . . ."

"Some people are very peculiar," said El Chamarís. "And women are naturally keener to save than to spend. Very often they don't know themselves why they're saving something like this rice, or when they're saving it for. They do it just because they've got a mania for saving or perhaps because they think it'll be more good to them another day. They imagine that they'll get more out of things in the future than if they use them right away."

"Yes, that's what they call 'looking ahead'," said Mauricio, "and I don't deny that it has its advantages at certain times. But most often it's just stupid pig-headedness."

"There's no doubt about that."

"Ha, ha! The rows my neighbour has with his wife on that very subject," laughed the Alcarrenian. "He's rather openhanded, by the way, and likes his victuals." He pointed to his mouth – "But as for her, I believe she counts everything down to the grains of salt. You can't imagine how they quarrel. The rows they have at night are worse than the Korean War. Korea's like a game in comparison. A friendly game."

"Well I never! And so you've been listening!"

"Him?" said the shepherd. "You don't know him. His ear's always glued to the wall."

"Don't you interrupt! As if you had to put your ear to the wall! Why you could hear them in the Casino at Guadalajara."

"That's a fine one!"

The others laughed.

"Sh! It's the sober truth. I wouldn't tell you anything that wasn't."

"You're a grand mischief-maker," said the butcher. "If there's one thing you hate it's gossip."

"But in this case," said the shepherd, supporting him, "there is some ill-feeling."

The Alcarrenian looked at him with his one eye.

"Why do you say that? Where's the ill-feeling? Tell me that."

"It's as clear as daylight. No mystery about it. If you hadn't been working with him up to a little while ago . . ."

"Now what are you driving at? I've forgotten all about that. I'm not one to harbour grudges. I only mentioned him because his case is an example of what we were talking about. I could just as easily have mentioned any other. I don't waste my time on grudges. You're quite wrong there, Amalio. You don't know me at all."

"Aren't you still working in Eliseo's orchard?" asked Don Marcial.

The Alcarrenian shook his head.

"Not for about two months."

"And the reason?"

"Things."

"Did you have some differences about money?"

"No. Not that. That wasn't it. So far as money was concerned, all things considered, the man behaved very well."

"What was it then?"

"The position I occupied there. Let's say I wasn't prepared to put up with certain liberties he took with me and all that sort of thing. If you have a partner you don't treat him as a servant. As things were, I got up at daybreak and I even slept in the orchard most nights because it's a long way to go in the morning, and for whole days and weeks on end he didn't even show up. Of course he wasn't obliged to, because it was my job to do the work according to the agreement we'd made. All he provided was the land and the nitrates. But, lord! In that case a man mustn't come afterwards and criticize everything you've done in his absence. You must admit that."

"Yes, of course. In a case like that you have to have a daily discussion, and make your decisions. You have to agree on policy."

"Yes, that's just what I say. And if you want to neglect the place as he did, all right, then you must give your partner a free hand. You mustn't come afterwards complaining and criticizing a man because he did this or that, right or wrong. If you want to be lazy and do none of the work, you must just keep quiet and say nothing. You agree?

Don Marcial nodded.

"Stands to reason."

"Then there was the question of food, when my wife went off to spend six weeks in her village. Over the food it was much the same thing. It was painful to see the meals his wife produced for me at their house. I don't think the poorest labourer in the district gets anything worse brought to him in the fields. You don't ask for delicacies, naturally. But damn it, at least you expect something decent to eat."

Coca-Coña raised his head from his paper.

"Don't you take any notice of him, Marcial. He's just never satisfied, and always saying so. He's not working you up for nothing, moaning about the bad treatment he got at Eliseo's orchard. He wants to get something out of you, make no mistake about that."

"You be quiet when grown-ups are talking," said Don Marcial.

"That's right, midget," remarked the Alcarrenian, going on with his story. "Well, as I say, I didn't like sweating my guts out so that he could spend the day catching flies and then come to me and find fault whenever he felt like it. So one day we had a row, and in the course of the argument I told him a thing or two. I told him I wasn't his servant or anything of the sort. And that's how it all happened."

"It was a pity because, financially speaking, the arrangement suited you very well, didn't it?"

"Yes, and for that reason, and for that reason alone, I stuck it as long as I could. If it hadn't been for that, I wouldn't have stayed with him all that time, I can tell you. But what can't be can't be, and there comes a day when things come up to the surface whether you want them to or not. You can't help it."

"I understand. And how are things with you now?"

"Not too good, but I'm getting along."

"Find him a job, Marcial," interposed Coca-Coña. "You get him a job with your young boss. Can't you see that's what he's after with all this long story of his life?"

"Are you reading the paper or what, you little weakling? It's a good thing we know you and take no notice of you. If you had your way you'd do more harm than a pack of wild animals. Do you think that we're all as wily as you are when there's something we're after? Don Marcial here knows very well that if I wanted his help . . ."

"Now we've caught you with your trousers down! Now we've caught you," shouted Coca-Coña. "With all your excuses, all you've done is give yourself away. What do you say to that, eh?"

"He's touched the spot," laughed the shepherd and dug the Alcarrenian with his elbow.

The Alcarrenian turned to him. "Are you on the side of that filthy bastard too?" he asked.

El Chamarís and the two butchers were talking to Mauricio and the others.

"You married men are always complaining," Lucio had been saying.

"But you've only got to look at the state of a married man's clothes, at his suit for example, after he's worn it for five or six years. Why, by that time a bachelor's suit is just a rag. You can't do anything with it. It's no good even for cleaning the brass. Now what's the reason for that?"

"And his shoes," said White Shoes looking at his uppers.

"And shoes cost a small fortune today . . ."

The truck-driver laughed.

"Well, get married then," he said. "Get married, all of you, since you're so fond of clothes and shoes . . ."

Now Carmelo was listening. His ears, which protruded on either side of his face like the handles of a cooking-pot, were straining to hear what the talkers were saying. The truck-driver directed his argument to him.

"And you too, Carmelo. You're so fond of that flat cap of yours. Why not look for a good wife then to look after it and give it a brush every night?"

The truck-driver laughed, and Carmelo laughed too, his bitter-sweet eyes flashing under the peak of his cap.

"It's a veteran now," he said. "It doesn't want much looking after. But I must say a female isn't out of place in any house."

His eyes turned to the calendars.

"You're right there. You've said it. Women are a good thing," said the truck-driver. "And not just to look after a man's clothes, as Señor Lucio says."

"At my age," he smiled from where he sat, "at my age they're no good even for that. Even my clothes are past praying for now."

"But you're not so old," said El Chamarís. "Don't exaggerate."

"Not old, no I'm not old, I wouldn't say that. But I'm beginning to fall into disuse, or, let's say into decay. Sixty-one is quite an age."

"Still your trousers aren't falling down yet."

"He doesn't give them time," said Mauricio. "They never get the opportunity to fall down, don't worry about that. He sits down from morning to night. How can they fall down? When do they get a chance?"

The others laughed.

"That's the truth all right," said Claudio. "There's no danger. You never show your behind for even a second."

"For all a man has to do here . . . I'm better sitting down than on my two flat feet."

"You know best about that," said the truck-driver.

Lucio waved his hand in the air, and El Chamarís said jovially: "Your dancing days are over, aren't they, Señor Lucio?" He gave him a wink. "That's just it. They're over, and no mistake. Your dancing days, aren't they?"

Lucio looked at El Chamarís almost seriously. He nodded his head and then said slowly: "Yes, my dancing days are over. That's what many men say at my age. My dancing days are over. Damn it! I don't agree. It's ridiculous nonsense. How the devil could I agree, eh? What I say is just the opposite. I've lost what I've lost, all right. I haven't got it now, have I? But what I want is to get it back. That's the point. I want my dancing days back again. What I say is, let me have them back again. Let me have them back again."

*   *   *

They looked all round cautiously, suspicious of the darkened waters. The sounds of people nearby reached them, mingled with the sound of music.

"It isn't at all cold, is it?"

"It's absolutely lovely."

A little moonlight touched the treetops, and the hushed chatter of voices hidden in the darkness of the wood came to them from downstream. A clear and crystalline music sounded a little lower down the river. On its black mirror-like surfaces were reflected flashes of moonlight and electric light. There in the darkness they felt the river running over their skins like some huge animal that caressed them as it ran silently by. They were submerged up to the chest in its smooth flow. Paulina had caught her fiancé by the waist.

"How lovely it is to feel the water flowing past your body!"

"You see? And you didn't want to swim."

"It feels even more luscious than it did this morning."

Sebas shivered.

"Yes, but now it isn't quite the same. This morning you could stay in as long as you liked. Now you suddenly feel cold, and begin to have gooseflesh."

Paulina looked past Sebastián. Up the river was the shadow of the bridge, with its great arches in darkness. Now a ray of moonlight revealed the parapet and its bricks. Sebas had turned in the other direction. Downstream the weir roared beside the lights of the *merenderos*. Paulina turned round.

"Lucita. What are you doing out there on your own? Come over here to us. Luci!"

"But there she is. Can't you see her, there in front of you?

Lucita!" She was silent. Then in sudden fear she cried: "Lucita...!"'

They heard the weak sound of someone struggling in the water ten or fifteen yards out. They heard gasps interrupted by a bubbling sound, in the midst of which there was a sudden hiccup like a stifled cry.

"She's drowning ... Lucita's drowning ... Sebastián! Call for help, call for help!"

Sebas tried to move forward, but Paulina's nails were deep in his flesh and held him back.

"No, don't! Don't Sebastián, don't," she panted. "Not you, not you, not you ..."

The piercing cries of Sebastián and Paulina rang out again and again, shouting for help, and were magnified by the echo from the water. Shadows gathered on the bank, bustling and shouting in alarm. Not far off a little disturbance, a blind struggling and the sound of stifled throat-noises in the water, drifted slowly towards the pool. There was the splash of divers and shouts of "Where? Where?" The strokes of three or four swimmers could be heard, and voices calling from the water: "Let's keep together, Rafael. It's dangerous to go on your own!" The voices sounded very clear in the river. "This way! Higher up!" called Sebastián, and Tito could be heard shouting from the bank: "Sebastián! Sebastián!"

He had plunged into the water and was leaping towards them. Sebastián had got free from Paulina and was swimming towards the others. "Be careful! For God's sake be careful!" cried Paulina, with both her hands clutching her face. The swimmers were confused. They swam about in all directions, searching the whole black surface of the water. "Where is she? Can't you see her? Can't any of you see her?"

Tito came up to Paulina and she clutched him tightly.

"Luci's drowning!" she said.

With his whole body he felt Paulina trembling. He looked at the swimmers confusedly exploring the river this way and that. "They can't find her ..." Their shapes could be seen moving across the surface of the water. The moon lit up the crowd that lined the river bank. "Can't you find her? Last time we saw her she was just here," cried Sebastián. "Is it a girl?" "Yes." They were now a long way off in the direction of the dam, but their heads were visible above the water, five or six of them, in the light of the low moon and the reflected lamps on the bank where the music came from.

"Take me out, Tito. I'm terribly frightened. Take me to the bank."

She stood erect, stretching towards Tito as if to hoist herself out of the water. She was shivering. The arm and shoulder of one of the swimmers flashed white for a moment, downstream, in a patch of light. Tito and Paulina made for the bank, painfully overcoming the resistance of the waters. "Here! Here!" cried a voice from beside the dam. "Here she is!" He had touched her body with his arm, had struck it almost on the surface of the water.

★ ★ ★

The dull solitary voice of Miguel sang beside the wall of the house into the empty garden. The cat's eyes glistened beneath the vine. Miguel stretched his open hands towards all their faces and slightly rocked his head. "And when you never came back – the path through the wood was choked – and when you ceased to drink there – the mouth of the spring was blocked." He lifted his smiling face and looked at them all; and they applauded him.

"Sentimental!"

"Now have a little drink. To wet the vocal chords."

They heard Mariyayo laughing. Fernando had told her that she spoke like a foreigner, "An Italian, for instance, or something of that sort."

"And how do you know what Italian girls sound like?"

"I can imagine. Listening to you, I can imagine how they sound." They both laughed.

"They seem to have got very thick. Just look at them."

Ricardo's eyes were fixed on the light that hung in the centre of the garden. Hawk-moths, common moths, big dark summer moths swarmed round the bulbs. The two Legazpi girls were debating which of them had got browner.

"What's it matter?"

Zacarías leaned back beneath the vine, tipping his chair till it rested only on its two back legs. The back of his neck was deep in the leaves.

"That's not the point. It's because she's so pig-headed. Anyone can see, but she won't admit it."

"All right. Just you look at my arm beside hers, Federigo. Just you compare them."

"Don't bring me in. You're both very nice and brown."

"There now, he won't speak the truth because he doesn't want to annoy you."

"Stop it, please."

"It's her pig-headedness. I can take the rest. But it makes me furious that anyone could exist who really won't be convinced."

"Don't make such a noise about it," shouted Zacarías. "I don't want to know. Treat me like an invalid – a dying man."

Someone had asked the time. Zacarías caught Miguel's wrist and covered the face of his watch.

"You're crazy, crazy to have anything to do with these contraptions!" he said. "Nickel-plated death I call them."

"All right, Zacarías, we've heard your joke. Now will you please let go."

"You're tough on me."

"Poor fellow!"

Zacarías turned to Mely with a smile.

"This man's a real pest. What a way to live! Impossible! It must ruin your health and everything else. Stands to reason it must."

"Tell me then, are you going back by train?"

"To Madrid? Of course, by train. How else?"

"I don't know. A silly question, forget it. And you get in at . . . ?"

"Look, if you leave here at ten-thirty, add twenty minutes and it's ten-fifty. At ten-fifty then. What are you laughing at?"

"Nothing. You're very sweet – and the things you say!" She paused for a moment and looked at him with a smile, "At half past ten he says . . ."

"Come on, you've made enough fun of me. A man can't say anything without setting you off howling like a jackal, girl." He shook his head. "Just look at her splitting her sides. It doesn't take much to make her laugh."

"But, gracious me, I wasn't making fun of you, Zacarías, I give you my word I wasn't. You're absolutely wrong. It's just the careful way you said it that amused me, don't you see? I liked the way you said it . . ."

"And how did I say it? Tell me."

"Oh I don't know, really I don't. What a question to ask! You said it just the way you said it. I don't know. That's all there is to it. There's nothing to explain. I was just amused by the way you said it. I liked the way you said it. What else do you want me to say? . . . All right, now listen, there's nothing to understand. If you don't get that, you're an idiot. And don't ask me any more, because it makes me cross to get in such a muddle when I'm trying to explain something."

"Yes, I can see that. Because this explanation of yours hasn't made me any the wiser."

"There you are then. That just shows you. Besides, it's very silly because I don't know what it was all about or what I was trying to say, or anything . . ."

"All right. No reason to get cross then, is there?"

"It makes me wild."

"What does?"

"What? Oh, nothing. I don't know. How do you expect me to know? It doesn't matter any way."

"Well, tell me why you're talking in this tone."

Mely looked at him and then said, as she lowered her eyes: "I don't know, Zacarías. I'm an idiot, but I like people to be patient with me. You can understand that, can't you? I'm spoilt and I suppose . . ."

"Good, good! Now stop! Stop, honey. Don't let's have it all now, please. This is what I call stampeding a man. It's not fair! You drop from Heaven and make a man's life purgatory – no, hell. How you twist and turn, girl! And every turn you make, you leave half your tyres on the track. I'm not exaggerating, I swear."

"But it's a fact. There's nothing to argue about. It's exactly as I said . . . I get furious with myself and take it out on somebody else. That's the truth and I know it. If only you understood now . . . I'll tell you what I feel like, really. I feel like having a good cry. Why don't you slap me hard, Zacarías?"

Mariyayo had propped her elbows on the wine-stained table top.

"He's right," she had said, putting her head between her hands. "I should like to stay here, I really should. I don't know the time! Just when you're beginning to live, everything's over, whether you like it or not. It's all wrong, isn't it? But it's tomorrow already."

"Life's like that," Fernando said from behind her. "It's no good breaking your heart about it. Good times go by much more quickly than bad ones, but they're no worse for that."

Mariyayo had given him a look.

"They're good but they make you long for more. That's what they're good for."

"Yes, as you'll see next Sunday," put in Marialuisa. "Listen to me. Next Sunday we'll come here again and we'll throw one of those parties that nobody ever forgets."

"For what, girl? Will that change anything? Next Sunday will be just the same. It'll go by just as quickly as today. How could it last any longer?"

The moon appeared. It gradually climbed above the wall of the garden, peeping over like a great dead face, till all its eternal features were revealed.

"No. We can't afford to forget the time even if you can," said one of the Legazpi girls. "We've got to be punctual. Because at five past ten, you know, we shall have to pack up and go to the station."

"Come on, what's the hurry?" Federigo protested. "We don't need to stand on the station platform for twenty minutes, do we, staring at each other's faces till it's time for the train? No need to be in such a rush. If we get there early we only have to wait. Why hurry away?"

"All right, you do as you like. But this girl is leaving here at ten-five on the dot. I'm not running the risk of losing the last train, and it'll be very crowded. No doubt about that, any fool knows that."

"It wouldn't matter if you did lose it. There's another at quarter past eleven."

"That's fine. You make me laugh."

"Is it so urgent then for you to be back at a certain time?"

"You ask my father that one, and hear what he says, boy."

"The old man's strict, is he? Tough?"

"Don't know, I'm sure. Never liked to try in case there was trouble."

"Must be an old-fashioned devil. Wears a flannel vest in winter, does he?"

"I won't have you making fun of my father, do you hear?"

"I didn't say anything nasty, did I?"

"If you don't stop laughing, I'll smash this bottle over your head. Idiot!"

The moonlight slid over the faces at the end of the table which the vine had shaded from the electric bulb. Mely tipped her chair backwards till her eyes were in the shadow again. The moonlight rested just on her neck. She had hung her arm over the back of her chair, and it dangled behind. Zacarías' hand was groping in the shadow, feeling for hers among the leaves.

"They ought to arrange for some Sundays to be twice as long as weekdays," Samuel had said. "Don't you think so, Mariyayo? Don't you? Nothing will be any good until they do that."

"Or three times as long. A working day's long enough, goodness knows. Yes, if they'd do that we could get along somehow."

"You're a funny lot. You want everything."

"Not everything. Just something."

"You expect a good deal," said Fernando. "Tell me, do they give you such a bad time where you work? I thought that life must be quite fun in a bar."

"What an idea! It's may be fun seen from outside. But from inside it's real hell. It really is hell, boy. Don't you think it's an easy job."

"You don't look too bad on it!"

"I'm fed to the teeth with it. You don't know how fed up I am. But luckily I only remember days like this. I forget all about the week. That's the only way we can get along."

"If you stick to it, it must be because you want to, a pretty girl like you," said Fernando with a smile. "It wouldn't be difficult for you to catch a big shot. Then with a bit of luck and a bit of skill you'd be out of your troubles for ever. Then you'd live the life, life in a big way."

"Spare us the movie stuff, please. There's nothing like that about me, and I've no need to start looking for any big nobs, thank you."

"That was just an idea."

"Thank you. But I'm all right as I am. If you go on in that tone then we shan't stay friends for long."

"I was only joking. Really I know better. Anyone could see what you are by your face. It's like a mirror of your soul."

"That's laying it on a bit thick. I think you're exaggerating."

"Now what's the matter with you?" asked Marialuisa. "Have you stopped being friends? Come, come."

"No, of course not," replied Mariyayo. "Does a girl have to take notice of everything this man says?" She looked at Fernando with a half-smile. "It's like soap-bubbles."

"You're an angel," he said.

The others tried to persuade Lolita to come out and dance.

"It's very late."

"There's time. There's still time . . ."

"Is she a good dancer, that girl?"

"Her? She's a whirlwind. Just you watch!"

"Come on, Lolita, do! Do your act. Just the right thing to bring the curtain down! Let's see you."

"Let them hear about you in Legazpi, my girl! Come on, take the stage, and don't waste time."

"Where does she dance?"

"Just as we were running out of ideas."

They had begun to clap their hands, and Lolita finished her wine with a gulp. "Come on then, and we'll see how you like it!" With flaming cheeks she climbed on the table. Once up there she ordered them to clear the glasses and bottles. "Get all this out of the way of my feet."

"Quickly now! That's what I call a girl!"

They cleared the table. They all looked at Loli. She corrected the tempo of their clapping and tried the table with her foot.

"That's a girl. There's nobody to touch her."

Their clapping was now in time. Lolita took a glance at all their faces. She stretched out a hand to Ricardo. "Come up here too." He was unwilling.

"I hardly know . . ."

"You don't have to," insisted the girl. "Come on. Don't be silly."

"But I don't want to, darling, really. I'm dead tired for today."

"Oh, these men! So frightened of making fools of themselves!"

Now Federigo got up to offer himself as a substitute; "Will I do?" His friends pushed him up on to the table.

"Up with him."

"Our Federigo is full of energy; that's obvious."

Lolita faced Federigo, and once again corrected the rhythm of the clapping. When they were right she began to dance. A great cloud of dust flew in everyone's face when her little shoes began to strike the table top. Federigo kept time with her movements and poses. His head brushed the festoons of honeysuckle that hung from the wire, and his hair got entangled with them. Their two shadows appeared huge and broken up on the main wall of the house and on Justina's shutters, and the shadows of their heads touched the eaves. Then Lolita's shoes began to bother her and she kicked them off without interrupting her dance. One after the other, they fell into the dark garden. "The girl's marvellous!" Now she was dancing barefoot. Their clapping echoed from the walls at the end of the garden, the bronze frog, the gramophone and the empty tables. In the centre the lighted bulb and its dusty shade bounced up and down, for the electric cables swayed as the vine was shaken, and the shadows swayed and danced with it, all over the garden. Lolita's bare feet trod on the spilt wine, and her black skirts swirled and flew in all their faces. Then quickly they fell, closing round her white legs and crimson swimsuit. Suddenly her feet slipped on the slime that the dust and the spilt wine had formed on the wood, and she was thrown off the table, to fall laughing and panting, into the arms of Miguel and Zacarías. She was shouting with laughter and quite unable to get up. She said that she could not stand on her bare feet, because the pebbles on the ground would tickle the soles, and she was dying of laughter already. "It's all over now," she repeated again and again. They tried to calm her. Faustina had come out, and noticed the marks on the table.

[291]

"Look here," she said. "It's all very well making a row and having a good time, but putting your feet where other people eat their food, that's really too much. You understand! Try and behave yourselves, because this is the second time I've had to come out to you. I shall have to complain about your behaviour to my husband, I really will. But let's see if you can't behave a bit better after this. Because I've had quite enough trouble with you this evening, coming out all the time to see what childishness you're up to . . ."

She went into the house, and they commented from the table: "I could see that coming. They won't let us have a really good time. People . . . That woman is a real old misery. She's an evil-minded old bitch, I think."

"It's her own place. You've got to remember that. It is, you know, after all."

"It's a place of amusement, a place that's open to the public!"

"I want my shoes! Somebody find me my shoes," cried Lolita.

They went to look for them in the middle of the garden.

"It depends on what you mean by public. It's an adjective that doesn't fit everybody, if you know what I mean. You have to exclude some people . . . What's the matter with Loli now?"

Suddenly she had begun to cry. They could not find her second shoe.

"All right, I shall have to stay barefoot, seeing that it's lost and you're not looking for it. It's lost all right, and I shall have to go barefoot. It can't be helped. But when I get home, and when they open the door and see me . . . and my mother asks me why, what am I to tell her? A lie? Yes, but what lie? No lie will be any good. There's no way out . . . a girl doesn't wander about barefoot unless she's a bad lot . . . shoes don't just get lost."

Marialuisa held her tight and began to stroke her.

"Calm down, Lolita, they'll find it in a minute. Don't you see what a silly scene you're creating? All this weeping and speechifying, it's really silly. Don't you see it's all nonsense? Your shoe will turn up in a minute. Just you see if it doesn't . . . Darling, what a fuss you're making, just at the end of the day!"

Lolita collapsed into her friend's lap.

[292]

"It doesn't matter. I won't worry. I'll go barefoot. I don't mind a bit. I'll say to Mother: 'You can beat me, but you'll get tired first . . .' I'll tell Mother I lost my shoe dancing and playing around. 'You beat me,' I'll say, 'and I'll dance again, and I'll show my legs too. You can beat me tonight and tomorrow and the day after. You can beat me till I'm sore, and I'll dance the *zambra* tomorrow and the next day and the next day and the next. I'll go out and let the boys kiss me in the movies, and I'll just give myself a good time . . .'"

The missing shoe appeared. Lucas knelt at Lolita's feet. "Let me put your shoe on, your Ladyship," he said.

The girl looked at him. "Lucas, you're charming, thank you very much . . . But I'm like an old rag," she laughed – "really I am."

She let him put on her shoe. Then she felt bad, and Marialuisa and Juanita took her over to the hen-run to be sick.

"She had a good deal to drink, and then she started whirling round and round, the way you saw. That explains it. Imagine how that must have churned up her inside! Awful!"

On her way back to the table she tried to walk alone, pushing away the arms of the two girls who were with her.

"I still know how to walk! What do you think I am?" she said. "I can't bear having you two always coming to protect me . . . always protecting people whenever you have the slightest chance . . . you're a pest." She addressed those sitting at the table. "Yes, you're a lot of idiots, all of you. When a girl ends by being sick just because she's been dancing to amuse you, you go and treat it as a spectacle and make her as miserable as you can."

She reached the table and sat down. Then she looked at them and laughed.

"What an odd crew you are! Isn't there anybody among the whole lot of you who can think of a good way of rounding off a party?"

*   *   *

The whole crowd stood motionless on the bank, in the moonlight, with their gaze fixed on one spot in the river. They had moved downstream at the same time as the swimmers in the water, and now they were gathered beside the pool, almost at the wooded point of the island. There was nobody there when Tito and Paulina reached the shore. He found his trousers at once, picked them up, and began to run with them in his hand. They ran beside the whitish treetrunks, past the shadows of human figures who were guarding their encampments and at the same time watching what was going on by the promontory.

A little dog jumped out of the darkness to bark at Paulina as she ran, and already Tito was running about ten paces in front of her.

"Wait for me, wait for me, Tito . . ." he heard her shout breathlessly behind him.

They felt the stones and bits of stick hurting their feet. More than a hundred people cut off their view of the water, forming a barrier of black backs pressed close together in front of them. They forced their way through with their elbows, pushing their damp bodies through the tight-packed crowd. Hardly anyone said a word. Tito forced a way through in front of Paulina.

"No shoving," said somebody. "We all want to see."

Tito did not answer. He took Paulina's hand and together they reached the first line. Here the music could be heard very loud, as if filtered by the echo from the pool. A certain light came from the water itself, diffused by the bright patches thrown on its surface from the electric lights of the *merenderos*. Opposite, about fifty yards away, on the other side of the water, the edge of the concrete dyke that formed the dam could be seen faintly gleaming, like a band stretching right across the pool standing little more than span-high above the water-level. Near it the heads of three or four swimmers could now be made out. Paulina shouted after Sebastián. The noise of the sluice resounded. There was no room to move towards the promontory in front of the people along the shore. To get along, they had to wade in the water. They passed in front of all those motionless faces watching the river, which were lit by the moon and the reflected patches of light in the water. A little farther down there was a group of people around a naked man who was huddled in the sand at their feet; it was Sebastián. Paulina threw herself on her knees beside him.

"Sebastián!"

He did not answer. They could hear him panting with exhaustion.

His whole body was huddled. His arms were clasped around his legs, and his eyes and brow were tight against his knees, concealing his face. Paulina caught him by his dripping hair and lifted his head to see the face.

"Sebas," she said.

She could scarcely make out his features in the darkness. She felt the whole weight of his head in the grip of her hand, as she held it up by the hair. She saw that he was exhausted from swimming. Then she clasped his head in both her hands and pressed it to her breast. Somebody's knees stuck into Paulina's back. A thick forest of legs surrounded their two bodies like a palisade, leaving them only the narrowest space. Paulina felt her ankles caught among other people's legs, and brushed by damp feet that sank into the sand. She raised her eyes and looked up in horror at the faces of the people standing over them, surrounding them in a close semicircle that was open only towards the river. Ahead of them was Tito with his back to them and his body outlined by the reflected light on the water. Paulina buried her face in Sebastián's neck and pressed herself against him. Now the music had stopped, and many people from the *merenderos* were crowding to the pool. Their silhouettes could be seen in front of them all along the water. To the right, long shadows, cast from the embankment itself, obscured the reflections in the river. Paulina felt someone's fingers touching her back. She raised her head. A woman asked her, pointing to the river: "A relation of yours?"

She could not make out the woman's face.

"She was one of our party."

The woman raised her chin, gasped, and then gazed once more at the river. Now apparently, they were closing the sluices opposite; the noise of the water diminished and then stopped completely. Everything was silent, and you could hear the people whispering. Somebody explained that it would have been dangerous if they had not closed the sluice because the current might drag at the swimmers and prevent their bringing the body to the bank. Suddenly Paulina felt a general impulse around her, and the whole forest of legs began to move. "There! Over there! They're bringing her out!" They could not get up, but were suddenly bowled over by the sudden and unexpected rush towards the promontory. People trampled on their hands and their feet, or jumped over them, raising spurts of sand. Tito was calling them from the crowd. Finally they succeeded in getting up and ran with the others. Now they had brought the body into shallow water. Five or six men were carrying it, pushing it along the surface like a boat that is being floated to the shore. The noise of people talking grew louder, and the three friends once more tried to edge their way through the crowd. Everybody was gathered on the point itself. Now they could get a direct view of the lighted *merenderos* to the right of the pool, on the other side of the backwater, which was spanned by the little plank bridge. Many forms could be seen outlined along the bank, and some people were apparently hurrying across to the trees, for the rotten planks of the bridge could be heard creaking under the hurried feet. Suddenly most of the voices fell silent; there was a great silence as the body was gradually brought ashore. Everyone could distinctly hear a weary voice saying: "Just lift the arm a bit, Rafael."

Under the immediate light from the *merenderos*, the clay colour of the waters could be distinguished again; they were the same orange as they had been by day. "Oh my God, how dreadful!" sighed a woman. Paulina clung to Sebastián's side. She looked back for a moment, gripped by fear. Behind, the trees were in shadow, the encampments in silence, and further still the peaceful light of the moon struck the bricks of the bridge. Very far away a man was riding a horse on the edge of the railway track, along the top of the embankment that crossed the stubble fields. A quiet "Make way there!" was heard, and the two black three-cornered hats of Civil Guards caught the light, as they forced their way through the crowd. Lucita's body was lying there on the sand.

They were listening for her heart. Boys and girls of various ages occupied the front position in the thick semicircle of spectators. Their eyes were fixed immovably on the bare flesh of the dead girl. Her face was hidden in the shadow of her hair, and her cheek was on the sand.

"Don't shove, you!" said one of the boys.

"But they're pushing me . . ."

They retreated again as far as they could, their backs to the crowd, as if afraid of crossing an invisible line on the ground that perhaps formed the border of the dead girl's territory.

The Guards penetrated the circle and cast a quick glance at the body.

"Isn't anybody doing anything?" the older Guard quickly asked the swimmer who had previously been addressed as Rafael.

Another figure, who was bent over the body, sprang up, tossing the damp hair back from his forehead.

"I'm a medical student," he said panting. "There's nothing to be done."

"Oh," said the Civil Guard.

He looked at the corpse once more, removing his hat and shaking his head.

"A bad business," he said reflectively. "Quite a kid. Terrible shock for her parents."

Tito stood there, with his arms hanging limp. Beside him was Paulina, who cast sidelong glances at Lucita but would not face her directly. She had one hand on Sebastián's arm.

"Anybody know her?" asked the Guard, loudly addressing the crowd and putting his hat on again.

After a few minutes of silence, he heard close beside him: "We do."

"You two?"

"We three. Him too."

The Guard looked at Tito, who pointed automatically at his own chest.

"She came here with you, eh?"

"Yes, sir."

"Fiancée? Sister?"

They shook their heads.

"Just a friend?" concluded the same Guard with a wave of the hand.

"Yes, sir." said Sebas.

Paulina began to tremble and to weep loudly and convulsively against Sebas' chest. All the crowd ceased their whispering, the better to hear the sobbing in the silence, and heads peered one above another to see who it was that was weeping. The swimmers looked towards the sand. The old Guard sighed.

"Some things . . ."

The other Guard stared at Luci's left hand which lay half open and palm upwards on the ground, and brushed her fingers with the toe of his boot.

The old one changed his tone. "Now listen to me, you three. None of you is to leave this spot, see."

He turned to the swimmers. "Now then, you and the other young man, the one who says he is studying to be a doctor, you will stay here too, if you please. Also . . . there was someone else who said something" – he looked from end to end of the crowd. "That's it now. You two. Or rather you four. That'll be enough. I shall require you to make a sworn declaration before the judicial authority."

Then he quickly turned to the crowd and said, raising his voice: "The rest will kindly retire! Everyone will please go back to where they came from in an orderly fashion, with the exception of those whose services are required. Move off, if you please. Will everyone go back . . ."

He clapped twice, and the young Guard began to move forward to help him.

"Move along. Move along. Get moving . . ."

He set them in motion, touching some of them on the shoulder.

"All right, I'm going. You don't have to push me."

"Come on, hurry up . . ."

Now the crowd was small. There were not more than forty in the end, retreating towards the darkness of the trees. Nine persons – the two Guards, the group of four swimmers, Tito, Paulina and Sebastián – remained on the bank beside Luci's body, beneath the direct light from the *merenderos* which struck them after crossing a short stretch of shining water. Their half-naked bodies, still wet, stood out white on the side where the light struck them and black on the other side. Only six or seven figures could still be seen on the bank. The old Guard looked at Tito and Sebastián's bodies and said: "Now listen to me. One of you can break off from each group, to pick up the clothes, his own and his companions', so that you can all get dressed."

One of the four who had dragged Lucita from the river looked at the soaking trousers sticking to his legs.

"And whichever one of you goes," added the old Guard, addressing Sebastián, "can make it his business to bring the effects of the deceased at the same time. Understand?"

Now Paulina had collapsed exhausted and was sitting on the sand. She was still weeping, though more softly, leaning her hands and forehead against Sebastián's knee. They had reopened the sluice, and now the water was roaring again. A very shrill voice sounded from the darkness of the trees, calling Tito and Lucita. It was Daniel; his shadow could be seen emerging from the trees. Now he was running up. He stopped, shocked, in front of the corpse.

"It's Luci," he murmured.

Then he raised his head and saw Tito.

"Tito!"

Tito came out to meet Daniel and threw his arms round his neck.

"It's terrible, Daniel. It's terrible!"

He rubbed his eyes against Daniel's shoulder and groaned with distress.

"Did this have to happen? . . . Just now there were three of us here, Daniel, and look what hit us. It's damnable. And now her mother . . . What are we to say to her mother? What are we to say to her mother, Daniel? . . ."

Daniel looked at Luci's body over his friend's shoulder. He said nothing. Once again Paulina could be heard crying. The old Guard got up and dragged Tito away from Daniel's shoulder.

"Come on, calm down, lad. Accidents happen. You have to take them like a man. Calm down, both of you, and fetch the clothes. Get a move on or you'll both catch a chill, and there's no need for anyone to catch bronchial pneumonia. Get moving. And come back at once, don't hang around."

Tito turned his face to the shadows and wiped himself down with his hands. Then the two of them went off. Rafael joined them on the road and walked in silence beside Daniel. Now there could have been no one left in the wood; they heard no voices. It was very dark among the trees. Suddenly a human shadow moved among the tree-trunks. "Hi, is that you?" called a voice.

"Yes, Josemari, it's me," answered Rafael. "This is my pal. If you need any help call on us."

"Thank you," said Daniel. "We'll manage."

"Just as you like."

Rafael stopped beside the other man. Tito and Daniel went on.

"What happened?" Josemari asked his friend.

"We brought her out dead."

"I'd heard that. And who are these two?"

"We've got to pick up all our things and take them down there."

"Tell me, who are these two?"

"Those two? Oh, they came with the girl that was drowned. They're completely shattered."

"Yes, I can imagine that. And how did the thing happen?"

"Look, ask me that later on. Now we've got to pick up our things and take them all down there."

"Everything? But why? Can't they come up?"

"No, they can't. Of course they can't. Don't you understand that the Civil Guards have called on us four to make a sworn statement?"

"You might have said so. How can I know if you don't explain? Fine kettle of fish. It'll take quite a time to go through all their formalities."

"I suppose so."

They reached their encampment.

"I say, they'll at least let us telephone home, won't they?"

"Yes, I expect they will. But come on, Josemari, let's pick up our things."

Tito and Daniel did not reach their picnicking place at once. They lost their way in the dark. Then Tito's feet struck something lying on the ground. He looked and recognized the dull shine of a food tin.

"Here's the place."

He leaned against the tree where they had all three stood that afternoon, and slid slowly to the ground.

"What are you doing, man?"

Tito was lying on his stomach and had buried his face in a pile of clothes.

"Come on. You're not starting again? Come on now, get up."

"I can't do any more, Daniel, I swear, I swear to you I can't. I'm absolutely done in . . ."

Daniel had stooped down and clasped him by the shoulder.

"Come on, you've got to. There's nothing else you can do. And what do you suppose the rest of us feel like?"

"The rest of you! But you don't know! You don't know! You don't know at all! You don't know anything about it! . . . I'll never come back here again, never, never, so long as I live, I swear I won't. Never so long as I live will I come back and swim in this damned river! I shall hate it to my dying day! You understand me, Daniel, don't you. Not if I live a hundred years! . . ."

He thrust his face into the pile of clothes, and his voice was muffled.

As Tito and Daniel were departing the old Guard had said to his companion: "Listen now. First I'm going over there to telephone and call the authorities. You understand? In the meantime you'll stay on duty, and when they come with the clothes you'll take charge of the effects of the deceased. You'll throw something over her too, so that she isn't left exposed like she is now."

"I understand."

Sebastián sat down on the sand beside Paulina. Now two of the others also sat down facing the water, their hands clasped around their shins. The medical student was standing beside the body some six or seven yards from the others. He squatted down for a moment to observe something, but was reprimanded by the Civil Guard.

"Hey, you. Move off from there."

And he signed to him to get out. Then he strolled along the bank, with his thumb hooked through the strap of his rifle. Paulina shivered.

"I'm cold, Sebastián. I'm cold through and through."

She pressed herself against her fiancé to get warm. Sebas threw Tito's trousers over her legs. He had left them there on the ground. Now the old Guard crossed the little wooden bridge, which was

only fifteen yards long where it spanned the water from the promontory. Then he walked downstream again along the other side of the
backwater, through the short patch of undergrowth and under the
mulberry tree on to the terrace of that same *merenderos* that over-
looked the embankment. Now only a couple of families were still
sitting at the bare tables. The Guard went into the first of the bars.
There was a great deal of smoke inside. It was like a complete veil
that fused everything together beneath the same sticky yellow light.
It smudged the faces; it deadened the sparkle of the glass, and the
nickel-plated trays and the little espresso coffee-machine. It dulled
the dirty figures on the playing cards, the illustrated advertisement
and the coloured calendars. The bar was full of people, hardly any
of them from Madrid, and of loud-mouthed Sunday drunkenness.
Something was frying in the kitchen. There was a disagreeable smell
of burning oil.

"Aurelia, I'm going to use your telephone, if you don't mind."

"By all means. Make any calls you want to."

"Thank you."

He left his three-cornered hat on the counter and went across to
the instrument. They heard the burr of the handle, and many of them
kept quiet to listen.

"Hello, this is Gumersindo, Civil Guard, speaking." He thrust
his finger into his other ear. "Listen, Luisa, I want you to give me
– this is urgent – Alcalá de Henares – an official call, the Secretary of
the District Court. Now listen again. If they don't answer at his
house, tell the operator to trace him wherever he is. You understand?"
He paused. "What? Oh, that's got nothing to do with you. You'll
hear soon enough." He looked at the people round the tables. "Yes,
of course something's happened. I'm not ringing him up to wish him
a Merry Christmas!" There was laughter at the tables. He was
listening again. "Wha-at?" As he listened his lips broke into a smile.
"Listen, my girl, I'm old enough to be your father twice over. Don't
start flirting with old men, but put the call through quickly, see.
You can get me here, at Aurelia's. See? I'm going to hang up."

He replaced the earpiece and returned to the counter, where he
had left his hat.

"What can I give you?" asked the woman.

"Some water."

"The jar's there behind you."

She nodded her head towards the window ledge and then added in comment: "It's a nasty business and no mistake, to leave a person lying there in that state until someone chooses to come. What harm would it do to show a bit of decency? Why can't they move the poor thing somewhere and treat her with a little consideration?"

"These are the regulations. We aren't allowed to touch anything or to let anyone go near."

"Then the regulations are wrong. That's no way to treat anyone."

"And how can it affect a person once he's dead? The dead don't feel or suffer," interposed one of the listeners who was leaning against the counter.

"That's a thing you don't know," replied the woman, "whether it affects them or not. And even if it doesn't it's ugly anyway. A dead person is still a person just as much as when he was alive."

"More so. More than when he was alive," said the Guard. "More of a person than a living person, if you come to think of it, because you pay him more respect."

"Stands to reason," said Aurelia, turning to the interrupter. "Now suppose someone insults your father, wouldn't you feel much worse about it if he was dead than if he were still alive? . . . Now there's your call, Gumersindo."

The telephone bell rang. The Guard hurriedly unhooked the receiver.

"Hello!"

Now there was another silence among the customers, a silence even greater than before. Almost all of them turned in their chairs to listen to Gumersindo.

"Hello! Is the Secretary there?"

Someone at a table hissed to silence a drunken buzz that prevented those in the far corner from hearing the telephone.

"Listen, sir, this is a call from San Fernando de Henares, Civil Guard, first-class, Gumersindo Calderón, at your service . . . What do you say?" He listened. "Yes, sir." He nodded. "Yes, yes, sir. The patrol on duty on the Jar . . . Hello!"

Now all the customers were listening; a card game had been stopped, and the cards were lying face-downwards on the marble table.

"Listen, sir," continued Gumersindo, "I have to report that this afternoon a drowning took place, as a result of which a young woman whom certain indications show to have been an inhabitant of Madrid, lost her life. It appears that she came here to swim in the company of . . . Hello, sir." He listened. "In the pool. Yes, sir, in the vicinity of . . ." He broke off again. "Very well, sir." Another pause. "Yes, sir. Very well, sir. Just as you say. I beg your pardon." He listened and assented. "Yes, sir, yes, yes, sir . . . Until you come, sir, at your service."

He waited for a few moments before hanging up the receiver. Conversations were resumed at all the tables. The Guard returned to the counter and picked up his hat. He put it on.

"Thank you, Aurelia."

He went out on to the terrace.

They came back with the clothes, and Rafael and his friend, having dressed, joined them in the darkness. As they emerged from the trees they saw the silhouettes of the others on the point. They were all sitting down. Only the figure of the Civil Guard was still pacing up and down the shore.

Josemari went over for a moment to look at the corpse. The Guard spoke: "Hand me the effects of the . . ." He indicated the corpse with a nod. "Cover her, for decency's sake."

They dropped the things on the sand, and Daniel squatted down to find what was Luci's in the bundle.

"Move away, Tito. You're in my light . . ."

He picked up the clothes so that they caught the light from the *merenderos*. Lucita's dress was there, done up in a roll.

"Give it to me," said the Guard.

As it passed from one hand to another, the bundle of clothes came undone and what was inside dropped out; a pair of sandals and her underwear.

"Be a little more careful," said the Guard to Daniel. "Pick it up. Is there any more?"

The other Guard was coming; his steps could be heard on the plank bridge.

"Yes, I think there must also have been a bag and a food tin at least."

Daniel searched again. Sebastián and Paulina looked for their things.

"Here they are. I think that's all."

The young Guard picked up all Lucita's things. The older was now standing beside the corpse. He took Lucita's dress and laid it across her body, covering her head. It was a printed cotton dress; red flowers on a yellow ground. Her legs remained exposed.

"Just look in the bag to see if there's anything more."

The young Guard found a small blue and white striped towel, and gave it to Gumersindo, who used it to cover Lucita's legs. Then they put her sandals and underwear in the bag and left it with the tin beside the corpse.

"I think I ought to go up and tell the others," said Sebastián. "Eh? What do you think?"

"Ask those two before you go, and see if they'll let you."

"Yes, of course."

Gumersindo had gone over to the two groups. He spoke in a loud voice, addressing them all: "Now listen to me. I have just contacted the authorities, and informed the Secretary of the District Court of the occurrence. I have been instructed that he and the examining magistrate will arrive at this spot in three quarters of an hour at the most. I give you this information so that you don't get impatient, but know the state of affairs. Nothing more to say. Now you may go away and dress."

The five others also sorted their things. Something fell with a bump on the wet sand, and there was the flash of a mouth-organ dropping from a trouser pocket.

"Be careful with that," one of them exclaimed. He bent down to pick it up and tapped it against the palm of his hand to knock off the grains of sand that had stuck to it. The man with wet trousers took an almost complete packet of Chesterfields out of his pocket.

"Pity about these," he remarked, showing the wet and broken cigarettes in his hand.

"Worse things have happened than that."

"You're right."

He threw the tobacco into the pool. Then he wrung out his trousers on the bank and watched the packet break up, floating down the lighted water towards the sluice.

"I'm frightened to go alone, Sebastián," said Paulina. "Come and stay near me while I go behind a tree and dress. I'm frightened to be alone."

The two of them went off to the trees, and Daniel was left talking to the Guard Gumersindo.

"Look, there were some other men and girls came with us, and they're waiting for us at the top. You see? I should like to go up and tell them. They don't know anything about all this. I should like to tell them if that's possible."

"Where do you say they are?"

"Up at the top, at that *merendero* that stands back from the main road. You know it?"

"Yes, Mauricio's place." He reflected for a few moments and took out his watch. "Look, just you go up, but come down at once, you understand." He pointed to the watch in his hand. "I give you fifteen minutes, altogether, to go and come back, on the understanding that you don't arrive back here any later on any account. It wouldn't do for the magistrate to arrive and you not be here. Is that understood?"

"I promise."

"Go on then. Off with you."

Daniel turned away and made for the little bridge. Tito had finished dressing and was lying on his side, with his elbow in the sand. The other five were standing, smoking with their faces to the bank, looking at the light on the water.

The man with the mouth-organ asked: "What way shall we have of getting back to Madrid tonight?"

"By the time all this business is over, I'm afraid none at all."

Rafael lifted his watch to his face and turned his wrist till it caught the light.

"Quarter past ten," he said. "We've got fifty minutes till the last train. They'd have to be pretty quick if they were done in time to let us go and catch it."

"Impossible," said the medical student.

"There we are. Either sleep in the village or walk to Madrid on our own flat feet. That's the alternative."

"So we're to walk, are we? That's a fine idea."

"How far is it by road?"

"Ten miles."

"That's not so bad. Three hours walking, or a little less."

"And with this moon," said the medical student, turning to look at it, "and a nice cool night, it would be perfect walking."

"Suppose it's all over by twelve, we should be home by three."

"But I don't know why you don't go, Josemari," said Rafael. "They haven't told you to stay. You can still catch the train. You'll be a fool if you don't."

"I shall stay with you. We all came together, and we'll all see it through together."

"Do as you like. It's up to you. But no one here would be offended if you went."

Paulina and Sebastián had come back dressed and sat down beside Tito. Sebastián hid his face in his knees, Paulina leaned her head on his shoulder.

"The next thing to do is to tell our parents. If we telephone one lot they can pass the news on to the others. What do you think?"

"Well, that can be your job. You're free. The Guard has just telephoned. Ask him where he did it."

"Yes, I'll ask him. It must have been from somewhere near. One of those shacks."

"That'll be it. Do you remember all our numbers?"

"It's not worth bothering to tell them at my pension," said the man with the wet trousers. "I don't think anyone would be worried by my absence."

"All right. But tell me, Luis, what's your number?"

"Mine? Twenty-three, forty-two, sixty-five."

Josemari went off muttering the number under his breath, and was afterwards seen talking to the Civil Guards. The older had raised his arm to give him directions.

Now the moon was completely up over the plain; and beyond the dam, downstream, the winding ribbon of the Jarama could be seen shining. At its curves it disappeared for a little only to reappear farther on, narrowing as it ran south, until it disappeared in the far distance behind the hills on the horizon, which closed the valley.

The planks of the little bridge creaked under Josemari's tread. Paulina sighed.

"How do you feel?" Sebastián asked her, looking up.

"How do you expect me to feel?" she asked almost in tears. "I feel awful."

"Yes, I understand."

Sebastián dropped his head again. Paulina's head rested against his arm. He could feel her sobs as she broke once more into silent tears.

The Civil Guards paced up and down the sand. They did not go far. Tito saw what appeared to be a single silhouette, coming and going against the light from the bank. The black shadow passed and repassed Lucita's shrouded body. Then several lights suddenly went out on the other side, on the *merendero* terrace.

"Goodbye," called the man with the mouth-organ.

The Guards stopped for a moment, noticing the increasing darkness, then resumed their silent pacing. Now only two lamps were still alight, hanging in the empty air, and the orange square of a door above the black line of the bank. A figure appeared in the square and entered the door; it must have been Josemari who had reached the shack. Now very little light came across the point. Only the aluminium-white moonbeams fell on the sand, revealing the outlines of shapes and figures, and throwing milky pools, patches and streaks like the brushmarks or splashes of whitewash.

Paulina sneezed twice. Sebas took a towel from the bag and threw it over his fiancée's shoulders. She pulled out the corners and tied them round her neck, spreading the towel across her chest. It was very wet

"Everything's wet," she complained.

Her voice sounded weak and snuffly from crying. She felt the towel all over and shivered.

"There's nothing at all dry," she went on. "Everything's wringing wet. Oh dear!" She burst out crying again. "I can't stand this any more, Sebastián, I can't stand it, I can't," she repeated, weeping into the towel.

*   *   *

"Men of my age nowadays aren't worth a penny," said Lucio. "No, not worth a penny when it comes to getting a job. But as for experience," he smiled, "in the matter of experience we could show some of you younger chaps a thing or two."

"You!" replied Mauricio. "According to you, you could open a school if only we'd listen to you."

"Yes, I could."

"I should say so. The quantity of information you offer us in the course of a day! You don't half fancy yourself. A pity that it's all wasted! It's too bad."

"It's no laughing matter," said Lucio, smiling. "It isn't that I claim any great credit myself. It's just a question of age."

"Age! You'd need to be a clever fellow to follow your advice to the letter. Might as well throw yourself under a train and be done with it."

"You haven't much respect for age, by the sound of it. What do you think the old are good for?"

"The old should shut up and get out of the light. That's all. Make way for the young. Don't you understand how different life is today? Our ideas are antiquated. They've been on the scrap heap for God knows how many years."

"Not so antiquated as all that. Men go on making much the same mistakes, after all, or there doesn't seem much difference."

"Well, you treat them the same way, and see how you end up!"

"Now listen. Supposing a man is really cautious, and avoids all the mistakes someone else made, don't you think he'd save himself from one or two knocks, whoever he was?"

Mauricio smiled in agreement.

"Yes, that's true. If he were to take you as a model of how not to do it – the other side of the coin. Yes, I think you're talking sense there."

"Well?" said Lucio looking at the others. "He's a fine one, isn't he? Only got to throw a bit of mud at yourself and he agrees. Now look, Mauricio. I was only thinking of all the troubles I've met with, nothing more. Don't get things confused. There's a lot of difference between saying that a road is dangerous because you've been attacked by a dog there, and saying that you're sorry you ever took it. There's a big difference, and that's a fact."

"Don't pay any blasted attention to him, Señor Lucio," cut in El Chamarís. "Just let him do his job and give us one for the road, because we must be going." He glanced at the butchers. "Isn't that so?"

"Yes, yes," said Claudio. "We're all going."

"So soon?"

Mauricio filled their glasses.

"Soon? They'll be waiting for us. Suppertime," answered El Chamarís. "What do you expect? Because you haven't got a family and you have the constitution of a saint, so that you don't have to put a solid morsel in your mouth the whole blessed day, do you think we can all do the same? Well, you're wrong."

"Let the family have their supper and go to bed," said Lucio. "Sundays were made for a man to have some fun. When he's spent all his money then he goes home and not before."

"But not him," said the little butcher, pointing to El Charamís. "He can't do that. If he's only ten minutes or a quarter of an hour late, you see how quickly they'll send a message to call him home. Remember his little girl came to fetch him this morning." He turned to the subject of his discourse, "Isn't that true, man?"

"So what? If they send for me it means they miss me, and can't get on without me. That's as it should be. And it speaks in my favour too. I'm not one of the sort whose wife is happier when he's out of the house, and looks relieved when he's away because she hasn't got to put up with his company all day long."

"But that's her freedom. What other freedom can she have?"

said the butcher. "That's her only freedom. Look, you've only been married a little while. You're a pair of lovebirds, as somebody or other said. But you see, you'll come to it, never you fear. You'll come to that stage too."

"He's flattered," put in Claudio with a laugh. "He's really flattered when she sends the girl, just as she did today, to call Father home, and all that stuff."

"Yes, he's flattered. I believe you. It makes him purr," exclaimed the other butcher. "You've only got to look at his face. But just you wait a few years, it won't be very long, or when she begins to be a bit sharp with him, you'll see, you'll see the turn things take. 'All right, darling, just as you say. But do give a woman a little peace, won't you? I do my duty by the house, don't I? Well, let me alone then. That's enough. And if you don't . . .' "

"Gracious me!" exclaimed Lucio. "You're trying to rob our friend of his marital bliss."

"What? Don't be ridiculous. No one in this world could rob him of that. When a man has a young wife no power on earth can destroy his illusions. Nothing on earth."

"It would be a hard job," agreed Claudio. "He's really keen on his Rosalía. Not much chance for anyone who tries to make him change his mind!"

"Haven't you finished yet?" protested El Chamarís. "I think I've served long enough as a subject for general conversation. You've given me a thorough going over today. See if you can't change the subject. Besides, I've got to go. Tell me what I owe you, Mauricio, please."

"Yes, man, you're quite right. We'll give you a rest until to-morrow."

"You owe me nine fifty."

El Chamarís looked for his money among the leaves of a notebook with worn yellow covers. Coca-Coña went on turning the pages of the Sunday *ABC*.

"They're singing through there," said Carmelo to Mauricio with a gleam in his eye, and his ears turned to the passage and the garden.

"I can hear."

He gave El Chamarís his fifty céntimos change. White Shoes looked down at the floor. His left arm lay along the back of Lucio's chair.

"See you tomorrow," said El Chamarís as he departed.

The two butchers went out with him.

"Goodnight."

"Goodnight, gentlemen."

"See you tomorrow."

"Goodnight."

They went out into the dark road.

The Alcarrenian was pursuing his argument. "As I said, Don Marcial, no joking, I often think of packing up once and for all, and taking the family to America."

"Why is it you don't go?" asked the shepherd.

"Tongue takes him everywhere," shouted Coca-Coña, "but he doesn't move his feet."

"Shut up, once and for all, you cripple. Aren't you capable of having a serious conversation?"

"Ha, ha! A serious conversation! Just listen to that," exclaimed the cripple laughing. "He wants us to take his plans for going to America seriously now. What do you think of that? A fine sort of seriousness. Makes you die with laughter."

"And what do you know about it?"

"Me? Nothing. Don't talk to me about it. Well, almost nothing. Perhaps you'll teach me? Because I've been listening to the same thing for God knows how many years. You've been going about with that story ever since I first knew you. Who do you expect to take you seriously, man? You've sailed for America more often than Christopher Columbus."

"But that doesn't mean anything," put in Don Marcial. "You turn over a plan for a very long time, until it's ripe. And the day you least expect it – bang, bang, bang! You carry the thing out."

"Yes, yes, when the time's ripe. My feet will be on the move, I swear though I am crippled, I'll be off before this fellow has moved an inch. Imagination, that's all he's got, nothing but will o' the wisps dancing through his top storey."

"You're right," said the shepherd. "It's that brain of his, that's it. It's always swarming and swarming like a wasp's nest. And the only person who believes in it at all is him. He doesn't take any of us in with his tale of sailing for America, because we all know it by heart. There's not a word of truth in the whole business."

"Of course, I don't deny that often a man just thinks of these things as a comfort, to escape from his troubles," answered the Alcarrenian, "but that doesn't mean they're just moonshine. How do you know that one fine day if someone always digs at the same hole he won't really get through the wall? You'll find you've been making a big mistake. I shouldn't be so positive if I were you. You never know."

"As sure as my name's Amalio you'll be buried here? Won't he now?"

"Not a shadow of doubt," agreed Coca-Coña. "No one could possibly doubt it. I'd sign a document to that effect this very moment."

They laughed.

"You all think you're clever. You take yourselves for King Solomons, by the sound of it. But you don't know me yet. You don't know me, I can tell you."

"Come off it," put in Don Marcial. "They were just trying to tease you this evening, to see if they could get your goat. You don't take that sort of nonsense seriously, do you?"

"What? Me? As if I didn't see what they were after! But if they think they can get me rattled they're very much mistaken. They've chosen the wrong man."

"They just like finding fault, that's all there is to it. As for going to America, haven't we all thought of it at one time or another – more or less seriously?"

"There you see, it isn't such a crazy idea after all. It's just a question of making up your mind."

"Yes, that's the whole question. You've just got to have the pluck to make a decision of that size. You've got to gird up your loins and carry it through once and for all."

"No doubt about that. Nobody's denying that it costs you something to uproot yourself from the place you've always known and where you were brought up. It's easy to say that you'll leave your home and all the local people. They may be good or bad but you've rubbed along with them all your life. Leave your home, and land one fine morning somewhere entirely new in a country that you've never seen before even in pictures, with a way of life you've no idea of. Unless a man's devoid of all human feeling he obviously has to fight against his nature to do a thing like that."

"The whole art is to get used to the idea," answered Don Marcial. "When you arrive, of course, you may find yourself a real outsider. Nobody can make contact overnight with something that's quite strange to him. But a man very quickly comes to terms with a place, that's what I say. He's forced to fit into the atmosphere, whether he wants to or not, and to dig himself in. Necessity itself, in fact, makes you adapt yourself, and soon feel as much at home as a native."

"I can well believe you. I've heard emigrants come back and use the oddest expressions, and you couldn't persuade them to drop it and talk naturally. They really laughed at them in the village, I can tell you."

"Yes, they must have sounded like Cantinflas or Jorge Negrete in the films, didn't they?"

"Yes, just like that. The same as those films. The first time you heard them you couldn't keep a straight face. Just like the pictures. Couldn't be more like. Even though the people I'm speaking of came from Venezuela, while Cantinflas, Negrete and the rest were born in Mexico, which is a very long way from Venezuela, as you know. Not just what we think of in Spain as a very long way, but a long way by their distances, and they're so enormous they take your breath away ... But even then you can hardly distinguish one sort of language from another. They all seem to speak the same kind of gibberish over there as far as I can make out."

"And it's catching too! Everybody ends up talking like that."

"Now supposing that every difficulty disappeared overnight, and I boarded the boat tomorrow, then my way of talking would be spoiled and ruined for ever, and I should be the laughing-stock of the village when I came back ..."

"There!" cut in Amalio. "Now he's realized! Here's the real difficulty. The whole thing's trickier than it looks, much trickier. That's the point. Nobody wants complications. I can see now why you don't go."

Coca-Coña had returned to his newspaper.

"Just wait until I get sick of everything one of these fine days, and then you'll see whether I go or not," answered the Alcarrenian. "If life just goes on battering me as it's been doing up to now, and we still can't find any other way out, then you'll see me cross the pond soon enough, and we'll be out of our difficulties once and for all. We shan't be leading this miserable existence any more."

"And what do you expect you're going to find over there, on the other side of the pond, as you call it? Tell me that. I suppose you imagine you're going to strike piles of gold as soon as you land off the ship."

"I should be better off than I am here. I'm sure of that."

"Good lord, the things some people believe!" exclaimed the shepherd. "They really imagine they've only got to go far enough and their conditions will automatically improve, in the twinkling of an eye. The farther they travel, the better they think things will be for them. Just cross what he calls the pond – although it isn't precisely a pond but a fair-sized stretch of sea, more than a gipsy can jump over anyway. Lying where it does, it will swallow up any chance he's got of ever coming back, even if he wants to beat a retreat. I don't know what sort of picture you've got of the ocean. You talk as if you could swallow it at a gulp every time you mention it."

"Nobody talks like that. All I'm saying is that things are very different in America. In America . . ."

"Stop talking rubbish," interrupted the shepherd. "You tell me all about what goes on in America when you get back. All right? Always supposing you do go off one day and have the good luck to come back, and also supposing you still find me here and that I'm not dead by that time. Let's agree on that, eh? But no more daydreaming for now. It's not good for either of us. If I want to turn my brains, the heat of the sun will do it for me, burning down all day long while I'm fagging after my sheep, and struggling over these infernal plains."

"And may you scorch there for the rest of your life, know-all. I'd like to see you split like a chestnut for imagining you're the only man that's right!"

"I don't pretend to know any more than I know. What I don't do is to go about with my head full of fantasies like some fools who believe that the farther they go the better off they'll be, and that if they only get far enough away from their own country everything will be fine. Because people like us have to work just as hard to earn their living wherever they are. And the only way to do that is by the sweat of your brow, here or in America, or on the moon, if anyone can fly up there. Poor bastards like you and me get absolutely nothing for nothing. That's the one thing I'll swear to. And if some people come back from America with more money than they took with them, they got it by the work of their hands, just the same as they do here or in Peking. But then what happens? Other people get wrong ideas into their heads. Ripe fruit doesn't fall into the laps of our kind – we live by hard work. It's time you woke up, and that's no lie. My head will get scorched and scorched again, as you say, in this damned country – and I won't miss anything by not going to America. But at least it can never get scorched any worse than it is now."

"Boy, how he goes on!" exclaimed Coca-Coña, raising his smiling face from his paper. "How this fellow Amalio does speechify!"

"Yes, he's a first class bore," said the Alcarrenian. "But luckily I know him very well and never feel tempted to take him seriously. He's like you. There's only one thing that you're both after when you try and score points off me, and that's to make me fly off the handle. But you can't draw me that way."

"You'd be a poor fish if you couldn't," said Don Marcial. "The gentleman whom you see seated before you" – he pointed to Coca-Coña with outstretched arm and forefinger – "that gentleman is the most spiteful creature to be found within a thousand square miles of this place. There's no good feeling sorry for him, you have to take a stick to him. Hit him hard and give him a good drubbing. I'm the best friend he possesses, let me tell you, this squashed beetle disguised as a man, whom they call Marcelo Coca, alias Coca-Coña and the Thing on Wheels, and the Broken Doll, and the Man from Mars, and a number of other names that he's collected in the course of his life . . ."

"Go on with you! All that old rubbish again!" shouted Coca-Coña. "I've forgotten about it entirely although it did refer to me, but he still remembers it. You're a fine friend, Marcial. You're a pearl among friends to remember all the nicknames people have ever called your beloved little Coca. Come, you deserve a kiss! Come on! ! !"

"And he's laughing into the bargain! Look how he enjoys it! Look how he's enjoying it all on his own and clinging to his chair! Take a good look at him! . ."

The four laughed. A little later they heard the Alcarrenian humming in the mournful accents of his district, a simple falsetto of a kind special to Alcarria.

> "Little red legs has the partridge,
> Little red legs I repeat . . ."

"Hark the lark singing in the fields," observed the shepherd.

"I think he's really inspired tonight," said Don Marcial with a laugh. "He's not very loud but the feeling's there."

"A local song," said the Alcarrenian with a modest gesture.

A man now entered whose clothes were much splashed with whitewash. He greeted everybody.

"Hello, Macario," replied the boss.

"San Roque, San Roque! Where have you come from at this time of night? Don't you know it's against the law to work on Sundays?"

"Couldn't be helped. Have to make use of the time. Get all the little jobs done that people give you. Get some money from anywhere. Necessity's the master."

He had difficulty in pronouncing r and instead made a guttural sound on the roof of his mouth rather like a g. Coca-Coña imitated him.

"It's very wrong in every way. You ought to rest, man, you ought to rest on Sundays, you know. You shouldn't drive the body too hard or one fine day it'll revolt and refuse to work. You'll explode!"

"If it revolts it revolts," said Macario. "Then it'll be everyone for himself. I mean it'll be their turn then to bear the hardships. The kids and the wife'll have to get down to it and shift for themselves as best they can. But until that happens there's nothing for it but to get every ounce out of myself, every ounce I can."

"How many kids have you got?" asked Don Marcial.

"Five and a sixth on the way."

There was a whistle of alarm.

"Another on the way already?" asked the truck-driver.

"Yes, indeed, if it doesn't miscarry."

"It won't miscarry, never fear," said Lucio with a smile.

"I know that all right. There's no danger. It'll arrive, God willing, just like all its brothers and sisters. It won't miscarry, God willing. No."

He said this in a cheerful voice, rolling his eyes as he did so.

They began to laugh. Only White Shoes remained serious.

"They've all arrived safely so far then?" he asked. "No mishaps?"

"Eh? That depends on what you call mishaps. They all arrived right enough. None got lost on the way."

They laughed again at Macario's expression.

"Good stock, all right!"

"I'm not the only one concerned, you know. She has her share in it too. She's like the hen of Coimbra who hatched out the whole of her brood, without losing one."

"Three or four too many, I should say," observed Don Marcial.

"We shall see!"

"Yes, you're right there," said the shepherd emphatically. "Wait till they grow up. You've only got to wait just a few years, and things will begin to look fine. Pesetas will start flowing thick and fast once they all begin earning and supporting the house. The poor man's reward. You realize that, all right."

"Yes, unless I'm overtaken by the fate that Coca's just been prophesying for me, and kill myself first by overwork. If that happens, and of course it's quite possible, then I suppose I shan't live to enjoy the very pretty picture."

Coca-Coña answered him from his chair.

"Forget about it. I withdraw my prophecy. Don't be frightened. May you reach the age of a hundred with all your hair."

"That's more than I ask for. Eighty will do nicely. It's greedy to want more."

Don Marcial turned to Coca-Coña and showed him his watch.

"Just look what the time is now, boy. I for one must be on my way. Supposing you want me to take you . . ."

"Wait, man. You would choose just this moment! Don't be such a nuisance."

"I can't stay a minute longer, Coca. Don Carlos is waiting for me. If you want to stay, stay, but you'll have to go back alone."

"No, I shall come with you if you don't make life so miserable for me. At least you'll let me finish this drink, won't you? You haven't got to turn a starting handle on me, anyway. The time will come when I motorize myself once and for all. Then I shan't have to rely on my own arms or anyone else's to propel me."

"What's this about motorizing yourself?" asked White Shoes.

"I could, you know. With all these gadgets that have come out, these Vespas and all the rest, it's occurred to me that I might motorize myself too. Just by attaching a little motor to this contraption and transforming myself into an atomic age shooting-star. I've been putting aside a bit of my income every month, you know. I've still got to study the technical aspects to find out what motor would suit me, and all that. You'll see, all of you. Soon I shall be moving faster than any of you."

"It's a fine idea. But it would be silly to carry it out."

"It would be a rare sight," said the Alcarrenian, "to see you going everywhere, up and down the streets of San Fernando and all around in your invalid-chair – toot, toot, toot!"

"But I've seen them all around here motorized, you know. Don't you believe me? Just you wait until the winter, and you'll come and beg me to give you a ride. You'll be calling out after me, all of you, 'Wait for me!' when we take our airing on the highway."

"Now come on, Coca, please come and don't be a nuisance."

"What a pest you are. All right, come on and get me out."

The Alcarrenian seized the cripple's chair by the back and pulled him away from the table. Coca-Coña raised his arms. Don Marcial leaned forward and picked him up by the armpits.

"Come on, dear," he said as he lifted him, imitating a doting mother.

He picked him up without any effort and held him in his arms.

"Take that, Mummy."

The cripple gave Don Marcial a resounding slap.

"Well now!" exclaimed the Alcarrenian.

The spectators laughed. There was a red mark on Don Marcial's cheek.

"And I have to put up with that!" he said. "Who would have the courage to attack this object?"

He displayed the little deformed body in his arms: the neckless head sunk into the thorax; the arms of almost normal size that were so out of proportion with the rest of his body, and the wasted legs that hung lifeless, swinging like pendulums, weighed down by shapeless black boots.

"Goodnight, gentlemen!" he said from Don Marcial's arms.

Then he stretched out one arm towards Macario and caught him by the lapel.

"Come here, my fertile friend," he cried with a laugh, dragging him towards him.

"What do you want? Take your hands off me!"

Macario had no shirt or anything under his jacket; nothing but his naked hairless chest. Coca-Coña grasped his whitewash-stained lapel tightly.

"Come on, San Roque," he said. "Repeat after me: 'San Roque ran around the ragged rock.' Let's hear how you say it."

"Come on now, stop your fooling," protested Don Marcial, "and let him go."

"Didn't you hear him ask you to let me go? Come on!"

Coca-Coña threatened him with his left hand.

"I'll give you one! Just you wait till I start being violent!"

The others laughed. Macario tried to free his lapel from the cripple's grasp, but Coca-Coña hung on with all his might and shook him hard.

"Come on: 'San Roque ran round the rragged rrock.' Say it now, say it!"

Don Marcial too was shaken by the cripple's violent efforts, and swayed backwards and forwards with Macario.

"Let him go now, damn you," said Don Marcial impatiently. "My arms are tired from holding you. I shall be back late and it will be your fault. Let him go. If you don't let him go this moment I'll drop you."

"Well, let him say it then! Let him say it! Say it!"

"Don't be a nuisance, Coca! I'm not going to say it, so don't go on about it. Will you let me go, yes or no?"

Coca-Coña let go of his lapel.

"Very well then, San Roque. You can despise my lessons . . . but you'll never learn to pronounce your r's so long as you live. And you'll never prosper, or make your way in the world, or do any good at all. You'll remain the peasant you've always been. No one will help you. You'll be a peasant all your life! . . ."

Macario had got out of Coca-Coña's reach and joined the others, who were laughing. Now Don Marcial stood by the door with the cripple in his arms. On the doorstep he turned back.

"Have you ever met a nastier creature? And I have to carry him in my arms, the little angel!" He nodded his head. "Goodnight to you all."

He prepared to go. But Coca-Coña was still clinging to the lintel and the curtain, and prevented him from moving. Hauling himself up by main force, and firmly grasping the curtain, he thrust his head over Don Marcial's shoulder and shouted at Macario:

"San Goque gan gound the gagged gock! San Goque gan gound the gagged gock!"

Don Marcial pulled, wrenched him away from the door, and Coca-Coña shouted and struggled in his arms. The curtain trailed after them and was still flapping in the night until its whole length had slipped from the cripple's claws. Finally it fell limp, and after swaying a little resumed its former position. Don Marcial's voice sounded from outside the door.

"My God, what a spiteful devil you are! What have I ever done to earn such a trial? . . ."

He installed Coca-Coña in his wheel-chair, and they could still hear: "Gound the gagged gock . . .!"

Now Don Marcial was pushing the chair down the road.

"What a devil the little man is!" observed the truck-driver. "He must have taken a couple of glasses too much tonight . . ."

"Don't you believe it," said Mauricio. "He's always as poisonous as that, even when he hasn't taken a drop."

White Shoes agreed.

"Poor little man! The only pleasure he's got in life is to argue. What else has he got? His one enjoyment is a bit of company and then he attacks people one after another, and makes fun of them and starts up a row."

Macario and the shepherd had come together, and Lucio said, pointing to Macario: "He can't forget that blessed nonsense of his, with the r's and San Roque and all the rest."

"You see how obstinate he is in his damned fool ideas," said Macario. "He gave me a real nightmare and no mistake."

"Yes, he expects you to spend your whole life reciting his rigmarole, just to make him laugh. He's just like a child."

"He's not very different," observed the man in white shoes. "Nobody with a handicap like his could help being rather childish in what he does, and in his demands too."

"That's the only reason people put up with him, because he is what he is," said Macario. "And because he's really very funny and good company too, you can't deny that. Apart from the fact that this evening he pulled a button off my coat," – he looked about him on the floor – "with all the tugging he gave me. And on top of that he calls me a peasant." He stopped looking for his button and raised his head. "And what else could I be but a peasant?"

They had stopped listening to him. "Well, so far as I'm concerned," said Lucio, "to be like Coca would be one of the worst things that could ever happen to me. I can't think of anything as bad. I'd suffer all that I've suffered over again and ten times worse, rather than wake up one day and find myself like him. Physical pain, no! I just can't take it. Mental pain as they call it, I can take as much of that as you like so long as it still leaves me a man. But a common or garden toothache shatters me completely. It's worse than all the misery and anguish that you find roaming about the world looking for a victim."

"You're right there," agreed Carmelo. "There's nothing worse than a toothache, nothing at all. No night on earth can be so bad as a night when you've got the toothache. Pills are no good, nor any fomentations or brandy. You can't take your mind off it with a cigarette or the newspaper or a radio or anything. All you can do is dig your head into the pillow and take quinine until the light comes and you see the dawn. And then you hurry out like a cat, to look for a dentist. Or rather an Odontologist, for that's what they've got written up on the plate at his door. Then there you are. He takes the forceps and it's out. That's put an end of your pain. It's drastic. But it's the only thing that works when you've got the jaw-ache. It's the only cure. Sedatives are no use, nor is anything else. It's the one certain remedy for a bad tooth."

He looked from one face to another and was silent. He then examined his fingers which were caught up in his sleeve. He observed them curiously, as if they were little creatures independent of his will, and watched their movements as they played with the gold of his municipality buttons. There was a great noise in the garden.

"What a row they're making out there!" said Amalio.

"Youth!" retorted the Alcarrenian. "It's a stage we all go through."

"That's true," said Macario. "The age of innocence. They play the fool all the time."

There was a silence. Then the truck-driver said: "Pour us out a last drink, Mauricio. The time has come to hit the trail."

Mauricio took the bottle and filled their glasses.

"There . . ." He looked towards the door.

Daniel came in.

"Are they here?" he asked.

They all stared at him.

"Tell me whether they are still here?"

"Yes, yes, they're still out there," answered Mauricio.

"Anything wrong?"

"An accident."

He made his way quickly between them and went into the passage.

"Look who's here!" exclaimed Lucas on seeing him enter the garden.

"And about time," cried Fernando. "Have you all come?"

"We were just going."

"Miguel!" said Dani. "Come here a minute, Miguel!"

They were alarmed.

"What's the matter, eh?"

"I want to talk to Miguel."

Miguel got up from the table. Daniel took him by the arm and led him into the centre of the garden.

"What can it be?" exclaimed Alicia. "All this mystery."

"Wants to make us curious."

"No, I'm sure something's the matter. Something's happened. You can tell by Daniel's face . . ."

They were all silent, watching the two talking under the light in the middle of the garden. They suddenly saw the expression on Miguel's face change. They saw him clutch Daniel's shoulders. He spoke to him jerkily. "Alicia, come here. Come here, all of you," he cried. "Something terrible's happened." They rushed over and formed a circle round them. Miguel was looking on the ground. There was a silence while he searched for words.

"You tell them . . ."

Mely began to shout. She shook them both by the arm, imploring them to say once and for all what it was. Daniel lowered his head. "Lucita's been drowned in the river." They trembled. They attacked Daniel. "But how? But how, for God's sake? How could it have happened?" They dug their nails into his shirt. "Daniel!" Mely hid her head in her hands. "I knew it! I knew it was Lucita . . ."

"A little while ago. In the pool. She was bathing."

"We'd better go down," said Miguel.

"One of the girls who came with you?" asked the man from Atocha, who was behind them.

[324]

"Let me go . . ." said Fernando. "Come on, Daniel. Let's go right away to wherever it is . . ."

They made for the door, and Mely tried to follow them.

"Don't you go," said Zacarías, stopping her. "You'd better not go. It'll only upset you."

"But why . . . ?" she said, looking into his face. "Why shouldn't I go down ? What do you mean ? Why don't you want me to see her, Zacarías ? . . . But it's only" – she burst into tears – "such a short time ago since she was with us . . . Why don't you want me to go, Zacarías ? Why don't you want me to go ? Why don't you want me to ? . . ."

The gang from Legazpi had moved away and were picking up their things.

"We shan't come down," said Lucas. "There's no reason."

"Better for us to start off. We shall be in time for the train. Pick up the gramophone, and come along."

Mariyayo had gone up to Zacarías.

"You go with her, Zacarías," she said. "Don't bother about me. Look after her, and go down with her. I'll go back with Samuel and the others. Really . . ."

He gave her a look.

"That's very nice of you, Mariyayo."

"It's only natural . . ." she said, and went back to the others.

Zacarías and Mely followed Miguel, Fernando and Alicia, who had already started out with Daniel on their way to the river. The others stayed to go back with the little Legazpi group by train. They finished picking up their things and went slowly towards the passage. The first group had gone through the bar without pausing, and Mauricio now asked the group going to the station: "What's happened ?"

"A girl has been drowned in the river," answered the man from Atocha.

"My God, how terrible!" exclaimed the Alcarrenian, turning his head.

"Which of the girls was it ?"

"I can't tell you. I didn't know her. She came with the other lot.

These two can probably tell you." She pointed to Samuel and Marialuisa.

"It wouldn't be the one who came on the motorbike?"

"Eh? On the motorbike?" said Samuel. "No, that was Paulina. This one was a smaller girl, with brown hair . . ."

"Was she in blue?"

"Oh, I don't know what she was wearing. I didn't see her today. Her name was Luci . . ."

"The one in blue was Carmen," put in Marialuisa. "She wasn't the one either."

"She was – what shall I say? – rather thin, and her face was rather . . . Oh, I don't know how to describe her . . ."

"Tell us, what do we owe you?" asked Federigo.

Mauricio turned towards him.

"What am I to take for?"

The shepherd shook his head.

"Lord help us!" he said. "Nothing ever stays good all the time. Just when you're enjoying a party something comes to turn your pleasure to dust and ashes. Just look at these . . ."

Zacarías and Mely had caught up with Daniel and the others. Now they were going through the vineyard. They walked quickly and in silence, almost at a running pace. Miguel was making for the little earth steps by which they had come up that evening, but Daniel prevented him. "Not that way, Miguel. Better on this side."

They went down to the *merenderos* and the little wooden bridge. Their steps resounded on the planks. They reached the point of the island. The shadows of the others stood out, those of the Civil Guards first. Mely recognized their faces at a glance in the moonlight. Paulina came to meet them.

"Alicia, Alicia!" she cried as she came, and wept once more when she kissed her.

The others went straight to the dead Lucita.

"Keep away from here," said the older Guard.

But Mely had already bent down beside the body and uncovered Luci's face. Sebas went to Miguel and grasped him firmly by the arm but said nothing. He put his head against his friend's shoulder.

Miguel was looking at the body. The Guards approached Mely and pulled her up by the arm.

"Go away, miss. Didn't you hear me say you mustn't touch?"

She tore herself free and turned on them furiously.

"Keep your hands off me! Don't touch me! Let me alone!"

They were all standing round the corpse, looking at Luci's uncovered face, almost completely concealed by her hair. Only Tito had not moved. He was still lying on his elbows in the sand. Mely bent down once more over Luci's face.

"Please do what I say, miss, and go away from here!"

"Let me alone, you beast!" she cried, weeping and struggling, and struck at the hand that had grasped her.

"Mind your language, miss. Pull yourself together this moment, or we shall be compelled to take measures!"

Zacarías and the others went across to her.

"Swine, that's what you are . . . !" cried Mely who was now free. "Swine! Do you know what they are, Zacarías? Do you know what they are?"

She collapsed weeping on his shoulder. The train passed; the white headlight, the string of lighted windows, on top of the bridge.

"Now miss, you'll have to give me your name," said the Guard Gumersindo, taking a notebook from his upper pocket. "You'll have to be taught not to show disrespect for Authority."

The other Guard bent over the corpse to cover it up again. The students had gone over to them.

"Listen, excuse me for speaking to you for a moment," said the medical student. "You'll be thinking it's none of my business to interfere . . . But the girl's over-excited, and its only natural after a shock like that . . ."

"Yes, yes, of course. Obviously she's over-excited and all that. But that's no excuse for insulting people. Especially insulting people who represent what we represent."

"Yes, I know that, and you're perfectly right," answered the student in a conciliatory voice. "The only thing I say is that it is very normal and natural for anyone to lose control in a case like this, especially a girl. Their nerves are easily . . ."

"But we are only here, as you must also understand, to carry out certain orders, to fulfil instructions applicable to the conditions arising in this present case, and we have sufficient responsibility already in this matter without having to put up with insults of the kind that this young lady has offered us."

"Of course, we agree. That goes without saying. All I wanted to ask of you was a little patience, to take into account the shock she has received, and to realize that she is not in a condition to know what she's saying. I only wanted to say that you might for once excuse her and not proceed against her."

"But of course we take that into account. But all this, let me tell you, is a very serious matter, as you must know. And people don't understand in the majority of cases how serious it is, or that we are carrying out our duties. If a man has been put on duty in a certain place, it's surely for some good reason. And when people come along, who think it's a joking matter, as some do, they fail to understand that they are committing an offence. An offence, neither more nor less, for which there is a punishment in the Code. Now, you must appreciate that we can't take this sort of thing as a joke . . ."

He put his notebook back in his pocket.

"We will overlook the question for once. But if it happens again, you understand . . . People must be more careful what words they allow themselves to use. The simple fact of excitement is no excuse for a person's saying anything he likes. But I think I've made the matter plain."

"Get along now . . ." said the other Guard. "Move away from here, all of you, and let's have no more trouble. Move along."

"Everyone go back to his place," said the first Guard, "if you please. And behave with proper dignity from now on, and kindly show the respect that is due to these mortal remains, also to ourselves as the representatives of Authority. His worship the magistrate should soon be here now."

"Those are the fellows who dived in after her," explained Sebas in a whisper. "They did what they could but it was too late."

"We'd gone into the water to get clean," continued Sebas, "to get rid of the earth that was clinging to us. We meant just to go in

[328]

and come out. It was she that complained of being uncomfortable with all that dirt on her." He raised his twitching hands to his forehead. "And it had to be me who had the miserable idea! It makes me curse myself, Miguel, every time I think of it . . . It makes a man want to knock in his head with a stone, I swear it does." He paused, before concluding in a dull voice, "But isn't this magistrate ever coming?"

Everyone in the group was quiet. They gazed at the water and the distant, scattered lights. Josemari had joined his friends after making his telephone call.

"That's all fixed," he said. "I just said we should be back late, because we had missed the last train. I did not want to tell them about it. I didn't want to say any more than was necessary so that they shouldn't get stupidly alarmed."

"That was very sensible. You know what families are. Someone has only to mention the word 'drowned', and they immediately start thinking and jumping to conclusions. And then there's no reassuring them until they actually see your face. They can be told tomorrow."

"And all these people?"

"They've just turned up. Other friends of the girl's apparently."

"Oh."

The Guards were pacing up and down again.

"They almost started some more trouble whilst you were telephoning."

"How?"

"Oh, nothing. One of the girls insulted the Guardians of the Law, because they wouldn't let her uncover her friend to see her face. They were rash enough to take her by the arm. And, oh boy, she turned on them like a panther! She used such language that the Guards pulled out their notebooks. They would have taken her name if that man hadn't interfered and persuaded them very diplomatically to drop the matter."

"They're much too high-hat. They ought to understand that people are flesh and blood, not the way they would like them to be."

"Yes, but the job they've got is no picnic either," said the man

[329]

with the mouth-organ. "And they've got a first-class reason for disliking it. It's no joke, I can tell you, having to mount guard over a corpse and take whatever's coming to you, and to do it on the pay they get. You wouldn't like it."

"Yes, that's true enough, of course. By the way, have you got any cigarettes left?"

Almost all the others had sat down. Only Miguel and Fernando were still standing, Zacarías, sitting beside Mely, was watching the shadows in the moonlight. His hands were playing with the sand.

"I can't believe it," said Fernando. "There are some things that you can't make yourself believe. It's here before my eyes. I can see it. I know it's a fact. But I can't take it in. I don't accept it for what it is. I can't get it into my head."

Miguel said nothing. Zacarías lifted his hand and let the sand run through his fingers. He saw a match glowing in the group of five students. They were passing it round, lighting their cigarettes.

* * *

"And they were so gay this morning . . ."

"Life," answered Macario, "is full of surprises like that. It shatters you just when you're not looking. When you're most off your guard, crack! the whip's caught you!"

Mauricio nodded his head.

"Who could have told the girl when she came through that door this morning, that she would never go back, that she'd come here to stay for ever?"

"For ever and ever, amen. That's it," said the shepherd. "And who could have told her father when he saw her off for this outing that it was the last time he'd see her and that he'd never give her another kiss?"

"You've said it! It's just that. That's what hits me hardest when I think about it," White Shoes suddenly exclaimed in a dull voice. "Fathers who see their daughters disappear like that, like lightning. Fss! You see her and she's gone, just like lightning. When it comes as the result of an illness, whether it's short or long, it's just as painful of course. Who could prevent it's being painful for a father? It isn't that. Death from illness is quite different. It's not like having seen her, that very morning, alive and kicking. Perhaps you've even laid her place for supper, as they certainly would have done in this case for the girl who's just dead. In fact, you're still counting her in the kingdom of the living, and in a second, before you can say 'Jack Robinson', a telegram, a message, a telephone call ... and she's ceased to exist." He made a gesture of extinction. "It doesn't bear thinking about."

"No, it doesn't," said the truck-driver. "It's a terrible thought."

"The same when someone's just died, and they begin 'Poor chap' and 'Poor old fellow', all that pity just makes me think: What about the others? What about those that are left? Those are the ones that really have the knife in their backs, sticking right into their guts! They're the ones we ought to pity. That girl must have had a nasty few moments, a very nasty few moments, poor thing, of course she had. But now she's not suffering. Her troubles are over. Finis! Now it's her parents, it's them we ought to feel sorry for. It's they who are going to suffer now, really suffer."

"How can you say a thing like that!" protested the Alcarrenian. "How can you shift your ground like that? And since when should we be sorrier for the parents, who aren't young any longer and have little or nothing left to expect from life, than for a young girl whose life has been cut short in her prime, just as she was beginning to enjoy it? She had left the world at the most exciting and the most promising moment when life has most pleasure to offer. That's the most terrible thing. It's far more tragic than her parents' sorrow, a hundred times greater. There's no comparison!"

"No, my friend. That's where we differ, you see. I respect your opinion, but I look at the matter from the practical side. One thing may be very sad, but it's over now. The other lasts. The parents are left to go on suffering."

"No, no, no, man, it's wrong to think like that! There's only one thing you have to remember, and it's this: however much the parents have to suffer today, at the end of eight, ten, x months, or years if you like, the day will come when they'll forget the girl and recover.

Do you expect them never to recover? But the girl now, she'll never be able to recover what she's lost, all that death has taken from her on a particular day, as it has today. Nobody can give all that back to her, can they now? You recover from anything else. It may be sooner or it may be later, but you recover in the end."

"Yes, there's no cure for that," said Carmelo, "no cure at all. There's nothing you can do about it. Whichever way you look at it it's a bad business. Bad through and through, like the Co-operative's farm. Death's like a bad bull. There's no way of fighting it."

The Alcarrenian spoke again, addressing White Shoes: "If it had just been some old cow I should have agreed with you entirely of course."

"I wouldn't be so sure of that," said Lucio. "It's a moot point whether life's more valuable to the young than to the old. I should say that a man's attachment to life grows as he gets older. There's less left for the old of course. But who's to say we don't cling on to the little bit that's left a great deal harder than we did in youth to the long life that was before us?"

White Shoes gave a look of agreement. He was about to answer but the truck-driver spoke before him, interrupting the argument.

"Well, it's been a long discussion we've had about it all. Some time ago now I said I was going, and here we all are still. So, if you'll excuse me, I'll wish you goodnight, and push off at full speed. I've paid you, haven't I?"

Mauricio nodded and the truck-driver drained his glass.

"Goodnight."

"See you tomorrow."

"No, I shan't be in tomorrow," he answered, turning round at the door. "I've got a journey to Teruel. I shan't be in probably until Wednesday or Thursday."

"Well, a good trip then."

"See you when you get back."

"Thank you. Goodbye."

And he went out.

"Restless damn life that chap leads!" remarked Lucio. "What an existence! In Teruel today, Saragossa tomorrow, and Timbuctoo the day after. Poor fellow, he never stops."

"Don't talk nonsense," answered Macario. "He couldn't have it better. I wish I could change places with him. I'd enjoy a sight of the miserable life they're supposed to lead all around the big cities." – He said "misegable and agound" – "Even if I could only see it through a keyhole. He doesn't do badly, believe me. Drivers are like sailors. You know what I mean."

"Don't you believe that nonsense. He just takes a beer or two. You don't think any the worse of him for that, do you?"

"A beer or two. I'd like to see him, that's all I say, and to see whether it's beers he drinks or what. If he's got the face to do it, all right, and good luck to him! But some of us are so badly off we haven't the courage to pinch even twenty-five pesetas from the family pocket. We can't silence our consciences, but he's better at the game. It depends on your character, like everything else."

"Look here," interrupted Mauricio, "he's a customer of this house and I won't have him abused here, Macario. So stop this line of talk, if you please."

"Ho! Well this'll be the one place then where he isn't talked about."

"People enjoy gossiping, I know that," said Mauricio. "That's up to them. But inside these doors, I won't have anyone abused. Once I allow a man in this place, from the moment he's admitted he can be a hundred per cent certain that his character will be respected in his absence just as much as if he were here. You have that guarantee and I'm sure you're glad of it. Well, give the other customers the same sort of respect."

"I don't give a damn what people say," said Macario with a laugh. "In a place like this half the fun's gone if there's no quarrelling and no gossip."

"Don't talk that way to me," said White Shoes in a reproachful voice. "Everybody in my barber's shop thought that way of going on was great fun, but the result wasn't pleasant for me, I can tell you. If every public place, barber's shop, bath-house, or eating-house, or what you like, were run on the same lines as Mauricio's here, manners would be very different, and a person's reputation would be far safer. And, believe me, relations between customers would be just as good. We should all treat one another in a much more civilized way."

Faustina had appeared at the passage door.

"Where have they all gone to, Mauricio? I've just been out in the garden to tidy things up a bit, thinking they'd started for home, and I found all their bicycles still there at this hour of night."

"Oh, there's been an accident. Didn't you know? One of the girls got drowned."

"What did you say? Who got drowned? They were there, in the garden . . ."

"Not one of those. Some of them stayed down by the river. They didn't all come up."

"Oh, my God, my God!" she shook her head. "What a dreadful thing! . . . Something was bound to go wrong . . . They were quite crazy . . . really irresponsible. How could they have avoided having an accident? But what a terrible thing to happen! How dreadful! I'm not surprised though, I'm not surprised! God knows I'm sorry. But surprised? No, I couldn't be surprised! I couldn't possibly be surprised! . . ."

She went off down the passage, mumbling.

"They'll look a fine sight when they come up again," said Lucio.

"Yes, a fine sight."

There was a silence. Then Macario spoke.

"That river, it's very treacherous. It always drowns somebody, every year."

"Every year," said the shepherd.

"And always somebody from Madrid," said the Alcarrenian. "It must be somebody from Madrid. Nobody else will do. You might say that it's got a grudge against people from Madrid."

"Yes," remarked Macario. "Of course it knows the people from these parts and never goes for them."

"Or rather we local people know the river. We are familiar with its ways."

"Yes that's the right way round," said Amalio the shepherd. "The river can't know anybody, and it can't have any consideration for anybody. But it's very treacherous. In the height of summer – and that's what it is today, isn't it? – you might say there was no water in it. But that makes no difference. Just when it wants to, it seizes someone by the leg, and down with him. He's drowned. It's done in a minute. Just as if it was hungry. And when it seizes anyone it holds on. And no one can save the victim from its grasp, not even Tarzan with all his mop of hair, and his knife, and his tigerskin breeches. Not on your life!"

"That's true enough. You've got to look out," added the Alcarrenian.

"They don't pay it enough respect, these people from Madrid, and they pay very dearly for their mistake. What they do is, they learn to swim in pools and then they come to the Jarama to practise. They see how shallow it is, they see that it isn't half as deep as a pool. It doesn't go up to their waist. So they get confident and think it's safe. Oh yes, it's shallow enough in summer time, but what they don't know, my friend, is that the waters of the Jarama have hands and claws like a wild animal, they can seize a person and gobble him up in a few seconds. That's what they don't know."

"Very different from a swimming pool!" said Amalio. "Watch out! It has twists and turns, and there's no end of them. It has different currents at different depths, and it's full of snags and cross-currents and eddies. It's like something alive. It's got more tricks than a fox's tail, and it couldn't be more treacherous if it had a brood of snakes running through its bed instead of water. It's quite a character, this river. But not a character you can trust. It's so mysterious and so full of tricks, it makes you tremble to think of it." He laughed.

"In winter," said the Alcarrenian, "now they ought to come and see it in winter, when it's running full and boisterous. Then they'd know what kind of creature they had to deal with."

"True," agreed the shepherd. "On one of those March days when it's running high, and puffs out its chest like a cock that's spoiling for a fight. It roars a bit when it's in flood. And it'll wash away an orchard, with the trees and walls and everything in it, and leave it looking just like the beach. All you need then are a few parasols and some of those painted huts, and you'd think you were at the seaside. And that's no lie."

Everyone laughed, and the Alcarrenian observed: "And don't let anyone say to me it hasn't got arms and claws. Why it even tears down the trees. Do you imagine water that was plain water could ever do a thing like that?"

"You wouldn't think so," said Amalio the shepherd.

He looked at them with a smile and was silent. Both his hands rested on the top of his stick, behind which his stomach shrank into the folds of his yellow cloth trousers. Leaning like this made him hunch his shoulders, for he was not tall, and the bones protruded beneath his tight shirt. His flat head was sunk between his shoulders, and his features, pressed between his huge bare forehead and his angular frog's jaw, were even longer when he smiled.

"Yes, it's wild when it wants to be," he said, swaying on his stick, "when it's trying to be the river it is. For it's not just a stream, oh no, and it isn't one of your big rivers either. When it says to you in March, 'Off we go!' then all the blood in its veins begins to circulate, and it starts boiling and bubbling like a cooking-pot. Then it sweeps down branches and bushes that hang above the current, and timbers and half-trees and dead animals, dogs and cats and hares, with their bellies tight as drums, and sheep and even an odd cow or two, and it leaves them stinking wherever it chooses to drop them when it's tired of carrying them on its back and has no further use for them." He spoke with animation. "It'll take a sheep at San Fernando and arrange a banquet at Vaciamadrid. It'll pick up a rye mill in the Sierra, and instal a flour and tapioca mill with modern machinery right in the middle of Aranjuez. And it's no good smelling the breath of the happy party at Vaciamadrid when they're belching after their feast, to see if it was your sheep or someone else's! It was a good meal and good luck to them!" He laughed. "If the river steals from you it can't be helped; you have to let whatever it is go to those who are lucky enough to seize it farther down. It gives and takes, and provides its own breakages and its own amusement."

"Now come off it," said Lucio. "Seems to me you're making it out bigger than it ever was after any storm."

"Yes, I thought we seemed to be in full flood tonight," agreed Mauricio with a smile. "If the river's like this in August, in February it'll wash the whole province away. I think you've been going in for some exaggeration."

The shepherd laughed.

"I'm not so far out. But I filled out the numbers a little, to improve the story."

"I can see you enjoy making it sound bigger," said Lucio, "although you say how much you loathe it you get very excited and enthusiastic when you talk about it. It's got quite a hold on you now, hasn't it? Tell us the truth."

"Yes, I pay it proper respect," answered the shepherd, "and keep my distance. I'll cool my feet in it and sit on its bank, but that's as far as I'll trust it. I've seen it at work, I've seen it charging like a red bull, carrying all it's stolen before it. I've seen that many times and I enjoy the spectacle, I mean it. Especially if I catch it when it's making the first charge. Then it's magnificent."

"Without your sheep, of course."

"With the sheep penned up, naturally. Oh no, they'll eat no more sheep at Vaciamadrid so long as I'm the shepherd, I promise you."

"But how could it carry a sheep so far down, however swollen the river was?"

"Very easily," said the shepherd with a laugh. "First of all because they're all so thin. They weigh less than a decent-sized grasshopper. And secondly because I invented the story. It's one of my inventions, you see, a story I told my boss once when he sent me at the height of a storm to look for the skin of a sheep the Jarama had washed away. It was the father and grandfather of a lie but it took him in. I said, 'All right, I'll go this moment.' And I spent the evening playing nap, one game of nap after another. Then I went to him next morning as solemn as an owl, and told him that some rascals from Vaciamadrid had cooked his sheep, and they'd sold the skin to the first man who'd offered them four pesetas for it. And my master swallowed the story entire. He said, 'Very well, I don't see what we can do about it,' and told me to drop the matter and give up the search. That shows you how little he knows about anything, and what a serious face I put on when I told him that lie. And that's my story."

White Shoes raised his head.

"You're very funny, Amalio," he said, "with all these stories you've got to tell about the river. But today it's costing some people a lot of tears."

"That's true," said the shepherd. "As luck or ill-luck will have it. It's bound to be like that. The same thing makes some people laugh and other people cry. And this story of the Jarama is nothing new. They've been coming here to swim for goodness knows how long, since a long time before the war. The custom dates from time immemorial, and every single summer three or four people from Madrid are drowned. How long have you lived in Coslada?"

"Nearly four years."

"So you've had three summers here, including this one. Now do you remember any one of them in which someone from Madrid didn't get drowned in the Jarama? It's an old story and we all know it. It's become almost regular. Today was its day. The river was biding its time, you know, waiting for today."

"Yes, somebody's number turned up, like in a lottery, and it was all up with that somebody!"

"True enough. The river claims its own," answered the shepherd.

"And if one day people gave up bathing in the river it would come up over its banks to catch them."

"It would be capable of that, all right," said the Alcarrenian.

The shepherd laughed.

"That would be frightening, eh? The river leaving its bed and starting to chase people like a great snake. That'd put the wind up you, wouldn't it, Señor Lucio?"

"I've got very tough, you know. It would spit me out again good and quick."

"It may like the old cock's flesh best, you never know," said the Alcarrenian with a yawn.

There was a silence during which Carmelo raised his glass and took a sip of wine. Lucio had signed to Mauricio to refill all the glasses.

"You're always behindhand," said Mauricio to White Shoes. "Drink up and let me fill your glass."

"No, Mauricio, don't give me any more wine. These things take away a man's taste for drink."

"Just as you like," said Mauricio, withdrawing the bottle.

"What things?" asked Macario.

White Shoes looked him in the eyes.

"This business," he pointed towards the door, "the things that happen, you know."

"Oh, I see."

"It may be silly of me, but it makes me quite upset," explained White Shoes, as if to excuse himself. "When things happen like that, quite close to you, even though they haven't any connection with you. I hadn't even set eyes on this girl, if it comes to that. But we've seen all her friends about here, and it gives me an odd feeling that I shan't get rid of till tomorrow morning. It's like a bad taste in your mouth, or something like that. I really can't explain it."

"I understand you," said Macario. "It just depends on how sensitive you are. Some are more so, some less. Some don't flick an eyelid when a thing like this happens or when they see people mangled to death in a bus accident. While others are different – like you."

"And every day," White Shoes observed, "you read about quantities of accidents in the newspapers, with the descriptions of the victims and the colour of their hair, and it doesn't worry you in the least. But on the other hand, if you come somewhere near witnessing one, as we have this evening, on the ricochet, as you might say, then it gives you this odd feeling in the body, that there's no way of shaking off. It's like a bad omen. That's it, that's the word for it. It's like a bad omen."

"Yes, I know what you mean," said Macario, paying no attention to what White Shoes was saying.

"Now tonight, for instance, I shan't be able to eat any supper, you understand," concluded White Shoes. "The idea of supper sickens me."

* * *

He found the magistrate among the dancers. His fair head stood out above the others. They were playing a samba. Now the magistrate had seen him and pointed to his own chest to ask, "Is it me you're looking for?" The man nodded. The magistrate stopped dancing and made his excuses to his partner.

"Forgive me, Aurora dear, but the secretary has turned up. I must see what he wants."

"Don't bother about that, Ángel, of course. I forgive you. Duty first." She gave him a half smile.

"Thank you, Aurora."

He left the floor avoiding the other couples, and stopped beside a long leafed plant, where the secretary was standing.

"It's not so urgent," said the secretary. "You could have finished your dance."

"It doesn't matter. What is it?"

"A telephone message from San Fernando. A girl has been drowned in the river."

"Oh dear!" he made a grimace. "Who phoned?"

"The patrol."

The magistrate looked at the time.

"Very well. Have you asked for a car?"

"Yes, sir, it's at the door. Vicente's car."

"Good lord, it fairly creeps."

"There wasn't another. You can't find a taxi on a Sunday, you know, especially today when quail shooting's started."

"All right. I must just tell them I'm going. I'll be with you in a moment."

He crossed the room and went up to a table.

"Sorry, my friends, but I must go."

He picked up a silver lighter and a packet of Philip Morris which were lying on the table.

"What's happened?" asked the girl he had been dancing with.

"Somebody drowned."

"In the river?"

"Yes, but not here in the Henares. In the Jarama at San Fernando."

"And of course you've got to go immediately."

The magistrate nodded his head. He was wearing a dark suit and had a carnation in his buttonhole.

"I think it shows very bad taste to drown at this hour and especially on a Sunday," said one of the men at the table. "I sympathize with you."

"He chose his profession."

"Well, see you tomorrow," said the magistrate.

"You've still got something in your glass there. Drink it up," said a man in spectacles, handing him a very tall glass with a slice of lemon floating in it.

The magistrate took it and gulped down the contents. The band had stopped playing. A girl in blue came up to the table with a young man in a light jacket.

"Ángel's had to go," they told them.

"Oh! What for?"

"Duty calls him."

"What a nuisance. I am sorry."

"So am I," said the magistrate. "Enjoy yourselves."

"I'll be seeing you, Ángel dear."

"Goodbye, everybody."

He waved his hand in farewell and turned away. He crossed the dance floor to join the secretary.

"I'm ready when you are," he said without pausing.

They went out together, walking down a wide passage with a coffered roof into the reception hall. The doorman, who was old and wore a braided uniform with gold buttons, put his cigarette away when he saw them coming and got up wearily from his rush chair.

"Goodnight, your worship, goodnight," he said as he opened the great glass door with engraved letters.

The music started up again behind them. The magistrate glanced back at the ballroom.

"See you tomorrow, Ortega," he said to the doorman, as he went through the door into the street.

It was a maroon Balilla. The chauffeur was in his shirtsleeves, half sitting on the mudguard. The magistrate stood for a moment in front of the car, and looked up at the night sky. Then he bent his tall body and got into the car. The secretary got in behind him and the driver closed the door. On the right they could see the doorman's face looking at them from between the elaborate letters on the great glass doors: CASINO DE ALCALÁ. The chauffeur had gone round behind the car and now sat at the wheel. It refused to go at first. It didn't spark. Then he pulled out the choke and the engine started.

"Vicente," said the magistrate, "stop a moment please as you pass my house." He turned to the secretary: "I'm going to leave a message for my mother to say where we've gone and tell them not to wait supper for me."

They went through the Plaza Mayor. It was empty. Only the thin silhouette of Miguel de Cervantes on his pedestal with his pen and his rapier, in the middle of the little gardens under the quiet moon. Light and smoke poured from the bars. Inside, men could be seen confusedly huddled around the counters. Then the car stopped.

"You go in, Vicente," said the magistrate, "please. Tell the maid we are going to San Fernando, and it may be a couple of hours before we're back."

"Very well, your worship."

Vicente got out of the car and rang a door bell. The door was immediately opened, and the chauffeur spoke to the servant, whose figure was outlined in the doorway against the light from the house. He finished giving his message, but the door was not shut because another woman's figure appeared behind the maid, pushed her aside and came across the pavement to the car.

"Haven't you had anything to eat, darling?" she asked, leaning through the car window. "Just stop for a mouthful. And you too, Emilio. Come in, both of you."

"Thank you very much, Señora, but I've had my supper," answered the secretary.

"What about you, darling? You'll be very late."

"No thank you, Mother, I'm not hungry. We've had snacks at the Casino. I'll eat when I get back. Leave my supper covered up for me in the kitchen."

The chauffeur returned to his seat. The lady showed signs of objecting.

"I don't know how I can let you go off like this. When you do get in everything will be cold and you won't enjoy it. And it won't do you any good or anything. This sort of thing is really bad for you. But if you won't eat, well don't stay here, don't stay. There's nothing I can do about it."

She left the window.

"See you later, Mamma."

The engine started.

"Goodbye, darling." She stooped for a moment to see the secretary inside the car, which was already moving. "Goodbye, Emilio."

"Goodnight, Señora," he answered.

Once out on the road the chauffeur changed into second, and the door of the magistrate's house was shut behind them. He changed into top a little farther on, then crossed the stone bridge on to the Madrid road. Not far away, on their left, the great black mass of the Cerro del Viso stood like an inverted trough. Around it was a band of milky, violet light from the moon.

"Have you warned the surgeon?"

"Yes, sir. He said he'd come in his own car, a little later or whenever we send for him."

"Right. It was a young girl, wasn't it?"

"Yes, so I understood from the telephone."

"Didn't he give you any more details? Didn't he say if she was from Madrid?"

"Yes, sir, as a matter of fact he did. He said she did come from Madrid."

"Yes, on Sundays the place is fairly infested with picnickers from Madrid. What time did it take place?"

"I can't tell you that. He must have phoned just after ten."

Now they were making straight for the lights of Torrejón. The magistrate took out his Philip Morris.

"Want a cigarette, Vicente?"

The chauffeur took one hand off the wheel, and stretched it back over his shoulder without turning his head.

"Thanks, Don Ángel, if I may."

The magistrate put the cigarette in his hand.

"Still no petty vices, Emilio, eh?"

"No, nor any major vices either."

On their left they saw the valley of the Henares, bathed in moonlight where it fell into the Jarama. The secretary squinted at the magistrate's lapel with the carnation in its buttonhole. The lighter-flame shone on the upholstery of the car. The chauffeur tilted his head, so as to get a light from the magistrate without taking his eyes off the beams of the headlights, which lit up the stones of the road as they drove on. On their left, very far behind them, was a horizon of distant tableland, standing out whitish in the dim moonlight against a deep blue sky veiled by dust. A succession of flat hills of chalk or marl projected, bone-white, above the valleys, like the fossil shoulderblades of the world. Then the Balilla was suddenly lit up by a very strong light overtaking it from the rear. The loud horn of a touring car was demanding the right to pass. The light sailed past them on the left, with a squeak of new tyres scraping against the curb. A second later the Chrysler showed its tapering black back and its red tail-lights, which quickly disappeared.

"Americans," said the chauffeur.

"What else could they be?" answered the secretary.

"They were. I saw the registration plate. With an engine like that they can go anywhere."

"Yes, they certainly can."

"By the time we get to San Fernando they'll have reached Madrid and be sick of it. That is if they don't get smashed up on the way, and end up a mass of wreckage against some post on the road."

"Too much speed leads to a bad end," agreed the secretary.

"That's one advantage we've got. With this old fruit box we're in no danger," said the chauffeur. "We must have some advantage."

"You're right."

The magistrate travelled in silence. They passed the Loeches road on the left, and made towards Torrejón de Ardoz. There was still a good deal of light on the stretch of the road that went through the town, and some groups of men scattered to make way for the Balilla. Others were sitting in lines or clumps at the doors of the bars. As they passed they saw the insides of lighted taverns, and the transitory

brightness of coloured calendars on indigo-washed walls. They left
the silhouette of the clocktower behind them with a streak of moonlight on its blue roof tiles. The tall, angular shadow of a pediment
towered above the roofs. Then the road dipped down to the uncultivated land beside the Jarama and at the bottom of the slope, on the
further side of the glistening vein of river, appeared Coslada. The
road ran in a straight line flanked by trees as far as the Viveros
bridge. On crossing the bridge they left the main road, and turned to
the left along the secondary road to San Fernando de Henares. The
car jolted in the ruts. Now the magistrate asked, "Where exactly did
the Guard say the accident happened?"

"At the dam."

"And are you sure you know the way down to the dam, Vicente?"

"Yes, sir."

They found the level-crossing open. The car gave a great jolt as
they crossed the rails. Ahead, on the left, the great dark trees of
Cocherito of Bilbao's estate hid the shadow of the villa, whose roof
glistened among the leaves.

"This will be the ninth corpse I've dealt with that's been drowned
in the Jarama."

The chauffeur shook his head in a shocked way.

"No, only the eighth that has been drowned, now I come to think
of it," the magistrate corrected himself. "Because one of them was
the girl whose young man pushed her off the railway bridge. You
remember that, Emilio?"

"Yes, I remember. It'll be two years ago."

They turned to the left again, on to a road between vineyards,
and then dropped down to the right, to the *merenderos* themselves.
The car stopped under a big tree. Some people came out of the
shack, and figures appeared at the lighted doors to see who was
coming. They retreated respectfully from the door when the magistrate went in. He half closed his eyes in the light of the bar. Vicente
stayed outside.

"Good evening."

They were quiet at the tables and looked on, listening. The magistrate had fair hair, wavy about the forehead, and was considerably

taller than the secretary or any of those standing beside the counter.

"How are you, your worship?" asked Aurelia.

"Very well, thank you. Tell me, where is the victim of the accident?"

"Here, just here, your worship," she pointed towards the left, to some place outside the door. "Almost directly opposite. We could see everything from here. You've only got to cross the little bridge. Otherwise . . . Here, boy!" she called in the direction of the kitchen.

A lad appeared instantly from behind a flapping cloth that did duty for a door.

"Now take that thing off, and accompany his worship to the place this minute," said Aurelia. "And be quick about it!"

"Thank you. I didn't really want to bother you."

"No bother at all, your worship!"

The boy had taken off his apron.

"One other thing, Señora. There's no light down there, is there?"

"No, there's no light. No, your worship."

"Well then, look, would you be so kind as to let us have a torch?"

"A torch? No, I can't, sir. We haven't got one. I'd have been delighted if we had." She thought for a moment. "I have got some lanterns though, oil lanterns, you know the sort. I could let you have one of those, if you could make do with it. You could have it in a minute."

"All right, a lantern then," said the magistrate. "Provided it works, it'll be quite all right."

Aurelia turned to the boy again.

"Did you hear that? Go down to the cellar, and fetch me a lantern. But quick as lightning! Quick. Bring the newer one of the two. But run! Run!"

The boy ran off.

"And wipe off the dust!" she called after his retreating back.

She then directed her shouts to the kitchen door.

"Luisa! Luisa! . . bring me the oil jar, quickly, and the new wicks. They're on the chimney shelf."

"Coming, Mother!" answered a child's voice from behind the curtain.

Aurelia turned to the magistrate.

"It'll be ready in a second."

"Many thanks, Señora. I've got a torch at home, but . . ." he shrugged his shoulders.

"Anything we can do here, you know . . . Nothing's too much trouble." She paused before going on with a shake of the head. "Unfortunately it's always when there's a tragedy . . . We should be glad to see you here and to be of assistance to you under other circumstances, pleasanter circumstances than have brought you here today."

"Yes, better not meet at all than meet like this."

"You're right, your worship. You're quite right. Much as we respect you it would be far better not to meet."

The magistrate absent-mindedly agreed.

"Naturally, yes."

"But all the same it would be very nice if you were to come here one Sunday with your friends, and then we could welcome you as we should like. It needn't always be . . ."

"One day, yes. Thank you."

The girl came in with the wicks and the oil.

"Well, we'll see if you keep your promise, your worship. Bring it over here and put it down. I wonder what that young wretch can be thinking of?" She peered down into the cellar. "Erneee! Ernesto! What are you up to? What are you doing down there, I should like to know?"

She listened for Ernesto's answer, and replied: "Well, bring it as it is then? Don't you know that his worship's waiting for it?" She came back to the middle of the counter.

"I'm sorry, your worship, but that boy's as much use as a sick headache. I'm always on at him."

"Don't worry."

The boy appeared.

"I told you to wipe the dust off the top, idiot, not to polish it like a church ornament. Bring it here, come on, bring it to me, half-wit!"

One of the men at the counter intervened.

"There's only one thing rattles that boy, Aurelia, that's having you shouting at him every minute of the day."

[347]

"You hold your tongue."

"That's not the way to make the boy lively. All you do, the way you go about it, is to make him more and more frightened."

"Did anyone ask you your opinion, eh?"

"It makes me wild! It makes me damned furious!"

He struck his fist on the marble and walked out of the bar.

"Well!" said Aurelia, turning to the other man at the counter. "Did you ever see anything like it? No respect for his worship here . . ."

They gave her an expressionless look and said nothing. Aurelia shrugged her shoulders. She opened the door of the lantern and took out the white metal box that formed the burner.

"Would you like me to help you?" asked the secretary.

"You'll make yourself dirty."

"Give it to me. I'll get out the burnt wick. Please let me."

Aurelia opened the burner and passed the upper part to the secretary.

"Careful! It's all filthy. It's six or eight months since it's been used. Not since the winter it hasn't."

She began to clean the bottom part with a rag, while the secretary used a little stick to extract the remains of the wick, which choked the tube in the top. Then Aurelia retwisted the strands with her fingers.

"Do you mind?"

The secretary handed her the cover, and she pushed the wick through its tube. Then she refilled the little container with oil, and caught with her finger the drip that was running down the neck of the jar. She put the two parts together, and the burner was now closed in its box and ready. She replaced it in the lantern, pushing it between the two flanges in the bottom which were designed to hold it. One of the men lit a match and applied it to the wick.

"Splendid!" said the magistrate when the oil took fire.

Aurelia closed the lantern, and the flame was now enclosed within the four glass panes. She lifted it by the handle and gave it to the boy.

"You carry it. Take it now, and mind you don't drop it!"

"But it's not necessary for him to come," said the magistrate. "We'll carry it ourselves."

"Come now, you mustn't carry it! Not in those Sunday clothes of yours. The boy can carry it for you. He's got nothing on that'll stain. Make him go in front, and then you'll see where you're treading. The path's very rough."

"Well, let's go. We'll see you later, Señora. Many thanks."

He addressed the customers: "Goodnight."

A murmur of reply came from the tables. Aurelia accompanied them to the door.

"This way. D'you see? You've only got to cross the planks. There's a little bridge, you know. You'll see the two Guards just on the other side. The boy will guide you?"

"I understand," said the magistrate as he departed.

The secretary took a brief case and a blanket from the car. They passed beneath a large tree, whose top hid the moon and threw a very deep shadow. Leaving the tree behind them, they followed a narrow path between weeds and brambles, which encroached on it and compelled them to walk in single file. The boy went first, with his long thin arm stretched upwards holding the lantern, that swung from his fingers. Next came the little shadow of the secretary, in his black suit, with his pink bald head and his steel-rimmed spectacles, and last the tall, fair haired magistrate, who had fallen behind and was advancing with the long strides of youth. They emerged on the edge of the backwater, and the secretary stopped two paces from the bridge.

"Wait a moment, lad."

The boy stopped. The secretary then turned back to the magistrate.

"Your worship!"

"What is it, Emilio?"

"I didn't care to mention it before, your worship. But have you thought about your buttonhole?"

"No. What's the matter?"

He looked down at his chest and saw the carnation.

"Good lord, you're right. I hadn't noticed it. Thank you for warning me in time."

He caught up with the secretary and proffered his lapel.

"Take it out, will you, there's a good fellow. It's held in behind with a couple of pins."

"Bring the light here, lad."

The boy obediently lifted the lantern as near as he could to the examining magistrate's head, whose golden hair shone in the light of the flame. The secretary got clumsily to work, bringing his glasses close to the magistrate's lapel. At last he managed to extract the pins, and the magistrate pulled the carnation out.

"Thank you, Emilio. Now we can go on."

The three figures crossed the little wooden bridge in single file. The boy remained in front, with the lantern swinging at the end of his arm. The magistrate crossed last and threw his carnation down in the mud. The planks creaked beneath their weight. As they left the bridge the Guard Gumersindo advanced to meet them. The patent leather of his three-cornered hat gleamed as he came into the light of the lantern.

"At your worship's service."

The sand had deadened the stamp of his heels.

"Good evening," said the magistrate. "Let us see her."

They reached the river bank. Everyone had got up and was standing silently around the body. The sluices roared. The magistrate seized the boy by the neck.

"Come here, my fine fellow! Stand there, and hold the lantern up for me. Nothing to be afraid of."

The little boy put up his bare arm, and held it horizontal with the lantern dangling over the shape of the corpse.

"Come on, uncover it," said the magistrate.

The young Guard approached to do so.

"No, not you. The secretary."

The secretary leaned over the body, and removed the dress and the towel that covered it. The skin looked bluish white beside the black of the swimsuit. Now the magistrate crouched down, and ran his eyes over the whole body, examining it closely.

"Lie her flat on her back."

The secretary lifted the corpse from one side and it fell inertly into the new position. Small grains of sand stuck to it where it had been touching the ground. The magistrate lifted the hair from its eyes.

"Give me that light."

He took the lantern from the boy's hands and held it to Lucita's face. The pupils shone with a dull light like bits of mirror that were covered with dust, or fragments of tin-plate. The mouth was open. The lips hung like those of a fish. The magistrate got up.

"When did you get here?"

"Us, your worship?"

"Of course."

"Well, we, your worship, we came to this spot at the critical moment, when these gentlemen were laying the victim on the shore."

"What time was that?"

"The event must have occurred at nine forty-five p.m. approximately, and allowing for error."

"Yes, at a quarter to ten roughly, in fact. Who are the gentlemen you are referring to?"

"Us, sir," the medical student came forward and stated. "The four of us."

"I see. Had she gone out to swim with you?"

"No, your worship, we only went in when we heard people shouting for help."

"Did you see her from the shore?"

"It was dark by that time, sir. All we that could see was some movement on the surface of the water."

"Who was shouting for help?"

"This gentleman and this young lady, from the river."

The magistrate looked at Paulina and Sebastián, and asked the student another question.

"Could you calculate what the distance was between them and the victim at that moment?"

"I reckon it must have been about twenty yards."

"No less?"

"I don't think so, sir."

"And there wasn't anyone else in the water who was any nearer to the victim?"

"No, your worship, there was nobody else to be seen in the river."

The magistrate turned to Sebastián.

"You are in general agreement with what this gentleman says?"

"Yes, your worship."

"And you, miss?"

"The same," answered Paulina, lowering her head.

"Don't say 'the same'. Say yes or no."

"Well, yes. Yes, sir."

There were tears in her voice.

"Thank you, miss." He turned to the students. "Now which was the first of you to reach the victim in the river?"

"I was, sir," answered Rafael. "I bumped into the body on the surface of the water."

"I see. And you couldn't tell at that moment whether she still showed any signs of life?"

"I could, your worship. She showed no signs of life."

"Thank you very much. That's enough for the present. Nobody who has spoken to me here is to go away, nor is anyone who has been previously instructed by the Guards. If anyone wishes to volunteer a statement concerning this matter, let him remain behind also."

He turned to the secretary.

"Secretary, proceed with the lifting of the corpse, and take charge of the clothing and possessions of the victim."

"Yes, sir."

"You may request three or four of these young men to help you transport it. We will leave it at Aurelia's for the present, until the mortuary keeper arrives. Now, one of you Guards!"

"At your orders, your worship."

"You will see the mortuary is advised by telephone. Go and see to it now. Tell the man in charge to come immediately and report to me."

"Yes, your worship. At your orders."

"We shall then put the body at the disposition of the examining surgeon at the earliest possible moment."

Rafael and his companions had approached the secretary. Wet Trousers said quietly: "Look, we will help you, if that's all right by you. The others knew the girl, and it might be rather painful for them."

"That's all right. You'll do. Let's get it done. Come here, lad, and bring the light."

The boy came up with the lantern in his hand. The secretary unfolded the blanket he was carrying, and laid it beside Luci's body. Then Rafael and Wet Trousers rolled it into the middle of the blanket, which they folded over the body from both sides, to cover it completely.

"That's right."

The Guard handed Lucita's bag and her food tin to the secretary, and he put them with her towel and her clothes.

"Is that all she had?"

"Yes, sir."

"Forward then. Carefully. You go ahead with the light, lad, the same way as you did when we came down. Your worship!"

The magistrate was looking at the river. He turned round.

"What? All right. Let the Guard make sure the required people follow us. Let's go."

The blanket was lifted by four of the students, one at each corner. The one with the mouth-organ supported the corpse in the middle, putting his hands under the blanket to prevent its scraping the ground. The whole group began to walk in silence in the wake of the boy with the light. Behind the corpse went the magistrate and the secretary, then Lucita's friends, followed by the Guard with his thumb through the strap of his rifle. They crossed the little bridge cautiously, and the four who were carrying the body had difficulty in negotiating the narrow path through the brambles. The boy turned the lantern on them, and walked backwards, to light the painful progress of the corpse. Their clothes caught on the thorns as their sides brushed the wall of undergrowth. They emerged by the great tree and the magistrate then went ahead.

"Wait here for a little," he said. "I'll be back in a moment."

They put the body down on the ground among the tables and chairs that covered the little terrace. Vicente the chauffeur came over to look at it by the weak light of the two electric bulbs still burning. The last of the party arrived, and now they all stood there waiting. Ten yards from them the light struck the machinery of the two sluice gates; two toothed wheels and some iron bars stood straight and tall at the end of the dam. It was here that the waters thundered. The magistrate had met the old Guard coming out of the bar.

"Have you advised him?"

"At your orders, sir. He's coming immediately."

"Good," said the magistrate going through the bar door. "Señora!"

"What can I do for you, sir?"

She came up obsequiously, drying her hands on her apron.

"Look now, I want to put the victim's remains somewhere until the mortuary keeper comes to take charge of them."

Aurelia glanced at him hesitantly.

"In here?" she asked in a low voice. "But your worship, remember I've still got customers in the place . . ."

"I understand that. But I have no alternative."

"Listen, your worship, if it was only me . . . at a time when the place was empty . . ."

"Just as you please. There's no compulsion. You have a perfect right to refuse hospitality to the victim's corpse."

"Oh no, sir. How could I do that? It would be dreadful. I can't do that either, your worship. I was only thinking of them . . ."

"Señora," interrupted the magistrate, "your motives have nothing to do with the matter. You haven't got to give me any explanations. All I want to know is whether you are willing or not."

"What do you expect me to do, your worship? How could I shut my doors on the poor thing?" She turned up her eyes. "You present me with a painful alternative . . ."

"I'm sorry, Señora. That's just what my job is, to present people with hard alternatives. I can't avoid it. Do you mind showing me the place?"

"The place? Why here in the cellar, don't you think? There at the back."

She jerked her thumb towards the sackcloth curtain behind her.

"Excellent. Thank you. I'll tell them to bring her in." He went out.

"You can bring her in here. The owner will tell you where to put her."

[354]

Then he shouted louder, pointing upwards to the group still on the terrace.

"Send me in one Guard. Everyone else is to stay outside."

"At your worship's orders."

It was the younger Guard. The magistrate acknowledged him with a gesture. The Guard came through the door backwards, in advance of the five who were carrying the body.

"Lift her a bit. Be careful, there's a step."

All the men in the bar got up and removed their headgear. They stood still, in deep silence, facing the corpse as it was brought through. One of them quickly crossed himself. The sound of his lips as he kissed his thumb lingered on the air.

"This way," said Aurelia. "There are half a dozen steps." She led them behind the counter.

"Be careful, you won't be able to see."

She joined the two loose ends of an electric wire that hung on the wall, and the cellar was seen to light up through the sack that served as a curtain. She hurriedly drew it back and held it aside while they carried Lucita's body through, and down the six steps. After them came the magistrate, the secretary and the Civil Guard. They found themselves in an artificial cave, hollowed in the limestone and running back into the high bank which stood behind the house and formed its rear wall. It ran twenty-five or thirty feet into the rock, and was fifteen feet wide and about the same in height, under a roughly vaulted roof. Both roof and walls were very crude. But the uneven surface of the rock had been persistently whitewashed, coat after coat in the course of years, and now the thickness of the lime had softened its projections and blunted its angles and ridges. They put Lucita's body down.

"Stay here, you. The rest go outside."

Rafael ran his eyes over the vault as his companions went out. The lime was not fresh but its whiteness was broken in only a few places, where patches of greenish ooze appeared on the roof and walls. From these stains hung swags of moss. Aurelia was still standing beside the curtain at the top of the six steps cut into the rock which led down to the vault.

[355]

"Another request, Señora. We need a table and three chairs, if you will be so kind."

"Only too pleased, sir. They'll be brought down right away."

The magistrate took out his cigarettes.

"We'll see that you get away as soon as possible. But there are formalities to be complied with. Do you smoke?"

"Thank you, not just now."

Against one wall stood three large casks, some barrels, and several earthenware jars in a line. In the far corners there were timber beams, soot-blackened stove pipes, and ropes of esparto grass, plus the trestles and planks of a builder's cradle, much stained with plaster. On the floor was an upturned boat whose timbers were warped and dry, an iron stove, a pile of broken chairs, a wheelbarrow, a door, some tins and a great number of small paint pots. Rafael went to help Aurelia's daughter and the boy, who had appeared on the steps with the table and some green-painted folding chairs. These they placed in the middle of the cellar, and the girl looked up at the light in order to put the table immediately beneath it. Then Aurelia reappeared, unfolding a newspaper.

"I'm sorry, your worship, but today I haven't a single tablecloth left. On Sundays they dirty every one I've got. And the more I had the more they'd dirty."

She spread the newspaper on the table top. The girl and the boy departed.

"You must excuse the shortage, but perhaps you can make do with this."

"Thank you. Don't worry," said the secretary. "That'll be quite all right."

"If there's anything you need, you know where I am. If there is anything just give me a shout. I shall be just at the top – " She pointed to the steps – "Behind that curtain."

"Yes, I know. Thank you," said the magistrate impatiently. "There's nothing more for the present."

"Don't be afraid to ask."

Aurelia disappeared up the steps, resting her hands on her knees to help herself, and went behind the curtain.

"Just like your mother, sir."

The two smiled. The young Guard looked at the pile of broken objects at the far end of the cellar. The magistrate stubbed out his cigarette on the side of a jar.

"Please sit down."

Rafael and the secretary sat down facing one another. The Guard poked something on the ground with the butt of his rifle to unearth it from the dust. It was the registration plate of a cart. The secretary had taken out his papers. The magistrate remained on his feet.

"Your surname and christian names?"

"Rafael Soriano Fernández."

"Age?"

"Twenty-four."

"Profession?"

The secretary wrote: "Next to appear before the Representative of Justice was one answering to the name of Rafael Soriano Fernández, twenty-four years of age, bachelor, by profession student, inhabitant of Madrid, domiciled in the Calle de Penascales, number one, seventh floor, centre, literate and with no police record, who, having been warned and put under oath, as the law provides, declared that he had not been adjudged guilty of any contravention of the law . . ."

"Now, let's see, Rafael, tell me what was the first evidence you had of this accident?"

"We heard shouts from the river."

"Right. And could you ascertain the place from which these shouts proceeded?"

"Yes, sir. We ran to the bank, and the shouts continued, and I saw that there were two people together in the water."

"One of them being the victim?"

"No, your worship. If the victim had been shouting as well, I should have distinguished her cries from the others. They were here and she was there, you see. That is to say that they were so far apart that their voices would not have been confused if the other girl had shouted too. I mean, this one." He made a slight movement of the head to indicate Lucita's body which was lying behind him.

"Good. And then you immediately distinguished the victim in the water also. Is that correct?"

"Not as clearly as the others. You couldn't see her so well. But there could have been no mistake."

"Good, Rafael. And what distance do you reckon there was at that moment between her and her friends?"

"Oh . . . Twenty or twenty-five yards I should say."

"Good, let's put down twenty. Now give me your account of what occurred. Go on."

"Well then, your worship, we saw the girl . . . When I say the girl I mean we saw what proved to be the girl, but we didn't know it was her till afterwards. At that moment all we could make out was a shape, just the shape of somebody moving up and down in the water . . ."

The Guard was now still, standing beside Lucita's covered body and listening to Rafael. The secretary was writing: ". . . distinguishing the shape of someone moving up and down in the water . . ." The magistrate had not taken a seat; he was standing listening to Rafael, leaning with one arm on a cask. The Guard yawned and looked up at the ceiling. There were cobwebs around the lamp, and their threads shone in the light.

Then the magistrate asked: "Now tell me, from what you could make out, do you believe you have sufficient facts to swear, without fear of error, that this was a purely accidental matter for which no one could be held responsible? Remember, of course, that negligence is a manner of offence in the eyes of the law."

"Yes, your worship. From what I saw, I have more than sufficient reason to assure you that this was an accident."

"Very good. Thank you. That will be all."

The secretary then wrote: "Read, affirmed, ratified, and signed by the said witness . . ."

A voice came from behind the curtain.

"Have I your worship's permission? . . ."

"Yes, you may go now. Next please! Send your companion in, please, the other man who was talking to me on the river bank."

"Yes, sir. I'll send him at once. Goodnight."

"Goodnight to you."

A man appeared from behind the curtain. He came down the steps with his cap in his hand and passed Rafael on the way.

"Good evening. The keeper of the mortuary, your worship, at your service."

He had halted three yards from the table.

"Yes, I remember you. Good evening."

The man approached.

"Now look," said the magistrate. "I sent for you because I want you to open the mortuary and get it ready to receive the remains of a person who has been drowned this evening. We shall leave very soon. See that everything's prepared. You understand?"

"Yes, your worship. It shall be done."

The secretary looked towards the entrance. The medical student had just come in.

"Right. And then you'll have to wait up until the surgeon comes. He'll be there tonight. You understand?"

"Yes, your worship."

"Well, that's all. You may go now. The sooner you go the better."

The student was waiting with averted eyes at the foot of the steps.

"I'll see you shortly then, your worship."

"Yes, goodbye for the present. Come over here, if you will, and take a seat."

The medical student gave a slight nod of salutation as he came up. The mortuary keeper went through the curtain.

"Your surname and Christian names?"

The secretary wrote in his memorandum: "The next to appear before the Representative of Justice was one answering to the name of José Manuel Gallardo Espinosa, twenty-four years of age, bachelor, by profession student, inhabitant of Madrid, domiciled in the Calle de Cea Bermúdez, number one hundred and thirty-nine, third floor, letter E, literate and with no police record, who, having been warned and put under oath as the law provides, declared that he had not been adjudged guilty of any contravention of the law. And that in the matter of this affair, that being on an expedition with several friends on the day of this report, in the vicinity of a place known as 'the Dam', at a quarter to ten in the evening he heard shouts for help coming from that part of the river, whereupon promptly approaching with three of his companions, he immediately observed from the bank the form of a person apparently drowning about thirty-five yards from the point where the witness and his companions were standing, and not less than twenty yards away from those persons who had uttered the aforementioned cries for help from the water. That, in view of this alarming situation, the said José Manuel with his three aforementioned companions plunged into the water without delay with the intention of coming to the aid of the person who was in danger, and having done so all swam to the spot where they had previously observed her. That in the interim, before they could reach the victim of the accident, this person had been carried away by the current of the river and could no longer be seen, and thus they were unable to fulfil their intention of promptly rescuing her from the water. Further, that despite the great zeal shown by the said José Manuel and by his comrades in their endeavours to rediscover the victim, their efforts remained fruitless. These companions were joined, as the witness affirms, by another youth, who was already in the water and whom he recognized as one of those who a few moments before had been calling for help, and whom he immediately advised to abandon his endeavours, having noticed that he was not an adequate swimmer. That a few moments later the victim was finally discovered, the previous witness Rafael being the first to touch her. On his information, the present witness, together with others who at that time were in the water, swam to the spot, and were able to discover immediately that the victim showed no signs of life. Then they carried her to the bank and laid her down there. On the shore, considering himself justified by his profession as student of medicine, the said José Manuel, after making a proper examination, arrived at the immediate conclusion that the victim was dead. Asked by His Worship whether in view of what he had seen he could affirm with reasonable certainty that the drowning he had witnessed was accidental and involuntary, involving no responsibility by any third party, the witness answered in the affirmative.

"Read, affirmed, ratified and signed by the said witness."

"Thank you very much," said the magistrate. "We shan't need

declarations by any of your companions. You are at liberty, therefore, to go as soon as you like."

"Then if you want nothing more . . ."

"Nothing. Goodbye."

"Goodnight, your worship. Goodnight."

The secretary nodded goodnight and the student mounted the steps.

"Oh, excuse me. Send me down the girl, if you would. The one who was in the river."

"Very well, your worship. I'll send her straight down." He disappeared behind the sacking.

"Now we'll deal with the girl. I don't think she'll take us very long. She doesn't seem in much of a mood for making a declaration."

He lit another cigarette.

"Oh, women! Women!" exclaimed the secretary, putting his head on one side.

The magistrate puffed out some smoke, and looked up, to examine the ceiling.

"A fine cellar they built here," he observed. "Must have cost them a lot of work to cut into the rock."

"Must be very old," answered the secretary. "Goodness knows how old it would be."

"Centuries old, probably."

"Very likely. Very likely."

They were silent for a moment. Then the magistrate spoke again: "A cool spot, eh?"

"Yes, it is. A good place to sit in the summer. If I had a cellar like this at home . . ."

"You're right. If I had one too. There won't be many spots as cool in this summer we're having."

"None at all." He looked up at the ceiling.

The curtain was drawn back.

"Here's the girl," announced the secretary.

The secretary stamped out his cigarette. Paulina came down the steps. She carried a wet handkerchief and was sniffing. The magistrate's eyes rested on the wide shapeless male trousers which had rolled up above her ankles.

"You wanted me, sir," said Paulina in a feeble voice as she came up to the table.

She was dabbing her nostrils with her crumpled handkerchief.

"Sit down, miss," said the magistrate. "Tell me what happened?" he continued kindly, pointing to her trousers. "Did you lose your skirt in the river?"

Paulina looked helplessly at her legs.

"No, sir," she answered, lifting her head. "I came like this."

She had no colour in her lips and her eyes were red.

"I beg your pardon," said the magistrate, "I thought . . ."

He looked away towards the end of the cellar and clenched his fists. There was a silence. The secretary looked at his papers. Paulina sat down.

"You wanted me, sir," she repeated nasally.

The magistrate looked at her again.

"Yes, miss," he said, making his voice soft. "We won't trouble you any more than necessary. Just sit quietly and try to answer my questions simply, please. Don't be alarmed, it won't be a long business, and I know how you must be feeling. Now would you, please, tell me your name, miss?"

"Paulina Lemos Gutiérrez."

"And your age?"

"Twenty-one."

"Do you do a job?"

"I help my mother in the house."

"Where do you live?"

"Bernardino Obregón, number five, just near the Ronda Valencia." She looked up at the curtain.

"Unmarried, eh?"

She nodded.

"Can you read and write?"

"Yes, sir."

"Never been convicted, eh?"

"What? Me, sir, oh no!"

The magistrate reflected for a moment and then said: "Did you know the victim?"

"Yes, I knew her. Yes, sir."

"Tell me, were you related to her in any way?"

"No, I was a friend, just a friend."

"Could you give me her surname and christian names?"

"Hers? Yes, sir. She was called Lucia Garrido."

"Do you remember her other name?"*

"Well, no ... I don't think I ever heard it ... If I had I should remember."

The magistrate turned to the secretary: "Remind me to get her full name afterwards. Perhaps one of the others will remember it."

Then to Paulina: "Lucita, what sort of name is that, exactly?"

"Lucia then. I suppose it was Lucia. Yes. But we always called her Lucita, or Luci for short."

"Right. Do you know where she lived?"

"Wait ... number nine, Caravaca."

"Did she do a job?"

"Yes, sir. This summer she was working for Ilsa's, serving at an ice cream stall. One of those stalls where they serve it to you by the slice. Do you know the ones I mean? Well one of those. Her stall was in Atocha, in front of the National ..."

"Yes," interrupted the magistrate. "Her age, do you know that?"

"Same as mine. Twenty-one."

"Thank you, miss. Now let's see what happened. Try and tell me in an orderly way, and don't forget any of the details. Keep calm and I'll help you. Please don't be frightened. Now, would you begin."

Paulina raised her hand to her mouth.

"Think for a moment, if you like, before you start. Don't be afraid. There's no hurry. Just keep calm."

"Well, your worship, we'd all got a lot of earth, you see, sticking all over us ... and they suggested that we went into the water to wash the earth off ... I didn't want to, and I told them so too, not at that time of night ... but they said, 'Oh yes, don't be so silly, it won't do us any harm ...' And they made such a fuss that I agreed

---

* The mother's surname is by Spanish custom appended to the father's. In the case of an illegitimate child, the mother's surname occurs alone. The presumption is that Lucita was illegitimate.

and we all three of us went in . . ." She was almost weeping as she spoke.

"Excuse me," said the magistrate, "but who was the third?"

"The other boy, the one you spoke to at the beginning, Sebastián Nabarro. He's my fiancé. So two of them and me. But I said to them, 'We won't go in too far'." She broke off in tears. "I said, 'We won't go in very far,' and he said, 'Don't be afraid, Paulina' . . . So we were close together, my fiancé and me, and suddenly I missed Lucita. Where was she? . . . You couldn't see her anywhere. The water was all very dark, and I called to her, 'Lucita, come over where we are! What are you doing all on your own? . . .' And she didn't answer. And we went on talking to her as if nothing was the matter, and all the time she was drowning . . . Then I called to her again, and my God! Lucita was drowning. 'Can't you see she's drowning?' I called out to him . . . And it was shocking what we saw, your worship, because the water was already choking her, and she couldn't call us or anything, but only struggle like this . . . It was dreadful. She was in her agony threshing about something like a whirlpool, and her arms going round, like this and this . . . and we two began to shout and shout." She broke off again, choked by her sobs. "Then we saw that the other boys were jumping in to pull her out. And I thought, my God, if only they can save her! But I wondered if they'd be there in time . . . and all the time Sebas my fiancé was struggling towards her, and he can hardly swim . . . And then suddenly you couldn't see her any more because the water was flowing very fast and dragging her down into the deep part of the pool . . . and, oh my God! I felt awful at that moment . . . They couldn't find her. They couldn't find her. It was all dark and they couldn't see her . . . " Now she was crying freely, covering her face with her hands and her crumpled handkerchief.

The magistrate went over and stood behind her. He put his hand on her shoulder.

"Calm yourself, young lady, calm yourself. Come, now, come . . ."

★ ★ ★

They had taken a last look at the lights in the valley. They were flickering down there in what seemed a huge swarming anthill of blue, red and green flashes from commercial signs. Blocks of houses stood out in huge verticals of violet shadow or clusters of prisms set in a rocky crust. Long strings of lights stretched out into the countryside and were swallowed up by the blackness of the land. The violet halo floated above it like an immense, ill-defined cupola of pulverized light. They came down the farther slope of Almodóvar. Only the moon, now high in the sky, lit the fields. They saw the chromium of their bicycle quietly glistening in the furrow. Santos picked it up and pushed it by the handlebars into the road. Carmen clung closely to him with her face buried in his neck.

"What's up?" asked Santos.

"Nothing. A burst of affection," she laughed.

"Come on now, let's be going. It's late."

They got on. Then as they came on to the Valencia road, Santos suddenly began to pedal hard, with a sharp burst of energy which increased the bicycle's speed. With the wind in their faces they went through Vallecas village, where a few people were still in the street. They came on to the main road again, and Carmen saw the village behind her. The moonlight presented it as a single profile, framed by a plaster moulding which ran along the line of the roofs. They rode at full speed, and the bicycle jolted on the cobbles.

"This is marvellous, Santos! Go as hard as you can!"

He felt Carmen's hair fluttering against his face. As they crossed the Vallecas bridge Carmen was surprised to find herself so suddenly surrounded by the lighted signs of cinemas and bars, by swarms of people and lights, and the din of the city.

"What's this?" she asked.

Santos had slowed down to the pace of the urban traffic.

"This? Vallecas City, the frontier town," he answered with a laugh.

They had to be careful not to run down the Sunday strollers who filled the streets.

★ ★ ★

The students had gone. Lucita's friends remained in silence, sitting on the terrace under the light of the bulb. They had rested their heads on the table, and their faces were hidden by their arms. Zacarías was staring at the old Guard, who was talking to Vicente the chauffeur. The din of the water prevented his hearing their words. The pair of them were standing on the embankment, beside the two cogs and wheels that raised the sluice gates. The chauffeur had taken out his tobacco, but the Guard refused to smoke. He was on duty, he said. They gazed at the turbulent water where all the current ran out.

"Just once in a while!" urged the chauffeur. "To hell with duty! You chaps have got enough to put up with."

"No, if his worship comes out and catches me smoking, it's a bad mark for me. Afterwards, when it's all over."

"God knows when that will be!"

"Everything has to be done at the proper snail's pace. It's no good being in a hurry."

"In a hurry? Who is? How could I possibly be in a hurry either, in a profession like mine? It's against regulations. You have to wait and wait. And when I do drive off I have to adjust myself to the speed of this Balilla. Everybody knows it can't do more than forty. You couldn't get it to do more if you beat it with a stick. So I don't know anything about speed. Still it's more restful that way, don't you think?"

"Yes, impatient people never get fat."

"That's right. At home they ask me when I expect to get back. Well, even if I knew for sure I should still answer, 'No idea!' Why should you make them anxious? Supposing there's an accident or some unexpected trouble crops up, then you know that nobody's expecting you, and you haven't got to worry about their being impatient or wondering what on earth can have happened to the man."

"Leading the sort of life you lead it's better like that," said the Guard Gumersindo, showing no interest.

Then after a silence, he added: "And now of course you'll have to take it to the mortuary. Who else could?"

"Yes, I was afraid of that. That's a thing I don't much like."

"But why, man?" asked Gumersindo. "That's silly. Nothing but superstition. What difference can it make to you whether you carry the living or the dead?"

"Call it superstition or what you like. But it makes a good deal of difference to me. And it would to anyone else, if he told you the honest truth."

He threw his cigarette into the black water and blew out the smoke very slowly, adding: "It's no pleasure to me to carry cold meat in my tin. I don't like it at all, I admit."

Now Gumersindo recognized the silhouette of his comrade's hat in the square of light that Aurelia's door threw on to the terrace. He had come to call Sebastián, who followed him between the tables and entered the bar. Gumersindo resumed their interrupted conversation.

"The living are more dangerous," he said. "They're the ones that give you trouble. The dead can't do much to you, poor devils."

"No, I agree with you. But they scare everybody stiff all the same, and there must be some reason for it. No one's very comfortable in their company, when you come to think of it."

"Well I'd much rather deal with the dead, than have criminals on my hands all day long, and keep in with my superiors. I'd change company without a thought, I promise you that."

"Well, I wouldn't. You may laugh at me but I don't like having to carry that object, I don't like it at all. I know all about it. I've done it before. Do you know how I feel after I've had a corpse in the car?" He paused before continuing. "I feel as if the seat has been left sort of dirty. I know you think it's nonsense. But I don't even like touching it. It gives me a queer feeling, like having to do with rats or snakes, and it stays with me for quite a time. Though after some days, of course, I do forget it."

The Guard put his head on one side.

"We all have our strange ideas," he said. "Different ideas with different people."

"I have my own reasons for disliking this. It's not just a question of transporting a corpse somewhere. That's soon over. It's all the days afterwards when I remember where it's been sitting, and imagine what it's left sticking to the material of the seat, or something of the sort, and I can't get it out of my head."

"If you'd been carrying someone infectious, there'd be a reason. But a corpse . . ."

"That's exactly it," said the chauffeur. "For me a corpse is like something infectious, there's no difference."

"That's nonsense. But once a man gets an idea in his head, it's a waste of time trying to argue him out of it."

"Yes, that's quite right, I admit. The sillier the idea, and the more unrealistic, the more impossible it is for a man to get it out of his head. That's what superstitions are. Yes, that's exactly what superstitions are."

There at the table they all sat motionless in a depressed, silent group. The boy with the lamp had come out to collect the folding chairs and tables, and was closing them one by one and putting them in a shed beside the house. The only tables and chairs left on the terrace were those occupied by Lucita's companions. They were like a redoubt in the middle of an empty space. Then the girl came out with a broom and began to sweep the ground all round them: trampled papers, fruit skins and paper serviettes, empty cartons; cigarette stubs and the tops of beer, orangeade and coca-cola bottles; cardboard plates and flattened cake-boxes with shop names printed on them, corks, peanut shells, and newspapers, all scattered and mingled with the dust now that the holiday was over. She gathered all this together with her broom and collected it into little piles along the embankment. Here it showed white for a moment, as it floated away to be swallowed into the black whirlpool of the sluice and disappear downstream.

The young Guard reappeared with Sebas and Paulina, and after exchanging a few words with his comrade, informed everyone in a loud voice that as His Worship had instructed him to release them, they could now go. They did not hurry but wearily got up, just as the boy came down again to collect the last chairs.

"We can go down now," said the young Guard to Gumersindo.

Vicente was left alone on the terrace. There was hardly anyone still in the bar when the Guards went through on their way to the cellar.

"At your worship's orders."

"You've sent them away?"

"Yes, sir."

"Good. You can wait here now."

The magistrate then picked up Lucita's bag and possessions.

"Let's deal with this," he said, turning to the secretary.

The secretary wrote: "Next an examination and inventory were made of the victim's possessions, clothes and personal objects, which were as follows . . ."

The magistrate opened the bag and dictated.

"A cloth bag, a printed dress, a neckerchief ditto." He laid the things on the chair as he named them. "Put down: underwear, two garments. Got that? Now, a pair of sandals . . . plastic. A pocket handkerchief. A blue striped towel. A red belt of plastic material." He stopped. "And the swimsuit that is on her. Now let's see what is here." He plunged his hand into the bag, and there was a chink of objects. "A comb," he continued, "an aluminium food tin, an ordinary fork, a table napkin, a pocket mirror, a tin of sun-cream." He laid the rest of the objects down one after another as he took them out, arranging them in a line on the table in front of the secretary's papers.

He stopped for a moment with a little purse in his hand, trying to open it.

"Right. A suède purse, colour blue." He emptied the contents on the table. "Let's see the contents." He counted the coins. "Now put down seven pesetas and eighty-five céntimos in small change, a postage stamp." He paused once more to examine something he was holding in his fingers. "An ornamental pin in the shape of a dog's head. Add in parenthesis, n dot, v dot – no value. A lipstick, and five photographs." – He looked them quickly over. "I think that's all. But go through them again with the list in your hand, just in case."

The magistrate took out his cigarettes and lit one. The secretary had completed his report.

"All correct. Nothing left out."

"Let's go then. Pick everything up. You may remove the body of the victim."

[369]

The two Guards picked up Lucita's corpse and took it on to the terrace.

"I've got a present for you," whispered the old Guard to Vicente as they approached him.

"I could have done without it!" he answered with a sigh as he opened the car door.

They placed Lucita's body in the back seat. Aurelia came out with the magistrate.

"You get in behind with the victim," he said to the secretary.

"And you know, your worship," said Aurelia in parting. "If ever you care to come in one evening we shall be delighted to look after you . . . And if . . ."

"Thank you, and thank you for your help. So long," he answered as he got into the car.

"Has your worship any orders?" asked the old Guard.

"No. You can resume your ordinary duties. Goodbye to you both."

The car doors slammed to, and Vicente took his seat.

"At your command."

"We'll see you again, your worship!" said the woman in farewell. "You know now . . ."

"Goodbye," said the magistrate, interrupting her.

* * *

Aurelia's daughter, the boy and a couple of men had come out on to the terrace. The Guards almost stood at attention as Vicente started the engine. The light of the headlamps struck the cog-wheels of the sluice gates and, passing over the empty water of the pool, picked out the point of the island and the little bridge. Weakly it lit up the mass of trunks and foliage of the more distant wood, then concentrated on the riverside slope and the great trunk of the mulberry tree in the foreground. At the end of its circle it came out on the road. Vicente changed gear and the car climbed the short slope that led to the road between the vineyards, leaving behind it the dust of its wheels and the motionless figures of the two Civil Guards who stood at attention and presented arms. After passing the vineyards, the Balilla turned to the left along the road to San Fernando. Now there were hardly any lights except the street lamps and an occasional bar door. It was barely half a mile to the town. No one spoke in the car. They took a road to the left and came out in a large round space, surrounded by low houses, with a statue, a fountain and a pine tree in the middle. On the farther side of this space they left the village again, passing a convent and a very large house, a school of dressmaking, and dropped down to the river. The cemetery was at the bottom, on a waste spot to the left of the road, and barely a hundred yards from the Jarama. The mortuary keeper came out when he heard the car, and opened the gates. Vicente stopped the car and they got out.

"Good evening. Is everything ready?"

"Yes, your worship, everything's ready."

"Well, let's get going."

The mortuary keeper helped the secretary to carry the corpse, and together they put it on the marble slab. After this they stripped it of the swimsuit. The secretary dictated a description of Lucita, and the admission sheet was filled up and signed. Finally the secretary picked up the blanket and the swimsuit, and the three men came out of the mortuary leaving Lucita's body stretched on the sloping marble slab. The keeper put out the light and locked the door.

"The surgeon won't be long," said the examining magistrate.

"No, your worship. Hope you have a good journey back."

"Thank you. Goodnight."

The mortuary keeper shut the car door, and the Balilla climbed the hill again to San Fernando, and on to Alcalá.

* * *

They went up the hill to the bar. The noise of the sluice grew fainter behind them. Tito and Daniel walked last, preceded by Zacarías and Mely. When they reached the main road Fernando turned back to say, "I tell you what you can do, Zacarías. You can ride her bike back."

"I had thought of that. But what do you think I ought to do with it afterwards?"

"What? Oh, I don't know. I don't know what we ought to do. But ..."

"Forget it," cut in Mely. "For God's sake, drop the subject. We can think about it later on."

Tito was hurrying after them.

"No, Mely," he said excitedly, almost shouting, "we must decide about that now. We must decide now who is to go tonight and tell her mother. Somebody's got to wheel the bicycle round and tell her. Who is it to be? . . ."

They had stopped in the road.

"Don't shout, for God's sake, Tito," Mely begged him with tears in her voice. "Drop the subject for now, drop it. We'll think about it afterwards. I can't stand it!"

"We've got to think it out now, Mely. Who is to tell her? Who?"

"Calm down, Tito," put in Daniel. "It's no good getting nervous about nothing. It doesn't help."

"But it's you who are getting nervous, Daniel, at just the thought of having to go up there and tell her mother . . ."

"It's got to be done," interrupted Zacarías.

"Yes, Zacarías," said Tito. "Someone will have to tell her, I know. The question is how. How is she to be told?"

They began to walk on.

"I don't think one way's any better than another," answered Zacarías, "when you have to tell a mother that her daughter is dead. Every way is bad."

"It just puts the fear of God into me," groaned Tito. "It panics me."

"Forget it . . ." said Mely. "We'll all go together, anyway. But don't think about it now, please."

"It'll have to be all together," said Tito. "All together. I couldn't face it otherwise."

"Nor could any of us," said Daniel. "If I had to go alone, I should run away. I shouldn't have the courage to climb the stairs. I should run away through the door."

Miguel, Alicia, Paulina and Sebastián were waiting for them beside the bar.

"Somebody get the things out," said Sebas, "so that we can pack them on the bike. We'll wait for you here. I'd rather not go in myself, if it's all the same to you."

"Don't you worry," said Zacarías. "We'll see to that."

Paulina stayed outside with Sebastián. The others went in.

"Evening!" said Miguel.

"Well, how are you?" said Mauricio. "I can't tell you how sorry we are, lad, about this tragedy. What a terrible way to end the day! God help her!"

Miguel looked at him as if about to say something, but did not know what to say.

There was a silence.

"These things happen."

"Yes. Will you tell us what we owe you, please. We're off now."

"In a second. Tell me if there's anything you need . . ."

"Thank you," said Miguel. "We're going to fetch the bicycles."

"Wait till I give you a light."

White Shoes looked on the ground. The Alcarrenian gazed into the bottom of his glass. Carmelo examined all their faces, one by one, as they went in single file into the passage to the garden. They were returning with the bicycles when the two women looked out of the kitchen.

"My goodness," said Faustina, "it's been a sad outing for you . . . What a tragedy! And such a young girl too! It's terrible, terrible! I can't tell you how sorry we are for you!"

Fernando quickly picked up the tins that Mauricio had laid on the counter for him. Miguel stayed behind with his hands on the handle-bars waiting amidst a general silence for Mauricio to make his reckoning. By the time he had paid and walked out, Sebastián had started up his engine.

"Wait for us at the end of the motorway, on the corner of the Calle Cartagena!" Miguel called to Sebastián above the noise of the engine. "Okay? We'll have a talk there."

"Right you are!"

Sebastián accelerated and started off. Macario and Carmelo had come to the door to see them off. Alicia sighed.

"And who feels strong enough now to pedal all the way to Madrid?"

"We've got to do it all the same."

The motorbike was already ahead. They could see the flash of its headlight as it took the main road. Daniel was the last to mount his bike, and the whole silent group rode swiftly off. Macario and Carmelo went back into the bar.

"Poor things!"

"They were fond of her," said Carmelo. "You could tell they were all very fond of that poor girl who got drowned. More or less all of them had been crying, I could see that right away. They'd all been crying right enough, not only the girls but some of the boys too. When a man cries like that, it's because he's really shattered. He's going through real agony." He spread out his fingers to imitate a spider and clenched them over his stomach.

"These sudden disasters can upset even the strongest stomach," said the shepherd, "especially when they happen on a holiday, when nobody's worrying about anything, and everybody's gay and only thinking of how to have a good time. It's rough, as they say. It gives you the feeling of going straight into darkness out of the light."

"It's the sort of thing that often happens to Madrid people," said the Alcarrenian. "They're always so mad about enjoying themselves. They have more accidents on holiday than ever they have at work. More of them are killed on Sundays than on any other day of the week. Madrid people are like that . . ."

"I agree," said the shepherd. "They're so keen to enjoy themselves that they try to pull the stars down from the sky, but sometimes they fall and break their heads. They behave like madmen, they get so excited and uncontrolled. They seem quite reckless of their lives. Din and chaos are the only things that give them any peace."

"That's certainly what it looks like," agreed the Alcarrenian. "It's true they like a good outing and a good spree, but you mustn't exaggerate. Madrid people are good for anything."

"Madrid's the best place in Spain," interrupted Carmelo with a categorical gesture.

"The best," said Lucio slowly, "and the worst as well."

[374]

Macario finished his wine.

"Right," he said. "Now I think we've seen all we're going to see today. Who's coming home?"

"All of us," said the shepherd. "This man and me, at least." He caught the Alcarrenian by the sleeve of his shirt.

"Wait just a second," said the Alcarrenian. "Nothing on fire, is there?"

"No, nothing. We just said we're going home. That's all. Got to be up early tomorrow. Sheep only graze before it gets hot. If you drive them out a minute too late, they won't take a mouthful because of the heat. They're obstinate creatures. I've got to be up at five in the morning you know. The alarm clock and a coffee and off I go, on my own two feet. You know how I live. So come on now, Liodoro. Don't be a nuisance but come along now. Every man has a right to his sleep."

"All right, man, all right. Let me drink the last drop in my glass. It's just selfishness, this. Because you have to get up early you want to send everyone else early to bed. Now let me go. You're tearing my shirt. What else have I got to cover myself with!"

The shepherd let him go, and went back to the counter.

"What do I owe you, Mauricio?"

"Fourteen glasses." He did the sum in his head. "Four twenty, that's all."

The Alcarrenian took a five-peseta note out of the little purse that he carried in his belt.

"Yours truly must be off too," said Carmelo.

The four who were departing paid their bills.

"Goodnight."

"See you tomorrow, all."

"Goodnight. See you tomorrow."

Lucio and White Shoes were left.

"Go and have your supper, man. Go and have your supper," said Macario to the latter.

"Perhaps I will," he answered with a wry smile. "Goodnight."

The four went out. There was a long silence. White Shoes looked at his uppers and went up and down on the tips of his toes. Mauricio propped his elbows on the wooden counter, with his jaw between his hands. His head looked like a solid walnut ball. His eyes were fixed on the middle distance. Lucio gazed up at the smooth yellow ceiling which sagged slightly in the middle like a great belly. It was split in one place and the lath stuck through. The shutters were painted a lead grey. The table legs seemed too delicate to hold up so much marble. The shelves were so overloaded with bottles that they looked as if they would fall on Mauricio's head. Little dark moths had flown in and were circling round the light. Outside the door, the ruined tower of the old San Fernando factory stood out in the moonlight. You could no longer see the subjects of the pictures on the wall, since their warped cardboard reflected the light. You could see in the narrow door-frame the thickness of the walls that pressed in on it.

"Tell me about this fellow Ocaña. Does he come to see you every summer?"

"Yes, he does," answered Mauricio. "Why do you ask me that now?"

"It just occurred to me. He must think a lot of you, then?"

"Of course he must," said White Shoes. "He doesn't worry what a visit costs him, does he? To give up a whole Sunday like that, with all that big family on his shoulders."

"He's a good fellow," said Mauricio, "a really good fellow."

"You've only got to listen to him. You can judge a man by what he says."

"A good man despite his name," said Lucio with a smile. "But I don't like his name."*

"What name?"

"Ocaña of course. What other name could I mean? It may say nothing to you but it does to me."

Mauricio raised his chin and smiled.

"Yes, I see."

There was a silence until Lucio spoke again.

"Your daughter told us that you two had made friends in the provincial hospital."

* Ocaña is the best-known political prison in Spain.

"Yes, we relieved the monotony for one another. We helped one another to bear our troubles."

"They couldn't have been very bad."

There was another silence.

"Aren't you going to have your supper, Mauricio?"

"Yes, in a little while."

"Don't stay on here on our account. I'll be off in a minute myself."

"No, don't worry about that. I'm not staying on your account. I know I haven't got to stand on ceremony with you. It's just that I'm not feeling like it yet."

"There's never any hurry for you. You get up at any time you fancy."

"I know what he's going to get tonight," put in Lucio. "He's smelt lentils just as I've smelt lentils. He knows they're cooking for his supper and they don't attract him one little bit. I'm right, Mauricio, aren't I?"

"That must be it. I'm not in love with them and I never have been."

"But lentils are considered quite a feast in many households. You're a bit fussy, you are."

"They're rather a heavy dish for summer," said White Shoes, and retched.

"What's the matter," asked Mauricio in alarm.

White Shoes breathed wearily and said: "It was just the thought ... of food. I was imagining those lentils ... Can you see them? Filthy stuff! As I was telling you, I'm squeamish about such things..."

Mauricio and Lucio looked at his face. He had turned pale.

"I'm sorry," said Lucio. "I didn't think what I said was going to upset you."

White Shoes was clutching his throat and breathing deeply. Another sharper fit of retching suddenly seized him, and he put his hand before his mouth and rushed out into the road, followed by Mauricio. There was a sound of choked coughing. He then came back holding a clean handkerchief to his lips. He had not unfolded it.

"Have you thrown up?" asked Lucio.

White Shoes nodded.

"Well now you've got rid of the trouble."

"Drink a glass of water," said Mauricio, going back behind the counter.

"I'm afraid I've been making a terrible exhibition of myself for this last hour or so," said White Shoes. "I'm ashamed." He smiled sadly. "I really ought not to be allowed out."

He took a sip from the glass of water that Mauricio had put out for him.

"Oh, rubbish! Don't be so silly. How can it be your fault if accidents upset you?"

"Do you feel better now?"

"Yes, Lucio, thank you. Excuse me for being so stupid."

"Not again!" exclaimed Mauricio. "As if you could control yourself on these occasions. Don't give it another thought."

"It's the limit. It's ridiculous to get oneself in such a state." He hesitated and was silent. "Well gentlemen, in view of my last successful performance I will now retire homewards. I will trouble you no more."

Mauricio lost patience.

"How pig-headed the man is! Why should he want to go away because of anything so silly? Come, sit down and don't be such a pest. How could you think of leaving for such a silly reason?"

"No, but it's late as well," replied White Shoes. "It must be about half past twelve." He tapped his wrist watch but did not look at it. "It's quite a way to Coslada, and the moon goes down very early. Haven't you noticed that it's full moon? I don't know whether I'm still in time for it to see me all the way home. If I'm not, I shall probably break my skull on these rough goat tracks."

"All right, just as you like then," said Mauricio. "If you're going to be so difficult there's nothing we can do. What really matters is that you don't break your skull. You mustn't do that."

"How much do I owe you?"

"Six forty altogether."

White Shoes took a wallet out of his back trouser pocket, and handed Mauricio seven pesetas, saying as he did so: "Here . . . but listen a minute, please. Don't tell anybody about this, if you don't mind. I mean about my stupid vomiting and all that. I should hate people to know about it. Okay?"

"Look here," said Mauricio. "I wouldn't have expected you to say a thing like that. You don't give me credit for much, do you? You didn't have to warn me. Surely you know your own friends. That's the first thing. But the second is that you don't seem to remember the custom of this house. We don't talk about people behind their backs. Come on now, that was a bad blunder." He gave him his change. "Sixty."

"I'm very sorry, Mauricio. You must excuse me once more," said White Shoes, picking up the six small coins. "Tonight I can't put a foot right. It's obviously not my night. Time for sleep, I think. Perhaps I'll get out of bed on the other side in the morning." He put away his wallet. "Sleep well. See you tomorrow."

"Goodnight," said Mauricio. "I always forgive you. I hope the moon lasts till you get home."

"See you tomorrow," said Lucio.

White Shoes stopped for a moment in the doorway to measure the height of the moon. Then he looked back into the bar, and observed with a serious smile: "Yes, it'll last me home. Goodbye."

He waved them farewell and set out.

"What an odd customer!" said Lucio when he had gone. "I do like him though."

"Yes, he's a grand fellow," said Mauricio slowly. "But he was very ashamed of himself for throwing up. It almost made me laugh."

"It hurt his pride," said Lucio. "It did, you know . . . Or perhaps he thought it was bad etiquette or something."

"I've known other men taken in much the same way. An accident like that would make them quite ill. Even if it hardly had anything to do with them, they were still upset."

"Yes, I know. Some people are more sensitive by nature, and it gets them somewhere, in some part of their anatomy. It may get them in the stomach, or in the liver, or in any other internal organ."

Justina suddenly came in and took them by surprise.

"Aren't you going to have any supper tonight, Father? It's quite cold, and there are hardly any coals on the fire to warm it through."

"Yes, I'll have my supper. Don't worry."

"Mother and I are just going to bed. Come on and clear things up."

She then turned quickly on Lucio.

"What's keeping you here, eh? Why don't you go?" she said severely.

"I was waiting for you to come in and chuck me out, beautiful."

"Come now, I like that!" She made a gesture of protest. "You've been here long enough, surely!"

"All right, then. Chuck me out if you want to."

"I? God forbid. That's my father's business. That is if you don't go of your own accord in the proper way."

"You're the boss here, not your father. At least so far as I'm concerned."

"Oh, I see. Well, I think you've got my father in your pocket. You won't let him eat his supper, or shut the place up, or come to bed, or anything. He has to stay here listening to you. Do you think everyone else is like you, that we all live on air like Indian fakirs?"

"You're libelling my character, dear little Justi," said Lucio with a laugh. "Yours truly eats just like anyone else, but he does it in his own time."

"Why, you've become a perfect skeleton! And don't you call me your little Justi either. I weigh twice as much as you do." She changed her tone. "All right. Stay where you are then and do as you like, both of you. I'm going to bed. Goodnight, Father!"

"Goodnight Justi darling, sleep well."

"What about me?"

"You?" Justina smiled as she looked down on Lucio in his chair. "Not even goodnight to you. You don't deserve even as much as that."

She went into the passage.

Lucio stretched his limbs.

"Well, I think I shall take your daughter's advice. I'm going home. I've got things to do in the morning."

"You?"

"Are you as surprised as all that?"

"Well now . . ."

"I wanted to keep it all quiet until everything was fixed up for certain. But now the appointment's made I can tell you what it's all about. It's only a trifling job, nothing more, just some chance work I picked up the other day, quite unexpectedly."

"Well, let's hear about it."

"It's just to mix the dough for the festivals in three or four villages round about here. Rolls and tarts, and all that, you know. The man's a pastrycook who goes from one festival to another, and he's going to take me round as his assistant. D'you see? There's six weeks' work altogether. We stay five days or a week in each place. Tomorrow I'm actually going to talk to the man, and if I like him I'll take it on. Now what do you say?"

"That's fine. If the fellow pays properly, it will be a decent little job for you."

"There's not much to it, of course. It's on a small scale, and it's not very grand on the financial side. But it'll be enough to keep me in my little luxuries, don't you think? The only thing that worries me is my age, you know. The fellow hasn't seen me yet, and nobody's told him how old I am. Our discussions have been through a third party. And that does worry me, because he may think he can get more work out of a young man and turn me down."

"I don't think that'll happen. It's the skill that counts. What's age got to do with it? The older you are the better the guarantee that you've got years of experience behind you."

"We'll see if you're right. I should be glad of the job, man. I don't know how many years it is since these hands of mine" – he spread them out in front of him – "have known the feel of flour and yeast. And now I've told you I'll beat it quick." He helped himself up with his hands. "It must be very late, and you haven't had your supper yet."

He got up.

"It's ten to one," said Mauricio.

Lucio stretched. He eased his creased trousers which had stuck to his skin. He lifted each knee in succession several times to get the life back into his legs.

"Well, goodnight. See you in the morning."

"Best of luck. Anything I can do to help."

"Yes, of course. We'll see if the whole thing doesn't just turn out to be eyewash."

Lucio went out into the road above the hills of Coslada. He heard Mauricio close the door behind him, and by the time he began to walk on again the bar had ceased to throw its square of light on the track. He followed the road between two olive fields as far as the walls of San Fernando, the roar of the river water in the sluice, sounding in his ears all the while, until it was cut off by the first buildings of the village. They were new little houses, whose bricks were still bare, and they were still for the most part uninhabited.

* * *

"*It then re-enters the tertiary field, and is joined by the Henares, which flows in from the left at Mejorada del Campo. At Vaciamadrid, the Manzanares flows into it from the right below the bridge of Arganda; and at Titulcia the Tajuña from the left. It then feeds the great canal known as the Real del Jarama, and on reaching the plain of Aranjuez discharges its waters into the Tagus, which carries them westward to Portugal and the Atlantic Ocean ...*"

Printed in Great Britain by Cox and Wyman Ltd
London, Reading and Fakenham